HAROLD COYLE'S STRATEGIC SOLUTIONS, INC.

PANDORA'S LEGION

HAROLD COYLE'S STRATEGIC SOLUTIONS, INC.

PANDORA'S LEGION

HAROLD COYLE
and
BARRETT TILLMAN

A Tom Doherty Associates Book

New York

PANDORA'S LEGION

This book is printed on acid-free paper.

A Forge Book
Published by Tom Doherty Associates, LLC
175 Fifth Avenue
New York, NY 10010

www.tor.com

Forge® is a registered trademark of Tom Doherty Associates, LLC.

Library of Congress Cataloging-in-Publication Data

Coyle, Harold, 1952–
    Pandora's legion : Harold Coyle's Strategic Solutions, Inc.
/ Harold Coyle and Barrett Tillman. 1st hardcover ed.
        p.   cm.
    "A Tom Doherty Associates book."
    ISBN-13: 978-0-765-31371-3
    ISBN-10: 0-765-31371-5
    1. Paramilitary forces—Fiction.   2. Terrorism—Prevention—Fiction.
3. Bioterrorism—Fiction.   4. Marburg virus—Fiction.   I. Tillman, Barrett.
II. Title.
    PS3553.O948P36 2007
    813'.54—dc22   2006033430

First Edition: February 2007

Printed in the United States of America

0   9   8   7   6   5   4   3   2   1

PART

I

1

HEATHROW AIRPORT, LONDON

The traveler had a secret.

He was a young man with an American passport; one of 155,000 travelers who passed through Heathrow Airport west of the city that day. The British customs official in Terminal Three personally dealt with scores of them at a time, and she had become expert at sizing up people. Patrice Assamba was Jamaican by birth and British by her first marriage. She was also the senior agent on her shift by virtue of thirteen years' experience.

Assamba accepted the youngster's dark blue passport and began her initial examination. *Another screwed-up American*, she told herself. His appearance was unremarkable: early to mid-twenties, slight build, close-cropped dark beard, blue eyes turning watery behind John Lennon glasses. He wore the headgear common to many Islamic males—a brimless cloth cap of nondescript shape, vaguely khaki in color, pushed back on his head.

The traveler standing before Agent Assamba held the passport of one Youssef Ibrahim, but he certainly had been born with another name. Apparently a convert to Islam, his hometown was listed as Berkeley, California. *That figures*, Assamba sneered. She had been through the "People's Republic" several years before, helping a friend guiding a U.K. tour group. Free airfare and accommodations in the San Francisco area for four days and three nights. Hell of a deal. The scenery was marvelous, and Fisherman's Wharf alone was worth the effort.

Young Mr. Ibrahim's hand trembled when passing his documents, but Patrice Assamba attributed that to initial nervousness. Gauging by the stamps in the passport, he was new to international travel. Apparently he had gone from California to Saudi Arabia, via Frankfurt, thence to Pakistan for two months. Evidently the boy was on some sort of personal pilgrimage.

Assamba looked closer at the supplicant. She noted his pale, clammy skin and the watery eyes that seldom fixed on her. She read the signs: *He's trying to appear relaxed by body posture but he won't look directly at me. Keeps glancing away.*

Youssef Ibrahim probably was hiding something.

Assamba's accent bore the carefree lilt of the Caribbean. "Welcome to Heathrow, sir." She gave him a gleaming smile and perky tilt of the head. "Are you staying in England for long?"

Ibrahim shifted his weight, placing his hands in his jacket pockets. "Uh, no. Ma'am. No, ma'am. I'll just be here a few days." He glanced away again.

Agent Assamba decided to play this strange fish before reeling him in. "After Pakistan, you must be glad to be going home."

A brisk nod. "Yes, ma'am. You bet." Mentally he excoriated himself. *You bet.* The slangy residual of a wasted California youth.

In fact, Youssef Ibrahim loathed the very existence of Berkeley, California. After all, that's where his parents lived. He felt an onset of queasiness, uncertain whether it was caused by parental disdain or the effects of his secret. He swallowed hard, keeping the saliva down only by conscious effort. His mouth now was drier than ever before. He damned himself for shivering visibly. The headache that had begun as merely annoying hours before was a growing, insistent pressure behind his eyes.

Now the customs agent was examining him more closely. *She suspects something. Well, let her look. They can't find what I'm hiding. No way, man.*

"Sir, you don't look well. Would you like to sit down? Could we get you some water?"

Ibrahim opened his mouth, intending to decline the offer, when he felt the sudden rumbling in his bowels. He contracted his sphincter, desperately needful of a lavatory. He turned away, not sure where to go, realizing it was already too late. He turned back to Agent Assamba, beyond embarrassment at confiding his crisis to a strange woman. An *infidel* woman. He felt the first liquid tracking down the back of his legs, squeezed harder, and failed. The eruption announced itself to everyone within twenty feet.

ST. EDMUND'S HOSPITAL, LONDON

Dr. Carolyn Padgett-Smith resembled a practitioner of neither medicine nor immunology, though she possessed a master's degree in the latter. Tall and slender, at forty-one she could have passed for thirty-five, and it took most of her male colleagues a while to get their egos around the fact that a woman with large, violet eyes and high cheekbones knew more about infectious diseases than most Ph.D.s. None would have been surprised to learn that she had paid much of her college tuition by modeling; few realized that beneath her stylish clothes she had the muscular agility of a passionate rock climber.

"CPS" had planned on grading some postgraduate papers but the call from the Home Office changed all that. Because she had been on the short list for notification in the event of a communicable disease crisis, she was summoned to St. Edmund's, a well-equipped teaching hospital of 1960s vintage.

Padgett-Smith was met by a security officer she knew slightly, Richard Eversole Carruthers. She knew him to be professionally competent but, like too many coppers of her acquaintance, prone to situational ethics. "Hullo, Mr. Carruthers. What've we got?"

"Nice to see you, too, Padgers." Carruthers had long since abandoned hope of getting anywhere with Carolyn Padgett-Smith, burdened as she was with conventional morality and an attentive husband. *Forsaking all others, that sort of thing. Pity.* "The boy arrived yesterday on the PIA flight from Islamabad. He collapsed at the customs station and was brought here because it's closest to the M4 access to Heathrow."

"Ebola?"

"Likely that or Marburg, I'm told."

CPS muttered some fervent Anglo-Saxon monosyllables, none encumbered with a fifth letter. Then she focused her attention. "I shall need to see a blood sample to confirm the virus."

Carruthers nodded in his curt fashion. "Right. They're ready for you in the lab."

———

Padgett-Smith pulled on a gown, mask, and rubber gloves before stepping to the microscope with the blood in the high-quality plastic tube. She appreciated the caution: Glass could shatter if dropped, possibly spreading a deadly virus.

CPS focused the eyepiece more sharply and looked into the microscopic world. She felt a slight chill run down her spine, as if she had locked eyes with a cobra.

A layman would have seen a riot of cells, hardly recognizable one from another, though the sick ones outnumbered the healthy. But Dr. Padgett-Smith immediately discerned the dying cells: discolored, pale, swollen. Some had already burst apart.

Something had caused them to explode.

Padgett-Smith looked up at the lab director. "Filovirus?"

The man nodded. "I'll show you the microphotographs. We're also running tests to see if the patient's blood reacts positively in other samples. We should know before long."

———

Padgett-Smith returned to the lobby, ordering her priorities to coordinate with Carruthers's.

"Who had contact with the patient?" she asked.

"Well, the customs agents of course. And the ambulance attendants; probably some others."

"I shall like to see all of them."

"Of course. You can start with the point of contact, Agent Patrice Assamba."

"Give me the short version first."

"She seems a reliable observer. At first she suspected this so-called Ibrahim fellow was merely nervous because he was hiding something. Then with the sweating and chills, she thought he had malaria or a bad fever."

CPS nodded slowly. "Yes, that's the trouble with Marburg and Ebola. The onset is similar to far lesser illnesses with comparable incubation periods." Then she focused those violet eyes on his hazel orbs, two inches lower than hers. "You said 'so-called Ibrahim.' Is that an alias?"

"Well, it's the name on the passport, for what that's worth. We're checking with the Americans." CPS suspected that when drinking with his mates at the Hare and Hounds, Detective Carruthers said "Americans" with the same sneering tone as "wogs."

"He's been in Africa? Exposure to monkeys?" she asked.

"Arabia and Pakistan. About two months, apparently." The dick shrugged his sloped shoulders. "Don't know about any bloody apes."

Dr. Carolyn Padgett-Smith extended a manicured hand and patted Carruthers's cheek. "Why, I'd expect you'd know all about the great bloody apes, dear. Friends of the family."

Jason Scott Lamunyon knew the end would be bad. Dr. Ali had warned him, but "bad" was a vast understatement. The Californian remembered collapsing in a pool of his own excrement, blood, and vomit, regaining consciousness hours later in the isolation ward. Nobody came near him without a biohazard suit and respirator. He realized that he was dying a putrid death: the kind of blight he sought to inflict upon arrogant, decadent Western Civilization.

A nurse approached the bed to replenish the IV drip. He wanted to raise an arm, beckoning her—or him—to bend closer. *So weak. Can't lift much.* He barely nodded his head, and the attendant leaned down. The patient's lips were moving; apparently he wanted to say something. Dr. Padgett-Smith would need to know about it; the American had been unconscious when she first looked in.

Through the morphine haze, which only dulled the soaring pain, Jason Scott Lamunyon tried to speak. It was doubly hard since the virus had attacked his tongue, which was shedding skin at an alarming rate. He croaked something almost unintelligible: "Sorry. So sorry."

With an exertion of will, he moved his right hand to his left forearm and flexed his right thumb. Then he raised two fingers.

The attendant had no idea what the pantomime signified, but she hastened to find Carolyn Padgett-Smith.

OFF THE MARYLAND COAST

"My God, this fish is a fighter!"

Rear Admiral Michael Derringer, USN(Ret) loved the sea. But now, after nearly seven hours strapped into *HMS Bounty*'s fighting chair, he was beginning to think fondly of a warm, dry place ashore. Preferably someplace where marlin fishing was unknown.

The 130-pound test line unreeled again as the big blue sprinted away. At *Bounty*'s helm, "Cap'n Bob" Bligh glanced back over his shoulder while the skipper's son Bobby shouted directions and lent encouragement.

With his feet braced against the strain, Derringer waited for his prey to broach again. When it leapt into the sunlight once more, he used the opportunity to reel in several more precious inches. Cap'n Bob had already pegged the blue at perhaps nine hundred pounds, and Derringer was glad that he had accepted the skipper's advice. Blue marlin had been landed on far lighter lines, but mainly in shallow water. Here at Poor Man's Canyon, fifty miles off the Maryland coast, the bottom was 1,200 fathoms. A big, strong fish like the one Derringer had hooked could use some depth to gain momentum and snap a lighter line.

This time the marlin changed tactics. Instead of running astern, tiring itself against the tension of the line, it abruptly turned and charged the boat. Bobby gave the "full power" signal and Cap'n Bob ran the throttle forward. Derringer appreciated the wisdom of the move: he did not want to give this very capable fish too much time at the end of a slack line. As *Bounty* nosed into the swells, the distance between fish and boat stabilized, then began opening. Derringer cranked furiously on his reel, taking advantage of the opportunity. When the line snugged up again, he pulled with both hands, relishing the physicality of the contest even as he felt the strain in his back and arms.

Bobby patted the client on his aching shoulders. "We're gettin' him, Adm'ral. Keep him comin'."

A couple of years before, Derringer had landed a 680-pounder in barely two hours. But that was in the Gulf of Mexico. This would be his biggest catch yet, maybe even a "grander." That would put Michael Derringer in elite company: thousand-pound marlins were getting rare these days.

"Adm'ral, there's a message for you." The scratchy voice belonged to Miz Alice, Cap'n Bob's "able-bodied first mate." In fact, her insubordinate actions late one night—declared mutinous by Cap'n Bob—inspired the name of his next boat. For a moment, Derringer could not imagine who could possibly reach him. He had left his cell phone turned off—it was a curse more than a help.

Miz Alice emerged from the cockpit with a thermos of vegetable soup. "We just got a radio call from the Coast Guard," she advised. "ComFifth says you need to talk to them right away."

Derringer tugged on his pole again. He could sense that at length the marlin was tiring. "Damn it! I've got my hands full here . . ."

"They're still on the horn, Admiral. Shall I tell 'em to stand by?"

Derringer nodded, then focused on the tactical battle. "Cap'n, you better back down a little and I'll switch with Bobby."

"Aye sir!" *Bounty*'s captain maneuvered to take some of the tension off the line while Derringer quickly unstrapped from the chair. Bobby, a muscular twenty-four, would have little problem keeping the fish occupied.

In the cockpit, Derringer keyed the microphone. He could not imagine why the Fifth Coast Guard District needed to talk to him. "ComFifth, this is Derringer in *Bounty*. Over."

"Ah, roger, *Bounty*. Sir, this is Captain Deevers, chief of staff. We have an urgent message relayed from headquarters in Washington.

You need to call your office immediately. Apparently they couldn't get you by cell phone."

"Hell no they couldn't get me by cell phone! I turned the damned thing off so I could go fishing."

Captain Deevers permitted himself a polite chuckle. "Understood, Admiral. All we know is that the Secretary contacted SSI and apparently some important people want to talk to you soonest."

Derringer thought for a moment. If the Secretary of Transportation had contacted SSI, something unusual was afoot. Unusual and likely unpleasant. "Thank you, Captain. I wish those people were as important as the blue marlin I've hooked out here."

The founder and CEO of Strategic Solutions, Inc. shouted back to Bobby. "Cast him loose, son. We're headed in."

HMS Bounty turned her stern to an exhausted blue marlin that happily dived on the continental shelf.

VIENNA, VIRGINIA

Dr. Phillip Catterly was accustomed to urgent calls at fearsome hours. This was the one he had always dreaded.

The clipped, upper-class tones of Carolyn Padgett-Smith snapped Catterly wide awake. Without bothering to apologize for the time, she said, "Phillip, check your email. When you've read my message and seen the attachments, get back to me straightaway."

Catterly blinked away the crusty feeling behind his eyes. "What is it, Carolyn?"

"It's awful, Phillip. Just awful."

WASHINGTON, D.C.

"Well, it's about as bad as it gets." Catterly spoke bluntly to the short-notice meeting of the Department of Homeland Security's Advisory Committee. Normally few of the attendees would have left home yet, but much of the federal alphabet was represented: DoD, DoT, FBI,

FEMA, INS, and TSA, as well as delegates from science, industry, and academia.

DHS Secretary Bruce Burridge stifled a yawn. It was barely 8:00 A.M. "We have some time, Phil. Please give us the medical background. I've already explained the carrier's travels and likely intentions."

"It's Marburg virus, similar to Ebola." The conference members stirred in their padded chairs; one or two uttered exclamations. The FBI representative emitted a low whistle. Catterly continued, "To give it its proper name, it's a family of negative-stranded RNA viruses, called *Filoviridae*. It's a hemorrhagic fever identified in 1967 in Marburg and Frankfurt, Germany, after researchers were exposed to African green monkeys or their tissues. The first two Ebola outbreaks were reported in Zaire and the Sudan in 1976, with mortality rates between fifty and ninety percent depending on conditions and locale. With Marburg we expect twenty to twenty-five percent fatalities."

FEMA and TSA exchanged glances. FEMA asked HSD, "Should we increase the national threat level?"

Burridge shook his head. "No, at least not yet. The fact is, most people don't pay any attention, even at the elevated level." He turned back to Catterly. "Phil, how is the virus passed along?"

Catterly seemed to bite his lip. "Frankly, we don't know much about Marburg's origins or mechanics of transmission. Other than dealing with infected monkeys, most documented cases are based on close contact with the carrier, including sexual transmission, exposure to small amounts of body fluids, or handling of contaminated objects. There is also evidence of respiratory transmission among monkeys, dating from 1983. Of course, that's what we fear the most."

"How do we prevent it?" Burridge asked.

Catterly glanced around the room. "I wish to God I knew." He allowed the sentiment to sink in. "There's a CDC manual for treating hospitalized patients, basically the same as other hemorrhagic fevers. Sterilization and isolation. But the long-term effects can be grim. Patients who recover still are susceptible to recurrent hepatitis, transverse myelitis, or uveitis. There is . . ."

The FBI's special agent, Jefferson Bethune, intervened. "Excuse me, Doctor. What's all that?"

"Transverse myelitis is partial inflammation of the spinal cord. It's a neurological disorder related to polio. It interrupts control of body movements and functions. Recovery may be total or partial over a period of months. Uveitis is serious inflammation of the eyes. There's also a record of inflammation of the testicles and other glands."

"So, even without a twenty-five percent fatality rate, this thing could overwhelm our entire healthcare network."

"Correct." Catterly continued. "The incubation lasts four to sixteen days with fever, chills, headache, anorexia, and muscle pain. It's often followed by nausea, vomiting, sore throat, abdominal pain, and diarrhea. Most victims exhibit severe symptoms between days five and seven with bleeding from multiple sites but mainly the gastrointestinal tract, lungs, and gums. Bleeding and lesions precede death by day sixteen at the latest, resulting from shock, with or without extensive bleeding." He paused. "That seems to be about where our mysterious young patient is. We don't know when he was infected, but he can't last much more than another day or so."

Secretary Burridge tracked his gray eyes around the room. "I'm meeting with the President, SecDef, and the Surgeon General this afternoon. We need to present some options right away."

Bethune asked, "Well, do we know enough to start looking for anybody?"

Burridge shrugged. "Apparently not. But we should at least formulate a couple of contingency plans."

"My God, Bruce, don't we have contingencies in place yet?" Virginia Governor Fitzhugh Parmenter was more concerned than most. The Old Dominion would take the brunt of a DC outbreak.

"Sure, for outbreaks of bio weapons. But if this Islamic kid was injected with a virulent strain of Marburg, as the Brits suspect, we need to get to the source ASAP."

The NSA representative spoke up. "If we're going to start looking along the Pakistan-Afghan border, we'll need thousands of people, or just a few who are really well informed."

Burridge nodded. "That's right. I'm talking to Donna over at State this morning. It seems there's concern about an increased American presence in Pakistan, and it looks as if we don't have enough assets to spare on the Afghan side. So . . ."

Bethune finished the thought. "We send a deniable asset."

Burridge remained expressionless.

"Who you have in mind, Bruce?" Parmenter thought he already knew.

"Mike Derringer and SSI."

———————

The afternoon meeting convened in the Oval Office, where President Patrick James Quincannon wasted no time on pleasantries. He had already consulted with SecDef Gregory Hooper, who shared Burridge's recommendation of employing a private military contractor: a PMC.

The president opened: "Allow me to save time by summarizing your info sheets. We have a particularly nasty situation brewing, probably the work of Islamic radicals operating in Pakistan. State says we can't insert our military without drawing more heat from the fundamentalists in-country, so that limits our options." Quincannon then addressed his Homeland Security czar. "Bruce, I don't know much about your friend Derringer other than he runs Strategic Solutions and he's reliable. What's he like, personally?"

"Mike Derringer is one smart son of a bitch," Burridge began. He briefly flushed in the obscure presence of Secretary of State Donna Lombardi. *Sailor's vocabulary,* he told himself. "We were at Annapolis together. I was in the upper half of our class but he graduated ninth out of 388 and just kept going. The guy was a water walker most of his career: astute and tough; a tad cynical. He was on the staff of the Joint Chiefs when the Soviet Union collapsed, and he saw it coming before most people. Even though he had one of the best records as an analyst in Pentagon history, hardly anyone believed him. He predicted the collapse about ten months beforehand, but where colonels go for coffee, a rear admiral doesn't carry a lot of weight."

"So what'd he do?"

"With his record he probably could've stuck around for a third star, maybe got a fleet command, but by then he'd had enough. In '89 he wrote me a letter and I wish I'd kept it. He laid it all out, almost month by month. He said that with the Evil Empire no more, the politicians would rush to dismantle DoD to placate the peace lobby.

Mike's nothing if not objective. He detested Clinton, but said the Republican-controlled Congress would roll over for major force reductions, and he predicted increased deployments that would lead to retention problems. He was right. He also said that few service chiefs—if any—would protest, let alone risk their jobs by standing up for the troops. He was right.

"Mike said there would be a major war in the Mideast in 1991 or 92: likely involving Iraq, Iran, and/or Saudi. He was right. When Bush wimped—ah, opted—out and left Saddam in power, Mike said we'd have to go back and do it again in ten years, but with fewer assets. He was wrong there—it was twelve years."

Quincannon grinned. "Doesn't he ever get tired of being right?"

"No. Never. But if you want to get his goat, just mention 'rightsizing.' Man, he hates that word."

"So how did all this lead to SSI?"

"Well, Mike foresaw that all the downsizing and rightsizing bull . . . was based on an absurd premise: just because the USSR collapsed didn't mean peace in our time. He knew we'd get caught short eventually, and he saw an opportunity. That's mainly why he put in his papers: he wanted to get a jump on other private military corporations. While outfits like Executive Outcomes were showing their stuff in Africa and elsewhere, he decided that he should form his own PMC. The result is SSI."

"Very well," the president said. He looked around the table. "Any comments?"

Secretary of State Lombardi leaned forward. "Mr. President, you must realize that even though they're legitimized as PMCs today, these organizations are basically mercenaries. That still carries a stigma in some quarters." She glanced down. "Especially in the UN."

"I know, Donna. But what's your point?"

"It's just that, well, we might lose some support in the international community."

Before the president could respond, SecDef Hooper intervened. "So what? The so-called international community isn't doing a hell of a lot to support us as it is. Besides, the whole point of using a PMC is deniability. A contractor is not operated by the U.S. Government. Any of us can go on CNN or Fox and truthfully state that no American military forces are engaged." He choked down a derisive snort. "But you already know that, Madame Secretary." It was an open secret in Washington that SecDef and SecState really truly disliked one another.

Ms. Lombardi's face reddened beneath her makeup. She half rose from her chair when the president responded. "I understand the concern about PMCs or mercenaries or whatever you call them . . ."

Hooper saw an opening and took it. "Excuse me, Mr. President. I remember the, ah, 'contradictions' in UN attitudes about Executive Outcomes, one of the early PMCs. In '93 when the Angolan army couldn't protect its oil fields against the rebels, EO was called in. It solved the problem with a few hundred elite troops, but then international protests arose. EO was recalled and several thousand UN 'peacekeepers' arrived but they couldn't keep the peace—or even defend themselves. The usual UN crowd was all hot and bothered because of EO's South African origins, but you know what? Most of the troops were black, and they were saving thousands of black lives. EO did the same thing in Sierra Leone and elsewhere, but the facts didn't matter then, did they?"

The Secretary of State returned her rival's gaze without speaking. As the ambient temperature in the room dropped ten degrees, the president resumed control.

"Well, there you go. State says the situation in Pakistan doesn't allow us to insert military forces, so we have two other options: rely on the locals, some of whom support the terrorists, or go with a PMC." He visually polled each secretary in turn.

Secretary Lombardi had recovered enough to find her tongue. "One moment, sir. I think we should know what we're getting into. I mean, have we ever used this SSI company before?"

Quincannon looked to Hooper, who said, "Sure, and several other PMCs besides. You know, Donna, in Iraq we don't have enough troops for convoy escorts and contractor security. In fact, our soldiers will tell you that the PMCs and military are working pretty well together."

Lombardi shook her head. "No, no. I mean, have you hired this firm for other covert operations?"

SecDef exercised his best press-conference blank face while the commander in chief regarded SecState for two heartbeats. President

Quincannon smiled and looked around the room. *Damned if I'll tell her what I don't know.* "Well then, if there's no other business, we'll adjourn. Turning to face Homeland and SecDef, he said, "Bruce, Greg: make it happen."

ARLINGTON, VIRGINIA
SSI OFFICES

Michael Derringer convened the briefing in SSI's most secure facility. There was seating for sixteen people in the room known as "the cone of silence."

"Gentlemen." He nodded at Sandra Carmichael, the firm's head of operations. "Lady. Dr. Catterly is one of the leading immunologists in the country. He's worked all over the world and now chairs a crisis response committee with representatives of WHO, CDC, and other agencies. He's here to familiarize you with the threat we face. You've all heard of Ebola; well, we're up against something almost as bad: Marburg virus.

"Three days ago, an American citizen collapsed at Heathrow Airport with advanced Marburg. He won't last much longer. We know a little about him and the feds are looking closer. Briefly, he was a disaffected youngster who converted to Islam and spent quite some time in Arabia and Pakistan. It's likely that he was intentionally infected with the virus as a means of spreading a serious disease in the western world. His travel plans included the UK, U.S., and Canada." Derringer turned to Catterly. "Doctor."

Phil Catterly cleared his throat. "I've spent a few years in Africa and Asia and I've seen some terrible sights. But based on the images I received from a colleague in Britain, this young American is far worse than anything I've ever seen. He had one of the worst cases of Marburg *anybody's* seen.

"While driving out here, I tried to think of a phrase to communicate the severity of this case for you. The best I've come up with is from a book called *Plague Wars.* Mangold and Goldberg said that Marburg turns humans into 'a digested slime of virus particles.' "

Derringer scanned the faces around the table, assessing the reaction. Most remained impassive. Sandy Carmichael covered her mouth
with one hand. She had two daughters.

Catterly stopped to gather his thoughts. "The worst cases are almost indescribable. The virus attacks nearly every system and organ
except the bones and some skeletal muscles. It replicates itself in the
body, and accumulates small clots in the bloodstream. Circulation
suffers. After a while, the patient develops red spots that are hemorrhages beneath the skin. As they grow, they burst through the surface, and often the skin just drops off. Finally, the heart begins
bleeding into itself. You can tell at that point because the eyes turn
red from excess blood." He spread his hands on the table, palms up.
"The pain is horrible. Just horrible. Without heavy sedation, the patient dies trying to scream, but sometimes the tongue is gone."

The firm's domestic ops chief uttered, "Jesus wept." It was a cross
between a whisper and a croak. Derringer knew Joseph Wolf, former
FBI assistant director, to be a devout Catholic.

SSI's president, Marshall Wilmot, tapped his pencil on the table.
"What's the likely mortality, Doctor?"

"Best case: about twenty-five percent."

Wilmot nodded, apparently unaffected. Derringer thought,
Marsh's home life isn't much cheerier than that prospect.

"There's something else," Catterly added. "It got little notice, but
there's already been an outbreak in the U.S. In fact, in this area."

Derringer already knew about it. "Reston."

"Correct. In 1989 a shipment of laboratory monkeys from the
Philippines was imported by a legitimate contractor. At least one of
them was a carrier and infected many of the others. CDC and the
Army were both called in. The only thing to do was euthanize all the
monkeys, decontaminate the facility, and close it up. We were just
damned lucky that no humans died, though a few were infected."

A chilly silence descended over the room. Finally Wolf asked,
"Okay. How do we fit in?"

Derringer leaned back, flipping some notes he did not need. The
hard drive of his memory was almost infallible, but a lifetime of
habit had sunk deep roots. "You heard about the C-130 crash in

Karachi a few days ago. It was loaded with disaster relief supplies for delivery up-country but it went down in a populated area. At least thirty people died on the ground. Of course, the radical elements in Pakistan turned it into an Evil Satan situation—never mind that we were trying to help the locals. The responsible agencies in Islamabad understand the facts, but there are unsympathetic people in the government. State says that an increased U.S. military presence in the country is not acceptable at present." He shrugged. "They've offered the job to us. I wanted a consensus before accepting."

Wilmot gave Derringer an arched-eyebrows expression with a slight nod toward Catterly. Derringer nodded, then turned to the researcher. "Phil, we need to discuss some discreet business. May I ask you to . . ."

"Surely." Catterly read the signs all too well. *They need to talk money.*

As the researcher closed the door, Wilmot continued. "Just as background, I think everybody should know that Mike and I haven't had much time to discuss this contract. He was still fuming about The One That Got Away when I picked him up."

There was laughter in the room; some knew that Wilmot was only mildly exaggerating.

"Anyway, because I'm working with Corin Pilong on contracts, I think it only fair to note that this is a seller's market. Now, maybe that makes me an evil bastard, considering what we're up against. But I'd be remiss if I didn't point that out."

"Marsh is right," Derringer added. "Because this is a covert op on a tight schedule, there's no competition. We can maximize the profits on this one because there's relatively little overhead. We envision probably three dozen operators and maybe a few helos. Plus the cost of getting there and back, of course."

Sandra Carmichael had enough experience with international PMC ops to raise a cynical question. "What are the chances we may run into other operators over there? You know, somebody working as a backup in case we fail." She shrugged. "And what about the Brits?" It was the kind of question that Derringer liked.

"Sandy, unless Greg Hooper is leading me on, it won't happen. And I've known him over twenty years. We have the lead on this project, but the administration is keeping London informed in general terms."

Derringer almost smiled at Carmichael's mission-oriented attitude. It was one of the things he appreciated about the small-town Alabama girl who finished her army career as a lieutenant colonel. He suspected that deep down, the rural squirrel shooter still stirred in her; she liked to play with subguns and pistols, which gave her credibility with Frank Leopole, chief of SSI's foreign operations division. The former marine O-5 looked the part: high-and-tight haircut and perennial scowl. While he enjoyed plinking with Carmichael, he still felt that it should be beneath a lady's dignity to kill anyone.

Derringer proceeded to the next items on the agenda. "Very well. We'll push the contract right along but we'll begin planning today to save time." He looked at Leopole. "Frank, unless we have an operator fluent in Urdu and Pashto, you'll want to put Omar on this one. Of course, he also speaks Arabic."

Leopole nodded, grunting, "Roger that." Though suspicious of all Muslims, he respected Dr. Omar Mohammed's awesome linguistic ability—the native Iranian was fluent in four languages and conversant in half a dozen others.

"One more thing," Derringer added. "Given the medical and scientific nature of the mission, we would benefit by having a specialist on the team. I'll talk to Dr. Catterly but he's on the shady side of sixty, and he wouldn't perform well at eight thousand feet. He may know somebody."

Leopole dexterously flipped his pencil like a miniature baton between his finger. *I could never do that*, Sandy Carmichael thought. "We could go through Dave Main; he probably has a couple of names from Fort Detrick."

Colonel David Main was SSI's "official unofficial" liaison with Special Operations Command. Leopole looked at Carmichael. "Sandy?"

Carmichael shifted awkwardly in her chair. Leopole knew they were acquainted from West Point and suspected they may have been something more than classmates. "Sure, ah, yes. I can call him today. But aren't we supposed to avoid U.S. military personnel?"

Derringer caught Leopole's expression and made a mental note. *Something going on there. No business of mine—unless it affects* my *business.* "Sandy's right. But go ahead and call him. Maybe the bio researchers in Maryland can put us onto a civilian immunologist who likes exotic places."

After the meeting, Derringer invited his golf partner to the office to consult with Leopole and Wolf. "Phil, you're now on the clock again. I need your help with immunology because we could use somebody who understands Marburg and Ebola. Can you suggest someone who could handle the physical challenge? It's likely to be high elevation for days at a time."

Catterly thought for a moment. "Well, let me ask: does the immunologist have to be a U.S. citizen?"

Derringer looked at Leopole, who shrugged. "I don't know. It's preferable for legal reasons, but from a practical viewpoint I'd think it's okay. Why?"

"I know a highly qualified person in Britain. In fact, she's the one who told me about the Marburg case at Heathrow. She consults for the British government and she's even investigating homeopathic remedies for Ebola."

Frank Leopole, erstwhile lieutenant colonel of marines, leaned backward as if reeling from an impact. Going on an op with a scientist, a foreigner, *and* a female. What in the name of Chesty Puller was Catterly thinking?

"Doctor, I don't think you understand," the operations officer interjected. "This mission will likely involve combat. It'll definitely involve strenuous physical activity."

"Then Carolyn Padgett-Smith is qualified, Colonel. She's a world-class rock climber, an excellent skier, and as far as I know, she's in tip-top condition. You should see her." Phillip Catterly unknowingly arched his eyebrows in a universal male gesture. *Hubba-hubba.*

"Well, how old is she?"

"Oh, early forties."

Leopole shook his head. "Doc, I'm in my forties, and this job might be a stretch for *me.* Most of our operators are in their thirties, and they work out all the time."

Catterly persisted. "It's just a thought. If you want to contact her, let me know. Otherwise, I can't think of anyone qualified both professionally and physically." He turned back to Derringer. "What about the army? Have you tried Fort Detrick?"

Derringer cleared his throat. "We're checking that out." Then he turned to Wolf. "Joe, I suppose the FBI has already talked to the boy's parents. I'll leave it up to you whether we see what the bureau will share with us or if we send our own people out there."

Wolf, who had been a rarity in the FBI hierarchy by advocating "civilian" training such as SSI's, had already alerted his domestic operations staff. A team was ready to fly to Berkeley on short notice. "I'll find out today, chief."

Derringer tapped the tabletop in a rhythmic tattoo. "Very well. Let's push this one, guys. Time is crucial."

————

After Leopole and Wolf left, Catterly remained. "Mike, I appreciate your trust in me, and I'll give you all the help I can. But if I'm going to work with some of your people I'd like some background."

Derringer sipped some raspberry iced tea. "Ahh, that's good. Sure thing, Phil. Where do you want to start?"

"Well, what's Dr. Mohammed's background?"

"Oh, he's an incredible linguist. You should read his Ph.D. dissertation: the effect of language on war. He grew up in Paris and was partly educated in Britain. His father was a diplomat for the Shah so Omar was raised speaking Farsi, Arabic, and French. He decided to concentrate on Mideast languages and picked up Hebrew just for drill. After 9-11 he read the map and concentrated on Pashto and Urdu so he could work both sides of the Afghan border. Besides that, he's conversant in Russian and I think he's studied Hindi. He said his next language is Indonesian."

"Indonesia?"

"Yeah. It has the largest Muslim population on earth, by about two and a half laps."

"So he teaches Islamic languages to your people?"

"Well, he can do that, of course, but Omar's a man of many parts. Actually he's director of training. A few years ago I brought him in for a couple of months to teach our operators about Islamic culture and some basic Arabic: asking directions, field interrogations, that sort of thing. Frankly, those segments were only marginally successful because Omar believes in immersion for really learning a language. We have better luck with former Green Beanies who studied at Monterey and worked in the Middle East. The Army was real cranky when we scooped up some of those guys, but that's another story.

"Anyway, Omar got along great with some of the door kickers, which kind of surprised us. I mean, he comes across as more an academic than an operator, and he's not exactly a boozer or a chaser. In fact, he's a pretty strict Muslim. But when he went on some exercises in Saudi and, ah, elsewhere"—Derringer raised his eyebrows—"the guys found that he kept making really good suggestions. After a few months we made him assistant training director, and he's run the department since last year."

"I'd never have guessed it. What's he do besides language and cultural stuff?"

"Oh, you name it. He's not an operator, but we have instructors for tradecraft. Omar coordinates all that with the specialists. He just knows a hell of a lot, and he has contacts throughout Europe and the Middle East. If you need somebody to teach alpine climbing or how to operate in a sand storm, he can get 'em. Basically, he's a big-picture guy: he knows what he doesn't know, but he can write a first-class training syllabus faster than anybody I've ever known."

Catterly sipped his coffee, absorbing the information. "How's he get along with the others?"

"Very few problems. Oh, Frank Leopole might still be suspicious, but he's leery of anybody who can't sing all three verses of 'The Marine Corps Hymn.' No, Omar's solid. He plays it close to the vest most of the time, but if you get to know him, he'll open up. Just don't get him started on how OBL and al Qaeda have hijacked Islam. You'll be there for hours."

BALUCHISTAN PROVINCE, PAKISTAN

The doctor known as Ali swerved his Volkswagen bus to avoid pot-holes in the road, which he thought probably owed its origins to a caravan track 'across the Toba Kakar Range bordering Afghanistan. Smugglers had been using the mountainous terrain for longer than recorded history, which suited Ali's purposes. He gave a rare grin that would have been nearly invisible amid his heavy beard. *Let them search*, he thought. *I am smuggling what cannot be detected.* He shot a sideways glance at the young woman in the passenger's seat. She sensed the doctor's gaze and turned to face him, her brown eyes peering above the dark-gray veil.

Ali allowed himself the intimacy of patting her shoulder. "Child, you are on your way to Paradise." She leaned back, absent-mindedly rubbing her forearm. She had begun feeling slightly weaker over the past two days, but bed rest compensated.

Dusk was approaching and Ali turned on the headlights. He

reckoned that three more hours on the rutted road would take him to the pavement and on to the rendezvous where other jihadists would take delivery of "the package." From there they would forward it to Karachi and thence to the realm of the Great Satan.

SSI OFFICES

Derringer's intercom buzzed, preceding Peggy Singer's announcement. "Colonel Main to see you, Admiral."

Derringer depressed the switch. "Thank you, Mrs. Singer. Please send him in." Lieutenant Colonel David Main knew enough about SSI to recognize the formalities. Having been around the office and attended a couple of holiday parties, he knew that between them, Admiral Derringer and Mrs. Singer were "Mike" and "Peggy."

Main strode into the office, again bemused at the minimalist décor for a retired flag officer. Derringer stood up, reached over the desk, and shook hands. "Thanks for coming, Dave. I appreciate it on short notice."

Main sat down, finding that the straight-backed chair resisted any effort on his part to slouch. Insiders thought that Mike Derringer believed in keeping visitors uncomfortable and thereby preventing the urge to linger and chat. "What can I do for you, sir? Sandy mentioned bio weapons."

"That's right, Dave. Uh, incidentally, she sends her apologies. Something about one of the girls."

"Ah, yessir." Main's tone and body language hinted at something beyond disappointment. Privately, Derringer felt that Ms. Carmichael had found a convenient reason to be absent when her former classmate arrived.

Derringer leaned forward. "Dave, everything today is off the record, but you've worked that way before. Now, confidentially, we're trying to track down the source of a Marburg virus that apparently was found in an American national visiting Pakistan recently. He collapsed at Heathrow a couple of days ago and he's now comatose but we're told that he indicated he was injected with the virus and there may be others."

Main's eyes widened slightly. His Been There Done That badges and ribbons testified to Ranger School, 82nd Airborne, Grenada, Desert Storm, and Bosnia. He had walked the walk and done the deed, but anything related to Ebola was an instant attention-getter.

"Ah, yessir. I understand that you might want somebody with field experience as well as an immunology degree. I guess you needed to discuss it in person."

"Correct. Now, Sandy's already observed that State will not permit any active-duty military personnel on this job owing to the current sentiments in Pakistan. So, as you've done for us before, could you reach out and find somebody maybe in the Guard or Reserve who could fill the bill?"

"Well, I'll try, Admiral. But you know, that's a rare bird you're hunting. And it might take some time. How soon do you need to know?"

Derringer sat back, his face passive. "Well, it's now 1540." Finally he grinned. "I realize you can't get anything today, but we're like 7-11. We never close."

Main stood up. "I'll let you know my initial finding by noon tomorrow."

Derringer walked the Army officer to the door. "We really appreciate it, Dave. And, by the way, my offer stands. If you ever decide to put in your papers . . ."

Main chuckled. "Thanks, Admiral. It's good to know I wouldn't have to sell my soul as a beltway bandit. But I think I'm probably doing you more good as your liaison."

Derringer patted Main's shoulder. It was partly friendly, partly paternal. "That you are, son! Oh, by the way. Long as you're here, would you mind talking to our chief pilot? I think you've met him: Terry Keegan. He may have, ah, one or two favors to ask. Frank will show you the way."

"Certainly, sir. Glad to help." It was a lie, smoothly accomplished. In truth, David Main wanted to see the start of his son's basketball game for once.

————

En route to the planning room, Leopole briefed Main on Keegan. "We keep a few critical personnel on full-time or retainer. Terry's one of the admiral's favorites."

"I think he'd just become your chief pilot when I met him before."

"Roger that. Terry's a jack-of-all-trades. He's rated for fixed wing, helos, and seaplanes: probably has more ratings than anybody I know. He and Derringer go way back."

"Really? Derringer's not an aviator, is he?"

"Nope, strictly blackshoe. But he made his name in ASW, and Terry was his star SH-3 pilot. I don't know the full story, but Terry got snagged in the Tailhook witch hunt. He asked the admiral for help, and Mike really tried, but Bush 41 wanted a head count to pacify the feminazis, who were never going to be pacified. Between you and me, I think Mike still feels some guilt about not being able to save a fine young officer's career, but it worked out for the best. Terry was one of the first hires when SSI stood up, and the firm has paid for most of his upgrades."

Approaching the technical library, Leopole and Main nearly collided with an attractive young woman. Leopole said, "Hi, Sallie. Ah, have you met Colonel Main?"

"No, I would remember." Main was briefly taken aback by the frank statement. His brain defaulted to the male ego programming that was linked to his emotional hard drive. *She thinks I'm a stud* flashed on his screen before he realized that Ms. Sallie might possibly be referring to an excellent memory.

She extended her hand. "Sallie Ann Kline," she said with a Peach Street hint in her voice. At five-foot-eleven, her green eyes were level with the officer's.

Main shook hands; Ms. Kline's grip was firm and controlled. Her beige suit and dark hair gave her a professional appearance that Main found attractive. He noticed that she quickly scanned his ribbons and badges. Apparently she could decipher the esoterica displayed on his chest.

"I've been talking to Terry about more pilot applications," Sallie explained. "He's all yours, Frank." She raised a manicured hand and waved bye-bye. "Nice to see you, Colonel."

The army man turned to watch her walk away in long, purposeful strides. "Wow. I'm married, but man, how did I miss *that*?"

Leopole chuckled. "Sallie has that effect on a lot of men. She's here for a couple weeks as a consultant. She won't accept a full-time position because she's the admiral's niece."

"Is she really as confident as she seems?"

"Oh, yeah. It's spooky, how quickly she sizes up people."

Main emitted a low whistle. "What's she do for the firm?"

"Sallie's background is marketing and personnel. She analyzes applicants and predicts their likely job performance. She tells some clients that she uses a special computer program, but mainly it's her gut feeling. She's highly intuitive; I'd guess she bats about .800."

The army man chuckled aloud. "Maybe I should introduce her to our recruiters."

They found Keegan perusing SSI's technical library where Leopole reintroduced the men and left. Rather than speaking his mind—*Whattaya want I wantta get going*—the army man said, "Say, I understand that you and the admiral served together. That's how you joined SSI?"

Terry Keegan nodded his crewcut head. "Yeah, I was in HS-2 when Tailhook blew up in '91. We were transitioning from SH-3Hs to SH-60s, and I really wanted to deploy with the Seahawk."

Main leaned on a table strewn with aircraft and engine manuals. Women in combat was a subject upon which he held devout opinions. "I heard that the Tailhook thing caught a lot of you guys."

"Hell, it caught everybody, including those who weren't even there. Just the accusation was enough to ruin your career. It was, like, 'ready, fire, aim.' CNO and SecNav were both there, but they claimed they saw nothing, and the admirals ran for cover. You know, the Tailhook Association is a civilian organization with no authority over military personnel, but Hook became the scapegoat. Nobody was standing up for the troops, and I mean nobody. Except Mike Derringer, and he wasn't even in the loop."

"What really happened, Terry?"

"Well, I couldn't stay for the whole thing and left Saturday morning. Next thing I knew, the JAG goons were beating down my door, saying they had 'proof ' I was there. Hell, I never denied it. What I did deny—and it's true—is that I ever saw any sexual harassment. Years later I learned that somebody said he'd seen a guy who looked like me with one of the women who complained. She was a pro, by the way; several of 'em hopped on the lawsuit bandwagon. Anyway, that was enough to red-flag me for promotion. It happened to lots of guys. I know one who was in San Diego that whole weekend but his name got on the 'suspect' list and that was that. No due process, no nothin'."

Main shook his head. "My god, I didn't know it was that bad. What else happened?"

"Well, I remember in 1996 Muhammad Ali went to Cuba to meet Castro, who he said he admired. That same year some politically correct captain invited Ali aboard USS *George Washington*, but the Tailhook Association—composed of naval aviators—was forbidden aboard navy vessels."

"You gotta be shittin' me!"

"No lie, GI." Keegan gave a sardonic grin. "The U.S. Fucking Navy catered to a brain-dead celebrity who seeks out communist dictators. Finally Clinton's SecNav decided enough was enough and gave his blessing to Tailhook in 2000."

"The admiral tried to help you?" Main could easily envision Derringer supporting people he valued.

"Yeah, he really did. I wrote him, not really expecting very much, but we'd had a good relationship on deployment. When he wanted somebody to follow a contact at night and maybe a high sea state, my crew usually got the call. By '92, almost a year after Vegas, it was obvious I had nothing to lose."

"Could he help?"

"Not much. He saw the handwriting on the wall and was already starting SSI. But my point is, he tried to help me and a couple of other pilots. Far as I know, Mike Derringer did more than any three active-duty flags. He called in markers, bent arms, and generally kept up the heat. I've heard that some admirals still resent him because he made them feel like wimps."

"I guess a lot of aviators are still bitter."

"Damn right. I was so disgusted that I changed my registration to Democrat and, so help me, I voted for Clinton in '92. I don't care who knows it."

Main grinned. "What about '96?"

Keegan shrugged. "Why bother? The difference between the parties is more a matter of degree than substance."

"Geez, you sound like the man without a country."

Keegan thought for a moment. "Yeah, there's something to that. Not many guys will say so, but what th' hell—I got no retirement at stake. Some of us feel that we have a government more than a country. That's why our loyalty goes to SSI. If the UN do-gooders are worried about PMCs taking the place of established governments, maybe they're right. Not that it'll happen, because at least forty percent of the population has been co-opted by perks and benefits. But I tell you what: in this outfit, loyalty up gets loyalty down. Mike Derringer says that his people come first, and he walks the walk. I could tell you a couple of stories—" Keegan slipped a knowing grin and left the sentence hovering.

Which reminded Main of his mission. "The admiral said I might be able to help you."

"Oh! Yeah." Keegan laughed at himself. "I get spooled up about what happened to us and the whole female thing."

"Roger that." Main was enjoying the male bonding, even with a squid.

Keegan picked up a manual. It was a translation of the pilot's instructions for the Russian Mi-17 helicopter, code name Hip H. "Reading the book is one thing but flying the bird is another. I know this is a stretch, but do you know if Fort Rucker or anyplace else has one of these machines? If we have to use 'em in . . . well, wherever we go, it'd be a big help to have some stick time beforehand."

Main leaned back, rubbing his chin. "Geez, Terry, that's a pretty big request, especially on short notice. It's also out of my league. If you wanted to drive a T-72, I could probably arrange it." He thought for a moment. "Let me see what I can do. I'll get back to you tomorrow."

"That'd be great, Dave. I really appreciate it, and so would the admiral. Oh, by the way, the Mi-8 would be almost as good. The 17 is the export Hip with the tail rotor on the starboard side. I'd be happy with either one."

BERKELEY, CALIFORNIA

The Lamunyon house was a low, rambling residence, a style that once would have been advertised as "ranch," but that description had long fallen into trendy disfavor. The rental car exited off Route 24 onto Alvarado and turned onto Hillcrest Road. Apparently the Lamunyons lived in the political-cultural no-man's-land between the Clairemont Country Club and the Berkeley-Clark-Kerr campus.

SSI's investigators were former bureau colleagues of Wolf's. James Mannock had finally resigned in disgust over repeated scandals in the crime lab, choosing to sell his skills in the private sector. Sherree Kim had graduated in the top ten percent of her academy class and, in the politically correct era of the '90s, seemed destined for success. But she had bumped against the FBI's glass ceiling and decided to look elsewhere rather than spend her most productive years fighting an entrenched male culture.

"Think they'll still want to talk to us?" Mannock asked.

Kim shrugged. "I dunno, Jim. Mrs. Lamunyon sounded more interested than her husband."

Mannock looked down at the five-foot-five Kim. He winked. "You're good on the phone, Sherree." She gave him a slight nudge in retaliation. It was a matter of faith in SSI that Ms. Kim had the silkiest voice in the firm.

Kim rang the doorbell as Mannock stood behind her. Without discussing details, both realized that a young Asian woman with an appealing manner would be more warmly received than a six-foot-one, balding ex-wrestler with a Joe Friday demeanor. *Just the facts, ma'am.*

The door opened partway and a matronly woman's face appeared behind the screen. "Yes?"

Kim took the initiative. "Good afternoon, Mrs. Lamunyon. I'm Sherree Kim. We talked on the phone again last night." She did not need to mention that Mr. Lamunyon had ended their first conversation on his wife's behalf.

"Oh, yes . . ."

Kim allowed Mrs. Lamunyon no chance to end the discussion so abruptly. "We really appreciate your taking time to talk to us, ma'am.

This is my assistant, Mr. Mannock." Before the burly former athlete could kick her from behind, Kim pressed on. "May we come in for a moment?"

Marian Lamunyon opened the screen enough to look up and down the street. *She's worried that hubby will come home*, Kim realized.

"I promise we'll only be a few minutes, ma'am. And we've had *such* a long trip." Sometimes a little guilt went a long way.

It worked.

Mrs. Lamunyon invited the visitors into the sitting room. While Kim worked her people skills, Mannock pretended to be interested in the family photos on the wall. Apparently Jason had a teenage sister—something of a babe—and the family swarmed with pets. In truth, the ex-fed knew that there were ways of gaining information without asking questions.

"I don't really know what more I can tell you," Marian began. "We already talked to those government investigators."

"Yes, ma'am. We're just trying to be thorough and maybe pick up some details that could help tell you more about Jason's, ah, last few weeks."

"Well, Keith talked to the detectives more than I did." She leaned close, feeling more comfortable with the friendly young woman. "He's still embarrassed that Jason went and joined those Muslims."

"Detectives, ma'am?"

"Well, I guess they were detectives. They had badges and everything. They wore suits, not uniforms, you know."

"Were they local police or federal agents? Maybe FBI?"

Marian sat up straight. "Oh, you're right. They were FBI men. I'm just used to those TV shows. Like *Barney Miller* and *Hill Street Blues*."

Kim and Mannock exchanged knowing glances. Both managed to avoid smiling.

"Mrs. Lamunyon, we think we can help you the most if we know more about Jason's time in Arabia and Pakistan. For example, where did he stay? Who did he see?"

"Keith gave those detec . . . er . . . FBI men a list of where Jason went. At least what we knew. But really, Miss Kim, I don't know much beyond that. We hardly heard from him after he left. Just a couple of notes."

"Did the other investigators take them?"

"What? The notes? Oh, no. Keith wouldn't talk about those. He told me not to mention them."

Mannock abruptly turned from the photo gallery and sat beside Kim. She decided to go for broke. "Ma'am, would you mind if we looked at those notes?"

Mrs. Lamunyon's composure, never serene, visibly tightened. She began rubbing her hands unconsciously. "You know, my husband is due . . ."

Kim reached across the settee and placed her own hand on the mother's. "If we could see Jason's notes, we'd be able to leave right away."

Without speaking, the grieving woman rose and left the room. When she returned there were tears in the corners of her eyes.

Mannock produced a notepad and copied everything: postal marks, type of paper, and exact spelling with errors. Kim scanned them twice; one was a single sheet, the other one and a half. There were references to a couple of obscure villages, and both letters mentioned "Dr. Ali."

Kim carefully refolded the papers and laid them on the table with the envelopes. She rose to go and Mannock stepped back to the picture gallery.

"Thank you *so* much, Mrs. Lamunyon. You've been very helpful."

Mannock, who had hardly spoken, seized one last chance. "I see that animals are popular in your family, ma'am. We have two dogs and some cats ourselves."

Sherree managed to keep a straight face. She knew that Mannock was allergic to most animals.

Marian Lamunyon beamed for a change. "Oh, yes. Jason just loves . . . loved . . . animals. He wanted to be a veterinarian, you know. He volunteered at the animal clinic."

Kim shook her head. "No, we didn't know that. Ah, what else was he interested in?"

"Oh, he used to like girls and cars and music. A California boy, you know." Her smile faded. "Then a couple years ago he got into that Islamic thing . . ."

Sherree Kim managed to keep a level tone in her voice. "Yes, ma'am. We know."

SSI OFFICES

The next afternoon Derringer convened a conference in his office. Typically, he went straight to the point. "Dave Main called me during the noon hour. He says we could probably get somebody who's professionally and physically qualified if we had more time. The AMRIID civilians were a good suggestion, but it's no go. He checked at Fort Detrick. A couple of the ones we'd consider are essential personnel. Others are out of the country or not interested in our, uh, adventure."

Derringer turned to Wolf. "What did you find at CDC, Joe? Don't they have some ex-military types?"

The domestic ops chief shook his head. "I talked to the assistant director myself. They have about 5,500 people just in Atlanta but that includes everything from admin types to birth defects and accident prevention. She didn't know of anybody with Marburg background *and* the kind of field experience we need. At least not in the time available."

SSI's founder leaned back in his chair, tapping his right-hand fingers in a rhythmic tattoo. Nobody but his few intimates knew that the young Michael had won a state championship playing snare in his drum and bugle corps. *Flam-flam paradiddle; flam-flam paradiddle; paradiddle-paradiddle, tap-tap-tap.*

"Very well. I'll call Phil and see if he can get his British friend. If it were up to me, I'd take the best-qualified military immunologist we could find and just keep our mouths shut, but the firm's reputation is on the line.

"Frank, you should talk to Phil, too. Your guys can start assembling the medical gear we'll likely need. I doubt if we have much of it in stock, especially biohazard suits and decontamination equipment. Check with Terry about loading the aircraft, because you'll be better off taking what you need rather than trying to get it from the locals."

"Roger that."

LONDON

Dr. Carolyn Padgett-Smith checked her emails before dinner and found an intriguing message from Phil Catterly. She phoned him immediately.

"Phillip, Carolyn here."

"Oh, thanks for calling, Carolyn. Ah, you can probably read between the lines, but is your passport up to date?"

"It is. And I have appropriate inoculations for Pakistan."

"Well, I'm authorized to ask on behalf of a U.S. Government contractor if you would be, uh, available for as much as a couple of weeks . . ."

Dr. Padgett-Smith did not want to assume too much. "Are you offering me the chance of a lifetime, Phillip? A view of barren vistas in the company of bronzed, hardy young men?"

"CPS, you've read too much Kipling. This could be damned dangerous, and . . ."

"Why, I should love the opportunity to climb some new rocks. Do tell me more."

Padgett-Smith never did get a proper dinner.

After ringing off, she phoned an unlisted number in Sussex. A familiar male voice resonated in her ear. "Why, Carolyn! What can I do for my favorite ex-sister-in-law?"

"Now, Tony. Don't be so cynical. Why do you always assume that I want something?"

"Because you always do, love."

Carolyn was reminded why Lydia had divorced the former soldier. He was inevitably so damnably *right* about everything. Not to mention that he was inevitably so damnably *gone*. If only the parachuting accident had occurred a few months earlier, their marriage might have survived. Tony insisted that he saw his ex more since the divorce than during the two-year duration, and Carolyn suspected that the once-unhappy couple had renewed conjugal relations.

"Tony, I need to ask a big favor, but I can't say too much. You understand how it is. Well, suffice to say that I shall be traveling abroad in areas where the locals are decidedly restless, and they do not take kindly to western females."

"That could cover a great deal of geography. The wogs begin at Calais, you know."

CPS relaxed. With Tony lapsing into the old, familiar banter, she was halfway home. "Ah, Tony, you recall when I addressed your colleagues about the emerging bio threat about a year and a half ago?"

"Certainly. You were a hit."

"Well, I wonder if the colonel's offer still stands."

"What offer was that?"

"He said, 'Dr. Padgett-Smith, if ever I may be of assistance in your counter terrorism efforts, do not hesitate to contact me.' Of course, I've long since mislaid his card."

Tony did the mental gymnastics. Foreign travel, exotic climes, hint of danger. SAS assistance. It was getting interesting. "I can call him tonight, Padgers. But what do you need?"

She told him.

3

SSI OFFICES

"Gentlemen, this is your initial brief on the Pandora Project." As head of SSI's foreign operations division, Frank Leopole had assembled the team for background briefing with other company principals on hand.

"We called this mission the Pandora Project because it's like Pandora's Box. Some radical Muslims apparently have injected suicide volunteers with Marburg virus, which is related to Ebola. There is no known cure for either. So, once the bug is out of the box—or the genie out of the bottle—there's no going back." He paused for emphasis, then said, "Dr. Catterly is our expert on the subject. I'll let him explain."

Catterly began. "Ebola can be eighty percent fatal, while Marburg runs twenty-five percent or more, if that's any consolation. Anyway, our concern is the first carrier, who was found in Britain a few days ago. He was a young Californian, a convert to Islam, who collapsed at

Heathrow Airport. When he was diagnosed with Marburg, the Brits contacted us and the job was offered to Admiral Derringer. Unfortunately, the host now has died without providing much information."

The former ranger called Bosco was known for his flippancy. This time was no different. "So when did this California convert collect his seventy-two virgins?"

Leopole glanced at Dr. Mohammed. "That's not funny, Bosco. The, ah, young man died three days ago."

Leopole returned to pertinent matters. "Mission: to find and capture, if possible, the source of the virus. Mr. Wolf's investigators have talked to the carrier's family in California, and they learned that he was staying with a Pakistani doctor known as Ali. We don't know if that's his real name but we're working both domestic and foreign intel sources.

"Op area: the most likely region is Baluchistan Province, on the Afghan border. Quetta, the capital, runs about 650,000 people. It's headquarters of the Pakis' XII Corps, nominally with two infantry divisions and supporting units plus police and border guards. I have street maps for everybody."

The ops officer turned on his PowerPoint display and clicked on the first subject. Satellite imagery of the area appeared on the screen. "Terrain is what you'd expect: high and often steep. Median elevation is 5,500 MSL.

"Local situation: increased border security has gone into effect with some checkpoints as much as one klick apart. There's usually long lines at the gateways but smugglers can nearly always get through. Drugs and weapons are the major contraband, though apparently some high-value assets have passed through. The border guards have been increased at each station but if the contraband is primo, it doesn't add a lot to the overhead to grease two or three palms.

"Equipment: we'll mainly take what the locals use. That means G3 rifles, Browning Highpower pistols, and some of our own special gear. Plan on suppressed MP-5s and a couple of precision rifles. Also nonlethal weapons including tasers and bean bags. Anybody who's not checked out for their use, see Chuck. Night vision will also be issued."

"Our contacts are supposed to provide suitable uniforms but

we'll have generic civilian clothes as well. Everybody start growing beards or mustaches. You'll blend in better.

"Comm: two common channels plus one for each team. Standard voice-activated headsets to keep our hands free. The respirators have limited comm, so we'll hold a couple of nonverbal refresher sessions. Because of the cross-border prospects, Dr. Mohammed is going with us. We don't have anybody else readily available who's conversant in both Urdu for Pakistan and Pashto in Afghanistan."

Moahmmed interjected to pursue the linguistic concerns. "There are two Urdu dialects, northern and southern. The northern uses a *kh* sound as opposed to the southern *sh*. We will likely be operating within the southern, Kandahar dialect." He gestured to a box full of manuals on the table. "I will distribute these Urdu phrase books after the briefing. They contain much useful information, such as how to pronounce 'hello,' 'thank you,' and 'drop your weapon.' " The audience laughed appreciatively as Mohammed sat down.

Leopole continued. "Navigation: the usual GPS sets but I'm taking a British Army terrain map. We'll add the known threat areas before liftoff.

"Transport: most likely we'll fly in and out, courtesy of the Paki army. We're also trying to pre-position ground transport but that's uncertain." He smiled at J. J. Johnson, who had done a stretch in the Foreign Legion. "If we need to commandeer local vehicles, J. J. can hotwire anything from an ox cart to a T-72."

"Casualties: Jeff and Jerry and Breezy are up to speed on combat medicine. We'll probably have a guest medic for advice on the bio hazard but don't know who yet. Personnel is trying to find somebody with scientific and field experience. Terry and his guys will be on hand for dustoff in case we need to air-evac. They're studying the Hip manual and may get some stick time. At any rate, one of our guys will be aboard each Paki chopper."

Leopole glanced at the screen and clicked on the next subject of his PowerPoint file. As an experienced staff officer, he preferred to show each topic in sequence to avoid his audience reading ahead of his commentary.

"Biohazard. As you've heard, the Marburg virus is a potential killer. We're getting biological suits from Dr. Catterly and we'll have a couple of trial runs so the entry teams know how to use them. We're also taking a couple hundred gallons of bleach and disinfectant plus a portable generator to spray everything that enters a likely hot zone. We'll burn the disposable portions of the suits as well as the hospital scrubs."

Bosco raised a hand. "Uh, why scrubs?"

Leopole nodded toward Catterly, who responded. "Any bacteria can host a virus. So you'll wear disposable scrubs with the bio suits but no underwear. I also recommend that you take several changes of clean clothes because there's a slight risk in wearing the same material after possible exposure."

The operators exchanged solemn glances. A few fidgeted in their seats. For once there was no joking.

"Friendly forces: we'll take three teams. I'll have Red; Steve has White, and Dan has Blue. Twelve men per team with six bio suits for each. The others will provide perimeter security and transport, and everybody helps with decontamination. Terry's divided the flight crews into Black and Green."

Steven Lee was a former army major with a two-inch-thick personnel file and two ex-wives. Other than Catterly, he was the only man in the room wearing glasses, which he described as "tactical eyewear." Lee lived for action, forsaking his father's computer fortune in San Francisco in favor of more exotic climes. He had operated in Afghanistan and spoke some Pashto. Leopole considered him the finest raid planner he had ever met.

Daniel Foyte was another divorced veteran. With two college-age daughters, he was originally drawn to SSI from the Marine Corps but soon found that he enjoyed working for Mike Derringer. His dossier showed seven years with Marine Force Recon, including four years as an instructor. Gunnery Sergeant Foyte and Lieutenant Colonel Leopole were closer than any other SSI operators. They had hunted, fished, hiked, and fought together. Every November 10th they observed their corps' anniversary with quantities of adult beverages. SOP was to take a cab to their favorite bistro, tear a fifty-dollar bill in half, and give Ulysses S. Grant's left half to the cabbie. He collected the president's right half at the stroke of midnight.

Foyte waved a hand. "Colonel, who do we work with over there?"

Leopole almost smiled. In the presence of others, the former noncom was scrupulously formal when addressing former officers. In private, whether hunting in Nebraska or hiking the Blue Ridge, Leopole was "Frank" or "Hey maggot."

"Coming to that, Dan. The admiral and Dr. Mohammed have contacts with our embassy and the Pakistani security force." Intentional groans met that bit of intelligence. Nobody in the room had any faith in the United States State Department, and Islamabad's ISI was known to sympathize with the *mujahadin*. "Pipe down, you guys. Our, ah, colleagues, are with the Paki army, not their intelligence service. Security is crucial if we're going to catch these bastards, and nobody knows exactly what we're after. But the admiral thinks we need the embassy for greasing the skids, and we might need the Pakis to get us out of Dodge. You'll meet our friends on the other end."

Leopole continued down his list. "Enemy forces: unknown. Our Pakistani doctor may or may not have a security detail. We'll likely outnumber them but we can't count on it. Anyway, the usual cautions apply. Take all the ammo you can carry and extra water. Local sources are always suspect."

Steve Lee raised his pen. "How do we get to Pakistan? SS Air?"

Soft laughter tittered through the room.

"Affirm. We'll use the company 727 and we'll lease another bird, half the operators on each plane." Nobody had to ask about the division of labor when SSI's "Jurassic jet" could easily handle the full team with room left over. Too much was at stake for the Pandora Project to lose all its personnel in one plane crash.

"Now, obviously we need more information but time is crucial so we're planning on wheels in the well day after tomorrow. Once the team is assembled in-country we'll have updates from Mr. Wolf and his domestic ops staff. In fact, they're in California right now, talking to the carrier's family." He surveyed the room. "Any other questions?"

Trying to redeem himself, Bosco asked, "Colonel, what about the medical aspects? I mean, if we're dealing with some really bad shit, how do we handle it if we find these guys?"

Leopole sighed, almost audibly. What he was about to impart was a sore point. "The government won't allow active-duty personnel on this job so our Pentagon liaison tried to find a Guard or Reserve member who's knowledgeable about the disease and able to keep up with you guys. We ran out of time, so Dr. Catterly contacted the British immunologist who notified him. Apparently Dr."—he checked his notes—"Dr. Padgett-Smith is a skier and mountain climber and she's willing to go along."

A low buzz flitted through the room. Bosco leaned over to Breezy. "Did he say *she?*"

When the meeting broke up, some of the operators gathered around the coffee pot, thumbing through a U.S. Army manual from the Monterey language school. A former cop named Phil Green was the self-appointed linguist of the SSI door kickers; he could say "don't shoot" in twenty-two languages. "Lessee," he murmured. " 'Hands up' is *laasuna portakra*. 'Stop' is *wodariga*, and 'Don't move' is *harakat makawa*." He shrugged, then deadpanned, "That seems simple enough."

Nearby, Mohammed overheard Bosco's partner, Breezy Brezyinski. "Seventy-two virgins? Man, I thought it was twelve."

"And I heard it was, like, twenty." Slouching against the table, ex-SEAL Jeffrey Malten was suddenly attentive.

Bosco shrugged. "Maybe it's virgin inflation or somethin'."

Breezy had just taken a gulp of coffee, unfortunately timed with the sudden ingestion of air in response to Bosco's irreverence. The result was a two-minute laughing-coughing fit.

Bosco pounded Breezy on the back until the affliction passed. Then he noticed Dr. Mohammed. "Uh. Sir, what's the Koran say about all those virgins, anyway?"

Mohammed shook his head in bemusement tinged with disgust. "Not that it matters to any of you . . . gentlemen . . . but it's not in the Koran. It is from a collection of traditional beliefs or sayings, the Hadith. It is similar to the Apocrypha for Christians, though there are different interpretations. The Prophet apparently referred to the righteous receiving eighty-thousand servants and seventy-two wives. But in French the passage reads *des belles aux seins arrondis*, or beautiful women with round breasts."

Regaining his breath, Breezy focused on the celestial plane. "Hey, I wonder if you could, like, switch the numbers, you know?"

Malten, uncharacteristically sensitive for a SEAL, elbowed the erstwhile paratrooper. "Quiet down, you jerk. Doc Mohammed will hear you."

Breezy would not be deterred. "Wow, man. With eighty-thousand virgins you could have one a day for, like, three hundred years! Besides, seventy servants would be plenty for me."

Bosco did the math. "Uh . . . more like 220 years." Whatever his social failings, former Sergeant Jason Boscombe predated outcome-based education. Friends knew that his penchant for numbers included baseball stats and Vegas odds.

Straightening up for a change, Malten asked, "Doctor, no offense, but does that paradise stuff apply to converts like this American kid?"

Mohammed almost welcomed the query as intellectual discourse. "Well, yes, I suppose so. You see, some believe that the surest way for a devout Muslim to enter paradise is to die in a *jihad*." His dark eyes swept the audience. "Any takers, gentlemen?"

ANNANDALE, VIRGINIA

SSI did not own a shooting facility, but Frank Leopole had a friend who did. Lock, Stock & Barrel often rented its indoor range to corporations, but this evening Leopole requested access after hours. It would not be politic to have the public observe men in "space suits" wielding submachine guns.

The door kickers tried on the Racal suits for Biosafety Level 4 protection. They had battery-powered oxygen systems with positive internal pressure to deter contaminated air from entering. The most obvious feature, apart from the bright orange color, was the futuristic plastic helmet. The "bubble" design permitted the user full range of head motion and all-round vision.

It was not meant for riflemen.

Dr. Phillip Catterly, who had hauled within three strokes of Admiral Derringer's golf handicap, did not share his partner's enthusiasm for firearms. But after explaining the workings of the Racals, he supervised each shooter's initial fitting, offering practical advice as he went.

Catterly held up a roll of duct tape. "Before you enter a potential hot zone, I recommend that you tear off a couple of strips and stick them where you can easily reach them. If you get . . . well, if you rip the suit, or something, you can slap on a temporary patch right away and probably be okay."

Leopole had complete trust in the other team leaders and allowed them to make their own assignments. Dan Foyte decided to remain with the perimeter guards to coordinate Blue Team operations while Steve Lee relished being first man through the door. He would lead White Team's door kickers and began wedging himself into the Racal.

Breezy was already suited up. He ambled around the room, impersonating Neil Armstrong on the Sea of Tranquility, though The Eagle had landed six years before Mark Casimir Brezyinski was born. Once accustomed to the fit of the Racal, he picked up an MP-5, cycled the bolt three times to ensure it was empty, and tried hefting it into firing position. As expected, the "space helmet" got in the way.

"No cheek weld, man. Bummer."

Leopole had long since tried to expunge the hey-dude argot from SSI's operators. Though most were in their thirties, some like Bosco and Breezy clung to the adolescent vocabulary of a bygone era.

"It's what I told you would happen," the former marine exclaimed. "That's why we're putting lasers on every long gun we take. You can shoot from a mid-chest position with good accuracy. Or you can shoot normally with a pistol."

He patted the three-magazine pouch on his duty belt. "Ordinary web gear won't fit very well with the pressure suit so we'll have to gin up something else. Best thing that occurs to me is a couple of bags slung over the shoulders: one for reloads and the other for grenades and a pistol."

Then Leopole raised his MP-5 from its tactical sling, stepped to the firing line, and called over his shoulder. "Lights."

As the building's lights dimmed, he inserted a magazine of 9mm frangible ammunition and called, "Going hot."

Leopole was already wearing pale blue Dillon hearing protectors. He glanced sideways at Breezy, who reflexively raised his hands to cover his ears. His palms collided with the plastic helmet.

Extending the Heckler-Koch straight forward against the limits of its sling, Leopole leaned forward slightly, pressed the laser switch on the forestock, and tracked the bright red dot onto the fifteen-meter target. Breezy had just shouted "Wait!" when Leopole pressed the trigger.

The MP-5 spat out three rounds on burst control. A cluster of hits appeared in the center of the cardboard target. Leopole then raised the aiming dot to the squared-off head and fired again. Two rounds punctured the nostril area.

Bosco stepped to the line beside his partner. "Way cool. The noise isn't so bad inside this helmet, ya know?" He held his weapon in his right hand, a loaded magazine in his left.

"Fershure, dewd." Breezy inserted a magazine in his HK and waited for the command from the rangemaster. In a few minutes their lasers were zeroed at twenty-five meters, and the rest of the team took its turn.

A dozen shooters went through two cases of ammo before midnight. At the end of the session Breezy exclaimed, "Man, I'm set. Six mags and I'm stress-free all week."

CREDENHILL, HEREFORDSHIRE

Carolyn Padgett-Smith sat in Tony Williamson's Austin while he chatted up the warrant officer in the armory. Fifteen minutes later he emerged with a soft rifle case and boxes of 9mm and 7.62x39 ammunition. He slid into the right-hand seat, put the car in gear, and drove off. "We've got about four hours," he said.

"What did you tell them?"

Tony looked at the immunologist. "I took the course of last resort. I told the truth, love."

She laughed and punched his arm. Though lacking specifics, she had told the SAS veteran all he needed to know when she said, "I am not going to be defenseless among people who cut off the heads of hostages."

At a twenty-five-meter pistol range Tony set up two silhouette targets, one with a bull's-eye and the other with the old "Charging

Hun." He placed Carolyn at ten meters from the bull and produced a Browning Hipower pistol.

"Right. Safety first, love. There are all sorts of regulations, but you only need to keep two rules in mind." He held up one finger. "First, keep your finger off the trigger until your sights are on target. Always. Forever and a day. In close quarters sometimes you can't avoid sweeping someone . . ."

"Sweeping?"

"Covering them with the muzzle of your gun. But if you keep your finger off the trigger, you'll be safe and so will they."

Carolyn nodded, regarding the Browning with ambivalence. She had never cared for guns, pro or con. Charles used to shoot grouse but that was ages ago.

Tony held up a second finger. "Two. If you can help it, never point the weapon at anybody you're unwilling to kill, including yourself. Common sense, I know, but cemeteries are filled with blokes who got careless." He handed the pistol to her.

"Right." He pointed out the salient features. "Front sight, rear sight, trigger, hammer, frame, and slide. Forget everything you've seen in the movies, love. Pistols are shot at eye level with the front sight centered in the rear sight notch. This is a common pistol, one you're likely to encounter . . . well, wherever. Most others work pretty much the same way. It holds a detachable magazine with thirteen nine-millimeter rounds but we'll come to that in a bit. This one has some modifications." He neglected to mention that it was his personal weapon, retained in violation of certain of Her Majesty's draconian ordinances. He relied on his status as a onetime Territorial officer to cover that topic.

Tony demonstrated the grip and stance, and walked Carolyn through a quarter hour of dry firing. Finally he demonstrated loading, safety activation, and firing. After donning eye and ear protection, he raised the Hipower with both hands, got a quick sight picture, and put three rounds in the six-inch bull in two seconds. "Now you. But take your time."

Tony called a break after thirty minutes. By then Carolyn was able to keep half of her rounds in the black at fifteen meters—better than he expected. "Too bad we don't have more time, though it'd be hard to get this range again anytime soon." He regarded her slyly. "Now, if you could get to America for a week you'd be safe as houses."

"How's that?"

"Well, those chaps can shoot almost anything they want, nearly anywhere. Especially schools like Gunsite and Thunder Ranch. Far different from here, you know."

She grinned at her former in-law. "Something about a difference of opinion regarding eighteenth-century Crown tax policy, I believe."

"Right. Here we go again. I've loaded some magazines with a few duds so you'll have to clear malfunctions as I showed you. Also, I want you to start firing doubles at the heart followed by one to the head. It's called the Mozambique Drill."

She shook her head. "Mozambique?"

"It was popularized in Africa in the 1970s. 'Two to the body and one to the head . . . every time . . . leaves 'em dead.' It's what we call a failure drill. About half the time, two nine millimeters to the body don't put the chap down. In that case there's no point in shooting him in the body again, so the next round goes between the lights."

Carolyn learned the procedure and did moderately well. However, her trigger control needed work, as she frequently pulled the third shot low and left. Tony checked his watch and made a decision. "I want to familiarize you with the AK-47 but we'll stick with this a bit longer. From now on, love, after you shoot, *move*. At least three steps diagonally backward, left or right. Preferably toward some cover like a building or rock."

After another rest, Tony produced the Kalashnikov. "This is the most common firearm on earth. You find it everywhere." Carolyn had seen the Islamic icon on television, but had never been near one. It struck her as businesslike, devoid of elegance, wholly functional. "I'm going to show you how it works," he explained, "and you'll fire a couple of mags so you can use one if you need to."

He demonstrated the curved magazine and how it was inserted and removed. He had her chamber a round and activate the safety several times. "This is a selective fire weapon, meaning it's both semi and fully automatic. There's no point in you trying to shoot full auto—that takes training. If you have to use one, push the selector lever to the *bottom* position, after safe on top and auto in the middle.

If it's fully loaded, you have thirty rounds semi-auto. Sighting is the same as before: front sight aligned with the rear."

Carolyn snugged the stock into her shoulder, using rearward pressure with her right hand on the pistol grip as Tony had explained. With her sights aligned on the bull's-eye, she pressed the trigger. The rifle barked and she issued a slight yelp. Tony's hand steadied her from behind. "That's an object lesson, love. Remember to lean into it a bit. This is not a heavy recoiling rifle, but it's much more than the pistol."

At the end of the session, Dr. Padgett-Smith was putting two rounds within five inches of each other at twenty-five meters, offhand.

Over drinks at a nearby pub, she asked, "So tell me, Tony. How'd I do?"

"For a complete novice, unusually well. But then you're more motivated than most. I could increase your speed with a couple more sessions, but that's tough. I owe the colonel a big one just for today."

She leaned close. "You know, it's sort of . . . fun."

Tony Williamson leaned back, regarding his beautiful sister-in-law. "I tried to convince Lydia of that, you know. Not much luck there, and my career was in the regiment."

"So . . . are you seeing each other again?"

He drained the last of his ale. "You know damned well we are!"

"Well . . ." She arched her eyebrows.

Tony set his empty glass down on the table with a forceful thud. "Well, as I was saying, pistol shooting is a highly perishable skill. If you get any chance at all, be sure to have your chums get you another session."

SSI OFFICES

"How's the voyage shaping up, Magellan?" Leopole seldom missed a chance to toss a jibe at his ex-navy counterpart.

Keegan glanced up from his aeronautical charts. He tried to appear nonchalant, but the ten-thousand-mile trip had him more interested than any recent event. "Pretty routine, actually, Frank. We'll be lightly loaded so we can use the 727's long-range tanks. Depending on the winds, we should make Dulles to Goose Bay no sweat, then

Reykjavik to London. I guess we'll be there for a day or so to pick up the Brit babe."

"Uh, you mean Dr. Padgett-Smith, the prominent immunologist."

"Yeah, the Brit babe. Then on to Athens and Islamabad via Oman. Too bad we can't overfly Iran. It'd cut half the time off our last leg."

"Well, we might ask permission but the admiral thinks we . . ."

"I know. And I don't disagree. Now, the 757 has a three-thousand-mile range. We could cut out most of the fuel stops. With the Jurassic Jet we're limited to two thousand miles nautical with any reserve."

Leopole laughed at the moniker. The Boeing 727-200 was still popular with some companies because it was relatively inexpensive, and SSI's had long since been amortized. "Take it up with the board of directors."

"Maybe I should. I mean, we might consider a lease-to-buy arrangement."

"Well, go ahead and work it up. Hell, I'll even support the idea. But remember, Terry, sometimes security outweighs the finances. If we want to lease a jet, and provide our own crew, and decline to say where we're going, the owners are going to get nervous." He shrugged. "I can't blame 'em."

Keegan laid down his old-fashioned Jeppesen E6B flight computer with its rotating dial and printed grid. There were easier ways to do the navigation but he enjoyed the way he'd been taught. "We're still splitting up the teams?"

"Affirmative. You'll take Red and White while the leased Falcon takes Blue and another flight crew. Everybody meets in Islamabad in three days."

"It might be tight with fourteen bubbas and some gear in a Falcon 200 but they should be okay since I'm packing most of the equipment. I already checked with maintenance. Our bird is good to go."

Leopole nodded. "Okay. Uh, how about the choppers?"

"I asked Dave about getting a Hip checkout but we're running out of time. I wish we had another helo pilot, too. That Guatemalan job took Dave and Morrie and we can't get them back soon enough. The new guy, Eddie Marsh, is fine but there's no backup. We'll have to rely on the Pakis to some extent."

"Concur. But I endorsed your memo to Pat Finch for two more

rotorheads on the staff. He hasn't got back to me officially but I think that Personnel will recommend approval to the board."

Keegan grinned self-consciously. "Yeah, that's what Sallie said. I told her it might help if they recommend dual-rated guys. Uh, you know . . . like me. Fixed wing *and* helos. Bean counters like getting more bang for their buck."

Leopole saw an opportunity. "Hey, Sallie made quite an impression on Dave Main."

The pilot smiled broadly. "Sallie makes quite an impression on everybody."

Leopole eyed his counterpart. He suspected that Ms. Kline and Mr. Keegan might have socialized at one point. If so, they were an odd couple: she was a spiritualist and he an agnostic. But as Mike Derringer always said, it takes all kinds to fill a battleship.

OUTSIDE KARACHI

Ali reached his rendezvous almost two hours late. Nobody objected.

The doctor stepped out of the VW van, leaving his passenger inside. Ali was greeted by his reception committee, headed by a Syrian expatriate named Kassim. "My brother, peace be with you."

"And unto you," Ali replied. He held few men in absolute trust, but Kassim was among them. If nothing else, the man's loss of a foot to a Soviet mine had earned him trust on earth and a seat in Paradise.

Kassim gestured behind him. "I have two good men, *mujahadin* who have proven their worth many times. We shall escort the woman to the airport and one of them will be her traveling companion."

"The papers are prepared, then?"

Kassim nodded gravely. "They are genuine. We have certain . . . friends. They travel routinely to Amman and then will enter the Zionist zone."

Ali's teeth showed as he smiled in the dark. "All is proceeding as planned, then. The first, ah, package, departed Islamabad a few days ago. When the westerners and their Jewish masters look into this case, they will have an even wider area to cover."

Kassim glanced at the van again; the woman's dark shape blended into the night. "Does she truly understand what awaits her?"

Ali nodded vigorously. "It is one thing to pull a pin or push a plunger and vanish in an instant. Before the warrior knows it, he awakens in Paradise. But this . . ." he nodded toward the young woman in the van. "This method requires vastly more courage and devotion."

Kassim's companion joined them, a carpenter known as Farrukh Awan. Ali had noticed that they spent more time together of late.

Looking at the woman, Kassim said, "Perhaps she will become a vestal virgin. She shames us all." Ali suspected that he offered the sentiment for Awan's benefit. The young man had potential.

Ali placed a bony hand on his colleague's arm. "She was going to die anyway, you know. And I would not save her if I could—she is far too valuable this way. Just remember, we cannot all be messengers, my friend. Some of us must prepare the message. But God will know his servants, and all shall receive his blessing."

Before handing over the woman to Kassim's team, Ali beckoned to her. She stepped from the van, moving slowly and with apparent difficulty. When she approached him he raised a hand in benediction. Obviously quoting from memory, he intoned,

"Pledge. O Sister, the following against the unbelievers:

"Covenant, O Sister . . . to make their women widows and their children orphans.

"Covenant, O Sister . . . to make them desire death and hate appointments and prestige.

"Covenant, O Sister . . . to slaughter them like lambs and let the Nile, al-Asi, and Euphrates Rivers flow with their blood.

"Covenant, O Sister . . . to be a pick of destruction for every godless and apostate regime.

"Covenant, O Sister . . . to retaliate for you against every dog who touch you even with a bad word."

The female jihadist placed her right hand on her forehead, bowed toward her benefactor, and walked toward the other vehicle. The rough-hewn men of Kassim's team stepped aside, watching her with reverential curiosity.

Meanwhile, the Syrian leaned close to Ali, speaking softly. "When shall we expect the next, um, shipment?"

"Most likely within a week. Such volunteers are rare, and I am adjusting the dosage to provide some overlap, but it is an inexact science. I would prefer to release all the carriers at once, but the most willing have terminal illnesses and their condition dictates the schedule. However, God willing, we shall have some to disperse among the Crusaders' accomplices as well as in the West itself."

"*Inshallah,*" Kassim exclaimed in his native Arabic.

"God willing," Ali translated in Urdu. Whatever the language, the sentiment was exactly the same.

SSI OFFICES

Mike Derringer felt that he walked a fine line before the teams left. He wanted to bid his operators good-bye and good hunting, but he did not wish to overstate the matter. Therefore, he decided on last-minute handshakes at the airport. Meanwhile, he convened a final meeting with his braintrust.

Inevitably, Derringer launched into one of his favorite subjects, ironically, one that usually left him depressed. He began, "The problem with the global war on terrorism—well, all right, there's a lot more than one. But in comparison with conventional war, there's no way to get a grip on the size of the problem. A few days ago the news reported that coalition troops killed or captured about seventy combatants in Iraq. A few days before that, twenty or so Taliban were killed in Afghanistan. Okay, let's take those numbers at face value. What do they mean?"

There was silence in the room.

Derringer nodded his balding head. "Exactly." Then he grinned. "You don't know, and neither do I. Hell, I suspect that nobody knows— maybe not even our enemy. The point is, we have no idea what the loss of ninety or a hundred men represents. Is it a lot? A few? Does it matter at all?" He shrugged. "Nobody knows."

Leopole rubbed his high-and-tight haircut—an unconscious sign of irritability. "Admiral, I see your point. But shouldn't we be careful about a body count mentality?"

"Yes, Frank, we should. And I would be well down the list of those who would ever endorse Robert Strange McNamara's approach to anything: from Edsels to Vietnam. Hell, the bastard didn't even believe in his own war. But at least in Vietnam we had a rough idea of the enemy's strength. Now . . ." His voice trailed off.

The retired marine picked up the retired admiral's thought. "Yes, sir. Apparently EOB estimates still run from several hundred to maybe twenty thousand." Establishing enemy order of battle had long been a sore point in the Pentagon; it still was.

Derringer found his voice again. "Let's look at it another way: reverse the numbers. If we or the coalition lost seventy men in Iraq and twenty more in Afghanistan in a couple of days, what would be the result?"

"Some kind of policy change," offered Wolfe. "We might even pull out."

"I tend to agree. But we know our force levels. One hundred dead represents, what? A fraction of a percent. In the overall scheme, it's tiny. But in a country where the press lives by the motto 'If it bleeds, it leads,' that tiny number could have enormous effect.

"Which is why this Marburg project is so important. In Clauswitzian terms, it's elegant: economy of force writ large. Sacrifice a handful of suicidal hosts in exchange for tens of thousands of casualties, and not just on the battlefield. People dying in droves in Heartland, USA. But you know what? The human cost would not be the decisive factor. The knockout blow would be economic. Let a pandemic loose in this country, and maybe Western Europe as well, and the Western economy would tank. It might take decades to recover."

Knowing he had made his point, Derringer surveyed the audience. He was met with level gazes of planners and operators who already shared his tacit sentiment. But he spoke the words anyway. "Find them, gentlemen. Find them and kill them."

5

"Tartan coming up." Keegan's first officer called the position as the 727 approached another waypoint. In a previous existence Earl "Hearty" Boharty had been an E-2 copilot, accustomed to landing Hawkeyes on carrier decks. Compared to that, driving a 727 across the Atlantic was almost a no-brainer. As another Tailhook orphan, he shared Keegan's low opinion of both naval leadership and the Republican Party.

Boharty fingered the next reporting point on the aeronautical chart, perhaps symbolically labled "Tartan." Over water, the 727 was mostly out of VHF range so voice communication was accomplished via high frequency. Therefore, Keegan switched from Ocean Control to Shannon for clearance into British airspace.

The pilot adjusted his headset and winked at Boharty. Few passengers ever knew—or cared—that Keegan had adopted the callsign of Helicopter Antisubmarine Squadron Two. "Shannon, Hunter One One. Position fifty-four north, ten west, flight level 370. Estimating

Tartan at 1825. SelCal Bravo Alfa Sierra Whiskey. Static air minus forty-two, winds 256."

The controller's Irish brogue came through the earphones. "Ah, roger Hunter. Squawk 2462."

Once Shannon had Hunter One One's transponder code, the jet would be funneled into a Standard Aviation Route for its ultimate destination. The flight crew knew that with the Selective Calling code, the controller could contact them with an audible tone that otherwise acted as call screening in the sky.

In the passenger cabin, Frank Leopole began rousing Red and White Teams. He reckoned that Blue was not far astern in the Falcon.

SSI OFFICES

After closing time, Derringer invited Catterly to the office. The sun was setting beyond the office buildings, casting long shadows across the concrete and glass edifices. Derringer poured their respective favorites and extended a glass to his golf partner. "Well, they're off, Phil." They clinked glasses.

"God speed the work," Catterly replied. "You can be proud of your people, Mike. All of them, not just the navy."

Derringer leaned back in his comfortable chair. He looked around, as if just noticing the sparse memorabilia on the walls and shelves. He took a long sip of his Wild Turkey, squinting slightly. Catterly knew the signs. Mike Derringer was about to become philosophical. "You know, Phil, there's no such thing as *the* U.S. Navy. It's actually a kingdom composed of four fiefdoms: surface, submarine, aviation, and special ops. Now, I'm a confirmed blackshoe: wouldn't deny it. I spent my operational career in ASW and amphibious billets. But sometime in the late '80s, it dawned on me that there were two principalities in the kingdom: warfighters and all the others. If you look at what the Navy does in combat, you quickly see where the casualties occur. I checked up and found that in Korea and Vietnam, eighty percent of Navy KIAs were aircrew. The next biggest segment was the SEALs and riverine forces in Vietnam.

"Now, logically you'd expect the warfighters to rise to the top.

Not so. The Navy is the only branch that's ever had five consecutive noncombatants as service chief, mostly submariners. In comparison, eight of the nine Air Force chiefs since Vietnam were combat veterans. Now, God love 'em, I like bubbleheads as much as anybody. Hell, I spent years earning my pay by chasing them around the Pacific. But the plain fact is, they haven't intentionally killed anybody since 1945, and over the decades far too many submariners developed an engineering emphasis. Managing a nuclear reactor has very little to do with fighting a war at sea, which is why the Brits make propulsion a separate career track. That makes enormous sense to me.

"Well, the interest on the U.S. Navy's engineering debt came due in 1991. CNO was a submariner who naturally did what bubbleheads do in a hostile situation: he dived deep and ran silent. Thousands of innocent aviators were persecuted—and I use the word advisedly—in the Tailhook witch hunt. The aviation community had just made a major contribution to winning Desert Storm, but the warfighters became political targets."

Derringer leaned forward, visibly gaining momentum as he warmed to his subject. His friend did not try to interject any comments.

"You know what? That's the best thing that could've happened to SSI. The avoidable failings of the administration in '91–'92 drove hundreds of good men out of the Navy and Marines. We could only take on so many, of course, but we got the cream of the crop, and not just pilots. Nearly all those guys are still with us. You know why? Because in this company, loyalty works both ways. Our people know that, and they're devoted to SSI because my corporate policy emphasizes loyalty down." He shook his head, smiling slightly. "What a deal. The services spend hundreds of thousands of dollars training smart, motivated people, then drive them out. So we turn around and charge top prices for the government to hire those same people with those same skills."

He spread his hands into an eloquent shrug. "My father said, 'Son, always remember that we are ruled by ambitious hypocrites.' He was right, of course. It just took me awhile to realize it." He took another drink.

Catterly had heard similar sentiments before, but seldom as vehemently expressed. "Well, Mike, sometimes I admit I don't know how you career men stood it. I mean, no matter how high you went, you were never going to be your own boss."

Derringer slowly nodded, glancing outside at the yellow glow on the offices across the plaza. "Yeah, I know. For a long time I told myself that I couldn't expect anything else. I spent years working under people who weren't as smart or as ethical as I was. But I had faith in the system, you know? There were usually enough good men to make it work. Then . . ." His voice trailed off.

"So now you don't have that problem."

Derringer snorted, then grinned self-consciously. "Well . . ." Then he laughed. "You know what? Now I call nearly all my own shots, taking jobs that appeal to me or that help the company grow, and I'm *still* working for other people. The board of directors!"

"Way of the world, my friend."

A silence wrapped itself around the room; it felt like an old, familiar blanket. Catterly finished his three fingers of scotch and set down the glass. "You still up to a game Saturday morning?"

Derringer looked up. "Ah, no. No thanks, Phil. I'm going to sit on this until . . ."

Catterly wondered, *Until what?*

". . . until the guys come back."

LONDON

Carolyn Padgett-Smith made a conscious effort to appear relaxed before the all-male audience. She was long accustomed to stares from men, and years of rock climbing and mountaineering had inured her to patronizing males. But her professional life usually included older men. This bunch ranged from approximately her age to twelve years younger. Her female receptors sensed the atmosphere as equal parts admiration, curiosity, and resentment.

Frank Leopole had introduced the immunologist to the three teams: thirty-six operators plus Keegan's two flight crews. There had been polite conversation with coffee, tea, and crumpets before Padgett-Smith got down to business.

She stood beside the screen, holding the slide carousel's remote button in one hand. After a few seconds to let things quiet down, she began. She thought: *As the Yanks say, "Here's the windup . . . and the pitch!"*

"Gentlemen. I wish to acquaint you with your enemy. This short briefing does not deal with our mysterious Pakistani doctor, but rather with the weapon he deploys." She clicked the button.

On the screen was a photo of a filovirus enlarged seventeen thousand times. Its long, ropey tendrils ended in a curlicue that might have been a pronounced shepherd's hook.

"Ebola virus contains seven proteins, identifiably different and strung together lengthwise. Three proteins are partially decoded but the others remain unknown. It's not clear what their function is. The virus attacks the immune system, somewhat like AIDS, but Ebola is far more aggressive. AIDS takes years to kill; Ebola takes days.

"That's not all. Ebola travels much faster than AIDS. The filovirus is like influenza; it can circle the world in as little as six weeks.

"Marburg likely began in monkeys but it's what we call a traveler: it jumps from one species to another. The first human hosts probably were bitten by infected animals or ate their meat."

Click.

"Here's a closer look. You will see the variety of shapes: some long and stringy and some circular." She traced an oval on the screen with her laser pointer.

"Looks like a Cheerio," somebody said. Chuckles skittered through the darkened room.

None of the SSI men realized that they had been set up. The dull clinical speech had lulled them into indifference. Here came the right hook, fast and hard.

She clicked the button again. Even some macho men gasped audibly.

"This is a patient in the terminal phase of Ebola. As you'll note from the red spots, he's bleeding through his skin. He died two days after this was taken."

Click. More mutterings. Someone gagged. Somebody else uttered a reverential "Shit!"

"And this is what he looked like when we opened him up." CPS was pleased: she was controlling her voice nicely. "You will note the partial liquification of the lungs and major organs." She traced the affected areas with her laser. "This patient died coughing up lung tissue

and brackish, dark blood. He also hemorrhaged from other orifices."
She allowed that image to sink in.

The clinician turned to face her audience. Gauging the expression
on most of the faces, she had made her point. *I'm one tough dame, boys.
Don't mess with me.*

"As you may know, Marburg and can Ebola affect the brain, so . . ."
Click.

A high male voice exclaimed "Holy Christ!"

"When we removed the brain we found these areas noticeably
degraded." She leaned close, as if admiring the wretched specimen.
"In the terminal phase, portions of the prefrontal cortex that control
personality are often destroyed or damaged, hence the erratic mood
swings often observed."

Dr. Padgett-Smith turned back toward her audience. "Now, Marburg is not as virulent as Ebola but I think you should know the
worst. We are now partners, gentlemen. I'll do as you say in the field,
but it would behoove you to defer to me in other areas."

In the front row, Bosco swallowed hard. "Ye . . . yes, ma'am!"

She nodded decisively, her light brown hair bobbing around her
ears. Then, nailing the lid on the male egos, she said, "Please excuse
me, gentlemen. I'm meeting my husband for dinner."

On the way out, the Briton heard someone ask, "My god! How
can she eat after *that?*"

———

During the salad course, Charles Padgett-Smith grinned at his wife.
"It sounds as if you laid it on a bit thick, Carolyn."

CPS sipped her champagne. "I intended to. I've only a day or so to
bond with these men. They need to know that I'm all business, and
they won't catch me in a game of slap and tickle. They may not like
me, but by God they'll respect me."

He slipped his left hand across the linen tablecloth and touched
hers. "I rather suspect that they respect *and* like you." His Rolex reflected the candlelight.

"They seem a competent bunch—what Tony would call a good
mob. And honestly, Charles, I wouldn't be going if I felt otherwise.
You know Phillip Catterly: I accept his judgment implicitly, and . . ."

"And you always liked adventure."

She squeezed his hand. "Charles, if anything goes . . ."

"It's quite all right, darling. Everything is set." The investment broker in him had ensured that Charles Padgett-Smith had read Carolyn's SSI contract forwards and backwards. The insurance provisions were more than ample.

Her violet eyes were moistening around the edges. "Oh, Charles. I miss you already."

LONDON

Loading Padgett-Smith's equipment took little time. But as some of the operators could have imagined, selecting her Pakistani wardrobe took longer.

Padgett-Smith accepted the help offered by some of the SSI hardies. Her field kit was more than she could easily handle, especially with two large cases. But Steve Lee and one of his White Team cronies one-handed the two large items without visible exertion. Padgett-Smith did not remember the other man's name, but she would not forget his physique. His friends called Ken Delmore "Mr. Clean" for his resemblance to the ad character: he was huge and completely bald with twenty-inch biceps. Padgett-Smith suspected he could bench-press a Yugo without visible exertion.

Leopole appeared at the doorway. "All set, Doctor?"

She turned at the sound of his voice. "Yes, thank you, Mr. Leopole. This is all I need, other than my personal items."

"What's in the cases, ma'am?"

"Oh, field test kits. Two microscopes, test tubes, the like . . ."

"Two microscopes?"

She shrugged her round shoulders. "Better too much than too little, don't you think?"

Leopole suppressed a smirk. "I would agree with you if we were talking about ammo. But all this stuff has to be man-portable, you know. We may not have pack animals, let alone vehicles in some areas."

CPS folded her arms and speared the American with her violet eyes. "Tell me . . . Frank. If you broke your only microscope in the wilds of Baluchistan, where would you get another?"

Leopole's gunmetal blue eyes lowered momentarily. "Point well taken." Painfully aware that he had been outscored, he sought to regain the initiative. "Now then, let's see about your mountain clothes."

In an adjoining room, Leopole sifted through a pile of miscellaneous clothing of approximate Afghan-Pakistan origin. All items were earth toned; most showed some evidence of previous use. He held up a shapeless shirt and not-so-matching vest. Padgett-Smith took the garments and held them against herself. She grinned. "The height of Pakistani fashion, no doubt."

Leopole looked her up and down in a manner devoid of appreciation. "The fit's okay, I guess. Loose is better, since it doesn't show your . . . ah, outline." CPS would have sworn that the retired marine blushed. Privately, Leopole guessed her at a 34B.

Leopole recovered quickly, turning to Mohammed. "Omar, what do you think?"

SSI's training officer stood with one arm folded, one hand beneath his bearded chin. "The clothes aren't the problem, especially with the long shirt and vest. The trouble is her face." Abruptly he looked at his colleague. "Oh, I'm sorry, Doctor. I didn't mean to imply . . ."

"I know what you mean," the immunologist interjected. "I can't very well grow a beard, and a false one would appear . . . false."

"There is one other option," Leopole offered.

Mohammed looked back at him. "Yes?"

"Women's clothes?"

The Iranian turned his head slightly. "Well, certainly. But then we have to ask ourselves what the locals will think, seeing a party of armed men with one woman. They're bound to be curious."

Padgett-Smith began to resent the conversation. The marine and the Muslim—products of two ultra-masculine cultures—were discussing her as if she weren't there. Or as if she were a mannequin. However, she reminded herself that much of her education had been funded in exactly that role: a living, breathing, walking, non-talking doll. Fashion runways; poofter photographers . . . and the other kind. *Work with me, darling! Show us some attitude!*

Leopole held up his hands. "Then I'm Winchester."

Padgett-Smith cocked her head. "You're *Winchester?*"

Mohammed laughed aloud. "Military shorthand, Doctor. It's a radio call that means, 'I am out of ammunition.'"

CPS rolled her eyes. Finally she realized she still held the grayish, tannish garments and let them drop on the table.

"As I see it," Mohammed continued, "we can take two approaches. On the one hand, yes, a lone woman with a scouting party will draw attention. But because she's 'only a woman' . . ." At that he drew quote marks in the air. "The locals won't bother talking to her."

She bit her lip. The PC phrase about Celebrating Diversity sounded in her mind, followed by a mental flushing sound from the loo.

"On the other hand, if she's dressed as a man, holding a weapon like everyone else, she might blend in. Especially if her face is obscured somehow, and she keeps in the rear of the group."

Padgett-Smith finally found her voice. "How about a big floppy hat, some dirt on my face, and I clip my nails?"

The men exchanged glances. CPS thought for all the world they resembled Professor Higgins and Colonel Pickering. *By jove, she's got it!*

Before either spoke, she pressed her advantage. "I prefer an AK, if that's all right with you, gentlemen. Thirty rounds semi-auto should get me through any scrape."

Tony, you're such a love.

AMMAN, JORDAN

Mideast News Bureau. Jordanian authorities briefly shut down part of Amman Queen Alia International Airport today after a Pakistani woman collapsed upon deplaning from an Egyptair flight. Authorities indicated that the woman showed signs of an infectious disease and was taken to a military hospital. The victim was identified as Hina bint Ahmed, twenty-six. Though she lapsed into a coma some hours later, investigation revealed that the young woman probably suffered from advanced pancreatitis.

Only one of the airport's two terminals was affected after the Egyptian Boeing 737 arrived. Laboratory tests on the stricken woman caused temporary concern that she may have had a communicable disease. Some flights were delayed several hours but were allowed to proceed when the crisis passed. An unknown number of passengers were inconvenienced, and reportedly some European diplomatic personnel had to reschedule trips to their home capitals.

Speaking on conditions of anonymity, Jordanian authorities stated that the victim's journey began in Pakistan and included an interim stop in Cairo.

OVER FRANCE

CPS sat on a canvas and frame seat that folded up for stowage. The 727's interior was optimized for utility over comfort, though six bunks were available for longer flights. She was re-reading the cargo manifest, keeping ahead of potential shortages. It was far better to know that the operators were lacking something before landing than minutes before they needed it. Leopole had insisted that most standard equipment could be obtained in Islamabad.

Satisfied with the inventory, Padgett-Smith turned her attention to personnel. She had been introduced to everyone and reckoned that she remembered about one-third of the names and faces. She was most interested in the medics: one fully qualified on each team plus at least one partially cross-trained. She had talked to that over-age adolescent called Breezy and determined that he was probably competent—at least he could discuss medical vocabulary while sneaking glances at her chest. The thirty-something ex–Green Beret,

Jerry Sefton, had impressed her as a near match for her ex-brother-in-law. *How he would love this job!* she mused.

That left the former SEAL, Jeffrey Malten. He seemed quieter and, whatever his age, more mature than most of the others. She waved to him and patted the seat beside her. That Bosco character saw the gesture and punched Malten's arm in a comradely manner. He mouthed something unintelligible over the jet noise; two syllables. American soldiers were forever uttering ferral grunts and tones: *Hoo-ah!* and *Ah-oo!* seemed most popular. She had even heard the former expressed with a rising tone: *Hoo-ah?* evidently was an interrogatory as well as a declarative. Carolyn inferred that to the military cognoscenti, one or the other was favored by the Marines and the Army. Apparently fliers and sailors communicated on a higher plane, occasionally rising to polysyllabics.

Malten sat down, looking alert and composed. "Yes, ma'am?"

"Mr. Malten, we had so little time before leaving that I didn't get to talk to you as much as I hoped. I should like to know a bit more about your medical experience. That is, if you don't mind."

Malten blinked. He thought of himself as a shooter who could keep WIAs alive long enough for a dustoff flight. "Well, ma'am, sure. I mean, I finished the combat corpsman school and got the refreshers along the way. But I don't know about these viruses, other than what we were told about the bio threat, and that wasn't much."

"Yes, I understand that. Mainly I wondered if you received information on the symptoms. In the early stages it's terribly difficult to distinguish between Marburg or Ebola and more common diseases, from malaria or dengue to the lesser hemorrhagic fevers."

Jeffrey Malten slowly shook his close-cropped head. "Ah, no ma'am. I couldn't tell the difference. To tell you the truth, Doctor, I know a lot more about penetrating and sucking wounds than anything else."

CPS absorbed that information, briefly staring out the opposite window. The evening sunlight glowed golden on the cloud deck. Then she turned to the earnest young man. "I'll see if I can organize a briefing for you and the other medics. Perhaps some of the nuances would be helpful. Until then, it's best to assume the worst and treat any likely patient with isolation and barrier methods."

"Yes'm. Gotcha."

Padgett-Smith regarded young Mr. Malten for a moment. He returned her level gaze; he seemed to regard her as an equal, and considering their vast educational differences, she was surprised to find that fact appealing.

"Would you mind if I asked a personal question?"

"No ma'am."

"Obviously you're quite good at your work. Why did you leave the Navy?"

Malten grinned almost shyly. "Well . . ." He seemed to squint, as if concentrating. Then he looked back at her. "Do you know what 'ruck up' means?"

"I would guess it's from climbing or hiking. As in ruck sack."

"Yeah, that's close. The guys say they ruck up by putting on their gear and sh . . . stuff. But it also means to get ready for an op—you know, a mission."

"Ah, I see." *Tony would have a far better idea.*

"Well, in the teams—in the SEALs—I was active for almost four years. We'd ruck up—and stand down. Ruck up—and stand down. Ruck up—and stand down. Ruck up—and stand down. I don't even know how many times we were briefed for a mission and then had it cancelled. The only two ops I was on, practically nothing happened. It was just surveillance. I was going nuts. So were a lot of the guys."

"So you were frustrated at the lack of . . . action?"

Malten nodded decisively. "That's it. Frustrated."

Padgett-Smith recalled only two such discussions with Tony. He had expressed similar sentiments. "Mr. Malten, my brother-in-law was SAS. He absolutely loved the regiment and would have stayed for fifty years if he hadn't broken both legs and ankles. But he was in the Falklands."

Jeffrey Malten almost grinned. "Cool."

"So . . . you left the Navy to join SSI?"

"Well, not really. I just knew I didn't want to spend more time training and training, and never really doing the job. Besides, I had no personal life. In the teams, the divorce rate is like eighty percent. I wanted to meet a girl and, maybe, you know . . ." He shrugged. "So I decided not to re-enlist. Then I heard about SSI and . . . well, here I am."

"You're happy with your work now?"

Malten's eyes seemed to light up. "Oh yeah. I've been . . . well, ah, I can't really say everywhere I've been. But the work's steady and it pays well, and the admiral's just a great boss. I even have time to chase girls again." He laughed aloud.

Carolyn Padgett-Smith bestowed a large smile on Jeffrey Malten. "I hope you catch one, then!"

BALUCHISTAN PROVINCE

Sometimes it was hard for Kassim to remember that Ali's degree was in medicine rather than theology. While the doctor practiced the former, he lived the latter. Had Kassim heard the word, he would have recognized Ali as a devoted evangelist.

Some of Ali's cell lacked the Syrian's ability to distinguish between lay teacher and cleric. Occasionally someone referred to the doctor as an imam, but only one time. Dr. Ali's piousness could turn into a wrath of stunning proportions, lest he permit himself to indulge in the sin of false pride. He considered himself a scholar, not a priest.

This evening the "sermon" turned on seeming contradictions in the *Qur'an* and the *Hadith*, though Ali insisted that The Prophet's compilations contained far fewer than the Christian holy book.

One *surah* in particular troubled Miam Tahirkheli, a youngster who wanted to follow his teacher into medicine. "Doctor, Sunan Abu Dawud quotes The Prophet that we may not harm any old person, any child, or any woman. If it is prohibited to make war upon women and children, how then can we use methods that destroy the innocent?"

Ali had never known a Jesuit but he had a seminarian's knowledge of polemical questions. "I believe there *are* no totally innocent victims among the Crusaders. Yes, children are blameless in and of themselves, but their parents are at fault for failing to protect them. Worse, for failing to guide them on the true path. America and the other Zionist nations all are ruled by democratically elected officials. Yet their governments are opposed to Islam and kill our believers in large numbers. Therefore, America and its lackeys constitute a legitimate target. If the populations would overthrow the Crusaders and the Jews, we would have little argument with them."

Tahirkheli, who had some schooling beyond the elementary level, accepted the logic. "Then we must strengthen ourselves to act in ways that might offend The Faith?"

Ali folded his arms and rocked back on his haunches. "My brother, what would you have us do? Either we can defend The Faith or we can watch it wither and die. World conditions permit nothing else."

Miam Tahirkheli realized that the other men and boys were watching him. Thrusting out his chin, which bore the beginnings of a fine beard, he forced his voice an octave lower than normal. "I will be a defender."

QUETTA, PAKISTAN

As the 727 braked to a stop and the three engines spun down, the parking ramp was dimly lit. Clearly the Pakistanis did not want to draw undue attention to the new arrival. Keegan knew that two hangars had been allotted to SSI: one for the company plane and another for the teams. The Falcon would unload and depart almost immediately.

A limousine was waiting from the American consulate as Frank Leopole and Omar Mohammed descended the stairs. Though the limo bore diplomatic plates, it flew no flags and showed no sign of the passengers' prestige. A tall American emerged in mufti with a uniformed Pakistani.

Brigadier General Bryce Hardesty was known as "Buster." As military attaché to Islamabad, his position carried more responsibility than his rank indicated. Mohammed had gleaned some useful information from the officer's bio, filling in the gaps with a couple of phone calls. SSI knew that Hardesty's previous experience and fluency in Urdu had gained him the position before he pinned on his star.

Introductions were made as the men walked to the office. Buster

Hardesty made a point of pronouncing the Pakistani's name slowly and carefully, though SSI already had the information via fax.

Major Rustam Khan wore a green uniform with the star and crescent of his rank on the epaulets of an immaculately pressed blouse. Leopole assessed him in one glance: mid-thirties, five-eight or -nine, generally fit. Professional-looking. He spoke English with a hint of a British accent.

Hardesty was businesslike but personable. He laid out the situation in more detail than SSI had seen previously. "This is a pretty secure facility, gentlemen. It was a training base until a couple years ago when the PAF consolidated some facilities. You have more than adequate barracks for forty men, and in fact you're welcome to spread out if you wish. Major Khan has already provided for chow and laundry services from the caretakers here."

Leopole took SSI's lead in the discussion, focusing on Hardesty while being careful to include Khan. The erstwhile marine considered the Pakis an odd bunch. Their army used conventional ranks while the air force was RAF. Their navy had ensigns and lieutenants junior grade but above the O-2 level they used army ranks. He tried to imagine majors and colonels commanding ships. He couldn't.

Keegan and Padgett-Smith arrived, having supervised parking the 727 and unloading medical kits. Hardesty and Khan rose to their feet as Leopole made the introductions. "Dr. Padgett-Smith is the immunologist I mentioned. She's really the reason we're here."

Carolyn extended a manicured hand to Hardesty. She was amused when Khan kissed her hand in a most un-Islamic gesture. With a sideways glance, she thought that she saw Leopole register mild disapproval. She was pleased.

Administrative matters took about forty minutes. At that point Keegan interjected. "Excuse me, gentlemen. Ah, I have another helicopter pilot with me. We hoped for some flight time in a Hip before we left the States but it wasn't possible . . ."

Khan nodded briskly. "Yes, yes. We have arranged to begin day after tomorrow. You shall have an Mi-17 with an instructor pilot and engineer."

Keegan expressed obvious pleasure. He arched his eyebrows at Leopole, who interpreted the message: *I'll be damned!* "Ah, thank you, Major. We've already read the manual so we should be able to transition pretty quickly."

As the meeting broke up, Khan introduced the base liaison officer who would care for the Americans. The two Pakis obliged Mohammed and Steve Lee with some Urdu conversation while Leopole commiserated with Hardesty. "General, I'd say that Khan is a capable officer. But isn't an O-4 kind of junior for a project of this priority?"

"Well, remember that in this part of the world a major carries more weight than his western counterparts. Besides, Rustam would be my choice in any case. Most of the senior officers here owe their allegiance to the ruling clique, and frankly some of them are suspect. They may not overtly support al Qaeda but they won't try very hard to defeat it, either. In a way, you can't blame them. They know that if the current regime is overthrown, they'll be at risk."

"So what's Khan's motivation?"

"He's a decent man and a good officer. But, just between us, he has more reason than most. A couple of years back there was a string of car bombings near military and government facilities. Rustam's wife was injured and their daughter was killed. There isn't much he wouldn't do to track down those people."

QUETTA AIRBASE

"Interesting bunch of lads. I'm getting to know them better."

Frank Leopole regarded Carolyn Padgett-Smith with renewed interest. In a few days his original skepticism had mutated into grudging admiration that now teetered on the verge of respect. "You mean they try to speak the Queen's English around you?"

"Such as one can discern from American mercenaries!"

"Yes, they're mercenaries," Leopole conceded. "Hell, *I'm* a merc myself, since I fight for money." He uttered a short male bark. Few strangers had ever seen Lieutenant Colonel Leopole actually laugh. "But then I did the same thing in the corps, when you think about it."

She returned the smile. "One man's mercenary is another's soldier of fortune, I suppose."

Leopole nodded. "Yes, ma'am, but the difference is damn . . . thin." He waved a hand at Blue Team kicking a soccer ball around the hangar. Gunny Foyte had given them a half-hour respite after unpacking and stowing gear. "The name 'mercenary' still has negative connotations, but that's just a word. It got a bad rap in the sixties when a lot of mercs were just drunks and gunslingers looking for a quick check. These men are entirely different."

Padgett-Smith turned her attention to the SSI men, some without shirts, all visibly fit. "How so?"

"Well, they're professionals to start with. Only one or two have no military experience, and those were police. Beyond that, they're pretty smart as a group. Don't let the clowns like Bosco and Breezy fool you, ma'am. These guys mostly have stock portfolios and they know what's up and what's down. If there's any adrenaline junkies, I'm not aware of it. And it's my job to know."

"But aren't some of them here for the excitement, the adventure? Like some of them say—for the action?"

"Oh, sure. Some of them, but not all. A lot of them would be happy if they never got shot at while others are looking to prove something to themselves. But I'd guess most of them are a lot like SWAT guys. They're more into body building and physical challenge than guns and explosives. SSI lets them do those things without the tedious aspects of military life." *Chicken shit* flashed on his mental screen, but Frank Leopole would never use that term around a lady.

The immunologist looked at some of White Team engaged in an arcane sort of male bonding. She had never seen anyone perform twenty-five one-armed push-ups before. That bald giant again; Ken something or other.

Leopole followed her gaze and read her mind. "It's like this, Doctor. Where else can a young guy without experience get paid for parachuting or scuba diving or handling expensive equipment? Only in the military, and each of these men had enough of that environment. Admiral Derringer was right there to pick up the people he needed." Leopole gave her a rare grin. "That's why he's an admiral and I was a light colonel!"

"I look forward to meeting him. Everyone seems to regard him well. Mr. Keegan especially . . ."

"Roger that. Terry's a very capable young man, but still bitter inside. Guess I can't blame him after the way the Navy treated him, but that was years ago. He should get over it and move on."

Because Leopole had never been so open before, Padgett-Smith sensed an opportunity and took it. She was tempted to call him "Frank" but resisted it. "Colonel, I'd like to ask about my personal protection. I know you can't assign me a bodyguard, and I wouldn't want to be dependent anyway. Besides, my contract was written so that . . ."

"Yes, ma'am. I meant to handle that for you." He rose, walked to his duffel bag, and came back with a green satchel. "This is for you, Doctor, if you can handle it."

Padgett-Smith opened the satchel and withdrew a holstered Browning. She was aware that the American was watching her closely. She hesitated a moment, focusing on what Tony had told her. *Keep three rules in mind, love.* She turned away from the soccer game and drew the pistol. It was a Highpower, just like Tony's. *Check if it's loaded. Keep it pointed safely. Finger off the trigger.* With the muzzle pointed at the floor and her finger along the frame, she retracted the slide. It locked back on an empty magazine.

Damn! She berated herself. *I should have dropped the magazine first.*

She made a point of looking in the chamber, then felt with the tip of a small finger. Satisfied, she set the Browning down, muzzle toward the wall.

Leopole looked at her closely, as if examining something through one of her microscopes. "Nicely done, Doctor. You've had some training."

"Well, not a lot, you know. But my brother-in-law was SAS."

"I'll try to get us a range session but that may not be possible. Anyway, you seem safe with firearms and I've seldom known a good shooter who wasn't a good gun handler."

He tapped the holster. "We'll get you rigged up so you can carry this on a belt. When you wear it, keep it concealed at all times. The locals disapprove of women with guns."

Leopole reached into his duffel and came up with a spare magazine and a box of fifty cartridges. "These are 124-grain hollowpoints. Best nine-mil ammo I know of. It's not approved by the Geneva Convention but we're not operating under their rules." He paused, focusing his thoughts. Then he turned to her again. "Doctor, if you ever have to shoot, keep shooting until the threat goes away. That's the best advice I can give you."

He wondered whether he should deliver the final advice about the Last Bullet. *Save it for yourself.* He decided against it. Carolyn Padgett-Smith had already decided that she would not be taken alive.

QUETTA AIRBASE

Terry Keegan settled in the copilot's seat of the Mi-17. The instructor, Captain Falak Mir, sat to his left; Eddie Marsh in the flight engineer's seat behind them. "Terrific viz," Keegan enthused, looking downward between the two instrument panels.

"Everybody says that," Mir replied. He spoke fluent English but did not bother mentioning that he also had passable Russian. "Believe me, it helps to see beneath your feet when you are trying to maintain a hover on a four thousand-meter mountain."

Keegan looked up from the glass panels. "Do you do that very often?"

Mir nodded. "We can, but that is fairly unusual. However, we have Alouette pilots with a thousand hours above six thousand meters. That is because our highest army positions are at six thousand."

"Well, my hat's off to you. I'm basically an antisubmarine guy. I get a nose bleed much over two hundred feet!"

Marsh interjected, leaning over Keegan's shoulder. "Captain Mir, I know we'll have some classroom instruction on systems and procedures, but what's this helo like to fly?"

Mir rotated the control stick between his knees. "The cyclic is heavier than you are used to. That's the Russian design philosophy—they do not want their pilots making abrupt control inputs at higher airspeeds. That might cause airframe stress. So the hydraulic reservoir dampens the motion." He shrugged. "After a little experience you learn to anticipate more than normal."

Marsh nodded, thinking ahead to the time he would sit in the left seat, contrary to American choppers with the command pilot on the right. "How's the collective?"

Mir touched the control lever on the left side of Keegan's seat.

"Nothing unusual. It has a friction lock so you can adjust tension to your liking."

The instructor ran practiced fingers across the right-hand instrument panel. "Engine gauges, fuel flow, flight instruments. Those are all metric, of course, but it goes without saying that you keep everything in the green. At higher altitudes you may pull more torque in the yellow, but not for long." He grinned beneath his mustache. "We only have thirty-eight of these machines, and the two squadron commanders are rather jealous of them."

He continued his explanation. "Autopilot, radio compass, radio altimeter, and communication panel. I understand from Major Khan that you expect to operate discreetly, so your Pakistani copilot can handle special communications."

"The Mi-17 cruises at 240 kilometers, which is—what? About 130 knots? Vmax is only ten klicks more so I do not believe in pushing it. Your main performance advantage is in lifting. The Seventeen carries four tons of external load, which I imagine is far more than you will ever need. Mainly, you can hover at normal takeoff weight at four thousand meters."

"The specs I saw said your range is about five hundred kilometers," Keegan said.

"Figure 250 nautical and you should be safe."

"Captain, I'm all for being safe!"

QUETTA AIRBASE

"Do you mind if I join you?"

Jeffrey Malten was pleasantly surprised to hear the dulcet voice of "the bug lady." That's how some of the operators had been referring to her. Weapons of mass destruction came in three flavors: chemical, biological, and nuclear, aka gas, bugs, and nukes.

"Why, no, ma'am. Not a bit." Malten and a Red Team operator were finishing their stretching exercises when Padgett-Smith arrived. She wanted to maintain some sort of jogging routine but realized that a lone white female was bound to draw unwelcome attention.

She pulled her warmup's hood over her head and quickly finished her own routine. Malten introduced her to his partner.

"Dr. Smith, this is Jeremy Johnson." The two shook hands.

"Mr. Johnson. How do you do?"

"Uh, just call me J. J., ma'am. Everybody else does."

Malten nudged his friend. "Hey, what'd the frogs call you, *Le Double Jay?*"

"Aw, knock it off, Malten."

Padgett-Smith cocked her head. "The frogs?"

Johnson clearly was embarrassed at the attention. When he failed to respond, Malten explained. "J. J. did a stretch in the Foreign Legion."

CPS straightened up, mouth slightly agape. *"La Légion étrangère?"*

Johnson nodded solemnly. *"Oui, Madame Médecin. 'Legio Pro Patria.'"*

The ex-legionnaire and the immunologist immediately established a rapport. Malten listened with growing impatience as they chatted—he would have said jabbered—with growing Gallic glee.

Johnson finished, *"Au combat, tu agis sans passion et sans haine, tu respectes les ennemis vaincus, tu n'abandonnes jamais ni tes morts, ni tes blessés, ni tes armes."*

"Bravo, mon vieux! Très bien!" Padgett-Smith exclaimed. She clapped her hands in appreciation.

Noting Malten's consternation, Carolyn turned to him. "Mr. Johnson just recited the Legion's code of honour. 'To fight without passion or hate, to respect vanquished enemies . . . never to abandon your dead, nor ever to surrender your arms.'"

The former SEAL tried to appear unimpressed. He rattled off, "Trustworthy, loyal, helpful, friendly, courteous, kind, obedient, cheerful, thrifty, brave, clean, and reverent."

"What'n hell's that?" Johnson asked.

"The Boy Scout laws."

On the way back to the hangar the joggers passed a young dog. Happy to find company, the mongrel capered after them, yapping along the way. Johnson tried to shoo the animal away, and though it cringed and held back, it trailed them at a respectful distance. Finally Padgett-Smith stopped. She quickly made friends with the dog.

"He has a collar but no identification," she said. Malten reached down to pat the animal, which tried to back away. "Jeffrey, I think he's shy of men. He's probably been abused, poor thing. You go ahead. I'll see if he'll come with me and maybe we can feed him."

Malten stood up. "I'm not sure that's a good idea, Doctor. He probably belongs to somebody who may not like us fooling with his mutt."

"Well, then. You start out and I'll keep you in sight. It's just a short way."

Malten exchanged glances with Johnson. Their faces read the tacit message: *Women!*

Outside the hangar, Padgett-Smith gave the stray dog some leftovers and water. Johnson kept her company; despite their different backgrounds, they found they enjoyed talking to one another.

"I still don't know why, but I wanted to join the Legion ever since I was a kid," Johnson began. "I took French in high school just so I'd have a jump on the language training. After that I spent a couple of years earning airfare and getting in shape. Besides, I wanted to travel some in Europe before enlisting. I signed on for one term, five years." He rolled his eyes. "That was enough!"

"Why didn't you re-enlist?"

"I'd seen and done everything I wanted to do. You know—got shot at and shot back. Besides, by then I was almost twenty-six and I wanted to start making some money."

"Are you still in touch with any of them?"

"No, not really. Still, it was an interesting bunch of guys. I learned everything you'd expect about soldiering and even more about people. My best friend was a Pole. The others in my section included a Canadian, two Italians, one or two Germans, a Greek, and even a Samoan. The best soldier I ever knew was Croatian, *Sergent-Chef* Dukovac. He'd fit right into this group."

"That's an interesting observation. What made him the best soldier?"

"Oh, I don't know exactly. It was just the whole package. He saw everything that happened, knew exactly what was going on, even in a nighttime firefight. Later somebody called it 'situation awareness.' Also, he took time to learn about his soldiers. Not everybody does. But he knew who could shoot straight, who could run the farthest, who was distracted and who was focused. And he could do anything the rest of us could, but better. Even though he was quite a bit older."

"Where did you serve, if I may ask?"

"Mostly in Djibouti. Thirteenth Demi-Brigade. Terrible climate but we had some excitement now and then. I'm making notes for a book."

She smiled. "Well, I know one or two publishers . . ."

"My dog!" The voice was harsh, grating, accented. Padgett-Smith and Johnson looked up to see an irate Pakistani NCO striding toward them. He was clearly agitated, exclaiming in high-decibel Urdu. He was also visibly curious as to what the hangar contained.

Johnson turned to the doctor. "You'd better get Major Khan."

"Oh dear, he's checking the shooting range with Frank Leopole."

"Then get Omar. He speaks the lingo."

Padgett-Smith disappeared through the partly open hangar door. When she returned with Omar Mohammed, the NCO was dragging the dog away.

"What happened?" Mohammed asked.

"Uh, the corporal says we stole his dog. That's not true, but somebody saw us heading back here with the mutt."

Dr. Omar Mohammed uttered an un-Muslim epithet. Then he went to find Frank Leopole before things turned worse.

BALUCHISTAN PROVINCE

Ali bowed a final time to the southwest, giving homage toward Mecca. Then he raised to a sitting position, hands on his knees, eyes still closed. Sometimes when he prayed, the spirit enveloped him like a warm, comforting blanket. Those were the moments he savored, for he knew that he had prayed properly: with true humility and reverence. He had been praying for his forty-nine years on earth, but still he managed to pray satisfactorily less than half the time. He would have to concentrate more; work even harder to become a deserving servant of God.

When he opened his eyes Ali saw a man striding toward him, perhaps fifty meters away. From the figure's awkward gait, the doctor recognized Kassim.

Ali gathered up his prayer rug and placed it inside the rude building. Then he went forward to meet his colleague. He knew the Syrian to be less than devout in matters of piety—Kassim certainly did not pray five times a day—but the man's loss of a foot against the Russians and his dedication to destroying the Crusaders were unquestioned.

Allah would make allowances.

Kassim limped to the door, where Ali invited him in for tea. But the Syrian declined with a perfunctory thank-you. "There is interesting news from Quetta."

Ali turned from the stove where the water boiled. "Yes?"

"Infidels at the old airfield. Working with government forces."

Ali forgot about the tea. He sat down, beckoning his friend to join him.

"We have eyes inside the perimeter," Kassim began. "Believers who share their knowledge with us."

"Yes, I recall." It was well known that the Pakistani armed forces had no shortage of al Qaeda supporters and sympathizers. Kassim's organization threw a wide net: The Base was global.

"Two days ago one of the faithful saw Americans there. They stole a dog."

Ali was slightly disappointed; he expected more. There were Americans and other westerners throughout Pakistan. "That is no secret, my friend. The Crusaders have contacts throughout our country."

Kassim waved a hand. "No, no. This is unusual. The Americans were soldiers but had no uniforms."

"Then how do you know they were soldiers?"

"My source works in the base facilities office. He says the soldiers are there disguised as security consultants. But they have the look and the bearing of soldiers: mostly young, very fit, with military haircuts, though most are growing beards. He saw weapons and . . ."

"How many men?"

"The corporal did not feel he could question them without raising suspicions. He saw six or eight, but he learned there are accommodations for as many as forty."

Ali absorbed the information, wondering if the Crusaders could be so fast off the mark after his first two failed "deliveries." While he was thinking, Kassim interjected.

"There is something else."

"What is it?"

"A woman."

QUETTA AIRBASE

Steve Lee was running White Team through some drills as Padgett-Smith finished some remedial pistol training. Jeffrey Malten had attempted to improve her speed with a manageable reduction in accuracy but finally conceded enough was enough. As the former SEAL cleaned the Hipower, Padgett-Smith regarded Lee's men with something approaching professional detachment. Most were casually dressed—some in cutoffs and T-shirts—while incongruously wearing gloves. She turned to Malten. "Why do some of them have gloves but so little else?"

"Oh. I know, it looks funny, but some guys prefer wearing gloves on an operation while others go bare handed. Whatever they do, they practice the same way. There's a saying, 'Fight like you train.' It can be a little hard to manipulate some guns or equipment with gloves so those guys practice with them on. There's a compromise, though. Fingerless gloves protect the hands but allow full use of the fingers. It's just personal preference." He tried suppressing a grin and failed.

"What?" she asked.

"Well, there's another reason for some of the young studs. The CDI Factor."

She cocked her head. "CDI?"

"Chicks dig it."

Padgett-Smith scowled at him. "That's absurd. Do they really . . ."

"Hey, Doc, it got your attention, didn't it?"

BALUCHISTAN PROVINCE

Ali and Kassim spoke in subdued tones. The other jihadists were men of proven commitment, but as the cell's intelligence officer Kassim took nothing for granted.

Ali bent close. "What of the American woman?"

"It is difficult to say. Apparently she is the only female with the so-called security agents." Kassim permitted himself a smile. "But I have learned her name."

"Well done, brother! Your sources must be praised. What is it?"

"Smith."

Ali's smile melted before Kassim's eyes. "My friend, that is of no use. Smith is as common among the Crusaders as Mohammed among the faithful."

"Oh . . ."

The bio-engineer placed an assuring hand on the Syrian's forearm. "Please tell your operatives that the leadership is pleased. Ask them to obtain more details, but not at risk of being discovered. Now, what else need we discuss?"

"I should start making plans for the next package. When do you expect the messenger?"

"Within one week."

QUETTA AIRBASE

The Hip lifted off the ramp, dipped its nose during translational lift, and chugged off to its pad across the field. Keegan and Eddie Marsh watched it with helmet visors lowered. They both relished the sound and smell of helicopters.

"Well, I feel pretty good about it," Marsh volunteered. He was a former Army warrant officer, several years younger than Keegan but with a comparable amount of helo time.

The Navy pilot lifted his visor. "Yeah, I do, too. Captain Mir knows what he's doing. Good stick, good instructor."

"They'll be back tomorrow, right?"

"Affirm. And likely every day after. We can use all the time we can get, and Frank's door kickers need to practice dismounts, too."

Marsh unzipped his jacket, which reminded Keegan of something. "Eddie, you'd better take that flag patch off the sleeve. Either that or don't wear the jacket."

"Hey, you know me. My theme song is 'Proud to Be an American.'"

"Well, that's fine, but we can't go waving the stars and stripes over here. We have to keep a low profile." He nudged the army flier. "You know that."

Marsh's tone became defensive. "Well, I care about what it means."

"C'mon, Eddie. It's just a flag."

"What do you mean, 'just a flag'?"

"It's only a symbol. Most people look at the starry spangled banner and see what they want to see. I know what it represents. Or doesn't represent. Not anymore."

Marsh felt his hair bristle on the back of his neck. "Like what?" There was more edge in his voice than he intended.

"Oh, hell. Forget it."

Marsh jabbed a finger at Keegan. "No, man. You raised it. Let's hear it!"

Keegan inhaled, exhaled, and briefly closed his eyes. He knew exactly what was going to be said in the next thirty seconds. "All right, Eddie. You're a good guy, straight arrow, red, white, and true blue. You look at Old Glory and you see Mount Rushmore or something. I see the federal thugs raising that flag over the ashes of Waco. And a lot more."

Marsh was incredulous. He almost stammered. "Well, to hell with Waco, man! Besides, it's not the flag's choice where it's raised."

Bingo. Gotcha, kid. "That's right, Eddie. It's not Old Glory's fault if it's raised over Waco or My Lai or Wounded Knee. Not any more than it's the swastika's fault it was raised over Auschwitz or the hammer and sickle's fault it flew over the gulag."

Now Marsh was visibly upset. The veins stood out in his head. "By god, Keegan, if you're comparing the American flag to those . . ."

"You're reacting emotionally, Eddie. Try thinking with your brain instead of with your glands." He resisted the urge to add *as usual.*

Frank Leopole strode within earshot, intending to get the pilots' assessment of their second day flying the Hip. As he drew nearer he saw Marsh's animated gestures and rising tone. Keegan, as usual, was calm and composed.

"What the hell's going on?"

Leopole's voice had the practiced tone of a Perturbed Marine Corps Officer. He reckoned it lay somewhere between an ordinary Parris Island DI and an outraged Catholic nun. Either way, it was a daunting performance.

Keegan thought fastest. Which meant he allowed Marsh to speak first.

"Colonel, I'm just about . . ." Keegan saw the light flick on in Marsh's eyes. The kid knew he'd been had.

"Yes, go on." Leopole had defaulted to Parade Ground Marine: hands touching behind his back, torso slightly inclined forward.

Marsh looked down. "Well, um. It's about the flag. The American flag."

Leopole gave an exaggerated shake of his head. "Say what?" He looked at Keegan. *The Navy sumbitch is almost grinning.*

"Frank, I was telling Eddie that he needs to take the patch off his flight jacket or wear something else. For obvious reasons."

"That's it? After all that?"

Keegan shrugged. "The rest is poetry."

Leopole's gunmetal gaze returned to the former Army rotorhead. "Mr. Marsh, this is a covert operation. We are in a foreign country, wearing foreign clothing, using foreign weapons, operating foreign aircraft. The American flag is a dead giveaway. I suspect you already know that. So what's the shouting *really* about?"

Edward Marsh, late of the 160th Special Operations Regiment, realized the consequences if he lapsed into a he-said-I-said defense. "Just a difference of opinion, sir."

Keegan folded his arms and rocked back on his heels. He was not enjoying Marsh's discomfiture as much as before. "Well, Frank, we were discussing the difference between symbolism and substance as it relates to national emblems."

Inside Frank Leopole's brain housing unit the mental tumblers clicked into place. *So that's it. Young Mr. Marsh met the Terry Monster. Gotta hand it to the squid. He sets 'em up and knocks 'em down every damn time.*

Leopole lanced Marsh with a gaze. "I don't give a flying fuck about your philosophical differences, gentlemen. You're paid to show on time and fly where you're needed. Everything else is secondary . . . or less. Is that clear?"

Marsh nodded earnestly. "Yes, sir."

Keegan straightened in a mockery of military protocol. "Sir. Yessir!"

BALUCHISTAN PROVINCE

Kassim stood at a respectful distance, waiting for Ali to finish the afternoon prayer. It occurred to the intelligence operative that he might profitably exercise his own prayer rug—wherever it was these days.

When Ali finished, Kassim quickly approached. "Doctor, some more information arrived today. I consider it urgent."

Ali paid close attention. Kassim seldom exaggerated. "Yes?"

"The woman at Quetta. She is probably British. Passport information confirms that a white female arrived the same day as the soldiers. Her full name appears to be Padgett Smith."

Ali figuratively shook his head. "Kassim, that cannot be her full name. Not unless her parents were extremely unconventional. 'Padgett' must be her middle name; perhaps her birth name."

Kassim consulted his notes, still hand-written by the cell's contact at the passport office. "My information is Dr. Padgett Smith." He looked up. "Does that make it any clearer?"

Ali's reaction was a tiny tremor across the back of his shoulders. "A doctor! You are certain?"

"Brother, I cannot be certain of anything other than the contents of this message. But the source has always been reliable."

Ali turned away, forcing order upon a jumble of new possibilities. "A doctor. A female doctor with a group of Crusaders. A British doctor with a group of American mercenaries. Why would they bring a foreign doctor instead of one of their own? And why a woman?"

"Perhaps she has special skills."

Ali spun on his heel. "Or perhaps she is not a medical doctor. She may be a scholar of some sort. A doctor of philosophy."

"It will take time to find out. And it looks as if the Crusaders are preparing to leave. Several soldiers were observed loading weapons and boxes into helicopters yesterday."

"Kassim, I must get into town. Tonight if possible. We need more information."

The Syrian's antennae sensed a risk, and risk assessment was his department. "Surely someone else can check on the details."

"No, not without undue attention. I need access to a computer."

"A computer?"

"Ten minutes on the internet should be all I need."

QUETTA AIRBASE

Leopole corralled Keegan after dinner.

"Another debate about patriotism, Terry?" The former Marine was chewing a cigar before lighting it.

"Actually, it wasn't much of a debate. I had him on facts and logic from the get-go. It was pretty much a slam-dunk." Keegan grinned wryly. "The benefits of a Jesuit education."

Leopole let it go. He knew that Keegan had been molested as a youngster and swore off religion for life. After an op that had gone south the two had stayed up late-late or early-early—Leopole forgot which—and Keegan had tied one on and vented his rage at the church. Leopole inferred that it was not the first time that an offending priest had been transferred to avoid prosecution. It was the only time Leopole had seen the pilot drunk.

"Terry, why in hell do you do it? Most of us understand your viewpoint. Hell, some of the guys *agree* with you."

The aviator grinned. "I guess because it's so easy."

"Cut the bull, mister. You're smarter than most of these guys but you're making a mistake. More than that, it's an avoidable mistake. You think that because logic is on your side, and because you got a raw deal, that you're untouchable. But damn it, Terry, this is a *team*. We have to rely on each other, which means we have to trust each other." He bit off the end of his cigar. "Do you think Marsh is as willing to fetch you back from deep serious as he was yesterday?"

"Hell, I don't know, Frank. But yeah, he probably is. He doesn't have to like me. But if he's really a pro, he'll come fetch me. And you know something more?" He didn't give Leopole a chance to respond. "When he's the one who needs a dustoff from a hot LZ, I'll man up and fly the lead bird." Now the Navy man grinned. "As long as he doesn't wave his damn flag at me!"

QUETTA

Ali leaned back in his chair, at once pleased and disturbed. The two al Qaeda bodyguards that Kassim had dispatched with him caught his mood but tried to appear nonchalant. The internet café was nearly vacant at 1:30 A.M. but the jihadists had long since developed professional paranoia. It was why they were still walking around.

Ali considered printing out the information but decided against it. He had a lengthy drive back to his base camp, and there might be surprise checkpoints. Besides, he was not about to forget the information he had gleaned.

He looked at the photo on the screen. An unusually attractive woman by western standards, with large, violet eyes. Dr. Carolyn Padgett-Smith, one of Britain's foremost immunologists.

She's after us, Ali repeated to himself. *We shall have to kill her.*

He mused at the wondrous ways of Allah. Simply because of a runaway dog.

BALUCHISTAN PROVINCE

Kassim usually reported to Ali without others present. It was the best way of preserving the security essential to longevity in his line of work. But this time was different.

Kassim made the introduction: "Qazi, this is Dr. Ali. Doctor, Sergeant Qazi is stationed in Quetta. He has information that I consider worthy of your ears."

Ali gestured for his guests to join him for tea. They sat at the rude table in his office, waiting for the kettle to boil.

Ali nodded to the visitor. "Proceed, brother."

"Doctor, I am a noncommissioned officer in the base facilities office. I have access to certain . . . information."

"Yes?" Ali sensed that the man was leading up to something. He glanced at Kassim, who appeared slightly on edge. That knowledge sent tingles up and down the doctor's spine. The Soviet Union had rarely made Kassim edgy.

Qazi proceeded. "Sir, I have obtained information about the

foreigners on the base. They are not soldiers, as Kassim suspected. They are hirelings, sent here because their government does not wish to draw attention to American troops."

Ali nodded again. "Yes, yes. Go on."

Qazi looked at Kassim, then back to Ali. "I have full information on their organization, their equipment, their capabilities. Everything."

Ali recognized a salesman when he saw one. He decided to put the sergeant on the defensive. "Then you are a servant of God."

Qazi spread his hands on the table. "Alas, I am but a *poor* servant . . ." He allowed the sentiment to dangle in midair.

As I thought, Ali told himself. He looked at Kassim, who nodded slowly.

Ali stretched a bony hand across the table. Touching Qazi's sleeve, he intoned, "Any information you share with us will be rewarded as befits you. We have many ways of expressing our gratitude." He smiled an ingratiating smile.

The NCO produced a notebook from his pocket. It contained a business card with the name of Lieutenant Colonel Frank Leopole, United States Marine Corps (retired). The man's title was Head, Foreign Operations Division, Strategic Solutions, Inc., in Arlington, Virginia, USA. Hand-written notes expanded upon the SSI arrangement at Quetta.

The kettle whistled and Ali turned to his assistant. "Tahir, please tend to our guest. I need to obtain some suitable gifts for his trouble." With that, he nodded at the door.

Outside, well away from the building, Ali said, "You did well to bring him here."

"He must die, of course. But first I thought that you should see him. He knew that I was not the chief of our district. He would not give me all the information he possessed."

"Offer him ten thousand rupees. If he balks at that, offer him two thousand American dollars. The man's greed will ensure his compliance. Then arrange to have his body found in ordinary circumstances."

Kassim almost smiled. "I favor traffic accidents. They happen every day."

"One more thing, brother."

"Yes?"

"You have contacts in America?"

"No, not directly. But The Base is worldwide, as you well know."

Ali thought for a moment. "Well, perhaps it is best if we have no direct line. It will be more difficult to connect us to any . . . incidents."

"You are thinking of direct action against the Great Satan?"

"They came here, hunting us. It is only fitting that we hunt them in their lair."

Kassim's wolf smile was back. "I shall see to it."

QUETTA AIRBASE

Officially, alcohol did not exist for SSI personnel in Muslim countries. Unofficially, the leadership invoked a policy based on "Don't ask, don't tell." Without realizing it, Terry Keegan brought attention upon himself when Leopole found him sipping something smooth in the cafeteria. He was alone, which Leopole recognized as a bad sign. He put an avuncular hand on the pilot's shoulder. "Come on, Terry. Time to turn in."

Keegan's eyes raised to meet his supervisor's. The pilot's eyes were bright blue; Leopole's were gunmetal blue-gray. "Oh, don't worry, Frank. I'm not flying tomorrow. Besides, I never drink within fifty feet of an aircraft."

Leopole ignored the attempt at humor. "You're still pissed about your flap with Marsh. Okay, you were right then. And I'm right now."

Keegan waved dismissively. "Shee-it, man. Don't get me started." He took another drink. *Oops, too late!* "Siddown, Frank. I'll tell you what's really got me pissed."

"Terry, I know about all that. We had this discussion before, remember?"

"Not all of it, we didn't. I want to fill in the gaps." He gestured at a chair, and for a moment Leopole considered dragging the tipsy aviator to bed. The 155-pound pilot could not win that contest with Franklin Puller Leopole, 180-pound professional warrior, enthusiastic martial artist, and erstwhile bar fighter. But that would cause more bad blood, and SSI needed its chief pilot up on the step and cruising. Leopole sat down. "Thanks," Keegan said. He dipped his head in gratitude, then began, "Frank, at age eleven I found out that my church was a lie, thanks to Father O'Brien and Bishop Farullo. At twenty-nine I found that the Home of the Brave was a lie: dozens of admirals were scared shitless of a few female politicians. Then at thirty-one I found that my marriage was a lie when my wife figured I must have done *something* in Vegas. All of them betrayed me; none of them lived up to the promise. It was lies and hypocrisy."

Leopole looked at his watch. He thought, *Are we really going to have this discussion again?* The aviator answered that tacit question. "Well, at about age thirty-three I finally found myself, Frank. I realized my whole goddam life has been a search for one thing. I've been looking for somebody—some*thing*—that I could trust." He grinned a private grin. "Do you like movies, Frank?"

Leopole sought to follow the logic. "Most anything with guns and horses."

Keegan laughed at the sentiment. "I like movies. Especially old ones, where everything works out in the last reel. But one of the best speeches in movie history was in *Conan the Barbarian*. Did you see it? At the start, William Smith is little Conan's father. He says, 'Put not your trust in man, not in woman, not in animals.' Then he holds up his sword. 'But *this* you can trust.'"

"I'm afraid I don't follow you, Terry."

"Sure you do, Frank. You must feel the same way. Sometimes, at least."

Leopole was about to agree in principle when Keegan continued. Tapping the table, he said, "Look, Frank, *this* is my sword. The admiral, SSI, you guys." He chuckled to himself. "John Milius got it right. Someday I'd like to shake his hand and tell him that Little Conan Keegan got the message."

ARLINGTON, VIRGINIA

"It will not be as simple as you imagine, brother."

Imam Mustafah al Latif sipped more tea and replaced the small cup on its saucer beside the thin wafers. His guest, whom he knew as Mohammed Shakir, occasionally paid a visit to the Islamic Fraternal Association on behalf of certain Middle Eastern interests. Shakir's position as an acting trade representative in the Pakistani embassy ensured freedom of movement and access to well-placed people. But he avoided al Latif's mosque.

"I recognize the potential for . . . embarrassment," Shakir said, choosing his words carefully. Whatever his faults, naivety was not among them. He always couched his messages in general terms, occasionally passing notes that were burned before he departed.

"It is more than that," al Latif responded. "As you know, Northern Virginia has an active Muslim population but few organizations are approachable for . . . your likely purposes. Other groups support

American initiatives and policies for a variety of reasons. In fact, one of our prominent artists designed a postage stamp for the United States government. Since there is every reason to believe that the more, ah, devoted groups and individuals are under scrutiny, you should seek men without obvious Islamic ties."

Shakir inclined his head toward the cleric. "Just as you say. Any references would be gratefully received, with a suitable donation to the association for its many good works."

Al Latif scrawled a list of three names with phone numbers. Handing it to the diplomat, he intoned, "One or two of these will undoubtedly consider whatever you propose. Copy these in your own hand and I will destroy the original. When you make contact, you are not to mention me or this organization."

"You are extremely cautious, father. I admire your diligence."

The imam raised his cup in salute. "And I commend your own good work."

QUETTA AIRBASE

Steve Lee poked his head inside Leopole's door. "Major Khan's here. Looks like he has some news."

Leopole was almost to the door when the Pakistani appeared. As always, he was impeccably dressed, reminding Leopole yet again of the differing emphasis between the two military cultures. They shook hands and sat down; Leopole motioned for Lee to remain.

Khan removed his hat and placed it beside his briefcase but that was the only deference to protocol. Unlike many officers in his army, he preferred substance to form. He got directly to the point.

"Colonel Leopole, I decided to come in person because I should not risk a security breach." He pulled a map from his valise and spread it on the desk. "Here. We believe that some of the men you seek are in this area."

Looking over Khan's shoulder, Lee noted that the coordinates were only about twenty-five miles to the west, along the border.

Leopole's gaze went from Khan to Lee and back again. "That's excellent, Major. Ah, may I ask the source of your intel?"

"I cannot be specific because I do not have that information my-self. But it comes from a very reliable conduit, one with excellent contacts in the Ministry of Defense. I could not inquire further with-out drawing suspicion."

Biting his lip, Leopole scanned the map again. High, rugged ter-rain. Remote enough to be a likely hideout for people who did not wish to be found. "What *can* you tell us, Major?"

Khan lowered his voice slightly. "I am informed that al Qaeda op-eratives have used this vicinity fairly recently, smuggling people and material in and out of both countries. It is reported that some of their cargos are sensitive materials. That seemed enough reason to bring it to your attention."

Lee stood up, obviously unconvinced. "Major Khan, please don't misunderstand. I have no reason to doubt your sources, but 'sensitive materials' could be almost anything. Weapons, drugs, or . . ."

"Yes, yes. I agree." Khan's enthusiasm briefly overcame his usual courtly manners. "But there is something else." He paused for dra-matic effect. "My source says that a doctor is involved."

Leopole sat upright. "Involved how?"

"I do not know exactly. But no mention of a medical connection has occurred before."

Steve Lee's eyebrows took an optimistic arch. "That's the best lead we've had, Colonel."

Leopole sat back, his fingers drumming on the desk. "Hell, it's the only lead we've had." He thought for a moment, weighing options. "Just one thing: if this is a false lead or a dead end, we risk tipping our hand. No telling who might be watching."

"We could send in a recce team, dressed like locals. You know— take a quick look-see, then call in the rest if it's promising."

Lee sensed that his boss was inclined toward taking action. Frank Leopole clearly wanted some action.

Several seconds passed. Finally, Leopole said, "Steve, I like the way you think. I'll call the admiral and recommend we go."

ARLINGTON, VIRGINIA

"No photos, man."

"Why not?"

"Because . . . when you take them to get developed, the store could get suspicious. That's why!"

The photographer, Marcus Garvey Jefferson, was a good-looking hustler in his late twenties. "Wow, man. Haven't you heard? This is, like, the twenty-first century."

"Say what?"

"Digital, my man. Di-gi-*tal*." When away from the sober, austere influence of the imam, the two brothers still lapsed into street jive.

The driver of the Honda Accord grasped the significance. "Oh. Right. No film." Hakeem put away his sketch pad.

"Riiight. We'll plug the disk into the computer when we have the briefing." The shooter double checked the exposure, framed the brick and glass façade in his viewfinder, and tripped the shutter again. By extending the zoom lens, he brought the shaded window into better view. He could now read the blue and white logo.

Strategic Solutions, Inc.

BALUCHISTAN PROVINCE

Ali knew that no plan worked to perfection. The Marburg operation was no exception.

Sitting with Kassim and two other al Qaeda operatives, the doctor considered his options. "It is as we expected in the beginning," Ali began. "The best way to begin our biological attack would have been with several hosts simultaneously. But volunteers are rare, and to wait until we had six or more would have posed security dangers." He frowned in concentration. "Besides that, most volunteers have limited life expectancy, so we are forced to launch them as they become available."

The other two men were recruiters, members of Ali's small cell who looked for potential jihadists burning with the desire to achieve Paradise—often before their own bodies burned themselves out. They had not been successful thus far. The youngest member, who adopted the alias Sted Nisar, worked as a hospital orderly. At nineteen he had found two prospects but one had died prematurely and the other became bedridden.

The second man was Farrukh Awan, who had helped send the vestal virgin on her journey. Ali accepted him because Kassim relied on him. It appeared that there was nothing the twenty-four-year-old carpenter would not do to please the cynical Syrian. Sometimes Ali wondered about that—what hold did Kassim have on the young man? *Do not look too closely unless you truly wish to know.* But Dr. Ali was a pragmatist as well as a theologist. Results were what mattered. Thus far both young men had done everything asked of them.

That made them valuable. Ironically, it also made them expendable.

Ali faced the pair across the rough table. "My brother Kassim has devised a plan to expand our attack against the Americans. But I wish to seek your counsel."

Ali caught Kassim's sideways glance. Ali hardly ever sought others' opinion. In fact, the plan was Ali's, but Awan would be impressed, and both leaders especially wanted to impress the carpenter.

Kassim took the hint. "I have studied the situation in Islamabad and Quetta. The Crusaders know that we are aware of them, and we cannot expect to strike them in their nest." He gave a wolfish smile. "So we shall draw them to us."

Nisar immediately saw the advantage. "Excellent! They will not expect a trap."

"That is what we hope. Certain information has already been planted with the infidels. Enough of it is accurate to attract them to a site of our choosing. Then it is a simple matter of devotion . . . and explosives."

Nisar asked the logical question. "When do we meet the sacrificial warriors?"

Ali's brown eyes bored into Nisar's. "My brother, Kassim and I are asking you and Awan to pledge yourselves to that task."

Nisar's guts turned to ice. He tried to think of a response.

Awan was more composed but remained silent.

Sensing that the mission lay in the balance, Kassim used his leverage to shove one or both of the young men over the brink.

"Hina bint Ahmed never balked at the chance to serve God. Farrukh, you watched her leave on her mission."

"But . . . but, she was already dying!"

"So are we all," said Ali. "So are we all."

ARLINGTON, VIRGINIA

"There's Carlito," Marcus said.

From the parking space, Hakeem Jefferson looked toward SSI's entrance where a well-built young Hispanic man entered the double doors. He was groomed for the occasion: high and tight haircut, polite, businesslike manner. What you would expect of a former Ranger looking for work with a PMC. At least that was his story. He hoped for a look behind the security door and perhaps a tour of the facility. With a pledge to return with appropriate documentation, he would tell the Jeffersons what he saw and then drop out of sight. No connection could be made.

The scout approached the desk, ignoring the uniformed security guard by the window. He nodded to the receptionist, being careful not to touch anything. "Good afternoon, ma'am. I'm interested in work with a military contractor and wonder if you have any openings."

Mrs. Grayson sized up the young man. He looked like a good prospect. "Well, I don't know if we're hiring right now but you could leave a resumé. We'd be glad to put it on file." She picked up a pen. "What's your name and address?"

Carlito Espinoza was ready for that. "I'm Rafael Castillo but I didn't bring any papers with me. You see, I'm from out of town and didn't know about your business. A relative mentioned it to me."

Emily Grayson picked up a business card and an SSI brochure. "Here's some information. You can send the required documents to this address."

Espinoza accepted the items without looking at them. "Thank you, ma'am. Ah, while I'm here, would it be possible to talk to someone? You know, so I could get a better idea of what's available." He flashed a white smile. "It'd sure save me a long trip back here again."

"Oh. Where do you live?"

"New Mexico, ma'am. Up near the Colorado border." Carlito Espinoza had never seen the Land of Enchantment but he knew enough to run a bluff.

"Just a moment, please."

Mrs. Grayson picked up the phone and buzzed personnel. In a few minutes Sallie Kline came through the security door with the keypad. She introduced herself, explaining, "I'm here part time, but I'm handling most personnel matters until our director returns." It wasn't entirely true but it was close enough.

After a few preliminaries, Sallie decided to invite the applicant into the anteroom. He followed her through the portal, admiring the way she moved. In other circumstances he would have pinched her in an act of machismo "valor."

"Sit down, Mr. Castillo." As they settled at a table Sallie produced an application form. "These are mostly self explanatory. It might help if I knew what sort of work you're looking for."

Carlito glanced around the room, taking a peek through the window of the next door. He noticed there was no keypad. A glance at the ceiling revealed no surveillance camera. He did not notice that Ms. Kline caught his visual sweep.

"Well, ma'am, I was in the Rangers. I've done all the light infantry duties but I'd be glad to do security work almost anywhere. I speak fluent Spanish."

"Any combat?"

The abrupt question took him aback. He blinked, thinking hard. Sallie waited two heartbeats, then knew that whatever he said would likely be a lie. "Well, you know." He grinned the white smile again. "I can't talk about it much."

"I see." *Let him sweat,* she told herself.

The awkward silence stretched into five, then six seconds. Espinoza's eyes went to the table top as he lost the staring contest.

"We'll need your DD-213, of course."

Nobody had briefed Carlito on DoD discharge papers. He merely nodded.

Sallie stood up. "Well, then. We'll wait to hear from you. Oh, where are you staying? Maybe we can arrange a follow-up interview while you're here."

"Uh, thank you, ma'am. But I'm leaving day after tomorrow."

"Very well, Mr. Castillo." She extended her hand. He accepted it and she squeezed gently, sensing his pulse with her thumb. "Goodbye, then."

As Espinoza left the lobby, Mrs. Grayson asked, "What do you think?"

She rubbed her chin. "He's a phony."

Grayson looked up. "What do you mean?"

"Oh, he puts up a good front. But he's an imposter. He didn't know about the DD-214, even though I gave him a chance to correct me on it. But he's also too smooth for some gonzo wannabe. No, he's up to something. Trust me."

"How can you be sure, dear?"

Sallie looked down at the older woman. "I saw it in his eyes and I noticed that he didn't touch anything—no fingerprints." She shrugged. "Besides that, I just *know*, Emily. I just know."

"Intuition?"

Sallie smiled. "We women *do* have it." She grasped a pad and scribbled some notes for Derringer. Uncle Mike probably would want to know of the peculiar visit from the mysterious young man.

QUETTA AIRBASE

With cross-border operations a possibility, Frank Leopole convened another briefing. He wanted to impress the SSI teams with what they might face, and he knew just the man to deliver the message.

Omar Mohammed did not require notes. He lived with his subject every waking minute, which is why Leopole asked him to address the operators. As always, Mohammed chose his words carefully.

"Gentlemen, I believe that you should understand something about our situation, the environment in which we will work. Though we will remain in Pakistan, you should remember that much of what happens there is driven by events across the border. Afghanistan is not only *a* Muslim nation, it is *the* Muslim nation. True, there are other nonsecular Islamic countries, but only the Afghans defeated the Soviet infidels. Nowhere else have Muslims defeated a western power in eight hundred years. How many of you ever gave that a thought?"

Mohammed allowed the rhetorical question to hang in midair. Knowing he had made his point, he continued. "You see the importance now? Well, the same point has been absorbed by Islamic peoples for nearly thirty years. They detested the Soviets as atheists who were harsh and tough. But you know what? They regard other westerners as infidels—not quite as bad as atheists—but less tough, even pampered."

Steve Lee interjected. "Doctor, what about Pakistan? Isn't that the center of gravity in this movement?"

"Yes, Major. Your war colleges do in fact identify Pakistan as the crucial player. If it goes fundamentalist, the cap is off the genie's bottle. From that point, it would probably be impossible to stem the rising tide of Islam. At least eighty percent of Pakistanis already are hostile or indifferent to America and the west. Now consider even an uneasy alliance between Afghanistan and Pakistan, with Iran sharing a common border. Imagine Pakistan *and* Iran with nuclear or biological weapons. I don't know about you, but that thought keeps me awake at night."

Seated to one side, Leopole allowed his door kickers to absorb that sentiment. Scanning the audience, he reflected that his squared-away career leatherneck attitude irked many of the operators. They were all technically competent and then some—otherwise they wouldn't be on the payroll—but several of them flaunted their civilian manners and dress. Neither was calculated to impress a former lieutenant colonel of Marines. He wanted to reinforce the seriousness of what SSI might face abroad, and interjected, "Doctor, I believe you have other intel to share with us."

Mohammed knew exactly what Leopole meant. "Certainly, Colonel. The following passage was lifted from an al Qaeda training manual found in a safe house in London. It provides as good a summary of radical Islam as I have seen anywhere else:

"'In the name of Allah, the merciful and compassionate.

"'To those champions who avowed the truth day and night . . .

"'And wrote with their blood and sufferings these phrases . . .

"'The confrontation that we are calling for with the apostate regimes does not know Socratic debates, platonic ideals, nor Aristotelian diplomacy. But it knows the dialogue of bullets, the ideals of assassination, bombing, and destruction, and the diplomacy of the cannon and machine gun.

"'Islamic governments have never and will never be established through peaceful solutions and cooperative councils. They are established as they always have been: by pen and gun

"'By word and bullet

"'By tongue and teeth.'"

Omar looked around the room, meeting every gaze. "I cannot state it more clearly than that." Then he added, "Mohammed fought twenty-eight battles and organized sixty-four raids, of which he led about half. Therefore, Islam is the only major religion founded and spread by the sword rather than by conversion."

Breezy raised a hand. "Doctor, I've heard that Muslims don't believe in suicide, like Catholics. So why do all these young guys blow themselves up?"

"That's a complicated question. The Prophet makes it clear that self-destruction is an offense against God. But He made allowances for the ignorant—those who had never received The Word. I don't know, but I suspect that the impressionable youngsters who become suicide bombers either have been misinformed by their leaders, or have intentionally been denied that knowledge.

"Either way, my friends, a naïve enemy can kill you just as easily as a dedicated one."

SSI OFFICES

Marcus Garvey Jefferson knew very little about the British Army. But he would have appreciated one of Her Majesty's Forces' favorite adages: "Time spent on reconnaissance is seldom wasted."

From the digital photos and Espinoza's bogus visit, Jefferson and his two accomplices knew much of SSI's layout before they walked through the doors. It was 10:20—a time chosen to optimize their one-shot option. Presumably most or all of the staffers would still be in the building before any left for lunch.

Jefferson and his brother Hakeem stopped outside the entrance to allow an army officer to enter. They waited a few moments, then pulled the balaclavas over their heads. They already wore latex gloves. Marcus nodded to Hakeem and their accomplice, grinning as he did so. If the imam's contact was true to his word, they stood to make at least $30,000 for perhaps five minutes' work. *Minimum ten grand for each shooter and everybody splits a grand a head for every corpse.*

The raiders strode across the polished floor to the reception desk. They noted that, as before, a uniformed security man sat astride a stool. *Rent-a-cop*, Hakeem sneered. He had previous dealings with the breed. This one was low-threat—a shade over sixty, more interested in his *Field and Stream* than doing his job.

Marcus focused his attention on the receptionist. He liked what he saw: pretty, mid-twenties, blue and blonde. Perky. He liked perky, up to a point. But she was not the gate guardian that Carlito had described. That woman was older, obviously more experienced. *Miss Perky is prob'ly a temp*, he told himself.

Marcus gave a high, guttural bark.

On signal, Hakeem pulled his nickel-plated Smith & Wesson 59 and grabbed the guard by the collar. The third raider, a naturalized citizen of Saudi extraction, produced a small spray can and leapt atop the counter. He quickly coated the lenses of both security cameras with a thick, viscous liquid. Then he unslung his folding-stock AK-47 from beneath his jacket and dropped behind the counter, covering the entrance.

Marcus pushed his Beretta 92 into Miss Perky's face. He registered her baby blues, now bug-eyed in disbelief, and glimpsed her name tag. Becky Nielsen. In his peripheral vision he glimpsed Ahmed pistol-whipping the guard into submission. With some difficulty the Saudi pulled the man's revolver from its thumb-break holster and tucked the .357 into his own belt.

Marcus placed himself into his dominance bubble. He knew from experience that violent intimidation went a long way, especially at gunpoint. "All right, bitch! Open that door!" He shoved Becky Nielsen against the wall, beside the keypad.

Speed was essential now. The plan held that if they did not gain entrance to the inner sanctum in two minutes, they would leave.

Becky Nielsen was screaming. She was certain of it. Her mouth was open, but somehow she heard no noise. Marcus knew he had achieved his goal: the girl was thoroughly cowed. Now he just needed to get her to perform a simple exercise. Speaking slowly, enunciating clearly, he said, "O-pen, the dooor."

In her twenty-three years, Ms. Nielsen had never confronted violence. Her eyes focused on the seemingly huge pistol wielded by the

young African American. She had African American friends; she
didn't even like to say "black," which sounded too much like "colored." She heard a loud moan and swiveled her gaze to nice old Ray,
bleeding on the floor. In their brief acquaintance she had learned that
they both liked coffee au lait. That was about all she knew of him.

Something stung her cheek. The skin felt suddenly rough,
bruised. Nobody had ever struck her. Never. She was stunned and
startled, not yet angered. "Do it!" the gunman was shrieking at her
again.

"I . . . I . . ." She reached for the keypad. Her hands trembling, she
tried punching in the five-digit access code: 19199. Twice the nine-
teenth letter of the alphabet, twice followed by the ninth letter. She
missed the one the second time. A red no-go light was illuminated.

"She's stalling, man!" Hakeem was checking his watch.

Keeping his voice low and controlled, Marcus grasped Becky by
the throat. "O-pen the dooor . . . or I will shoot him."

The blonde head vaguely nodded. She tried entering the five
numbers again, going slowly to concentrate. It was too slow.

"Do him!"

Without hesitation, Hakeem pulled Ray's Smith & Wesson
Model 28 and executed the gray-haired man with one round to the
head. The noise pealed off the high ceiling of the lobby. Becky began
to scream, but the fear rising in her throat choked it off. It emerged as
a desperate cry of helplesness. She realized that she had wet herself.

"You're next, bitch. Do it right!"

19199. The green light glowed. Hakeem's watch ticked through
the sixty-eighth second.

———

"Security breach, main entrance!"

Joe Wolf was the first to notice that surveillance of the lobby had
gone blank.

"We never should've hired that twinkie," Sandy Carmichael said.
Obviously Becky Nielsen had forgotten the rehearsals for such occasions. She had not even attempted to input the 20000 code that would
flash audio and visual alarms to every console in the office, let alone to
the security firm that would automatically summon the police.

Eighteen people were present at SSI headquarters that morning. One was dead, one now paralyzed with fear. Several of the eleven men picked up the nearest phone and dialed 911. None of them were armed.

Wolf immediately ran to the rear of the building, intending to open the "toy box." The walk-in gun vault contained rifles, pistols, and submachine guns. He fervently prayed to Saint Christopher that at least one had a loaded magazine.

In the executive offices, Michael Derringer learned of the threat and stood motionless for an eternal three seconds. Then he strode to his corner gun rack and pulled down a Browning Superposed, the world's first over-under shotgun. It was a collector's item, beautifully engraved by a factory artisan in the 1930s. Derringer had only taken it to the skeet range a few times. He would never take it hunting. Now he scrambled to find some twelve-gauge shells—any kind. Four rounds of birdshot beat a sharp pencil all to hell.

Lieutenant Colonel David Main had attended two wars and numerous firefights. He had his army briefcase and a Benchmade knife with a three-inch blade.

Joe Wolf, retired FBI agent, had a Sig 228 in the company safe.

Sandra Carmichael had a compact .45 Kimber Ultra Carry in her purse.

Things were going well. If Imam Mustafah was true to his word—and he always had been—Marcus and Hakeem stood to make ten grand apiece for a few minutes' work. It was almost too good to be true: shoot up the place, destroy computers and anything else worthwhile, and split before the heat rolled in. Ahmed didn't seem concerned with money. He was one of those true believers.

Into the anteroom, Marcus made straight for the door that Carlito had described. The gunman shoved his hostage through the portal, then brought her up short. "Where's the computer room?" If he didn't find living targets right away, he would destroy as many hard drives as possible.

Becky had been pushed over the brink. She collapsed in a heap at Marcus's feet, sobbing loudly, uncontrollably. Without blinking, he shot her in the back of the head and moved on. *A twenty-cent bullet gets you a grand. Bitchin'.*

At the next door Marcus went left and Hakeem went right. It was the misfortune of a visiting consultant to encounter Hakeem, who shot the man in the chest. Struck by a 115-grain bullet, he staggered backwards, tripped over a wastebasket, and fell to the tile floor. Hakeem stepped over him and continued down the hall.

It was his misfortune to encounter Sandra Carmichael.

Hakeem made the tactical error of leading with his gun hand around the door sill, and the nickel plated Model 59 gave her all the warning she needed. Crouched behind a steel desk, Carmichael raised her sights to chest level and waited, finger on the Kimber's trigger.

Hakeem Jefferson saw the open door and swung left into the room. He did not realize he had been shot until he found himself on his back, looking up at the fluorescent lights. Two 200-grain slugs had punched through his sternum into his heart; the second round of the double tap had clipped the aorta. He raised his head off the floor, trying to focus on whoever had decked him. He saw a light-haired woman behind a desk about twenty feet away. Then the world went fuzzy, gray, dark, black.

Sandy returned her focus to the door, expecting another shooter. When none appeared, she took stock of herself. She was mildly surprised to find her pulse only slightly elevated, breathing under control. She quickly tested her peripheral vision; little of the tunneling she had been told to expect.

Way down deep she felt a tiny electric thrill. Then she moved down the hall, trying to control her breathing. Her thoughts went to David Main, somewhere amid the shooting.

————

In the armory, Joe Wolf seized his Sig 228 and searched ravenously for a loaded magazine. Finding none, he dumped a box of 9mm cartridges on the bench. He scooped up several rounds, dropped a few, and loaded the others into the magazine. Working quickly, he forced himself to concentrate as he thumbed the ammunition into the double-column mag. He stopped at ten and put the others in his suit pocket.

Then he chambered a round and flipped the decocker, rendering the Sig safe. He was acutely aware that he had not shot a pistol since retiring.

More gunfire. More screams. The sounds of panicked people running.

Wolf turned into the hallway leading to the financial offices. Two men dashed past him; he recognized them from the research division. More gunshots; a woman shrieked.

SSI's domestic ops chief flipped off the safety and began checking each cubicle, "slicing the pie" as he methodically searched each wedge-shaped segment that came into view. It was slow going if done properly.

At the third cubicle he found a woman's body. She was a fifty-two-year-old grandmother named Harriet. Wolf knew her as an excellent accountant. He choked down the anger he felt rising inside him and stepped into the hall.

Forty-five feet away, Marcus Jefferson walked calmly away, pistol raised, ready to shoot.

The cop in Joe Wolf urged him to issue a verbal challenge. Then he thought of Harriet. He put his front sight between the gunman's shoulder blades and pressed the trigger. The eight-pound double action conspired with lack of practice to force the muzzle downward and left. The first round struck the wall at waist height.

Marcus jumped at the unexpected sound. He pivoted on one foot, turning to face the threat.

With the Sig now cocked, the second round was single action. Wolf stroked the four-pound trigger but the difference in pressure spoiled his aim. His next round went as he fought the recoil from the first. It missed Marcus' right shoulder by two inches.

The raider's Beretta came around, pointing at the white man's chest. Wolf knew he had no time for a third shot and threw himself sideways into the right-hand cubicle. A 9mm round snapped past his left arm.

Rolling to an upright position, Wolf leaned toward the entrance, intending to steady himself on the corner when he heard more shooting. Multiple rounds—a prolonged exchange—then momentary silence.

As Marcus advanced on the latest defender, he sensed that he was winning. This dude, whoever he was, had flubbed a dead-meat setup.

Two blasts impacted Marcus's back, lurching him forward. He caught himself on his right foot and spun to face the new threat.

Michael Derringer instantly knew his mistake. Dashing to the nearest shootout, he had caught a perpetrator from behind and fired both barrels of his 12-gauge, aiming at the man's torso. Both patterns of birdshot struck where intended, but they were not lethal.

Derringer ducked behind the doorway. He thumbed the release, bent the barrels downward and saw the empties ejected. He reached for the reloads in his pocket and tried to control his hands. One cartridge slipped into the upper barrel; the other resisted his fumbling efforts. He looked up again. The shooter was still upright, turning toward the late arrival.

The shotgunner backpedalled, removing himself from view and temporarily stabilizing the fight. The damnable second round would not drop into the Browning's lower barrel. Derringer let it go and closed the action, acutely aware of the fight-or-flight conflict raging behind his eyes. He wanted to turn and run.

Pride and survival fought for dominance of Michael Derringer's brain while the gunfight continued apace.

Joe Wolf poked his head around the corner of the cubicle. The assailant had turned away from him, slowly advancing on the doorway down the hall. There had been other shots—somebody else had engaged the man—but Wolf saw only the masked intruder.

With a temporary advantage, the lawman in Joseph Matthew Wolf shouted the oft-used phrase. "Freeze! FBI!"

Marcus swiveled his head, saw the man behind the partition again, and realized a no-win situation. Fully exposed in the hallway, he ignored the challenge, lowered his head, and charged eight steps to the cover of the doorsill.

He made it. For whatever reason, the man with the pistol did not try to shoot him in the back again.

The man with the shotgun centered the bead sight on Marcus's nose and, from eighteen feet away, mashed both triggers. One chamber emitted a soft *click*. The other detonated the primer on an ounce and a quarter of number 7½ birdshot.

When Ahmed heard more shooting in the rooms behind him, he suspected the worst. With a parting glance at the double doors in the lobby, he went through the security door that Hakeem had kept open with a chair. The Saudi-American sprinted down the first corridor to the left, noting spent brass on the floor, and began hunting. He glimpsed movement farther down the hall: a man and a woman, a green uniform. He spun on the targets and triggered a quick burst from his AK. The rounds impacted a conference room, sending shards of glass tingling to the floor.

Behind the thin wall, Dave Main leapt on Sandy Carmichael. He covered her body with his own, taking some of the glass pieces on his back. Beneath him, his erstwhile classmate strugged against his weight. "Lemme up, goddammit!"

"Sandy, stay down!" Main raised his head, only then noticing her compact .45 Kimber. He reached for the pistol. "Gimme the gun! Gimme the gun!"

Lieutenant Colonel Sandra Carmichael, U.S. Army (retired), was in no mood to negotiate. She tightened her grip on the weapon and tried to elbow Colonel Main off her. Another burst of automatic fire stuttered across the wall, eighteen inches over their heads. The shooter knew they would be on the floor.

"Sandy, he's coming!"

"Get off me then!"

The shooter had to be close. Main did the only thing he could. He rolled off Carmichael's slender frame, low-crawled six feet and risked a peek over the ledge.

Ahmed saw the head pop up to his left front. He swung the muzzle and fired again. The Kalashnikov's bark rang painfully off the walls, though he had inserted soft earplugs. Four rounds punched through the imitation wood paneling to Main's left as he dived for cover again. *Sumbitch missed from fifteen feet!*

But now there was nowhere to go.

Sandy Carmichael saw Main duck the next burst and knew she

had to shoot. She inhaled deeply, got both hands around the Kimber, and popped up, looking for her sights.

She found them. *Front sight's elevated, but he's close.* She pressed the trigger twice. *Got 'im!*

The .45-caliber rounds left the three-inch barrel at 800 fps. Both struck within four inches of one another. The AK gunner reeled visibly from the impact but kept his feet.

Sandy was stunned. She knew where the rounds went: mid torso. She could not know that Ahmed wore a typical AK chest pack with extra magazines beneath his windbreaker. They were almost as good as Kevlar.

Failure drill! The Kimber's sights came up again, seeking a place above the neck line. The man was moving slightly, making a head shot more difficult. She pressed the trigger, felt the compact pistol recoil, and awaited results. The AK barked again. Sandy felt something smack her right arm. She ignored it. She fired again. No good; low left. She fired again.

Then she noticed her slide had locked back. *My god, I'm empty!*

David Main could stand it no longer. He saw Sandy's slide locked open, leaving only one choice. Hunching low, he swung right, cleared the cubicle, and charged.

The green shape entered Sandy's vision as she prepared to fire her seventh round. Ahmed, aware of the closer threat, stepped back, giving himself time to engage the army officer. The muzzle brake came up and around. The 7.62mm bore looked huge. Main leapt from his feet, hands extended.

A gunshot went off. He did not feel any pain.

Main and Ahmed went down together in a tangle, Main grasping for the rifle. Sandy left the cubicle, knowing she had to get close to avoid hitting David. *Gotta get close.*

Main intended to bash in the assailant's head with the rifle, but it was unnecessary. Finally the colonel noticed the hole below the corpse's right ear. The last shot was Sandy's. He heard her exclaim, "My thumb must've hit the slide lock! I've got one round left."

Main looked up, saw Sandy wide-eyed, mouth agape, sucking air. He found his feet, reached for her and took her in both hands. "Honey, are you alright?"

She shook her head as if clearing cobwebs. "David . . ." Then she handed him the pistol and ran down the hall.

––––––––

The Arlington police and sheriff's departments responded quickly but too late to intervene in the shootout at Strategic Solutions. The sirens had convinced Marcus's driver to stop circling the block and seek employment elsewhere. At least he had the five-hundred-dollar advance. He drove away from the plaza, being careful to obey all traffic regulations.

The backup driver, in a rented station wagon, was not so circumspect. He busted a stop sign and drew the immediate attention of Arlington's finest. They had no reason to detain the Pakistani until it was realized that he had a forged driver's license and Immigration was interested in him.

––––––––

"Where's Sandy?" Derringer asked his niece.

Sallie Kline said, "Oh, I think she's still in the restroom. She keeps throwing up."

"What about you?"

She took a swig of mineral water. "I'm fine, Uncle Mike. Trust me." The faint tremor in her arms belied the words.

Derringer realized that the young woman was riding the peak of an adrenaline high. Eventually she would crash, but for the moment she was surprisingly composed.

He put an arm around her shoulders. "What do you want to do now, honey?"

Sallie Ann Kline leveled her gaze at SSI's founder. "Well, this week I'm going to call some numbers Sandy gave me in Arizona. Apparently most of the top instructors are there, including the best pistol shooter who ever lived. I'm going to sign up for a class with Firebase Phoenix or Morrigan Consulting. But for now I'm going home and screw Harold's wheels off."

With that, she kissed her uncle and walked to the parking lot. As she left, Derringer heard the detectives talking.

Sergeant Leo Forbus checked his notes. "Well, there were three shooters, all dead. Looks like they were pros: two of 'em had body armor. Six SSI people dead and four wounded, one critical."

His partner looked at the last body bag as it trundled out the door. "It would've been lots worse. If that Carmichael gal hadn't been here . . ."

"Man, she is something else. You know she was an oak leaf colonel?"

"I can believe it. A deputy told her he'd never known a woman who carried a gun, except female cops. You know what she said?"

"What?" asked Forbus.

"She said, 'Hey, if most women don't want to defend themselves, it's no skin off my vagina.' "

———————

David Main sat down beside Sandra Carmichael, who had stopped shaking almost two hours after the climax. He nodded at her right arm in a sling. "How you feeling?"

"Oh, I'll be alright. There's a big-ass bruise and contusion but the bullet hit the metal stanchion in the cubicle before it hit me." She looked at his bandaged neck. "How about you?"

"I got cut by some glass. No big deal." He looked at the floor, then turned back to her. "Sandy, we need to talk."

She looked at him through eyes still moist with fear and emotion. "You called me 'honey.' You never did that since . . ."

"Since I got married." He touched her left hand and she gripped his, hard.

"That's right." The Alabama inflection came out "raaaht." He still liked to hear it.

"Sandy, I love my wife and I adore my kids. But I love you, too. I knew that all along, but today when I thought you would be killed . . ."

"My god, David, that was the bravest thing I ever saw. Twenty years in the army and I never saw anything like it, how you charged that AK bare-handed."

"Honey"—he gave her an ironic smile—"what're we going to do?"

She had no answer, so she rested her head on his shoulder.

QUETTA AIRBASE

As SSI's resident rappelling authority, Jason Boscombe drew the not unpleasant duty of instructing Dr. Padgett-Smith in military techniques. Holding a tactical harness, he pointed out the features.

"The main difference from what you probably use is location of the carabiner," he began. "I think most sport climbers use a waist-level attachment but we put it higher, at the chest or shoulder. That way . . ."

"You can't fall backwards with your feet above your head," she interjected.

"Right." He liked the way she said *cawn't*. Male English accents sounded condescending but female accents were a turn-on. "Uh, would you like to show me how you rig the line?"

She gave him an indulgent smile. "Surely, Mr. Boscombe." She couldn't blame him; the operators had to satisfy themselves that their medical charge really did know something about climbing.

Taking the 11mm line and a steel figure eight, she talked her way through the process. "I pull a bight of the rope through the big hole and loop it around the stem; then clip the small hole to my harness with a locking carabiner or two opposing standard 'biners." Deftly completing the motion, she pulled the line tight to demonstrate it was safe.

"Good, ma'am. Now . . ."

"However, there's another option. On single lines, I can feed the rappel rope through the smaller hole, as long as it doesn't cause excess friction. I've used a petzl stop on occasion, but I don't suppose you lot have much need for them because you don't need to go upward, do you?"

Bosco smiled in spite of himself. "No, ma'am. Usually we just blow a hole in the wall and walk up the stairs if we need to."

Padgett-Smith had to laugh. "Well, I'll leave that part to you, lad."

For a moment the ranger was taken aback. He could not decide whether "lad" was an endearment or a put-down. Sometimes it was hard to remember that Dr. Padgett-Smith was ten to twelve years older than most of the SSI men.

"Um. Ma'am, we have use of this tower for an hour or so. I've already secured bases at the middle and upper decks so we can rappel down the wall. Once we've done that okay, Terry Keegan will lift us to a hundred-foot cliff and we'll also rappel from the helo with some of the other guys."

"Oh, splendid. I should enjoy that."

Bosco gallantly opened the door to the abandoned control tower and allowed his student to precede him up the stairs. He had already noted that she was dressed for comfort, with low boots, hiking shorts, and a T-shirt in addition to helmet and gloves. He decided that the immunologist looked as good from behind as she did from the front.

During the last practice session they decided to race to the ground. Bosco won by four feet, but he had to make a kamikaze descent to do it.

––––––––

At the end of the day Bosco commiserated with some of his friends. "Well, Dr. Smith sure knows her way around a cliff face. She moves slow, but with economy of motion."

Breezy nodded. "And she sure looks good doing it."

"You noticed that, did you?"

"Bosco, in case *you* haven't noticed, that lady has a gorgeous pair of buns following her around."

Bosco punched his partner. "Hey dude, why do you think I let her go first through doors all the time?"

―――――――

When they returned to the hangar, hardly anybody was around. Bosco inquired and was told to report to the meeting room. It was crowded with anxious SSI operators.

"Well, they beat us to the punch," Leopole announced. "This morning three men attacked the office in Arlington. They killed six of our people before they were taken down."

The listeners sat stunned for a microsecond before their emotions kicked in.

"Oh my god!"

"Sons of *bitches*!"

And a fervent "Holy shit."

Daniel Foyte raised his voice above the din. "Who were the shooters?"

"Evidently they were black Muslims with a naturalized Saudi. That's all we . . ."

"To hell with them, Colonel. Who's dead?" Breezy Brezyinski shouted to be heard.

Leopole raised a hand, motioning for quiet. "Most of you don't know the KIAs, but here's the list: Harriet Billingsley, Tom Grant, Becky Nielsen—she was brand new—Aaron Marks, Ray Treater, and Chuck Werblin. One of the electronics consultants, Jay Poor, is in critical condition. Sandy Carmichael was wounded but she's recovering. A few others also were hurt, including Dave Main, who was in the office at the time."

Steve Lee found his voice. "By God, it sounds like old Ray took some with him." Lee, an army officer, admired Ray Treater as a Vietnam Marine.

"I'm afraid not, Steve. Omar talked to HQ right after we got the email. Details are still sketchy, but nearly all the shooting was done by Sandy and the admiral."

Gunny Foyte exchanged wide-eyed glances with Lee. "Well I'll be go to hell."

Leopole sought out Carolyn Padgett-Smith and found her in the third row. She returned his look with a level gaze. *I am woman, hear me roar!*

Leopole continued. "All right, pipe down. I'll pass the word when we get more info. But for now, we need to keep our heads in the game, gentlemen. It's obvious that they know more about us than we do about them. Major Khan is investigating but I doubt he'll be able to learn much—it's impossible to keep our presence a secret. We knew that all along. We just didn't have a way to anticipate they'd take the offense in our home court."

Lee stood up. "Frank, aren't we likely to get hit right here?"

"Yes, that's possible. It's why I deployed most of my team as perimeter security during this meeting. We'll draw up a watch bill for additional sentries and rovers until further notice. Khan also is arranging for some reliable Pakis to help out."

"How do we know we can trust them, sir?" Foyte voiced the tacit concern of many SSI operators.

"All of them are vetted by Major Khan and our attaché office. But we're spreading out to avoid bunching up. From now on we'll bunk each team in a separate building."

SSI OFFICES

Michael Derringer made his way around the workmen patching holes in the walls and replacing shattered glass. The noise of power tools and the bustle of strangers in SSI spaces upset his routine but not his equanimity. He still had work to do.

Derringer walked past Wolf's office and paused a moment. He set down a zippered case that drew the domestic ops chief's attention. "Packing more artillery, Mike?"

"Damn right I am. When I was fumbling through my drawer

for some birdshot the other day, I realized that I was as personally unprepared as we were organizationally. Now I have some leverage, but I doubt I'll ever need it."

"What'd you get?"

"You know me, I'm a shotgunner. Remington 870 with an extended tube and poly-choke barrel. It takes eight rounds of double-ought buck with six more in a butt cuff."

"Have you shot it yet?"

"Sure did. With Hornady Tactical it patterns eight inches at fifteen yards."

Wolf swiveled in his chair. "I guess I need some range time myself. I still can't believe I missed that guy twice."

Derringer grinned. "Maybe that's why it's the Federal Bureau of Investigation rather than the Bureau of Marksmanship."

The ex-fed regarded his friend and employer. "You look better, Mike. How you feeling?"

He shrugged eloquently. "Oh, I'm all right. Not four-point-oh but good enough to get underway." After a moment he added, "You know, Joe, I spent a good part of my career training to kill submarines. Maybe a hundred fifty men at once. It hardly occurred to me I'd have to shoot somebody in the face."

Wolf leaned back, hands behind his head. "Yeah, I know. Even in my work . . ." His focus went soft, as if seeing something beyond the wall. Then he gathered himself. "I've been thinking, Mike. We know why those bastards were here. We just can't prove it. This was in effect a terrorist attack on American soil." He spread his hands in frustration. "But there's no way the government will admit it. Not publicly."

Derringer decided to take advantage of his colleague's contacts. He shut the door and sat down. "Joe, you know that any of us could be a target for kidnap or murder, especially those of us on the masthead." He hefted the zippered bag. "This is fine at the office or home. But what about traveling? What about just between here and the District?"

"You mean, packing in the car? Going to a restaurant? That sort of thing?"

"Exactly."

Wolf said, "Well, you can get a concealed carry permit in Virginia. But as for the District . . ." He spread his hands again.

"Yeah, I know. Get caught with a firearm and you're in deep trouble. It's absurd! Every gang banger has a gun but their victims are prosecuted for owning one. Are we supposed to go unarmed when there's a specific threat against us?"

"Well . . . legally, technically, yes."

"And another thing. We do business in government offices all the time. The so-called security people at the metal detectors are Barney Fifes, and you know it. But they carry sidearms while I go to jail if I'm found with a can of Mace."

"Right again, chief."

"So what can we do? Even if we get federal bodyguards—U.S. marshals or whatever. That's no solution. What's the worst that could happen if they screw up and get me killed? *Maybe* they'd lose their job. Not much incentive, is there?"

Wolf felt defensive at the implied criticism. "Well, Mike, you know, I'd like to think that our people in federal law enforcement are all professionals."

"Well, *I'd* like to think I can defend myself against the next hit squad that comes gunning for me. So we're back to Square One. What can we do, if anything?"

"I'll make some inquiries, Mike. I don't know if I can do anything, but I'll try. It's going to take time, though."

"Time's short and the clock's running, Joe."

"Well, I do have one immediate suggestion."

"Yes?"

Wolf grinned. "Don't go anyplace without Sandy."

BALUCHISTAN PROVINCE

"The Crusaders have been struck in their nest."

Ali received the word with dispassionate interest. He turned to Kassim and said, "Tell me."

"We have monitored press reports from Washington. Our operatives entered the headquarters of this . . . Strategic Solutions . . . and did much execution." His tone changed as he added, "All three now rest with God."

The Pakistani knew that his Syrian colleague was not devout, and briefly wondered at the man's choice of words. *Small matter—he serves our cause better than most.* "What damage was done, Kassim?"

"At least six Americans were killed and others wounded. Damage to the facility is unknown but said to be extensive."

Absorbing that information, Ali reckoned that it was good news but not decisive. Unless . . . "Who were the Crusaders that were killed?"

Kassim shrugged. "We have the names from the electronic sources but they mean nothing to me." He cocked his head. "Do you have knowledge of their leaders?"

"No, but it should be a simple matter to compare the corporate managers with the dead. Should it not?"

Kassim realized that he could have gained that information before making the return trek to the border. Ali was nothing if not thorough, but this matter of pulling information off the internet was a vexation. Kassim understood radios and small arms and explosives—and loyalty and ruthlessness and courage. Little else had mattered in his life.

"Doctor, shall I return to our safe house? I can obtain the information you desire and return in . . ."

"No, brother." Ali waved a placating hand. "Do it on your next scheduled trip. Meanwhile, what of the Crusaders in Quetta?"

"My men now watch them day and night. They have not moved. When they do, we will know."

Ali rested his chin on his folded hands. Kassim recognized the sign: the doctor was thinking. Finally he said, "I believe we should issue them an invitation. Call for two trustworthy men."

Kassim straightened, his face now drawn at the implied criticism. "Doctor, *all* of my men are trustworthy."

"Of course, brother. Of course."

SSI OFFICES

Rear Admiral Derringer met Homeland Security Secretary Burridge at SSI's entrance. They warmly shook hands, exchanging Annapolis incantations.

"Go Navy," Derringer intoned.

"Beat Army," Burridge replied.

"Thanks for coming out here, Bruce. I know it's inconvenient, but as I said, I can't protect myself in the District."

Burridge punched his classmate's arm. "Hey, it's good to get away from the office, and officially I'm in Florida. Besides, I'm traveling with more security than Gorbachev did."

Derringer looked outside, scanning the street and buildings. "I didn't see anything besides a couple of patrol cars."

DHS grinned. "You're not supposed to."

In the secure briefing room, Burridge and his two senior bio threat officers settled down with SSI's management team. The visitor opened the discussion. "Gentlemen, ladies, thank you for your cooperation. Ordinarily I wouldn't inject myself into operational matters, but you appreciate the urgency of this case. There's just too much at stake to risk something getting lost in the shuffle."

Derringer lapsed into officialese. "Certainly, Mr. Secretary. Now, I believe we've both seen the reports from Pakistan and Jordan. Is there anything more recent?"

Burridge turned to the well-groomed woman on his left. "Ms. Ramirez is tracking our intel on this case."

Consuela Ramirez was a biologist out of USC and Stanford. What she lacked in warmth—reportedly she was devoid of humor—she made up in dedication. "We're doing it the hard way because there's no recourse yet," she began. "We're working back-channel with a few Pakistani health officials, trying to narrow the search for doctors named Ali in the frontier areas. As you may imagine, that's a huge job. Our best information shows about 108,000 doctors in Pakistan, but apparently the database is not wholly computerized."

Derringer nodded. "Well, our teams are in-country, ready to go with a few local officials. All they need is an op area to start looking in Baluchistan. Or elsewhere, for that matter."

Ramirez was visibly frustrated. "Excuse me, sir. We could work so much better if we could put more personnel on the ground. This way, we're so limited."

Burridge touched her arm. "We know, Consuela. The proverbial needle in a haystack. But State is adamant: there was eighty percent anti-American polling throughout the country before the plane crash. If anything, it's higher now. We're lucky to have the support we do."

Joe Wolf tapped his pencil on the polished tabletop. "I'd like to discuss the Jordanian case. Is there anything linking that woman to the American boy? Had they been in the same areas?"

"Not yet, Joe, but that's the way to bet." Burridge had been out of the trenches for years; now he remembered why he had accepted a cabinet position with such reluctance. "We know the American definitely was in Baluchistan. The young woman's extended family is from Peshawar but she left there weeks ago, presumably for treatment of pancreatitis in Islamabad. She could've gone anywhere, including Baluchistan."

"Any similarities to their travel arrangements?"

Burridge looked again at Ramirez. "No. He left from Islamabad while her flight originated in Karachi. But when it turned out that she had Marburg, that was too much of a coincidence so we assume both carriers were injected by the same people. Obviously she was headed for Israel, though how she was going to enter the country is unknown."

Derringer caught Burridge's eye. "Then we must make another assumption: there will be more carriers, maybe from other countries. Back-tracking multiple suspects will be even harder."

Burridge inhaled, held his breath, then expelled it. *Here comes something else*, Derringer thought.

"Mike, that's not all. We're heard from reliable sources that other bio weapons are actively under development. The most serious seems to be a plant virus that attacks grain, especially wheat. Now, obviously that's not of immediate concern to SSI, but I think you should know that we're possibly facing a multi-axis attack from well-organized, competent forces that may not even be working together."

Wolf emitted a low whistle. He looked around the table and noticed that Sandy Carmichael's hands were now clenched fists. "How might we become involved, sir?"

Burridge produced a short document and slid it across the table. "We cannot afford an attack on our food supply any more than we can afford an oil boycott. Depending on what might turn up, SSI could be deployed to other countries for purposes of deniability. That paper contains names, numbers, and the CVs of scientists and field agents who could prove helpful to you. Feel free to contact them—they've all been vetted." He looked around. "We won't be scrambling for last-minute scientific help next time."

Derringer exchanged glances with George Ferraro, his chief financial officer. Both men realized that SSI had just been offered an open-ended contract. Discussion of that happy prospect would have to wait.

"Bruce, just for background. If Marburg or something else explodes here, how's the government going to deal with it?"

"Well, that's more FEMA's bailiwick, but there's contingency plans for local, state, and federal agencies. Most of the players know each other by now. Meanwhile, we're still working up to full strength of thirty-two National Guard emergency response teams. They're trained to deal with WMD attacks, though something like anthrax in a major metro area probably would be impossible to contain. As far as nukes . . ." He shrugged. "Hell, a couple of backpacks could come across the border on horses or burros."

Wolf sat upright in his chair. "Animals!" He smacked the heel of his hand against his forehead—what he called "the marine salute" when Leopole was not around. He rifled through a stack of papers. "Why didn't I think of it before?"

Derringer asked, "Think of what, Joe?"

"Here! I thought I remembered it!"

"For petesake, *what?*"

"Animals! In Mannock's notes, Jason's mother said he worked in an animal shelter. The kid wanted to be a vet but didn't have the grades. One of his letters goes into some detail about sheep and goats."

"Yeah? So?"

Wolf unleashed a grin that could in fact have been called wolfish. "So . . . maybe our Dr. Ali is a veterinarian!"

PART

II

SSI OFFICES

Joe Wolf had done his homework, and then some.

He had been up almost constantly for fifty hours, working the internet, maintaining email contact with Pakistan and Britain, and making phone calls at rude hours. At 0845 he walked into Derringer's office.

"My god, Joe, you look awful!"

Wolf laughed. "You should see me from this side of my eyeballs."

Derringer stood and offered his domestic ops chief some coffee. Wolf waved it away. "I've lived on the stuff since yesterday afternoon and I'm still wired. I may not come off my caffeine high for days."

"I'll whistle up some juice and rolls."

"Okay. Thanks." Wolf slumped into a chair and plopped a notepad on the desk.

Derringer picked it up. "What've we got?"

"What we've got is Dr. Saeed Sharif, DVM. At least I think that's who we want. Everything fits: geography, timing, and known activities. The other prospects are far less likely."

"What about our mysterious Dr. Ali?"

"Looks like an alias. Sharif is a leading veterinarian in Baluchistan. Very highly regarded—does all kinds of good work among the heathen. If he were Catholic, he'd be an odds-on candidate for sainthood."

Derringer nodded. "Okay, but what's the al Qaeda connection?"

Wolf massaged his temples, blinking his reddened eyes. "It's a long story. Sharif attended veterinary school in England during the 1980s. Evidently he had a real good time. That's not unusual for Muslims. I knew a couple of Saudis in college, and they burned the candle at both ends because they knew once they returned home the good times would come to a screeching halt."

"Yeah, so?"

"So . . . Sharif had a very good scholastic record—what we'd call an A and B student without much effort. And here's the kicker—he took some optional classes in microbiology. Anyway, he had time to play, and he played the field. He got a couple of girls preggers, as the Brits say, but his family bought them off. He was also a boozer, evidently a borderline alcoholic. But he got his degree in '88 and returned to Pakistan and opened his own practice."

Derringer rubbed his chin. "That doesn't sound like a candidate for a Muslim fanatic."

"Well, somewhere along the way he got religion. I've not been able to track that yet. But he pops up as a player in 1991, about the time . . ."

"Desert Storm."

"Check." Wolf looked around. "Uh, Mike, about the juice and rolls?"

"Oops, sorry." Derringer buzzed the outer office and relayed the request. "Go ahead."

Wolf sat up straighter, ordering his thoughts. "At first he was more vocal than active, but after the Russians left Afghanistan in '89 he became more interested in the Taliban. He disappeared for several months in '92 and again at odd intervals. Apparently he was back and forth across the border. He may even have known bin Laden. Anyway, he was certainly no friend of the U.S. He resented the American presence and our support of the Northern Alliance, especially since Afghanistan had mostly been a Muslim theocracy before 9-11."

"Any idea what turned him around?"

"Just a theory. I've been working with Dave Dare—or at least I think I have!" Wolf chuckled at the insider's joke. Allegedly Derringer was the only SSI member who had ever met the mysterious intelligence chief. "The contact has all been by email and phone. Anyway, you were right about him. Whatever the reason he left NSA was a real bonus for us. He put his research people on the case and they gave me some promising leads. I was able to track a couple of Sharif's vet school classmates and one of them kept in touch with him for about a year and a half afterward. He says that Sharif began to regret the good times he spent chasing and boozing, and was trying to redeem himself. I've had a couple of emails with Omar, who says that makes sense. He says that Islam accepts those who repent their evil ways and devote themselves to spreading The Word."

"Well, it looks like this Sharif is spreading a lot more than The Word."

"Damn straight. He's spreading the Marburg virus."

QUETTA AIRBASE

Leopole sat at the head of the table in SSI's improvised headquarters, joined by Omar Mohammed and the team leaders. "Gentlemen, I've heard from Arlington again. I asked them what we really know about Sharif or Ali or whoever he is, and the research division has been working overtime."

"What'd they find out?" Foyte asked.

"Mainly what you'd expect of somebody with his background. He's smart, maybe brilliant. Just getting into vet school is an accomplishment—sometimes it's easier to get into medical school. He had excellent grades and conducted some independent study in microbiology. That fits with bio terror, but of course that came years later."

Steve Lee appeared relaxed, polishing the lenses of his glasses. "Okay, that's the doctor. What about the man?"

"That's the best of it," Leopole responded. "Dave Dare and Joe Wolf worked up a likely profile. We know from Ali's college pals that he was a boozer and a chaser in his youth. At some point, likely in the early '90s, he became a born-again Muslim, probably because of his work with the Taliban in Afghanistan. He maintains a successful clinic in Islamabad but that's evidently a way to fund his pro-bono work with poor farmers and tribesmen. Dr. Mohammed says it's likely that the do-gooder in him led to the Marburg project as a way of redeeming his misspent youth." Leopole nodded to his colleague.

Mohammed consulted his notes. "According to the Hadith, if a Believer repents his evil actions and resolves not to repeat them, he can atone for his past by performing many righteous deeds." He looked up from the paper. "I think that's important—there's a distinction between righteous deeds and good deeds, or *hasanaat*. Ali obviously believes that his Marburg project is righteous—beyond mere good deeds. He certainly doesn't think he's performing *sayi 'aat*, or bad deeds."

"That seems the size of it," Leopole said. "Apparently Ali is trying to save his soul, and that's a powerful motivation. It tells us that he's not going to roll over."

Fidgeting in his chair, Gunny Foyte grew impatient with the psychological mumbo jumbo. He had cheerfully capped an assortment of dinks, spics, and ragheads in his career, and he never found that their motivation made the slightest ballistic difference. "Why don't we pay a visit to his clinic?"

Leopole permitted himself a rare smile. "We're going to—at 0200 day after tomorrow. Depending on what we find, we'll turn things over to the Pakis or we'll lock the door as we leave."

"So you don't expect to find the good doctor on-site," Foyte said.

"No, near as we can tell, he's still in Baluchistan, somewhere around Chaman on the Afghan border."

Lee put his military-issue glasses on again. "Okay, who goes to the big city?"

"I'm sending this your way, Steve. Pick the men you want— probably about six or eight—but leave your snipers and best field operators in case we need them here. Then check with Terry. He'll have the 727 ready this afternoon. I'm coordinating with General

Hardesty, who will clear things with the Paki police via the embassy."

"You mean we're working with the locals? I don't think that's . . ."

"No, no. Negative." Leopole waved a hand. "He's merely on call in case they get involved. Obviously, we won't risk a security breach just for the sake of being courteous to our hosts."

Lee sat back, mollified. "Roger that. If it goes like it should, nobody will know we've been there. But I'd like to arrive in time to survey the site in daylight, probably with my B and E guy."

Mohammed wore a quizzical expression. "B and E?"

"Breaking and entry, Doctor." Lee grinned at the seeming irony. "Yeah, it's illegal as hell, but we're not stealing anything unless we find the virus. In which case we're doing some righteous work ourselves."

"Quite so," Mohammed chuckled.

"Rix is really good at picking locks and neutralizing security systems, so the whole op should be covert. If we're busted, I imagine that General Hardesty will arrive in the nick of time."

Leopole nodded again. "Roger. He's tight with the chief of police and other security agencies. You'll meet him right after landing." Leopole almost adjourned the meeting. "Oh, it goes without saying that Dr. Padgett-Smith will go. She's needed to ID any suspicious elements in the office."

"Can she do it right there? I'd think it'll take some time."

"You're right, Steve. She'll have some biohazard containers to transport anything suspicious, and Hardesty is arranging for access to a government lab. She said that's likely to take several hours at least."

"Where is she, anyway?"

"She's at the range with some of Red Team, getting more trigger time."

Lee shook his head. "Now why can't *I* find a girl like that?"

ISLAMABAD

The pointed white dome of King Faisal Mosque stood in startling contrast to the rocky ruggedness behind it. Flanked by four tall, elegant spires, the architectural masterpiece drew hushed respect from the mostly agnostic Americans.

Looking in his rearview mirror, Buster Hardesty indulged in a knowing grin. "It affects everybody that way. I see it almost every day and I still gawk at it."

Things were crowded in the rented minibus, far more so than during the seventy-minute flight on the 727. But most of the passengers turned in their seats as Hardesty drove eastward on Siachin Road. "Man, that's big!" exclaimed Kenny Rix. "How many people will it take, sir?"

"Oh, about seventy thousand. I've never been there during prayer, but my Paki friends say that sometimes it's full up."

Padgett-Smith sat on the inside in the third row, her head covered with a shawl. She wanted a better look but still was impressed with what she glimpsed. "Winchester Cathedral has nothing on that," she murmured. "Except nine hundred years."

"Whole lotta prayin' goin' on," said Brian Guilford, a lapsed Presbyterian and practicing former Marine.

Lee, riding shotgun, consulted his city map. He had tracked the route north from the airport as Hardesty had taken Shaharra-Islamabad to the mosque before turning right at the mosque. His finger sought the F-6 area in the northeastern part of town. "If Ali's clinic is on Ataturk Avenue, that's not far from the diplomatic enclave."

"Correct," Hardesty replied. He took his time, avoiding the manic driving habits of many motorists in the capital. For a moment, Major Steven Lee, U.S. Army (Ret), mused on the irony of an active BG playing chauffeur for a retired O-5. But Hardesty seemed a mission-oriented type—something of a rarity among attachés. "The embassy is up ahead of us, on Ramna in the complex, but we'll pass the turnoff to Ataturk along the way. It'll help get you oriented."

Lee asked, "Sir, when's a good time to look at the clinic?"

"Probably around closing time. There's more traffic, you can drive slower and blend into the crowd better. I also have some overhead imagery for you." Hardesty braked abruptly to avoid rear-ending an ancient Volkswagen. "Who's your second-story man?"

Rix leaned forward from the second row. "That'd be me, General."

Hardesty's gray eyes went to the rearview mirror again. "Outstanding, Mr. Rix." The B and E specialist was impressed: the general had had only the briefest introductions at the airport but seemed to remember everyone's name. *Must be all those diplomatic parties*, Rix surmised.

Hardesty continued. "I've, ah, obtained some information about the clinic's security system. Because the vet has medical drugs, there have been a couple of attempted break-ins. Your Dr. Ali, or Sharif, installed electronic sensors linked to a security firm that can roll the cops in a couple of minutes. But it's a pretty basic system: you can probably run a wire around it in short order."

Rix sat back, appreciating the attaché's efficiency. "Roger that, sir."

Entering the diplomatic enclave, Hardesty turned into a tree-lined area and stopped the bus. "We're quartering you in some rented bungalows a few miles from here, strictly for security reasons. Obviously we can't put you up at the embassy. I'll get you set up and then Major Lee and Mr. Rix and I will take a look at the clinic. There'll be a full briefing after dinner, and you'll meet one of our medical assistance people who'll go in with you to read the labels. Any questions?"

Lee turned in his seat. "Yes, sir. Uh, General, I do wonder about your direct involvement. Isn't that risky? I mean, our running orders stressed that no military personnel were to be involved."

A grin ghosted across Buster Hardesty's face, then vanished as quickly as it had appeared. "That's odd. The Secretary of Defense never mentioned that to me. Maybe I'll have to check with him to clarify his orders in, oh, a week or so."

Lee realized what the attaché had actually said. *This is too important a mission to cater to the Secretary of State, and if there's any trouble, it'll take a well-connected general to sort it out.* He wanted to give Hardesty an ooh-rah punch to the shoulder. "Good to be back at the operator's level, isn't it, sir?"

Hardesty leaned over and winked. "Never been out of it, son. Never been out of it."

ISLAMABAD

Steve Lee ran the final comm check from his position atop the building across the avenue from the veterinary clinic. Beside him were

Padgett-Smith and an embassy doctor, wearing biohazard suits in case a hot zone was established inside. Another man stood by in a trailer in case decontamination measures were called for. That left two pair as lookouts and backup at both the front and rear, covering Rix and his two partners. The sentries used night vision to check the dark corners away from the streetlights.

"Front door, clear."

"Back door, clear."

Lee checked his watch: 0143. He keyed his mike. "All clear. Stand by."

Almost two minutes later the wailing of sirens stabbed through the night. Lee looked over his shoulder and glimpsed flashing lights as police and emergency vehicles sped to the south. *Buster's diversion, right on time.* Lee knew that the police patrol schedule was upset by two large fires in the G6 area along Hakeem Road.

"Echo Team, go."

On the west side of the building, Kenny Rix threw the switch activating the temporary circuit he had built around the alarm system. He punched in the test code, got a green light, and gave a thumbs-up to his partners. "Echo One here. We're moving."

Because the windows were barred, the team had little option but to enter through a door. The men moved to the nearest access, away from the avenue. The door was still illuminated by streetlights, but only indirectly.

Rix knelt at the door, adjusting a red-lensed Surefire on an elastic headband. He opened his kit, selected a likely probe, and inserted it in the lock-picking gun. Getliff and Skowen knelt six feet to either side of him, covering their respective zones with suppressed pistols. Each operator also carried a Taser for lesser threats.

Rix began mumbling to himself, a sign that Tom Skowen knew well. Apparently the lock picking was not going well. *Kenny's usually inside in thirty seconds.* The sentry glanced at his friend and saw Rix remove the pick from the gun, replacing it with another. The motions were calm, methodical. Take your time in a hurry.

More seconds passed, each with its own beginning, middle, and end. Corry Getliff backpedalled a few steps, risking a spoken query. "Kenny, can I help?"

"Get back," Rix snapped. He resented the solicitous gesture as much as he regretted the tone in his voice. *Take it easy*, he told himself. He lowered his hands and rocked back, resting on his heels. He flexed his fingers and popped his knuckles. Skowen heard the noise in the still night air. He was surprised at how loud it seemed.

Rix turned the adjustment wheel on the gun, selecting full engagement. Then he inserted the pick again and flexed the gun's mechanical trigger. The probe elevated four centimeters, engaged the tumbler, returned to horizontal, and sought the next detent. The pressure told him he was there.

Rix pulled the door open and Skowen stepped inside. As Rix followed, he heard Lee's voice in his ears. "Echo, contact! Two items headed yours. Twenty meters." All three operators dived inside. As last in, Getliff twisted the lock and scurried away from the glass door.

Two uniformed men came around the corner, chatting idly. Getliff spoke no Urdu but judged from their tones that they may have been discussing soccer or women. Something innocuous.

One man idly pulled on the door, ensuring it was locked. Without breaking stride, the pair continued its rounds.

Rix exhaled. He realized that he had stopped breathing. He whispered, "That was close!"

Skowen croaked, "Who the hell are they?" The irritation was audible in his voice. "Damn if I know. They must be some kind of security firm. No guns so they're not police."

"Damn it, Hardesty never mentioned rent-a-cops!"

"He prob'ly didn't know."

"There's always somebody doesn't get the word," Getliff said.

Rix spoke into his headset. "Control, Echo One. We're in. Send the doc."

"Roger that, Echo. You're clear."

Rix did an interior survey of the alarm system, looking for a secondary circuit. Finding none, he quickly unlocked the door leading to the lab area. He passed some empty cages, recalling Hardesty's briefing: Dr. Sharif, aka Ali, did not board his patients.

Moments later Padgett-Smith entered with her embassy counterpart who would double as interpreter. Skowen led them to the rear. "The storerooms are back here, Doctor. That's where you'd start, right?"

"Quite right. Thank you," she replied. Wearing her bio suit minus the helmet, she strode to the lab.

CPS would have liked to turn on the interior lights but Lee had cautioned against it. Somebody might see a tiny glow from outside and become suspicious. Everyone used subdued illumination, moving slowly and cautiously in the semi-darkness.

Padgett-Smith opened the first cabinet, revealing several shelves of containers. Her newfound partner, a communicable disease specialist named Carter Fox, read the labels. He found most in English. "Allwormers, roundwormers, ectoparasiticides, you name it. Dog and cat treatments."

"Ovine miticides and lousicides. Sheep stuff."

Padgett-Smith's violet eyes scanned the well-stocked room. "If he's keeping any filovirus here, it's likely in deep storage, not on the shelf. Let's have a look at the refrigerators."

There were three large units, labeled according to the family of serum they contained. Starting with the nearest, Fox noted that about one-third were labeled in Urdu. He read each one in turn, examining the contents for apparent consistency with the label. "Clostridium perfrigenes C and D. That's antiserum, likely for goats."

Padgett-Smith started on the next refrigerator, looking at the English labels.

After fifteen minutes neither doctor had found anything untoward. Rix called a progress report to Lee. "Control, Echo. Negative items so far."

"Roger that. You're still clear."

Another half hour passed. Lee made two calls in that time, using the cell phone that Hardesty had provided. The distractions to the south had begun to wear off; most of the police cars had returned to their usual patrols and the fire trucks were preparing to leave. Lee knew that the two roving guards were bound to return but he had no way of learning when.

A Honda sedan with light bar on the top cruised by. Lee saw it coming a block away but wanted to keep transmissions to a minimum. He relaxed a bit when it turned north, parallel to the clinic.

Then Rix's voice destroyed his composure. "Boss, we got something here."

ISLAMABAD

"Okay, Doctor. What did you find?" Lee was more relaxed after the entry team was en route to the safe house. But long habit told him it was too early to ease up. The unmarked van still could be stopped for any reason, legitimate or otherwise.

In the rear seat Padgett-Smith held up a biohazard box; she might have raised a trophy trout. "Mr. Fox found it, actually." She pronounced it "*ek*-chually." "He noticed the plastic container behind some specimen bottles in the second refrigerator. It seemed unusual so we decided to treat it as a possible hazard."

"Why's that?"

Padgett-Smith nodded to Carter Fox, a thirty-something lab tech who seemed to relish the clandestine arts. "Plastic is used for potentially dangerous samples because it won't break like glass. And there was no label identifying the contents," he said in his Boston accent. "The only notation is in Urdu *and* Arabic. Basically it says 'handle with caution.' "

Lee shrugged while his driver negotiated the last turn to the sanctuary. "Well, I don't know a bug from a germ, but 'handle with care' sounds pretty innocuous."

CPS gave an exaggerated smile. "It certainly does."

The American nodded briefly. "Oh. Gotcha."

————

Buster Hardesty was waiting when the SSI team arrived at its destination. He had an official of the Pakistani Ministry of Health with another unmarked vehicle and a small security detail from the embassy. All the men wore civilian clothes, but Lee noted that most carried concealed weapons. "Imprinting" was the word in firearms circles—the telltale bulge or outline of a weapon beneath a shirt or coat. However, it was obvious that the guards were unconcerned about being detected.

"Well done, Major." The attaché shook hands with Lee and nodded his appreciation to the other operators. He motioned to Lee and Padgett-Smith; they walked several yards away to speak privately.

"My Pakistani friend is, ah, well placed. For obvious reasons, he doesn't need to know your names and you don't need to know his. But he'll take your sample to a military lab for evaluation. The scientists will never know of our involvement. If the sample is benign, we may try to replace it, but I'm told that tests could take a couple of days. If it's hot, the security services will start looking for our suspect while you continue your own searches.

"Which reminds me." Hardesty pulled a scribbled note from a pocket and handed it to Lee. "Khan called on the discreet line this evening. He thinks he's on to something. Frank Leopole is organizing an op in the border region. He says he'll go with the people he still has in Quetta, but you folks might want to hustle back there."

QUETTA AIRBASE

Omar Mohammed found Padgett-Smith in the hangar. She was exercising when she heard his footsteps on the cement behind her. "We just heard from General Hardesty," he said. "He wants you to call him right away."

She straightened up, arching her back and stretching her arms over her head. Though a Muslim and happily married, Mohammed noted the muscular upper arms and slender torso. CPS had taken to exercising in the main hangar more often: she could dispense with bulky clothes and avoid unwanted attention. She caught his glance, knew its meaning, and accepted the tacit compliment.

"Roger that," she quipped.

Mohammed rolled his eyes in exaggerated fashion. "Oh no. Not you too!" He grinned in appreciation of the humor.

"Well, I spend all day with Type A commandos. Apparently that's the only kind there is. What should one expect?"

"I suppose it *would* be a welcome change if you had one or two ladies to talk to."

She picked up her towel and headed toward the office. "It would be perfectly delicious, Omar. But I knew the lay of the land when I signed on."

He paced beside her. "You know, the Soviet Spetsnaz were rumored to have twenty-five percent women. Many of them were Olympic athletes."

CPS absorbed that information, processing it behind those violet eyes. "It makes a certain amount of sense. Undoubtedly there were covert missions that required disarming guile rather than force." *Brains over brawn*, she thought. She turned to face him. "What does the general need?"

"Oh. I didn't talk to him. He just left a message asking you to call as soon as possible."

"Maybe he has a report on the sample we took. It's been a couple of days, and that's probably long enough to have run the tests."

———

Rustam Khan's presentation was concise and professional. Leopole expected no less, but thought that the Pakistani probably felt some pressure to make a good impression on the Americans. Leopole already had addressed the usual waypoints along the well-traveled route of a mission briefing: objective, intelligence, communications, and support, plus command and control.

In his clipped accent, Khan ticked off the known or suspected hostile forces and their capabilities. "I should emphasize that my sources are varied and do not always agree in details. That is to be expected. Additionally, some of the information is at least a few days old. But there is enough similarity on locale and previous sightings to justify launching an operation against this cave complex." He circled an area on the map, a five-kilometer area on the Afghan border.

Lee raised a hand in the front row. "How many caves are we looking at?"

Khan arched an eyebrow. "In that area, there could be dozens. But relatively few would be suitable for the terrorists' purposes. I shall accompany you to evaluate each site. I am familiar with such things and I can save some time. Unless we encounter an unexpected situation, the search should take little more than a day."

Mohammed opened the door at the rear of the room and got Leopole's attention. The team leader waved him in.

"Excuse the intrusion," Mohammed began. "But Dr. Padgett-Smith just talked with General Hardesty in Islamabad. The laboratory confirmed that the sample you found is in fact a filovirus. As yet it has not been identified, but the doctor believes we need look no further. Saeed Sharif is the man we want."

"Well, where is he?" Foyte asked.

Leopole stood up. "Let's hope he's in one of those caves. Ruck up, gentlemen. We launch at 0430 tomorrow. Blue Team's up front, White in reserve."

––––––––

After the briefing, Lee essayed a literary comparison for the benefit of those who read something besides *Soldier of Fortune*. "The terrorists we're after frequently hide in caves. The area is full of them, and some are huge. It's a lot like the Morlocks in H.G. Wells' novel . . ."

Delmore interjected. "Morlocks? You mean, like, the underground gooners in *The Time Machine?*"

"Oh, yeah," Breezy exclaimed. "The '60s flick with that really cute blonde babe. Yvette whatshername."

"Yvette Mimieux?" Bosco asked.

"I guess so. Little bitty gal."

Lee gave an exaggerated sigh. "As I was saying . . . there's a similarity between the terrorists and the Morlocks in the H.G. Wells novel." He nodded toward Breezy. "From which the movie was made."

"Uh, yessir."

"The comparison is, the Morlocks lived underground where they mutated into semi-human form. They came to the surface to prey on the people up there. Er, well, up here . . ." He felt growing frustration at trying to educate some of his knuckle-dragging door kickers in the finer points of literary-cinematic comparisons with the current world situation.

Bosco, a science-fiction devotee, turned to his partner. "Major Lee is saying that the terrorists are like the Morlocks; they can't stand the light of day so they dwell underground, like where we're gonna look for 'em in caves. They can't win a stand-up fight so they seek helpless victims like the Eloi, who were unable to defend themselves. The difference, of course, is that H.G. Wells' novel was set in a post-industrial world whereas we're merely in the post–Cold War world." He turned toward Lee, keeping a deadpan expression. He knew that he had just astonished the bejabbers out of the former Army officer.

"Boscombe, sometimes you freaking amaze me."

"Yes, sir. Sometimes I amaze myself."

BALUCHISTAN PROVINCE

Blue Team was deployed along a narrow crest overlooking the likely cave complex. It was chilly in the morning air at that elevation, but most of Dan Foyte's operators were dressed for mobility rather than warmth. They knew they might have to move fast.

Foyte glassed the largest entrance from 450 meters out, then handed his optic to Khan. After a few moments, the Pakistani returned the binoculars. He nodded. "Yes, that is a good spot to begin."

The scouts returned to the assembly area and Foyte called for a huddle. "Okay, here's the drill." He had checked off each item in his prebrief review though he knew the items cold.

"After we establish security and scout the area, we'll make a go-no-go decision. If we go, the entry team will search as far in as possible." He looked at the team leader, a former SEAL named Darryl Logue. "Darryl, keep me informed of your progress. We won't know about radio reception until you get inside, but if we lose contact for more than a minute or so, come on out and we'll reposition."

Logue nodded, working on a stick of gum. "When will you want to bring Mrs. . . . ah, Doctor Smith in?"

CPS shot a discreet grin at Foyte. She had long since accepted most Americans' inability to grasp hyphenated names.

"We'll do that only if there's sign of recent activity. Otherwise, we won't waste the time. We can start looking in other places."

"Gotcha, Gunny." Logue glanced over his shoulder. "Entry team, on me."

Foyte deployed the perimeter team below the ridge line to avoid unseemly silhouettes. He decided on a compromise between terrain and tactics, placing his two snipers to cover either side of the cave entrance, eighty meters out, and the other three men watching their rear and flanks. He kept Dr. Padgett-Smith nearby, noting that she watched the balletic actions of Logue's team with interest.

The tactical choreography unfolded. Hank Haywood and Jake Swetman were on point. They entered the mouth of the cave, within arm's reach of one another, advancing in a splay-footed gait they called "duck walking." Foyte watched approvingly as they alternately searched high and low, using the lights on their suppressed MP-5s to look into the recesses and darkest corners. They kept their night vision goggles up on their helmets for now. If necessary, they would lower the NVGs farther in.

Still in sight of the security team, Swetman pointed downward with his left hand, making a walking motion with two fingers. Foyte read the tacit shorthand. *Footprints.*

The last pair "pulled drag," watching the rear. Jim Boyle and Joel Hall had practiced "backwards dancing" until it was second nature.

Forty seconds after the "drag" team disappeared, the cave erupted.

QUETTA AIRBASE

"Oh my god." Omar looked up from the phone as Leopole entered the office.

"What is it?" Leopole asked.

"We lost half of Blue Team."

"What?"

Lee slumped in his chair. "Apparently the cave was wired. When the entry team was about twenty meters in, the ragheads blew it."

Leopole felt an emotional smack to his consciousness. He grappled with his professionalism to focus on the consequences. He heard his own voice. "Jesus. Who?"

Omar checked his scrawled notes. "Boyle, Cashius, Haywood, Hall, Logue, and Swetman."

"Carolyn?" Leopole realized it was the first time he had used her given name.

"No, she's all right."

Leopole thought for a moment, forcing the anger and grief to the back of his mind. He had conducted that exercise before. "Can they recover the bodies?"

"They don't know yet, Frank. The security team's working with the Pakis to see about excavating."

"Well, we can't do much good with six guys operating independently. Let's transfer the others to Red and White."

"Alright. I'll send Hendricks, Norton, and O'Neil to White. Gunny Foyte can bring Champlin, Santo, and Reynolds to us."

Leopole scratched his close-shaven head. "Omar, you know what this means . . ."

"Yes." The training officer looked at the former marine. "They knew we were coming."

"You think we were set up?"

Omar shrugged. "If we weren't, the results are the same. Maybe they dropped some false intel; maybe they just knew where we'd search."

Leopole stalked toward the door. "Frank, where you headed?" Omar asked.

"I'm gonna talk to Khan. Up close and personal."

ARLINGTON, VIRGINIA

Michael Derringer gripped his bedside phone. He reached for his nightstand notebook and began writing, forcing himself to focus on the words he transcribed from the familiar voice rendered scratchy from eight thousand miles away. He still blinked from the unwelcome light that probed his sleepy eyes but his mind was wholly, violently awake. "Repeat the last two, Omar." He looked at the freshly inked names: Logue and Swetman. He tried to put a face to each; he could not.

After Mohammed hung up, Derringer rolled back on his pillows. His wife's manicured hands went round his neck, her graying hair against his cheek. "It's no good trying to sleep, is it?"

"No, Karen, it's not. No good at all."

QUETTA AIRBASE

Major Khan appeared at Leopole's improvised office early the next morning. In contrast to his usual appearance, the Pakistani looked unusually rumpled. Leopole assessed him at a glance and concluded that he had been up most of the night.

"Please come in, Major." The American had not tried crossing the line with his colleague. Theirs was still a professional relationship; first names would only come in time, if at all.

Khan pulled up a chair and sat down, visibly tired but erect. He rubbed his mustache, then leveled his gaze at Leopole. "Colonel, I have investigated the tragedy that your team suffered. At least to the extent possible. I believe that I have an explanation, but . . ."

Leopole leaned forward, hands folded on the desk. "Yes?"

"But it is not meant as an excuse. You understand? You acted on my information. You took me at my word, and . . ." Khan's voice choked. For a moment Leopole wondered if the Paki would begin crying.

"Of course, Major. Of course I understand."

"Thank you." Khan cleared his throat, regaining his composure. "I, ah, talked to my sources several times." His obsidian eyes hinted at some severe "conversations" during the night. "What I believe happened is this:

"Military intelligence works with various agencies, especially where terrorism is concerned. Police and border guards deal with smugglers and that necessarily involves those who cross back and forth into Afghanistan."

Leopole nodded. "Yes, terrorists and smugglers are interrelated."

"Correct. After some preliminary—interviews—I suspected that one of my police contacts was too well informed on certain aspects of al Qaeda operations. I mean, he mentioned a sensitive detail that he would not ordinarily know." Khan shrugged. "The sin of pride, Colonel Leopole. Some men reveal themselves in order to appear intelligent or influential.

"Anyway, under further interrogation he, uh, admitted that he might have 'accientally' provided information to people who had no authority for such things." Khan licked his lips.

"Would you like some water, Major Khan? Or maybe some tea?"

The Pakistani wiped his mouth with a handkerchief, then nodded. "Water, please." As Leopole poured from the bottle on his desk, he wondered what had transpired in the past several hours that would make an experienced operator like Khan so unsettled. The erstwhile Marine decided not to pursue that subject.

Khan set down the empty glass and nodded his thanks. "After that interrogation, I contacted two trusted colleagues and told them what I had learned. They checked their sources, which took some time—most of the rest of the night. They called me just before I came here.

"This is my assessment: a mid-level customs official was eager to please his superiors with arrest of certain smugglers who have long evaded capture. In his haste to succeed, he worked without authority to consult with other sources, some of which had low-level security ratings or none at all. From there the trail grows cold, but I believe that at some point the terrorists connected me to your operation and—help me—seeded false information."

"Oh, planted. They planted false information."

"Quite so." Khan nodded. "That was the information I provided to you. And I am at fault for not checking it more thoroughly."

Leopole leaned back. "And we—that is, I—decided to act on your information, Major. I suggest that we take this as a lesson learned, and move on." He paused for effect. "What do you say?"

Khan almost smiled. "I say, thank you, Colonel Leopole. From my heart."

BALUCHISTAN PROVINCE

Kassim rapped on the door, greeting Ali with a rare grin. "Praise be to Allah!"

The doctor realized that it must be very good news indeed if the Syrian were becoming devout. "And to you, brother, for bringing His Word."

Kassim almost executed a jig despite his false foot. "Our messages produced results. Several of the Crusaders have been sent to hell."

"The Americans came to the cave?"

"They did, my friend. They did indeed. At least five—maybe six."

Ali gestured toward a rude chair. "Be seated, Kassim. Tell me more." He reached for the teapot and began to pour.

"It went much as we planned, but better than most plans actually produce." Kassim related the trail of hints and clues that had drawn the SSI team to the desired cave complex. "Awan and Nisar—the ones you met—waited with twelve kilos of explosives. One operative would have been sufficient but I convinced them that both had reached the time for Paradise."

"Blessings be upon them." Ali mouthed the words more perfunctorily than usual. His accomplice noted that the Samaritan tended toward minimizing such sacrifices of late. "Did the cave collapse?"

"My observer says that the mouth fell in. He watched the Americans trying to dig through the rubble for quite some time. Then he left when he heard a helicopter. But he counted at least five men entering the cave."

Ali sipped some tea, not really tasting it. He was thinking downstream again, trying to stay at least one step ahead. "We will learn the actual number of dead infidels shortly. An event such as this cannot be kept secret for long—not at Quetta."

Kassim leaned forward on the table. "Of course, this will only enrage the Crusaders. They will come after us harder than ever."

"That is certain, brother." Ali smiled.

QUETTA AIRBASE

The Hip air-taxied to the designated spot, then set down in response to the ramp director's signal. Terry Keegan allowed the helo's weight to settle onto its wheels, then began to shut down. Nobody approached the Mi-17 until the rotor nearly stopped. There was no hurry.

Leopole, Mohammed, and some others walked to the aircraft as an unmarked truck parked nearby. The Pakistani crew chief opened the helo's door and turned back inside.

The first body bag was handed down.

SSI operators carefully loaded their six friends in the truck, which drove to the company's hangar for temporary storage. Rustam Khan and Buster Hardesty had arranged for access to a civilian mortuary. They did not want a military facility to handle the casualties for security reasons. A certain handling fee offered better security than military protocol.

Padgett-Smith felt somehow obliged to witness the operation. She had seen the men enter the cave seconds before they died, but now with a start she noted that four of the rubber bags were marked "Human remains: nonviewable."

Leopole appeared at her side. She inclined her body slightly toward him; he resisted the impulse to hug her. After an awkward silence he intoned, "It's always like this. Sadness and anger."

She nodded slowly, unable to turn her gaze from the six forms. "I suppose it must be." Finally she looked up at him. "My god, Frank. Whatever will you tell their families?"

The former Marine emptied his lungs, his cheeks sagging inward. "Fortunately, I don't have to handle that chore. The admiral probably will do it. He always has in the past."

Padgett-Smith worked up the nerve to ask, "Have there been many others?"

He fixed his gaze on her. "This almost doubles the previous figure. It's not many, considering all the man-days we've logged over the years. But if you're the one going home in a box . . ."

"Yes." She touched his arm.

BALUCHISTAN PROVINCE

"Whatchutink, Gunny?"

Foyte shot a frosty DI glare at Bosco, then turned back to the compact Zeiss binoculars. Ordinarily Foyte would not choose to affiliate with the brash ex-ranger, but Bosco was SSI's rappel master. And the cliff face before them screamed for rappelling expertise.

"I think there's only one frigging way into that cave," Foyte allowed, fine-tuning the focus knob. Even from half a mile away, the gaping entrance looked large—Foyte estimated its width at thirty meters or more—but the approach offered any occupants a beautiful field of fire. The slight incline would expose attackers to both direct and grazing fire, depending on the defenders' deployment.

Foyte rolled onto his back and eased himself off the narrow saddleback. Bosco followed, notebook in hand. At the bottom they consulted with the others.

"It's like we thought, Colonel." Foyte addressed Leopole. "No way to get close without being seen unless they're drunk or asleep. Boscombe's sketched the layout. It's gotta be a vertical assault."

Bosco laid his notebook on a rock so the others could see. "I think we can get two teams down there at once. I'll know more when I recon the top, but there's at least one good-sized boulder to secure a petzl stop. I'd prefer a tree but there's none in sight. The other team may have to rope off of some expanding bolts. If the rock over there is like this stuff here, it'll hold."

Leopole nodded. "Roger that. So we're talking about eight assaulters?"

"Right," Bosco replied. He only used *sir* when joking. *It's great being a civilian.* "We might consider another assault element to attack on foot, but they'd have to cover some open ground, so they'd only go after the rappellers secure the mouth."

Foyte caught Leopole's attention. "That makes sense to me, Colonel. We don't know how big that cave is or how many people might be there."

"All right. That's eight men from the top and six or eight from below. The rest of Red Team will provide security so that should do."

Frank Leopole conducted the final briefing that afternoon. He stood before a large sketch of the cave, showing the top of the hill and the approaches. The operators were seated on the ground or standing for a better view. "All right, people, listen up. Paki intel says this cave complex is currently being used. Major Khan passed reports to us indicating recent activity, so we treat it as hot." He pointed out the terrain features. "Here's the drill. Because of the exposed terrain leading to the cave, we have to assault down the cliff face to achieve surprise." Audible groans skittered through the audience but he ignored them. Tracing the distance from the cave to the crest, he continued. "It's about sixty feet from the top, and we'll use two teams: one on each side of the mouth. You rappellers—remember to take your leg bags so you don't drop the ends of your lines and warn the gomers inside. I'll coordinate by radio so we'll have a comm and equipment check before we go. Bosco is running the show on top; Gunny will take the ground element." He nodded at Foyte. "We go at 0715."

Breezy waved a hand. "Sir, wouldn't we have a better chance of surprising them if we went at dawn? Maybe catch 'em praying or something?"

"Ordinarily I'd agree with you," Leopole said. "It's always advisable to take advantage of enemy habit patterns. But none of us have ever worked this area, and we can't afford to go stumbling around in the dark. Also, I don't want to spend any more time than necessary scouting the terrain. If we get caught in the open, we're in deep serious."

Jeff Malten called from the back row. "Sir, do we take bio suits?"

"Negative. There's no reason to believe there's any hazard in this remote area, unless it's naturally occurring, and there's no indication of that. But Dr. Padgett-Smith will be on hand in case you find anything suspicious, and Dr. Mohammed will conduct the interrogation." He surveyed the crowd. "Anything else?"

Nobody responded, so Leopole wrapped it up. "Remember the objective, people: we want prisoners. *Live* prisoners." A few door-kickers chuckled at the implication. "Just don't take any unnecessary risks. Any POWs or casualties will be air-evaced back to base but Keegan and our helos will keep out of earshot until we need them."

Foyte stood up to complete the briefing. "Listen up! We saddle up at 0500 and drive within two klicks of the objective. The rappelling teams won't move into position until the security element is in place, so the schedule might slip somewhat. If so, Colonel Leopole will coordinate by radio." He glanced at his watch. "Equipment check in three-zero mikes, then chow. Let's move!"

———

"Comm check. Control is up."

Leopole listened for the responses. They came promptly over the lightweight headsets that the operators wore.

"Red is up." Jeffrey Malten was crisply professional.

"White is up." Somehow Bosco's laid-back tone belied his attentiveness.

"Blue is up." Foyte's ground assault team was ready.

Atop the rocky tor, Bosco had secured 150 feet of yellow assault line around a large boulder fifty meters down the reverse slope. He was confident that the weight of four men would not dislodge it, especially since its bulk lay in the opposite direction of the rappel.

Next he screwed two expanding bolts into the rock above the other side of the cave mouth: a primary and a backup. Then he cinched them down tight with a crescent wrench from his backpack.

With the bases secure, Bosco and Breezy attached four-hole extension plates to each rope with extension lines off each plate. The eight operators ran their lines through the carabiners on their tactical harnesses, and Bosco checked each for tension as the assaulters leaned back, allowing the gear to take their weight. They were ready in minutes.

Breezy's team took the left side of the cave entrance; Jeff Malten's the right. Besides the rappelling gear, each operator wore a headset beneath his helmet plus goggles, gloves, and tactical vest. Most had MP-5s with suppressors and lasers or lights; all had pistols with lights. Malten favored a fourteen-inch Benelli shotgun. Every weapon was loaded and safed.

Breezy also had his medical kit.

After the two teams lined up shoulder to shoulder, Bosco tacitly queried them. He got eight thumbs-up.

"Control, White's a go."

Leopole heard the quiet statement and keyed his mike. "Blue?"

"Blue's a go." Foyte's ground team was in position, cocked and locked, eighty meters from the entrance.

"All teams, countdown begins." Leopole paused, then initiated the process. "Five, four, three, two . . ."

He waited five seconds—an automatic hold in case a last-second glitch developed. Hearing nothing, he continued. "One . . . execute!"

As double insurance that the ball started on time, Bosco pointed two fingers of each hand at the rappelling teams. On "execute" six operators pushed off with their legs, dropping toward the earthen rock sixty feet below. The more expert made the descent in three drops, braking themselves by extending their rope hands outward, increasing friction on the double loop in the steel figure-eights hooked to their harnesses.

Three men from each team hit the ground within a few seconds of one another, leveling their weapons and scanning for targets. Almost immediately the fourth man from each team arrived, covering the others who disengaged from the ropes. Without a word, the six initial assaulters then stalked forward while the backups slipped the lines from their harnesses.

Eight shooters were up and ready in less than ten seconds. By then, Foyte's "legs" were hustling across the open space, ready to secure the entrance or provide reinforcements inside.

Breezy and Malten led their teams on either side of the cave entrance, each man scanning left or right, high or low. They found that ambient light was ample within thirty meters of the wide entrance, gradually diminishing as they hunted farther in.

The point men were careful to watch for booby traps or warning devices. Finding none, they proceeded another ten meters when Breezy stopped. He touched his nose with his left hand, keeping a firing grip on his MP-5. Behind him, Delmore nodded. *He smells something.* Breezy pantomimed eating; the others caught the scent. He looked over at Malten, who repeated the gesture. *They're having breakfast.*

The cave narrowed slightly, curving left. As briefed, Breezy's left-hand team stopped in place, allowing Malten's to search the curve. With his short-barreled Benelli at eye level, Malten began slicing the pie, advancing a step at a time, shoulder to shoulder with his partner.

Malten stopped abruptly. Breezy thought: *He sees something.* Malten's left hand went to his chest, mimicking a child's gun with thumb and forefinger. *Danger, close.* Then, with his left hand on the shotgun's foregrip, he took the next step.

Four shooters swung around the rough-hewn corner, confronting an astonished Pakistani with an ancient Enfield slung over his shoulder. The man's eyes went saucer-wide, his mouth forming a pink oval in his thick beard. Breezy's partner took six steps forward, lifted his left index finger to his mouth, then motioned the man forward. As the bewildered gunman complied, he was relieved of his weapon and escorted to the rear. There he was gagged, frisked, and hands bound with tie wraps. The last operator in line shoved him toward the entrance and turned him over to Foyte's Blue Team. The gunny then sent two men inside to handle any additional prisoners.

The smell of a cook fire grew stronger but there was little smoke. Breezy surmised that the cave had some sort of natural ventilation. He continued his methodical advance until the cavern widened. Then, from the darker approach, he saw a well-lit area with several men talking, cooking, and eating. He did a quick head count and raised his left hand: five fingers followed by one.

The cooking area was roughly twelve meters by twenty with bags and boxes stacked along one wall. Most of the men appeared armed. Breezy made a fist, raised it to ear level, then made a gesture like pulling a chain.

Six operators stepped into the open area, those on either side checking for laterals off the main corridor.

Breezy and Malten had been briefed on the Urdu phrase for "hands up." Neither could recall "*laasuna portakra.*" Wondering at the silence, two other operators shouted the phrase in English. Then Delmore spoke the surrender demand: "*Taslim sha!*"

The Pakistanis looked up in stunned amazement. A few immediately raised their hands; one sank to his knees and began wailing.

Two went for their guns. Phil Green shouted "*Wodariga!*" Stop!

Breezy and Delmore put their front sights on the nearest man, who raised his AK on its sling. They pressed their triggers simultaneously. Breezy had selected three-round burst; Delmore went full auto. Between them, the suppressed HKs spat out eight 9mm rounds. Six struck flesh, punching small red gouts in the man's khaki vest. He dropped the AK, half spun on one foot, reeled awkwardly, and collapsed. He rolled a few feet, then stopped, holding his belly.

Other Pakistanis began shouting or sobbing. Most went to their knees.

Malten instantly placed his Benelli's bead sight on the other shooter's midsection. The ex-SEAL fired twice, and at twelve meters thirteen of the eighteen double-ought pellets carved a ten-inch circle in the target. The man went down hard, twitching and screaming. The screams turned to loud, thick gurgles, then ceased.

Most of the other hostiles now were face down, hands over their heads. Green, the former cop, thought, *They know the drill. They've done this before.*

As the SSI men secured the prisoners, Breezy made a preliminary call to Leopole. "Control, this is White. Over."

Only static responded. Breezy said, "We're too far in." He directed

one of Foyte's men to return to the entrance and radio a status report, adding, "And tell Frank we're still searching."

Fifteen minutes later most of the operators were back at the entrance with their prisoners. Breezy met Leopole, who wanted to see
the results up close.

"What've we got, Brezyinski?"

"Five tagged, two bagged, Skipper." Breezy knew that Frank
Leopole disliked being called "Skipper."

"Any sign of bio gear?"

Breezy shook his head. "Negative. I was talking with Jeff and Ken.
They don't think these gooners are al Qaeda. I think I agree."

Leopole frowned. "Explain."

"Look at their gear, their whole setup. No heavy metal—no RPGs
or belt-fed stuff. Some of 'em only have bolt-action rifles. They had
piss-poor security, and for Islamic fanatics they gave up pretty damn
quick."

"So what do you think they're up to?"

"Well, Skip, there's evidently some drugs and other contraband
but nothing like we want."

"Are you saying they're just smugglers?"

"Looks like, Boss."

Breezy turned away, intending to start an inventory, when he
bumped into Malten. "Hey, Jeff, how ya doin'?"

Malten patted his Benelli. "I was just thinking. Four years in the
teams and I never popped a cap. Now I come ten thousand miles to
whack one sorry gooner just so I can say I scored." He shook his head.
"Hell of a cover charge to get into this club!"

As the prisoners were led away by some of Major Khan's men,
Omar Mohammed consulted his notes. "It's as Brezyinski suspected,
Colonel. They are smugglers, though one of them has been wanted
by local authorities for some months. He was a suspect in a couple of
murders."

Leopole nodded. "So that's why he went for his weapon."

"Surely. At that point he had nothing to lose."

The ops officer tipped back his hat. "All right, then. We need to
talk to Khan and maybe Buster Hardesty. Obviously these guys have

nothing to do with bioterrorism. Looks like we were snookered . . . I mean . . ."

"I know what snookered is, Colonel." Mohammed managed to excise most of the derision from his voice. "But it could be merely the result of poor intelligence."

"Well, either way, we need to know. And damn fast."

QUETTA

To SSI's operators—and all others in the world—everything was a
contest. Except perhaps running. Daily jogging inevitably turned
into a race for second place because nobody could keep up with J. J.
Johnson. The ex-legionnaire had spent five years running everywhere: to and from meals; uphill and downhill; through sand;
through water; on the obstacle course. The only time *La Légion* did
not run was when it marched to the slow, patient cadence of *Le
Boudin*.

It was a point of pride with Jeffrey Malten that he usually finished second to Johnson. But today Breezy was in fine form. He beat
the ex-SEAL to the last corner by eight strides, then slowed. When
Breezy overtook him again, he noticed that Malten was barely loping,
turning his head left and right.

"What's wrong, dude? Lose somethin'?"

Breezy stopped, leaning forward with hands on his hips. He

inhaled and exhaled twice, then straightened. "It's weird, man. Where's J. J.?"

BALUCHISTAN PROVINCE

"We have one of the Crusaders."

Ali sat bolt upright on his cot. It took him a few pulses to absorb the implications of Kassim's announcement.

The Syrian stepped farther into the room, almost apologetic for the unprecedented intrusion. Few people had ever seen the interior of The Blessed Doctor's lodging. It was much like its owner: spare, clean, functional. The only adornment was an Islamic tapestry on one wall beside a bookcase.

Ali swung his feet onto the floor and picked his robe off the hook. "Tell me."

"One of my agents noticed that many of the Crusaders run for exercise around the perimeter every day. I told him to track their activities in his intelligence reports. One in particular seemed stronger than the others and usually finished one hundred meters or more ahead of them. For a brief time he was often out of sight of the others." Kassim shrugged eloquently. "It was simple."

"Where is he?"

Kassim's face showed a rare expression. It was a wolf's smile. "He is on the way here."

Jeremy Johnson, late of the French Foreign Legion, blinked at the sudden light. He had been bound and gagged for three hours, bouncing painfully in the Toyota's trunk. When the sedan lurched to a stop, the trunk was opened and the blanket pulled off him. Three men lifted him out and unbound his bare feet. The manacles and tape over his mouth remained.

Kassim met the group, displaying obvious pleasure. One of the kidnappers handed him the American's identification, which Kassim took inside the building. He knew that Ali would want to acquaint himself with the captive's particulars before the interrogation began.

Minutes later Kassim beckoned to the escorts who shoved their prize through the door. Johnson saw the grinning bastard who had taken his dog tags plus one other man. *That's the boss*, Johnson told himself. This one was somewhat older than the others; cleaner, more composed. He beckoned to a chair. *More polite. More dangerous.*

Johnson sat down, pointedly leaning forward to accommodate his hands behind his back. Ali took the hint and gestured to one of the acolytes. The man handed his Makarov pistol to a partner and released the manacles. "Thanks," Johnson said, rubbing his wrists.

Ali set a bottled water on the desk and Johnson drained almost half. He realized that he was getting dehydrated after hours in the trunk.

"Now then," Ali began. "Mr . . . Johnson." He gave the American a smile intended to cause more fear than confidence. "I will do you the honor of being direct. If you tell me what I wish to know, I will release you tomorrow. You may tell your friends whatever you wish—perhaps that you were the victim of a ransom attempt. It does not matter."

Johnson nodded, keeping a straight face. *Lying bastard. You're going to snuff me.* He had already judged the situation and decided to cooperate in hope of living long enough to escape. But that would be difficult without his shoes.

"Why are you here?" Ali asked.

From experience in *La Légion* and extensive reading, Jeremy Johnson knew that good interrogators seldom began by asking for information they did not already possess. "I'm hired by a security firm. But I think you know that, Mr . . ."

Ali waved a dismissive hand. "My name is unimportant. But yes, Mr. Johnson, I know that you belong to Strategic Solutions." He paused long enough to gauge the captive's reaction. Seeing none, he proceeded. "I know that you are a bought dog. You sell yourself to the highest bidder like a common harlot."

Johnson shrugged. "Girl's gotta make a living."

Ali barked a harsh phrase. The guard behind the chair responded instantly, bringing a frayed fan belt down in an overhand strike. It split the skin of the American's neck, searing exquisite pain through his upper torso. Johnson's composure melted in the hot rush of shock, blood, and rage. He cried out despite himself, sagging in the chair.

"One," Ali said, holding up a finger. "From this moment, every time I dislike your response, you shall receive an additional stroke."

Johnson pressed his left hand against the right side of his neck, felt the blood, and realized that he had few reserves. He knew that he could not tolerate many blows.

Ali read the signs. "Now, Mr. Johnson. I see in your face that you wish to kill me. You are free to try. But you will be shot in both legs and beaten more severely. In that case, before we allow you to die, you *will* tell us all we need." He leaned back, pointedly casual. "Or . . . you may walk out of here in your own shoes in a few days." Ali thought: *Always give them some hope.*

The legionnaire's glare contained equal portions of hate and resignation. Ali recognized the signs and knew he was winning.

"To repeat, Johnson: what is your mission here?" Ali waited for a slow five count. Then he held up two fingers.

The blows came in rapid, vicious succession: a stroke from the right, a quick reversal, and one from the left. Johnson screamed in pain and fury, leaping to his feet and turned to face his tormenter.

Something hard smashed into his right knee. He went down, groveling on the board floor, holding his patella. The other guard recovered to a ready stance, pointedly tapping the police baton against the palm of one hand.

Ali stood up, leaning on the desk. "Mr. Johnson? I am waiting. If you ever want to walk again . . ."

J. J. Johnson tried hard to choke off the sob rising from his core. He tasted a salty warmth and realized that he had bitten into his lip. He thought: *Maybe I can stand three, even four. Not five. Not ten. They have all day.*

"Bugs."

"What?" Ali gestured and his men set Johnson in the chair again. "What's that?"

"Germs." Johnson inhaled deeply, trying to keep his wits in the game.

"Go on, Johnson."

"Water." It came as a croak as he crawled onto the chair.

Ali shoved the bottle across the desk again. Johnson took his time sipping the water, then rubbed some on his stinging neck. *Gotta have time to think.*

"One . . . two . . ."

No time, man. No time. "Germ warfare," Johnson blurted. The Korean War phrase leapt to his mind from a long-ago book called *Honest John*. It was written by an Air Force pilot, a kickass fighter ace who was tortured into saying he dropped bugs on gooks.

Ali sat down again. "What kind of germs, Johnson? Do not test me!"

Johnson looked up, his vision blurring from the tears of pain. "I don't know! Okay? I don't know about the germs!" *Nice touch*, he congratulated himself. *Not too specific.* He shuddered visibly. *Not yet.*

Ali allowed himself to slouch in his chair. He wanted to appear calm, in control. He thought for a moment. He had to admire the American's fortitude. Many men would have spilled all they knew by now. He had seen it before. Then he played his trump. "Tell me about Doctor Carolyn Padgett-Smith."

Johnson's eyes betrayed him. They widened in astonished recognition. Then he recovered. "Who?"

Ali turned his head, showing the wolfish smile again. Slowly, almost elegantly, he raised a hand. Five fingers.

Then he raised the other hand.

Johnson was on the floor after the fourth blow. He felt his back flayed open, then more strikes whipped across his buttocks and upper legs. He rolled in hopeless desperation, shrieking in pain. The two tormenters boxed him in, taking turns and leaning into their work, imparting every ounce of energy to each lash.

When he was able to stop sobbing, Johnson stretched out a hand. "Water."

Ali was on his feet, taking long strides toward the wretch on the floor. Grasping Johnson's hair in one hand, he flicked open a knife and held it against the victim's cheek. "You get water when I have my answer. Or I take your eyes one at a time."

Jeremy Johnson levitated. He was seeing himself from above, as if hanging from the rafters. His alter ego called to him. *J. J., he means it, man. He'll do you.*

He heard himself say, "She's a British doctor."

Ali shook Johnson's head, pulling some hair out. "I know that! Why is she here?"

Johnson told him.

Ali was washing his feet in preparation for evening prayers when Kassim reappeared. The doctor beckoned him in.

"He is secure, Doctor. He cannot escape, and I doubt that he could walk far."

Ali looked up from the basin at his feet. "Has he eaten?"

Kassim was taken aback. The alien was a shredded figure of bloody tatters who limped along on one leg. What did it matter if he had eaten? "He has been fed. I do not know if he partakes."

"What did you give him?"

Kassim shook his head ever so slightly. "Rice with some mutton. And a cup of tea, as you ordered. Why do you ask?"

"Merely because he is our prisoner does not mean he should be starved. The Prophet requires it."

"With respect . . . the man has been sliced to ribbons. He lies in the dirt trying not to cry out. I doubt if he has much appetite."

"He will eat if he desires." Ali turned back to his ablution.

Kassim nodded, then turned to go. The doctor's voice brought him up short. "I must leave with my men. Meanwhile, remember this: no one is to approach the infidel alone. There must always be at least two guards, both armed."

The Syrian furrowed his bushy eyebrows. "Truly? You believe he is such a threat in his condition?"

"He is an elite soldier. Regardless of his cause or greed, we must not underestimate him. If he escapes, he will tell the others of this place. That in turn could lead—elsewhere."

Kassim did not share his colleague's respect for the whipped dog in the pen, but the doctor's judgment was seldom wrong. "I shall tell the others." He shifted his weight to his good leg. "Will you question him tomorrow?"

"I do not believe he has much more to tell us. But I shall tend his wounds tonight. I have some veterinary cephalhexin to prevent infection."

"Then . . . what shall we do with him?"

Ali raised his hands from the basin, palms up. "God will decide."

QUETTA AIRBASE

"Well, he's just not here. That's all we know."

Leopole slumped against the table in the briefing room, tacitly conceding the obvious to a roomful of operators. Omar Mohammed remained seated but appeared no less subdued.

Leopole continued, "We've tried every source we know: police, military, embassy. Even some back-channel contacts." He decided not to mention that an attractive sum had been offered in certain quarters for any information leading to the missing American, no questions asked. "We have to notify headquarters. Maybe they can try something in Washington."

Malten spoke the question on everyone's mind. "Colonel, do you think that al Qaeda got him?"

"I don't know how else to explain it," Leopole replied. "You and Brezyinski were closest to him, weren't you?"

"Yes, sir. Like I said, he disappeared around the corner and when I got there maybe twenty seconds later, he was gone."

Mohammed had a theory. "This was almost certainly a kidnapping. We suspected that the opposition had observers on the base, and they saw a pattern and took advantage of it." He stopped long enough to visualize the scene. "It wouldn't have been very hard: drive alongside him, point a gun at his head and tell him to get in."

Breezy would not admit it, but he began feeling pangs of regret for the way he had ribbed the former legionnaire so often. "So what do we do, now? Looks like all we can do is wait."

Leopole eased off the table and stood with his arms akimbo. He realized that he needed to demonstrate some leadership, even if he lacked confidence in the case of Jeremy Johnson. "We keep planning and training, gentlemen. Same schedule: training starts again at 0700."

BALUCHISTAN PROVINCE

J. J. Johnson tried to reason it out.

The Muslims had fed him and even tended the appalling wounds on his back and legs. That fact seemed to indicate a willingness to keep him alive, if only briefly. But the vicious, smooth-talking bastard who fancied himself a doctor was obviously a religious fanatic. Johnson had no doubt that the man's threat with the knife was genuine. Maybe he was taking a dual role: good cop, bad cop all in one. Maybe he was just playing mind games.

Johnson had no intention of waiting to find out. He realized that, having given the sophisticated sadist the desired information, there was little reason to keep an American alive. The mercenary tallied his likely fate. Plan A: his captors would keep him indefinitely. Plan B: they would sell him back to his employer, or, Plan C: they would kill him.

Briefly he wondered about Plan B. *How much is an ex-legionnaire worth on the open market?* Admiral Derringer would meet any fee, but the odds of completing the deal looked slim.

He pondered Plan C: would they take time to cut off his head or merely put a 7.62 round through his cranium? Since neither Alfa, Bravo, nor Charlie were acceptable options, he went to work on Plan Delta.

———————

Abdullah Hussain was restless. Like many of Kassim's operatives, he was young and headstrong, feeling a need to prove himself among the veteran *mujahadin*. Too many of them treated the youngsters with something between tolerance and disdain. Abdullah had discussed that unfortunate tendency with his youthful compatriots more than once.

Here was an opportunity.

When Sheikh Tahirkheli went to relieve himself, the twenty-year-old guard decided to show his mettle. Pointedly ignoring the older man's warning to delay feeding the prisoner, Hussain unslung his AK and opened the wire gate to the pen. He shoved the rice gruel ahead of him with a sandaled foot, keeping his distance from the reclining infidel. The man had barely moved all morning, leaving most of his breakfast untouched.

Hussain noticed the whip marks on the American's back, the shredded remains of the shirt. As he rested on his side, the man's slow, regular breathing showed that he remained asleep.

Despite nearly fourteen months with Kassim's cell, the youngster had never seen an infidel so close before. This was too good a chance to pass up: a minor test of manhood, facing an enemy eye to eye. He poked the Kalashnikov's muzzle into the prisoner's back, ordering him to rise. The only response was a half roll onto the stomach.

Abdullah Hussain wanted more. He kicked at the prone form, again ordering the captive up.

J. J. Johnson shot a glance between the guard's feet. As he expected, the young one was alone. *Stupid kids,* he thought. *They all think they're smarter than adults.*

Now or never.

In the upward glance he permitted himself, Johnson took in two salient facts. The kid's finger was on the trigger but the selector remained in the upward position. *Still on safe.*

Johnson had mentally rehearsed the disarming technique dozens of times during the night. In a fluid movement he used both hands and one foot to knock the guard down. Hussain hit the ground with a muted *thud* that briefly winded him. In that moment, Johnson was atop him, grabbing the AK and twisting it in a figure eight. The American's position gave him superior leverage; the guard's grip broke and the rifle was freed.

Johnson reversed the weapon, butt down, and stepped on the guard's right arm. Three solid blows to the head rendered him immobile. Two hard vertical strokes, more carefully delivered, fractured the skull.

The SSI man knew time was crucial. He flipped the AK's selector to full down—semi-auto—and pulled the bolt handle back. A live round was ejected. *So it was loaded after all.* He scanned the area, saw nobody else, and quickly removed the magazine. He guessed that it held about twenty-five rounds.

The legionnaire was breathing hard from the exertion. Forcing himself to concentrate, he pulled off the corpse's sandals and scooped up both the meals in their tins. He combined them into one container, losing some gruel over the side. With one more glance around, he noticed a cheap ornamental dagger on the guard's belt. Johnson took it and made for the rocks behind the hut.

Water. He paused, weighing the prospects of finding a bottle inside against the other guard's likely return. He also realized that he needed a sack to carry his plunder. *Well, here goes.*

The hut's contents were disappointing: two nearly empty water bottles and a burlap sack containing some grain. Johnson deposited his goods in the sack, unconcerned about spillage. Then he took a worn quilt off a cot, threw it over one shoulder, and checked outside through the cracks in the door. Seeing no one, he stepped out, the rifle shouldered, muzzle low.

Sheikh Tahirkheli came around the corner, fifteen feet away.

Both men stopped dead, requiring a heartbeat to absorb the situation.

Johnson held the initiative; he was ready to shoot, whereas the

Muslim held his rifle at waist level. But a gunshot could be heard for a mile or more, and the man was too far away to take him with the knife.

Johnson's mind raced, trying to retrieve the Urdu word. It came reluctantly, sulking amid the pain and fear inside him. *"Taslim sha!"* *Surrender!*

Tahirkheli was an experienced fighter. He dropped his rifle and raised his hands, instantly changing the dynamics of the situation. Johnson nodded slightly in acknowledgment of his opponent's intelligence. *Smart dude: he knows if I'm gonna kill him he's a goner no matter what he does. This way, he's still got a chance.*

Johnson stepped aside to let the Pakistani pass. Then, picking up the man's rifle, the American pointed his prisoner uphill into the rocks where they could not be tracked.

As they began the ascent, the former legionnaire began musing whether he had it in him to commit murder.

BALUCHISTAN PROVINCE

Forty minutes from the farm, Johnson called a halt. He motioned for the Muslim to squat, then opened the burlap sack. The American drained the contents of one water bottle and part of the next. Then he offered the remainder to his prisoner.

Tahirkheli paused, then accepted the bottle. He raised it to the American, muttered, *"Shukria,"* and drained the water. He handed the bottle back, then reclined against a rock. Johnson maintained several feet between them, his AK pointed at the Pakistani's belly, clearly indicating that the safety was off.

Since the escape, Johnson had tried to approximate his location. He had a general impression that safety lay to the east, but even in the hills behind the farm, he saw mainly more hills and rocks.

He picked up three stones and arranged them at his feet. From right to left, he pointed to them in turn. "Quetta, Chaman, Kandahar."

Tahirkheli leaned forward, studying the arrangement. Slowly he raised his left hand and rearranged the stones in a northwest-southeast axis. He nodded. "Quetta, Chaman, Kandahar."

Johnson made a circular motion, then pointed to the Muslim and himself. "Us? Where?" He suspected he was near Chaman but did not want to venture that option.

Tahirkheli cocked his head and rubbed his bearded chin. He picked up a pebble and placed it beside the middle stone. *"Yahaan."*

Johnson assumed that the man meant *here* but was uncertain whether to believe him. Offering water and remaining unthreatening seemed more in keeping with the Muslim virtue of hospitality. Johnson remembered Omar Mohammed's briefing: often in tribal cultures one was obliged to return a good deed. He realized that he was fortunate that the inquisitor had taken his two goons with him: the erstwhile ex-legionnaire would cheerfully have executed any or all of them.

Looking at the sky, Johnson assessed that it might rain later in the day. *Not a bad thing: cover my tracks in the dirt and maybe get some fresh water.* He had already decided to forego standing water except for emergencies.

Time for a command decision. Johnson realized that he could go directly to Chaman and probably find help, but he discounted that option. There were almost certainly people looking for him there, and in any case a beat-up westerner would draw attention. He thought again of the map he had studied on the previous operation: a road paralleled the border northeast of town while a rail line ran back toward Quetta. Spin Buldak was just across the border from Chaman: there would be a crossing station in between. *Hell with it. If I can't walk right up to the border, I'll get myself captured trying to sneak across.*

Johnson stretched himself upright, feeling the stinging pain in his back. He wanted to rub his knee but did not, lest his captive see an infirmity. As a military athlete, Jeremy Johnson knew his limits, and the vicious beating had taken its toll. *I need a short walk downhill,* he told himself. He handed the sack and quilt to his captive, allowing him to carry the load. Then they pushed on, heading west.

BALUCHISTAN PROVINCE

Kassim had never seen Ali genuinely angry. Ordinarily reserved and composed, the doctor seemed to accept bad news as equitably as good.

This was different.

"The fools! The damnable, stupid imbeciles!" He kicked the leg of a chair and nearly tipped the seat backwards. Glaring at his colleague, he caught the Syrian's defensive stance, the lowered eyes. Ali inhaled, exhaled, and regained most of his composure. "Tell me. Everything."

"I must accept full responsibility, Doctor. I chose the men . . ."

"Enough of that!" The words were spit out like high-velocity rounds, more harsh than intended. "Brother, we need to know if we can recapture him."

Kassim sat down, still angry with himself and saddened that his men had disappointed the cause. "I do not know the full story. When

I returned there, I found Hussain beaten to death. There was no sign of Tahirkheli. At first I thought perhaps he fled, but he is a proven fighter. I have seen him destroy two Soviet armored vehicles and several Northern Alliance trucks. He would not run away." He shrugged. "Perhaps the infidel took him with him for some reason."

"Were there any tracks? Any indication of where the American went?"

Kassim shook his head. "None. I checked the entire area so he must have gone uphill in the rocks. It is impossible to track him that way."

"So we must assume he has food and weapons."

"Yes, Doctor. He took the boy's sandals and rifle. As you warned, he was a dangerous man."

Ali drummed his long fingers on the table. "I doubt that he knows where he was, but with elevation he can see the surrounding area. He will likely head east, toward the plain."

"Possibly."

The veterinarian lanced his colleague with a glare. "Why 'possibly'?"

"The geography, Doctor. The nearest town of any size from the farm is Qila Abdullah, about thirty kilometers. The border is much closer, with Spin Buldak on the road to Kandahar. In any case he will avoid the roads. But we do not have nearly enough men to search the hills in either direction. As for the rivers, if he follows the Zhob or the Nari, which bank? Upstream or downstream?"

Ali asked, "But to the west the border is guarded. So what do you suggest?"

Kassim looked closer at the map, visualizing the topography. "Use our men as efficiently as possible. Have them watch the approaches here . . . and here." His blunt finger stabbed the places printed Qila Abdullah and Spin Buldak.

The doctor regarded his partner admiringly. "Yes! Rather than searching hundreds of square kilometers, wait for the rat to arrive at the bait."

Kassim's fist struck the table with a resounding *thud*. "Then spring the trap."

"See to it, brother. He has a wide start."

SSI OFFICES

Sandy Carmichael was going to knock on Derringer's door when she heard his voice inside. "Okay, thanks, Frank. Keep me informed."

She rapped politely before opening the door. "Excuse me, sir, but . . ."

He motioned to her. "It's alright, Sandy. Come on in. That was Frank. He figured I'd be in this morning so he phoned rather than sending an email." Derringer drummed his fingers on the desk. *Paradiddle-paradiddle tap-tap-tap.* He stared at the polished wood for a moment, then looked up. "One of our guys is missing. It looks like he's been kidnapped."

Carmichael slid into the chair nearest the desk. "Oh my god. Who?"

"Johnson. Jeremy Johnson. They call him J. J. I know him somewhat—good kid. He did a stretch in the Foreign Legion."

"Well, what happened?"

"Johnson's team was jogging around the perimeter to keep in shape. J. J.'s quite a runner, apparently. He got ahead of the others, turned a corner, and disappeared. Nobody saw anything."

"When did this happen?"

"Yesterday. Frank didn't want to worry us unnecessarily, but when nothing turned up overnight, he decided to call. He's done all the right things: checked with the locals, police, and the embassy. He's even dropped some hints offering a big reward, but nobody seems to have any leads."

The professional in Sandra Carmichael nudged aside the caring female half of her personality. "Well, sir, I have a couple of recommendations. First, we should decide how much longer to wait before notifying Johnson's family. That is, I assume he has some family. Then we need to prepare a response in case he turns up on Al Jazeera or some other media outlet."

Derringer slumped in his padded chair, one hand on his forehead. "Both accepted, Sandy. I'll call a meeting so we can hash out other options. But . . ."

"Yes, sir?"

He inhaled, then blew his breath out in a long, audible whisper. "I'm visualizing an on-screen decapitation, or something just as bad."

Carmichael had seen two such videos; she could not envision anything comparable. The first had taken thirty-five seconds, and she wondered at what point in the process the victim had died. She had not bothered to time the second one. Finally she asked, "Is there anything we can do here, maybe with the Pakistani embassy? I mean, anything that Frank and Omar can't do in-country?"

"I doubt it, but we need to consider all angles. I'll call Mark at Moritz and Moritz to see if they have any legal suggestions."

"Yes, sir." Carmichael stood up and turned to go. Then she caught the look in the admiral's eyes—something she had seldom seen before. *He's scared. Really scared.* She knew why: Michael Derringer always assigned himself the dreadful task of delivering terrible news in person.

BALUCHISTAN PROVINCE

The sun was setting and Jeremy Johnson had to make a decision.

Overlooking the approach to the border crossing, the fugitive American with his erstwhile captor figured the percentages. *If I go straight down there, I'll save time. But I gotta assume the terrs know I'm missing, and they can read the map. They could be waiting.*

He turned toward his prisoner. The man was impassive, as usual. They now knew one another as "Yonson" and "Kelly." Without seeing it written, Johnson could never get his tongue around "Tahirkheli." Again the question arose: how much to trust the Pakistani. *He probably can't go back to his people, but I don't know that for sure. He might give me away if things get tense.*

Looking at the topography again, Johnson sorted the odds. He would be harder to spot after dark, but he would also be more vulnerable to ambush. A close-range firefight against multiple enemies was a nonstarter. And he doubted that he could expect help from the Paki border guards. To them, a shootout would likely be interpreted as an outright attack. Anyone beyond the perimeter fence would be considered hostile.

And the guards might be on somebody's payroll.

So many questions; damn few answers.

He decided to try having it both ways. He would work within a klick or so of the border and proceed to the checkpoint with about half an hour of daylight remaining. That way, presumably he could spot any interlopers and, if necessary, evade into the gathering dark. A few rounds toward the guard station should elicit further interest.

It looked like six or seven hundred meters, maybe a bit more. *Hard to tell in this terrain.* Johnson turned to "Kelly" and made a shooing motion. "Go. You go away!" Whatever the man's previous faults, he had been more a companion than a captive. He deserved a chance. Tahirkheli nodded, apparently in comprehension of the generous sentiment, but pantomimed his intention to stay with Johnson.

They set out at an easy lope, approaching the border crossing from the southwest. That seemed the least likely avenue of approach from the starting point east of Chaman.

Johnson kept the AK at high port, holding the magazine from Tahirkheli's rifle with his left hand. They had left the sack and quilt at their starting point in case they had to move fast. At 4,300 feet the evening air had an edge; both men saw their breath as they exhaled.

A few moments along the way, Tahirkheli pulled up. Johnson almost overran him. The Pakistani squatted, shading his eyes against the sunset. To his left the American took a braced kneeling position, the AK's selector on semi-auto. The Pakistani said something that sounded like "dish man," looking at Johnson and gesturing to their right front.

Johnson did not know that *dushman* was Urdu for *enemy*.

"*Bhagna!*" Tahirkheli bolted from his squatting position like a sprinter. His exhortation to run required no translation. He began eating up the ground toward the checkpoint.

Semi-automatic fire erupted from the gathering dusk. Johnson glimpsed muzzle flashes, guessed the range at 250 meters, and held slightly high. *Damn! Shoulda taken the chance to check zero on this thing.* He fired two rounds to let the terrs know that he was armed, then took to his feet. But Johnson was slowed by his injuries and ill-fitting sandals.

The Pakistani showed surprising speed, quickly pulling away from the mercenary. *He's one tough sumbitch; spent his life in the mountains.*

Abruptly the other man stopped, throwing himself prone. Johnson looked ahead and saw the reason. Two men raced toward them from a cluster of rocks. Johnson took a glance toward the border crossing. No visible motion yet.

Johnson looked again to his right. Two more gunmen had emerged from cover. *They gotta get me before the guards arrive.*

Both hostile pair were about 150 meters out. Johnson felt relatively safe at that distance: *Most of 'em can't shoot for shit.* He squirmed into a prone position, facing the right-hand threat first. With no idea where his rifle shot, he took a center hold on the nearest opponent, focused on the front sight, and pressed the trigger.

The 7.62mm round snapped out—and vanished. Johnson could not tell where it went, other than it had missed its target. Briefly he wished that he could get Kelly to spot for him, but there was no time to pantomime it.

Both the gunmen approaching him were upright, alternately firing and running. Ballistic cracks popped over his head; a few rounds hit the earth around him. Johnson's mind was racing: *There's still time. Try something else.* Reckoning that his first round likely went high, he held on the target's knees. He pressed the trigger and the Kalashnikov bucked in recoil. Johnson's focus went from his sights to the target and saw the man flinch. *Nicked him or it's real close.* Applying Kentucky windage, he held low on the target's right side and fired twice.

The terrorist staggered, turned away, and tumbled sideways.

Immediately Johnson shifted targets. The second opponent was inside seventy meters, now kneeling. Johnson applied the same sight picture and pressed the trigger twice. No good. The man kept shooting.

He's not as tall a target. Hold lower. Johnson put his front sight on the man's left foot and fired again. Nothing. *I think I flinched. Try again.* Two more rounds went downrange. One connected. The target rolled onto his side and began crawling away. Johnson let him go.

More firing erupted from the second pair, now dangerously close. Johnson estimated they were no more than fifty meters out. As he swung on them, he felt a sharp impact. *I'm hit—keep shooting.* He put his front sight on the right-hand man and fired. No good. He fired again. And again. Sweat blurred his vision and the gathering dusk degraded his sight picture.

The rifle jammed.

Johnson's pulse, already elevated, hit high C. He recognized the physiological signs: tunnel vision; short, shallow breaths; leaden feeling in the arms; fine muscle skills diminished. He glanced down at the AK and was appalled to see a neat hole in the magazine. *That was the hit!* The wonderfully reliable weapon had continued functioning until the warped follower and deformed cartridge had reached the chamber.

Immediate action drill. Johnson released the magazine, pulled the charging handle twice, and scooped up the reload. Belatedly he remembered to roll the rifle on its right side and repeated the drill again. Small metal particles were ejected downward.

Johnson's trembling hands reseated the new magazine and he chambered the first round. Firing now was heavy and close. Rock fragments and clods of earth spattered his face. Rolling away from the impacts, Johnson was vaguely aware that he had wet his trousers.

"Kelly" leapt to his feet and began shouting frantically at the assailants. One paused, uncertain of the Urdu speaker's intent. The other continued firing from twenty yards. Johnson put his sights squarely in the shooter's middle and pulled the trigger two, three, four times.

Kelly screamed and went down. More gunfire split the dark.

––––––––

Johnson shifted his aim to the remaining threat. The man was getting close—terror close. Firing from an under-arm assault position, the gunman hosed a long, scything burst at the prone American. Johnson felt the sonic pain as 7.62 rounds barked past his head. He wanted full auto—now—but there was no time. He raised his muzzle toward the assailant's middle and began mashing the trigger. He kept firing until the man dropped. The conventional wisdom came to him: *Shoot until the threat goes away.* He fired some more.

When he came up for air, Johnson looked at Kelly, who was trembling visibly. *He's in shock. Gotta get help.* The legionnaire rose to his knees and scanned the darkening landscape. He saw three men jogging toward him, perhaps seventy meters out. They were armed, rifles at high port.

Johnson went prone again, wondering how many rounds he had left, and asking the most important question of his life: *Are they friendly or hostile?*

22

"Say again?" Leopole held the phone tighter, hardly daring to believe what he heard. After a pause he exclaimed, "My god!"

Mohammed caught the excitement in the team leader's voice as Leopole hung up with a fervent "Thank you, sir. Thank you *very* much." His eyes were wide, fixed on his associate. "Johnson's alive!"

Mohammed shook his head as if clearing a fog from his brain. "Jeremy Johnson? He's been missing for three days!"

Leopole was on his feet, grinning hugely. "Damn straight it's J. J.! Who else?" He clapped the reserved Muslim on one shoulder.

"Tell me!"

Leopole began pacing, uncharacteristically excited. "Buster Hardesty didn't have the full story, but we can send one of our helos for him. J. J. should arrive later today."

"Frank, tell me!"

"Oh, sorry, Omar." After so many losses, Leopole felt part of the emotional burden drain away. "C'mon, let's tell the others."

Minutes later, Leopole convened an impromptu meeting in the hangar. About half of the operators were present.

Breezy leaned toward Bosco. "Frank's smiling like the fucking cat that ate the fucking canary. What's up?"

Bosco hunched his shoulders. "DamnifIknow, dude."

Leopole stood at the front of the room. "Listen up, people!" The chatter and speculation instantly died away. "I just had some good news from General Hardesty in Islamabad." He paused for effect, then grinned again. "J. J. Johnson is alive! Marsh is flying him here this afternoon."

The room erupted in shouts, cheers, and male barks. Bosco and Breezy exchanged multiple high fives. Padgett-Smith, standing alone at the back, raised both hands to her mouth. Her violet eyes misted over.

Questions snapped toward Leopole, who had to wave down the increasing din.

"Alright, alright! Settle down!" When silence returned, he began the tale. "General Hardesty spoke to Johnson via land line, so all I know is what he told me. Briefly, J. J. was held and tortured in a remote area near Chaman. Somehow—I don't know how yet—he killed a guard and escaped." At that word, the calm evaporated again. *Ooh-rah* shouts and feral sounds erupted from young male throats.

Leopole allowed himself a grin at the sentiment. "After that, Johnson made his way overland to the border, which was closer than the next Pakistan town. The terrorists were waiting for him near Spin Buldak and it turned into a running gun battle. But he made it to the border station and was able to call the embassy."

Jeffrey Malten stood up. "Colonel, what's J. J.'s condition?"

"Well, he's strong enough to climb hills and run some distance. Buster . . . General Hardesty . . . said he'd been badly whipped and will need a hospital. But J. J. wanted to come here before anything else. And we need to debrief him."

More questioners waved for attention but Leopole decided enough was enough. Besides, he intended to treat himself to some discretely stashed Tennessee sippin' whiskey.

QUETTA AIRBASE

"There he is!" Jeff Malten's exclamation stated the obvious to the SSI crowd.

Jeremy Johnson appeared in the door of the Hip as Eddie Marsh shut down the engines. Wearing a borrowed flight suit, Johnson accepted help from the crew chief and descended to the tarmac. Stooped over, he walked carefully beyond the rotor diameter to a raucous reception.

As the troops crowded around him, Johnson raised his hands. "Hi guys. Don't touch my back. It's a mess."

Taking his directions literally, some of the operators scooped up the returnee and carried him shoulder high to the hangar. The abrasions on his legs were rubbed painfully, but Jeremy Johnson, late of the Foreign Legion, did not care.

———

Once in the office, Malten and Padgett-Smith convinced Johnson to allow them to see his wounds. As he peeled off his flight suit and shirt, the giddy mood changed instantly. It seemed that the ambient temperature dropped fifteen degrees.

"Oh, Jeremy," CPS muttered.

"Ah, shit, man." Malten's tone matched hers.

Johnson winced, then said, "I sorta got used to it. The back of my legs and . . . butt . . . also got worked over."

The salve previously applied to the long, deep welts clung to the thin shirt. Malten exchanged glances with Padgett-Smith. "It's best not to use salves on lacerations," the medic said. "You can, like, use Neosporin but that's usually for developed infections."

Padgett-Smith offered, "Some soap and warm water is best to start. Maybe some Keflex for later, if it's available. It's a good antibiotic."

As Malten worked on him, Johnson turned his focus to Leopole and Mohammed.

"Colonel, you need to know. I told them everything. I mean, not everything I knew, but everything they asked." His voice turned to a croak. "I . . . I couldn't take any more."

"My god, J. J. Nobody could stand that. Not half of it."

Padgett-Smith sought to alleviate some of Johnson's grief. "Jeremy. You need hospital treatment. No wonder . . ."

He interrupted her. "The head guy put a knife to my eyes and said he'd blind me if I didn't talk. I believed him, Colonel. I . . ." He began to sob.

Padgett-Smith wanted to hug the young American. But she merely placed a hand on his good shoulder.

Mohammed touched Johnson's knee. "Jeremy, believe me. Nobody thinks ill of you. *Nobody*. We're just glad to have you back."

Johnson inhaled deeply, rubbing his watery eyes with one hand. "I know, sir. I know . . ."

Mohammed continued, "Do you feel like talking? We can debrief you later if you like."

A decisive shake of the head. "No, Doctor. I want to get it out. All of it. Go ahead."

"This head man, who was he?"

"I don't know. He wouldn't tell me his name. He asked questions, not answered them. But he spoke good English."

Leopole asked, "What did he look like?"

"Oh, mid to late forties. I think he was kind of tall, though he sat most of the time. Long, thin face with a full beard."

"We'll have some mug shots for you a bit later." He stopped, then asked in as sympathetic a voice as possible, "J. J., what did they want to know?"

"They already knew about SSI, and they thought we're involved in chemical or biological work. But . . ."

"Yes?"

Johnson turned his head toward CPS. "They wanted to know about Dr. Padgett-Smith."

She sucked in her breath. A hand went to her throat. "Oh my god. How did they know my name?"

"They didn't say, ma'am. But when I tried to stall, they whipped me even harder. Then the head guy grabbed my hair and said he'd cut my eyes out. So I told him what I knew."

Mohammed sat beside Johnson, sensing the younger man's self-imposed guilt. "Jeremy, this man. You said he spoke good English."

"Yeah. He's fluent."

"Did he speak with an accent?"

"Sure, he's Pakistani far as I know."

"No, I mean, did he have a foreign accent? Something other than Pakistani." Johnson stared at the floor, trying to conjure the tonal nuances. He raised his head. "He has sort of a British accent."

Leopole looked at Mohammed. "What do you think, Doctor?"

"Just a moment. I'll be right back."

As Mohammed left the room, Malten continued working on Johnson. "J. J., can you stand up? I'll see what I can do for your . . . lower back."

Padgett-Smith took the hint. "I'll see if I can help Omar."

She caught him returning from the room that served as administrative office. "Omar, do you think that . . ."

"Great minds, Doctor. We'll find out."

When Malten finished his medical chores, Mohammed laid a file binder on Leopole's desk. "Jeremy, this is from Major Khan. It includes photos of some known and suspected al Qaeda operatives and others of interest to us. Do you recognize any of them?"

Johnson flipped the pages, studying each face in turn. He paused at the eighth one. "This could be one of the bastards that whipped me. Kinda hard to say, though."

As Mohammed made a note of the suspect's name, Johnson continued looking, moving faster. Near the end of the file he came to an abrupt stop. He felt his pulse spike.

"I think that's him."

"The head guy?" Leopole asked.

Johnson looked again. "Yes, sir. He's older, and he's got more of a beard, but I'd bet that's him."

"How certain are you, J. J.?"

"Eighty-nine percent, sir."

Leopole chuckled. "Well, that beats house odds anywhere I've ever been." He turned to Mohammed. "Good work, Omar."

Johnson turned the file to read the caption. "Saeed Sharif, DVM."

BALUCHISTAN PROVINCE

Kassim brought a gift. In fact, two gifts in one package.

"Doctor, I would have a word."

Ali set down the veterinary kit he was assembling for his day trip. "Surely." He gestured to a chair.

Kassim did not bother to sit. "One of my men has approached me with an offer. His youngest son and a cousin both wish to join us. He says they are committed in the highest order."

Ali blinked. "What does that mean?"

"One of the boys is sickly. He does not seem likely to outlive his father. Because of his faith, he believes he should offer himself to the *jihad*."

"And the other?"

"They were raised together, much as brothers. The man—the uncle—says they wish to enter Paradise together."

Ali thought for a moment. It seemed too good to be true: two volunteers presenting themselves at an opportune moment. No other bio couriers were readily available, and that fact made the veterinarian suspicious.

"You know these boys?"

Kassim shrugged. "I have met them; I have broken bread with them. If you ask me what is in their hearts, I cannot say. But I know the father and uncle, and I believe him."

"Who is he?"

"Razak Sial. He fought against the Northern Alliance for perhaps two years, then returned to farming. He has two other sons to help him. The youngest is the weakest but the most devout. For that reason I thought you should meet him."

"The father approached you?"

Kassim nodded.

"How much does he know?"

"He only knows that I am a fighter against the infidels. Nothing more."

"How old are these boys?"

Kassim thought for a moment. "Eighteen and twenty, give or take a year."

Ali thought again, weighing the options. "My friend, I thank you for your attention in this matter. I will see the father and the boys, but not in context of the *jihad*. I shall approach them as the veterinarian and feel them out." He peered at the Syrian. "They must not know of our dealings. Not yet."

"Brother, I understand your caution. But you will find that the boys are as I have said. They are willing to die in God's service. They do not seem to care just how they enter Paradise."

SSI OFFICES

"Mike, J. J. Johnson's back in Quetta. He's pretty beat up but okay."

The expression on Joe Wolf's face magnified the heartfelt gratitude evident in his voice. He raised the email printout that followed Mohammed's preliminary phone call. "Frank and Omar are debriefing him right away. Apparently he wants to tell his story before he goes to the hospital."

Derringer shook his head. "If he's okay why's he need a hospital? Observation or something?"

Wolf referred to the printout. "Omar says they used a fan belt on him. Severe lacerations of the back, buttocks, and legs. There's concern about infection."

"Okay, Joe. Thanks." The SSI executive flexed his fingers, forcing himself to relax. He had been composing a letter to Johnson's parents, but in truth it would have been used as reference notes for the phone call. Now Derringer scribbled some additional comments in the margin. Wolf could see the relief on his face. When Derringer finally talked to Mr. and Mrs. Johnson, he could assure them that their son was safe and would return to Montana as soon as he could travel.

The admiral put down his pen and regarded Wolf. "Joe, I'd like to convene a meeting about this episode, maybe as soon as tomorrow. Depending on what we hear from Frank and Omar, I think we should draft a corporate policy for the future. We always anticipated losing people, but hostages and MIAs are another matter. What do you think?"

"I agree." The ex-FBI man gave a sardonic grin. "One thing that occurs to me is long-term hostages or, as you say, MIAs. How long can we keep missing operators on the payroll? I mean, of course we're going to look out for our people, but the board will want to have some input. Undoubtedly Marsh Wilmot and Regina Wells and Matt Finch will all have a say about policy and finances."

Derringer almost finched at Finch's name. Matthew Finch, guru of the administrative support division, had allies on the board that backed many of his personnel decisions. Derringer and Wolf exchanged knowing glances. *We should've dumped him when we had the chance.* Now he was firmly entrenched.

Wolf looked for the silver lining. "At least Regina sees things more or less from Frank's perspective. She almost seems to understand operations lately."

"Yeah. You remember how Frank bitched and moaned when the board insisted on assigning him a budgeteer? To tell you the truth, I think she'd approve almost anything he proposed but she has to recommend denying some requests to satisfy the bean counters. Frank won't say so, but I suspect he's making some big-time equipment proposals that he knows won't fly. Then it's easier to get what he really wants."

Wolf winked. "And they say marines aren't very smart."

Derringer raised his hands. "Not me. I never agreed with Sir Walter Scott."

"Scott? What's he got to do with it?"

"He wrote, 'Tell it to the marines. The sailors won't believe it.' "

QUETTA AIRBASE

Padgett-Smith checked on the patient the next morning. She found him bare-skinned on his stomach, sheet pulled up to a modest level. "You look much better," she said. "I brought some tea and rolls."

Johnson rolled onto one side. "That's British hospitality. Tea in bed." *Only thing better would be you in bed, Doc.*

"I understand you'll be transferred to hospital today."

Johnson sipped from the small cup merely to be polite. He had never cared for tea.

"Yes ma'am. That's what Colonel Leopole said." He reached

toward the plate but she picked up a scone and handed it to him.

"Jeremy, I probably won't have a chance to say a proper good-bye later. But I did so much want to see you . . . alone."

Johnson perked up. Then he mentally slapped himself. *Down, boy.* "I appreciate that. Carolyn."

"You've been through so much. But I remember that you said you might consider writing a memoir. I hope you do. Even if it's not published, it could be . . ."

"Therapeutic."

She glanced down. Then those violet eyes were on him again. "Yes. Quite right."

"Well, I haven't thought about it much. But I've learned a few things.

"Yes?"

He cleared his throat. "I meant to talk to Dr. Mohammed about this, because of the Muslim connection. But . . . I, ah . . ." He coughed, taking his time. "I took a prisoner with me when I escaped. One of the guards. I could've killed him no sweat, but he dropped his rifle and . . . well, there were other factors, but I just couldn't cap him, standing there with his hands up."

"He didn't try to escape?"

"No, ma'am. We sort of became, like, friends. It was weird. We couldn't really talk but we got to understand each other. I shared what water I had with him and he gave me directions. When we got within sight of the border, I said he could go. I tried to chase him away but he stayed with me."

"So he's with his own people?"

"No ma'am. He was shot protecting me in the firefight. When it was over, and the Pakis arrived, he was hurt bad. I went to him and he grabbed me and said something over and over. One of the guards spoke fair English and he translated." Johnson's voice trailed off.

"Jeremy, can you tell me what he said?"

A tear tracked its way down the ex-legionnaire's cheek. His voice cracked as he said, "The debt is repaid."

She patted his arm. "Well, maybe you can see him again."

"Not in this life, ma'am. Not in this life."

QUETTA AIRBASE

Khan had an idea. But first he had to sell it.

During an afternoon lull in SSI activities the Pakistani sidled up to Omar Mohammed. Though Khan's plan had little to do with Islamic culture, he felt more confident broaching it to a fellow Muslim. "Doctor, I have been thinking about our efforts to date. I believe we should consider another approach to finding the Marburg operatives, and I would welcome your thoughts."

Mohammed knew when he was being courted but he respected Rustam Khan enough to hear him out. Besides, to do otherwise would be rude. "Certainly, Major."

"I know the Chaman border area well—not intimately, but I have walked and climbed hundreds of kilometers in that area. If the people we seek truly are working there, it seems unlikely that we will find them by overt methods. They have eyes and ears everywhere, and they only need a few minutes notice to elude us."

Mohammed nodded slowly, pondering the officer's sentiment. "Yes, I see what you mean. What do you propose?"

Khan turned toward the map on the wall. "Our intelligence sources have been able to place smugglers and even al Qaeda within areas of a few square kilometers, but finding the exact spot is extremely difficult, especially for outsiders. There is no substitute for boots on the ground. At least, that is my belief."

"Do you think we should keep search teams out full time? Obtain greater coverage of the area?"

"Not exactly, Doctor." Khan swung back to Mohammed, obviously warming to the subject. "Instead of seeking our prey, I propose that we draw it to us." He waited for the inevitable response.

"Yes?"

Khan's hand swept the map again. "Since we seek men with medical or biological knowledge, we might draw their interest if we drop some hints that other medical people are working the area. People with pharmaceuticals and other items of interest."

"I see." Mohammed's attention expanded beyond the theoretical to the practical. It was part of his psyche as a paramilitary trainer. He began to see possibilities. "I think that it might work. But it could backfire—I mean, it could draw attention from people we do not want to find."

"Yes, yes." Khan nodded briskly, sensing an ally. "The main threat would be smugglers—that region has been active for centuries. But I believe we might have it both ways. Field a team strong enough to deter bandits but small enough to seem what it claims to be—medical missionaries or the like."

Mohammed was spooling up, growing more enthused. "If we find the people we seek, our field force might be able to hold them or at least pursue long enough for aerial reinforcements." He looked at Khan. "Major, let us develop a more detailed plan, then we will see Colonel Leopole."

BALUCHISTAN PROVINCE

Ali finished the morning prayer and remained sitting upright on his rug. As leader of the *Fajr* he had selected a particularly long *surah* from the Koran. Upon completion of the ancient ritual, he nodded to his colleagues on either side. "Peace be upon you and the mercy of Allah." They replied in kind.

This morning Kassim had joined the faithful. It was the first time in many days. After reverently stowing his rug, Ali felt especially good after the devotion. He believed that he was praying more fervently and devotedly than ever. It was surely a good sign.

One of Kassim's men appeared nearby, standing aside while the ritual was concluded. Then he approached the Syrian. They walked twenty meters away, and stopped to talk. Ali noted that the messenger—if he was such—spoke briefly but animatedly. Kassim seemed to ask a few questions, then passed some coins, shook hands with the man, and sent him back the way he had come.

Ali waited for the inevitable report.

"Interesting news," Kassim began. "We may have some visitors to interest you."

The veterinarian focused his gaze upon his acolyte. "Friends or enemy?"

"We do not know yet, brother. But Shaukat is usually reliable, and he reports that a medical assistance group is coming to this area in the next few days."

Ali rubbed his bearded chin. "Medical assistance, you say? Nothing more?"

Kassim shook his head. The evening sun illuminated his dusky face in an orange-yellow tint that exaggerated his angular features. "Only a few details. But I rewarded him and asked him to obtain more information. Especially the composition of the group and its sponsoring organization. He has enough money to purchase it if necessary."

"What details are known?"

"The group will likely travel on foot, visiting the remote parts of this district for a few days. It is assumed to be a government program but we have no previous knowledge of such doings."

Ali's mind sorted the myriad possibilities, potentially discarding some while saving others for consideration. He pondered for fifteen seconds, staring at the skyline. Then his gaze returned to his partner. "What is your sense?"

"I wonder why we have not heard of such a program before. I wonder why this group of samaritans appears *now*. And I wonder why they travel afoot, unless they bring only quinine and bandages."

"So do I, brother. So do I."

QUETTA AIRBASE

Padgett-Smith had a favor to ask. At least that was how she phrased her demand to Frank Leopole. After a couple of weeks with the SSI operators, she had learned how to work the system. Since she was loath to make overt use of her feminine wiles, she took the road less traveled: the ruck-up, hit-the-trail approach.

Like any good huntress, she bided her time before leaping upon her prey.

After softening up her victim with some pleasant dinner conversation, the immunologist followed the former Marine back to his office. She stepped inside and closed the door. "Frank . . . if I may call you Frank."

Leopole's male receptors extended and locked in the full-up position. *She wants something.* "Well, sure. Carolyn. After all this time." He motioned to a chair and she accepted, smoothing her skirt as she sat.

"Thank you. Ah, Frank . . . I've been thinking about my situation here. I must admit that I'm feeling rather a fifth wheel, you know? I fear that I've not really earned my way and was wondering, well, whether I should return home."

He leaned forward, hands clasped on the desk. "I don't understand. I mean, you've not had much of a chance to apply your talent yet." He grinned self-consciously. "And I know that you'd be missed by the other guys."

"Yes, well, that's just it, you see? I'm feeling like an ornament, or some sort of mascot. Oh, the chaps have been marvelous; no mistake. I've actually become rather fond of some of them. Jeffrey and J. J. . . . even Bosco and Breezy at times." She smiled and flipped her hair in her most engaging fashion. *Not bad, eight point five out of ten,* she told herself.

Leopole suspected he was being conned. He enjoyed the hell out of it. "Well, then, what's the problem with staying?"

"Actually, Frank, it's my sense of self-worth. I accepted this contract with a specific purpose—to evaluate filoviruses. The fact that we've found so little after so long makes me feel that I'm accepting payment for no services rendered. That's why I wonder if I shouldn't go home until . . ."

"Yes?"

"Well, perhaps I could come back if you do find something. I could be here in barely a day."

Leopole leaned back, hands behind his head. He was not as relaxed as he appeared. "Yeah, I suppose you could. But Admiral Derringer and Dr. Catterly want you on the job. And so do I." He grinned at her. "For whatever that's worth."

The violet eyes lowered demurely to her lap; she wished she could blush on cue. "Thank you, Frank. I do appreciate it. Truly." She raised her gaze to him again. "But there's only so much I can do here. While the lads are dashing about, I'm mostly cooped up here. I can't go out on my own, and it's inconvenient to get an escort every time I feel like shopping or sightseeing." She spread her hands. "Frank, besides the medical inactivity, I'm going stir crazy. I believe that you Americans call it cabin fever." She found the right tone for the occasion. "If I don't get some outdoor activity, I shall burst!"

He nodded, assessing what was coming. *So that's it! She wants to go on the next mission.* "Carolyn, I understand your position. And it speaks well of your professional ethics. Some people would be happy to fort up here and collect their check. But you know we can't send out a crew just for you to climb some rocks or cross some hills. The only way is to send you on foot with one of our teams."

She inhaled, held her breath, then pressed the attack. "That's what I've been thinking. Now, the upcoming search of the Chaman area is expected to last, what? Three or four days?"

"Affirm. But . . ."

"That would be marvelous! I'm perfectly fit—ask any of the boys I exercise with. And if they find something, I'd be right there. You wouldn't have to fly me in."

"Carolyn, are you saying that if you don't go on this op you'll take the next plane to London?"

She shook her head vigorously. Her light brown hair swirled around her ears. "Oh, Frank . . ." *That's exactly what I mean.* She gave him a patented CPS How Could You? look. "I am merely saying that I'm not earning my keep just lazing about here, and that I may as well go home unless there's something really useful for me to do."

Leopole stood up and turned away, looking into the evening. When he pivoted, his mind was made up. "Carolyn, have you really thought this out? You'd be the only female in the most desolate countryside you ever saw. You'd be traveling with some hard cases— Americans and Pakistanis—who may like and admire you, but they won't cut you any slack. And they shouldn't. Furthermore, if you get separated from our people, you'd be a white woman, alone in a Muslim country. You need to think about that. You really do."

"I have done. Truly."

"What would your husband say?"

Padgett-Smith was taken aback. She felt an emotional bump; it was a legitimate question. She realized that she had given Charles little thought over the past few days. *He encourages me to follow my dreams.* She rose to face the American. "He would tell me the same thing he would tell you: she's a woman grown. She can make her own mistakes."

Leopole almost flinched. *Yeouch. You are one tough lady.* After four seconds of locking eyes with the Britisher, he heard himself say,

"Alright. I'll check with headquarters for an okay." Before she could respond, he added, "I just hope that you don't regret it. And neither do I."

QUETTA AIRBASE

Leopole had an announcement. "We're moving to search an area near Chaman."

Bosco perked up. "Where's that, Boss?"

"It's the area where J. J. was held. About sixty miles northwest, halfway to Kandahar. You would know that if you ever looked at a map, Boscombe."

"Uh, yessir. Rightyouaresir."

Leopole turned his attention to the rest of the room. "Chaman is right on the border, so it's prime smuggling territory. Major Khan and Dr. Mohammed have developed a plan that I think has possibilities. Khan's sources indicate that al Qaeda operates around there, playing both sides of the border, and there's indication of a veterinarian who's active in the region. So that's where we're going."

Steve Lee shifted in his seat. "All of us, Colonel?"

"Ah, no. We can't have too many foreigners running around so we'll send part of White Team. But you'll have Dr. Mohammed and Dr. Padgett-Smith owing to their specialties."

Lee nodded his assent. Whether he agreed with the extra baggage was problematical.

"And there's one other specialty," Leopole added. "Major Khan has offered a couple of military mule skinners, since you'll be packing some bio gear. A few of our local contacts have dropped information that a medical aid team is going to be working the area. Major Khan will bring along an army doctor for realism. We reckon you'll draw less scrutiny with low-end transportation rather than running up and down the highway with a paramilitary convoy. Besides that, Khan has enough horsepower to handle any suspicious types you may meet."

"Roger that." Lee glanced around at his team, sorting out which operators to take. "Ah, Colonel, what about a quick trip up there to scout the terrain?"

"Steve, I agree that recon is time well spent, but we're short on time. With the guides you'll have, there shouldn't be any big surprises. I'm told that the uphill climb is fairly easy on this side of the pass but pretty steep on the Afghan side. The scenery is supposed to be spectacular."

"Okay, roger the scenery." Lee grinned at his colleague. "Ah, what about extraction? I mean, if we find something, there's not much point coming out by mule."

"Right. Depending on what turns up, we can send some trucks to your area or we can have at least one helo there in less than an hour. Just keep us informed. I'll coordinate frequencies and comm schedules with you."

After the briefing, Lee waylaid Leopole. "Frank, I'd like to talk about Doc Smith."

Leopole had expected some resistance. He folded his arms, nodded his head, and said, "Fire away."

Lee glanced over his shoulder. Seeing no one nearby, he said, "Don't get me wrong. She's an impressive lady, and I have no doubt about her professional ability. But I gotta wonder what's the point in taking her along? I mean, if we find something out there, we can secure the area and you could fly her in."

"Steve, I understand your position. Hell, I agree with you. But she's really concerned about pulling her weight. She told me she doesn't think she's earning her pay, and unless something turns up pretty soon, she wants to go home."

Lee rolled his eyes. Behind the blue orbs an exclamation flashed on his mental screen. *Women!* "Damn it, she's like the rest of us. She starts earning her keep when and if we find something. Until then, we're all just warming our motors at the start line."

Leopole shook his head. "Actually, she's in a different boat than the rest of us. You know she's not a regular SSI employee. Well, I checked on her status when she told me she's thinking of going home. Because of her research work in England, she inserted a clause saying she could back out if she's not needed here. Corin Pilong's in charge of contracts, and she confirmed what Padgett-Smith said."

Lee's shoulders sagged visibly. "And there's nobody else."

"No lie, GI. We're buyers in a seller's market." Leopole then moved to the next order of business. "Who do you want to take with you?"

Lee already had his preferences. "I think some of the original Blue Team guys would benefit from being in the field again. So I'm picking Norton on radio with Hendricks and O'Neil. But Bosco and Breezy are a strong team and it makes sense to keep them together."

Leopole thought for a moment. "What about Ken Delmore? He could come in handy."

"Yeah, he's strong as two oxes, but he's just so damn big. He'd probably draw attention." Lee laughed. "Besides, we have three mules, remember?"

QUETTA AIRBASE

Padgett-Smith overheard Terry Keegan's latest rant. The tone of his voice caught her attention as much as his words: he remained an angry young man.

Rustam Khan signaled the Brit with his eyebrows. The meaning was clear: *Help!*

"Oh, there you are, Major." CPS winked at the Pakistani behind Keegan's back.

Obviously grateful, Khan took the hint. "Ah, Dr. Smith. Yes, I was just . . ."

"Looking for Colonel Leopole?"

"Ah, yes. Quite so. Quite so." He nodded to the American. "Please excuse me, Mr. Keegan. I, ah, look forward to continuing our conversation."

Padgett-Smith folded her arms and regarded the pilot. "I heard part of the . . . discussion. Perhaps you can explain a few things for me."

"Yes, ma'am. I mean, I'll try."

She shifted her weight and concentrated on Keegan's face. *Rather a nice-looking chap. Frowns too much, though.* "I've heard about the situation on your border with Mexico. Now, I've traveled widely in the States but not much in that area. I take it that the continuing problem is more political than anything else."

Keegan nodded vigorously. "That's correct, Doctor. We could seal the border in a couple of weeks if we wanted to. But the politicians won't do it."

"Well, why ever not? I mean, the threat is obvious, apart from all the economic and cultural concerns . . ."

"Well, it's like this, Doctor. The Democrats *want* illegals in our country. They talk about Mexicans doing work that Americans won't, but that's just a smoke screen. A guest worker program could handle that problem. No, those illegals who get the right papers are eligible to vote—some of them vote anyway—and they nearly always go Democratic. That's because they know the liberals provide funding and dispensation. On top of that, our constitution says that any child born in the U.S. is automatically a citizen. Even if the mother is there illegally. That's insane. But it'll never change."

"Then what about the Republicans? Don't they ever . . ."

"No, ma'am. Hardly ever. See, they mess their diapers at the thought of being accused of racism by the Democrats. And the Demos know that, so they use it like a club to beat the Goopers down."

"Goopers?"

Keegan laughed. "Oh, that's my expression. I sort of made it up. GOP: Grand Old Party. The Republicans." He shrugged. "Goopers."

The Brit shook her head slightly. "I still do not understand, Terry. If the Republicans—your Goopers—have the majority, why do they cater to the illegals and the political opposition? I mean, those people won't support the party anyway."

"I guess you'd have to ask them, ma'am. I'm a former Gooper myself, for a lot of reasons. Probably the biggest, though, is that the Republicans don't really stand for anything, except election. They want to get along with the Democrats, and the Demos are bent on destroying the country."

"That's a bit harsh, isn't it?"

The aviator shrugged again. "Probably. But it's also accurate. I think we're going to end up like Canada. Two cultures in one country, with neither having much use for the other."

"You're referring to the French influence?"

"Sure. Just substitute Spanish for French. You want to know how absurd it is? At one time on their military aircraft the port side said 'Canadian Armed Forces.' The starboard side said '*Forces Armées*

Canadiennes.' I don't know much, but I know that's just plain stupid. Even the Canucks finally agreed. Now they just paint 'Canada' on their birds."

She smiled. "Maybe there's hope." Before he could respond, she added, "Terry, because you feel so strongly, have you ever thought of going elsewhere?"

"Oh, yeah. Lots of times. But where would I go, Doc?" He thought for a moment. "No offense, but my ancestors were driven out of Ireland in the eighteenth century so they went to New York. But things were pretty bad there. Like, 'No dogs or Irish.' A couple of them got killed fighting for the Union in the Civil War, and the others migrated west. Eventually they ended up in California. The only thing that stopped them was the Pacific Ocean." He almost grinned. "There just isn't anyplace else. So I'm stuck."

"Well, all things considered, there are far worse places."

"Yes, ma'am. I know. That's why the rest of the world is moving there."

BALUCHISTAN PROVINCE

Much as he loved animals, Ali had a hard time feeling paternal toward goats. He much preferred horses and dogs—even sheep. The Kamori doe he had just inoculated expressed her displeasure with a bleat and a kick to Ali's left leg. The farmer's young son released the animal, which scampered across the pen to join her friends. Sometimes the veterinarian wondered if the smelly, messy creatures were worth domesticating. Not that it mattered: the feral variety, *capra hircus*, was less common these days.

Ali patted the boy's shoulder, thanking him for his help. At eleven years old, the youngster looked up at the tall stranger who brought a mysterious kindness to remote farms and settlements—all on behalf of God's creatures. "I like dogs," the boy declared. Ali almost laughed; the youngster seemed to share the doctor's opinion of goats. Seeing an opportunity to spread The Word, Ali replied, "The Book mentions dogs five times; they are our oldest friends. But God said to the horse, 'Thou shalt cast thine enemies between thy hooves, and thou shalt carry my friends upon thy back.' "

The boy nodded solemnly, uncertain what to make of the short sermon. Ali decided not to press the matter. *Patience in all things,* he told himself. In three or four years the youngster might become a candidate for the jihad.

Ali picked up his kit and walked toward the family home. He knew that, true to Islamic virtue, the boy's father would offer the hospitality of the house.

The host poured tea for the veterinarian while the farmer's wife kept a respectful distance in the kitchen. The father and husband, Shaabani by name, treated his woman more respectfully than some men in the area, but her options did not extend to participating in male discussions.

"Doctor, your benevolence does you much credit. I cannot offer you more than some grain and a few chickens but please know that my family is grateful. We shall remember you in our prayers of thanksgiving."

Ali waved a dismissive hand. "Brother, I am doing God's work. One does not seek praise for helping His creatures. But I thank you for your prayers—and your chickens." He smiled over his teacup. The barter system had much to commend it, especially when hard money could draw unwelcome attention.

Shaabani raised his head. "That reminds me: it is said that other medical volunteers are nearby. It is said that a group of doctors will be in our region this very week."

That was exactly the point that Ali had intended to raise with the farmer. "Yes, I have heard the same reports. Do you know anything about my mysterious colleagues? Who sponsors their good work?"

"One of my neighbors mentioned it. He said that a government program has just begun, traveling to remote areas with pack horses or mules."

Ali nodded. "Ah, that makes good sense. They can reach some of the needy without limiting themselves to roads." In truth, Ali wondered why pack animals were necessary in an age when all-terrain vehicles surely were available to government agencies. He sensed something odd—but what? He made a mental note to pursue his curiosity about the new makers of good works.

And something more: Kassim's friend who had offered a son and a nephew in the fight against the Crusaders. It was time to meet them and consider new options.

QUETTA AIRBASE

Rustam Khan supervised the outfitting of the small caravan, with an eye toward concealing details that could tip off a competent observer. CPS rated high in that regard.

"Doctor, your clothing is fine. From a distance of twenty or thirty meters you blend in with the others." He almost said "with the men." Studying her face, he concluded, "What you need is a dark complexion—and a mustache."

The immunologist managed a chuckle. "Well, Major, I can apply makeup for the former but I shan't be able to produce the latter in the time allotted. Do you have a mustache laying about?"

"As a matter of fact, I do." He emptied his knapsack and produced a theatrical makeup kit. "It's in here. I will leave it to you to decide whether to use it, Doctor."

CPS held the item with a mixture of curiosity and disgust. "I suppose I could manage. How long does it have to stay on?"

"Perhaps three or four days—no more. You can refresh it from time to time. Oh, and one more thing. Your hands."

"My hands?" She held them up, and Khan admired the manicure.

"If I may say so, Doctor, you have perhaps the loveliest, most feminine hands I have ever seen. Anyone would notice them. So you should wear gloves most of the time."

"Well, all right . . ."

"Besides, you may want some protection when dealing with the animals."

"The mules? What about them?"

"Oh, you should stay with the beasts of burden with one of the handlers. You are less likely to be noticed."

She shook her head. "Why is that?"

"Many Muslim males have a condescending attitude toward those with menial jobs. Any smugglers or al Qaeda operatives will be more interested in the mules' cargo than their handlers." He shrugged eloquently. "You will understand, I'm sure."

CPS shot him a frosty smile. "I'm sure."

Leopole intervened with another item. "Doctor, you can carry this. It's lighter than a standard AK-47."

He held out a compact assault rifle that resembled the AK-47 she had fired in Britain. Padgett-Smith accepted it, hefting the weight. "It *is* lighter. And it's so short!"

"It's an AKS-74U, better known as a Krinkov. It fires the 5.45mm round instead of the standard 7.62. With the stock folded it's only about twenty inches long and seven pounds loaded. That's almost three pounds less that you'll pack around the hills."

"Well, I'm sure it's useful, but I'm familiar with the full-size version that Tony . . ."

"Doctor, just trust me on this. I don't want to insult you, but no woman I've ever known can carry a full-size rifle for more than a couple of hours, let alone uphill at high elevation. Besides, the Krinkov works just the same as a '47."

"Maybe I should just carry the Browning."

"It's up to you, Doctor. But where you're going, a rifle is mighty handy. And you can sling it over your shoulder so you don't have to hold it all the time."

"Honestly, Fr . . . Colonel. I'm not such a weakling, you know."

Leopole drew her aside, guiding her by the arm. "Look, Carolyn, like I said, it's up to you. But women don't have the upper-body strength to carry a hunk of steel all day. As somebody who's humped a rifle up a hill or two, I know what I'm talking about."

She touched his arm, almost absentmindedly. "I'm not arguing, Frank. It's just that I have more confidence in the pistol. I've shot it more."

"Doc . . . okay, Carolyn." He leaned closer. "Look, I'll level with you. I don't expect you to hit anybody with a rifle you've hardly ever fired. But if for some reason you get separated from the others, if you're seen as a woman, in bandit country . . ." He let the image dangle in her imagination. "With the shorty you'll have thirty rounds to keep the bad guys away from you, at longer range."

He saw the dawn of recognition in her violet eyes. Finally she said, "You're very persuasive, Colonel Leopole. Very persuasive, indeed."

Leopole inclined in a slight bow. "My compliments, ma'am." He straightened and whistled at Brezyinski. "Breezy, will you help the doctor get zeroed?"

———————

At the range Breezy set up a twenty-five-meter target and supervised CPS in zeroing from prone. After the first three rounds she safed the Krinkov and looked up. "It's so easy to shoot! Far less recoil than before."

"Yes, ma'am. Less muzzle flip so you can get back on target easier." He shielded his hazel eyes against the sun, squinting downrange. The 5.45mm bullets made damnably small holes at that distance. He grunted to himself—something about eyes over thirty—and produced a compact pair of Steiner binoculars. He scanned the bull's-eye and found a neat group at eight o'clock, maybe three inches out. "Nice shooting, Doc. Unload and I'll move the sight."

After making the adjustment with the front sight tool, the paratrooper returned the rifle and watched while CPS fired a verifying group. The Steiners came out again. "A tad right but it's plenty good. You can hold dead on to about two hundred meters, which is more than you'll ever need."

As Padgett-Smith removed her ear plugs Breezy asked, "Do you want a spare magazine?"

Padgett-Smith hefted the loaded Krinkov and measured its weight against her Browning Hipower. After a moment she shook her head. "I should think that thirty in the rifle and thirteen in the pistol will be ample."

Breezy nodded. "Ma'am, if you need forty-three rounds you're not in a gunfight, you're in a war!"

"I suppose I could put some extra magazines on one of the mules."

"Yeah . . . ah, yes, ma'am. But there's not much point. I mean, if there's any shooting the mules are gonna head for the far horizon, if you know what I mean. That's why I'm humping about twelve pounds of 7.62 in loaded mags. One in the rifle, four in my chest pack and six in my ruck."

Before she could reply he took the AKS and said, "Lemme show you something."

Removing the curved mag, he said, "If you're in the dark and can't see your rifle very well, you can still tell if you're loaded. If there's no round in the chamber but you want it loaded, drop the mag and feel the top cartridge. Say it's on the right. Reload, chamber a round, and pull the mag again. If the top round is on the left, you know you're set. Reload again but remember to pull on the magazine to be sure it's seated."

"I'll practice that drill this evening."

"Good. Oh, there's another thing. Do you have tracers?"

"You mean, illuminating bullets?" she asked.

"Yeah. They light up when you shoot 'em."

"No. Should I?"

"Well, they're useful for signaling. But if you get lost or something, there's a standard signal. Shoot three rounds one minute apart. Everybody will hear the shots but only we'll know it's you. Just sit tight. If you don't hear a reply after ten minutes, do it again. Your pistol's best for that. Save the rifle ammo for when you really need it."

"I certainly shall."

BALUCHISTAN PROVINCE

Steve Lee had chosen his crew with efficiency in mind: Rustam Khan, four shooters, a radioman, CPS, a Pakistani doctor and medic, and three mule skinners—one for each animal. With himself that was thirteen in all: a group presumably large enough to deter brigands yet flexible enough to adapt to changing situations. If the team had to break up, Khan would lead the second section.

Lee briefed his team again the night before leaving. "We're committing most of our linguists to this op: Major Khan and the Paki doctor both speak Urdu, of course, while the major and I have passable Pashto. Dr. Mohammed is staying here in case we need somebody fluent with the locals." In truth, Lee and Leopole doubted that Mohammed was up to the physical challenge, and neither was enthused about their female colleague's prospects.

Following the briefing, the operators were introduced to their four-footed colleagues. Carolyn Padgett-Smith, for one, had never met the business end of a mule. For that matter, neither had any of the other SSI personnel, though Breezy voiced pretensions of equine ability.

Padgett-Smith did not know which was more cantankerous: the mules or their handlers. All possessed two things in common: unpronounceable names and an attitude.

The SSI men put their suppressed MP-5s in the mules' panniers; submachine guns would draw attention or envy where the team was headed. To blend in better with the locals, everyone had full-size rifles: the Americans carried AKs and most of the Pakis used G3s. The pistol-carrying types had Brownings beneath their vests. Other gear included night vision, tactical radio headsets, MREs and bottled water plus some fodder for the animals. The area where they were headed was rocky and low on vegetation.

Even with the mules, most of the men were burdened with more than they preferred to carry. Padgett-Smith's early confidence wilted visibly when she hefted Bosco's gear. "My lord!" she exclaimed. "That must be fifty pounds."

"More like seventy, ma'am," Boscombe replied. He knew that it was twenty-eight kilograms, but he believed in rounding up from sixty-two pounds.

The immunologist immediately sensed a male-female tiff brewing. She decided to defuse it by defaulting to her Scarlett O'Hara mode. "My *goodness*, Mr. Boscombe, how *do* you ever carry such a *huge* load?" *You great big hunk of man, you.* She batted her eyelashes at him.

Bosco was bright but he was also susceptible to feminine wiles. "Ah, you get used to it, ma'am. I . . ." He caught himself at the last second. *Jerk! You've just been had.* He recovered by cataloging the contents of his ruck. "Uh, I carry extra ammo plus at least a day's MREs, a couple gallons of water, night vision, rain gear, sleeping bag, shelter half, first aid kit, and a change of socks and underwear." He pondered asking Dr. Padgett-Smith about her extra undies when his testosterone poison was diluted by an influx of embarrassment.

Lee came by, saving Bosco from further discomfort. "Ah, Dr. Smith, if your gear is ready we'll put it on the mules." The bespectacled officer was careful to maintain a neutral tone in his voice, lest Padgett-Smith infer veiled criticism. She had prepared a day pack with enough food and water for twelve hours at a stretch; the rest went on the reddish jenny known as Taqat. CPS inferred that the name indicated strength or endurance.

Rustam Khan also was attentive to the mules. "Doctor, the handlers say this animal is the steadiest, so we will put your equipment and personal items on her. The other two will carry extra food, water, tents, and weapons. They will also have some medical supplies in case we meet people who might need help, which is of course our cover story. Dr. Chaudhry will deal with those cases, of course."

"Of course." Padgett-Smith had only briefly met her Pakistani colleague. He was courteous but remote, probably uncomfortable with a female of any variety taking the field. But since he was subordinate to Khan, she surmised that the major would continue running interference for her.

BALUCHISTAN PROVINCE

Kassim had news of the newcomers.

"My scouts found the medical team yesterday and remained hidden when it stopped for the night. There are more than twelve people, including foreigners. One of my men saw an armed guard dig a hole and void his bowels." Kassim paused for emphasis. "The guard wiped himself with his right hand."

Ali sat back, rubbing his chin, reflecting that Satan eats with his left hand. "So the guards are infidels. Maybe all of them are."

"No, Doctor. The animal handlers all seemed to speak Urdu. And there was at least one man who is almost certainly a Pakistani Army officer. But several men spoke English. So did the woman."

Ali sat bolt upright. "What?"

"Yes, one of the strangers is female. She wears men's clothing and tries to disguise her face. She is definitely not Muslim—I questioned my men closely."

"One woman traveling with a dozen men, on foot, in rough terrain. Presumably bringing medical aid to the poor." Ali's eyes tracked back and forth, as if seeing the camp layout. "Did these strangers treat any people?"

"Some. But they kept moving most of the time. They only seemed to provide the most basic treatment to a few farmers or travelers they met." Kassim organized his thoughts, focusing on evidence rather than supposition. "One of my scouts doubled back and talked to a few people who had dealt with the medical team. They had received bandages, water purification tablets, a few pills for diarrhea and the like."

"What did the woman do?"

Kassim shrugged. "I do not know. But as I said, my scouts only trailed them from late afternoon onward."

"Very well, Kassim. Your men did well. Please tell them that we will arrange a surprise meeting with these people tomorrow."

The Syrian turned to go. Abruptly he stopped and turned. "Oh, there is one thing about the woman. She carries a rifle."

Kassim's tone was flat, unemotional. Ali's blood pounded in his temples as he absorbed the blasphemy.

As Kassim departed, Ali raised his hands and eyes to the heavens, giving silent thanks for what had been delivered to him. When his senses returned to earth, he said, "So nice to meet you, Dr. Padgett-Smith."

BALUCHISTAN PROVINCE

Kassim had doubts.

"Doctor, I understand your eagerness to eliminate these strangers, especially if they are as you suspect. But I have few reliable fighters anymore. It takes time to grow *mujahadin*." He paused for emphasis. "As you know."

Ali exuded cool confidence. In truth, he had anticipated his colleague's objections and was prepared for them. "You are correct, my brother. Nor would I dispute your knowledge of . . . such things. But consider this: your new men are excellent at scouting and observation. This opportunity will give them small unit combat experience. Their numbers almost equal the infidels: with surprise they will surely succeed."

The veteran *muj* slowly shook his head. "I have seen it work the other way too many times. These Americans are almost certainly experienced. If they survive the initial volley—and some of them will—it could go badly." He was setting up his final argument. "Allow me to accompany them. I can make the difference between success and failure."

Ali rose from his rough desk and placed his hands on Kassim's shoulders. "My brother—my friend—I shall do you the honor of speaking bluntly. I cannot spare you, and with your wooden foot, you would be at greater risk." The vet shook his head. "No, Kassim. You must remain behind."

Kassim capitulated with atypical good grace. He was accustomed to having his way in tactical matters, but he recognized the wisdom of his superior's argument.

He also realized that Dr. Ali was willing to lose every man the Syrian had recruited and trained in the past several months in exchange for comparable losses among the Americans. And their British she-devil immunologist.

BALUCHISTAN PROVINCE

Lee was going to call a halt for the evening when the RPD gunner opened fire from barely forty meters uphill. Ollie Norton went down hard with the radio. Depending upon their training, judgment, or inclination, everybody else returned fire, hit the deck, or assaulted through the kill zone.

The mules brayed in panic, whipped their leads from the handlers, and fled as fast as four hooves would take them.

Lee had been on the receiving end of an ambush before. He knew that delay could be fatal, so he shouted for the nearest men to follow him. Bosco, Breezy, and a Pakistani joined him, sweeping the nearest rocks and foliage with full auto fire, clearing a path twenty meters wide. Reaching temporary safety, they knew the drill. "Cover!" Lee shouted.

"Covering!" Bosco replied.

Lee dumped his empty magazine, speed reloaded, chambered a round, and yelled "Ready!"

Bosco and Breezy hollered "Cover!" simultaneously. Lee responded,

"Covering." He scythed a short burst in the direction of the RPD. Seconds later the two partners called "Ready!"

The Pakistani soldier drew a G3 magazine, then calmly reloaded. Bosco thought, *Either he's a hell of a mule skinner or he doesn't have a nerve in his body.*

Lee looked around, trying to assess the situation. He badly wanted to regroup his dispersed team, lest it be destroyed in detail. He called out. "Rustam! You there?"

Khan responded from fifteen meters to the right rear. "Back here! We're covering Hendricks." The firefight had quickly stabilized, neither side now possessing an advantage.

Low crawling, Micky Hendricks was first to reach Norton and pulled the quick release clasps on the harness. He saw that the radio set had taken at least two 7.62 rounds; it looked useless.

The PRDC-150 was a high-end piece of gear: ten pounds without batteries and barely a foot square. Voice and data encryption, frequency-agile VHF. Now it was several thousand dollars' worth of assorted spare parts.

Hendricks safed his weapon, slung it around his neck, and began the laborious process of dragging Norton to cover. Occasional AK rounds spattered the hard earth around him, but Lee's and Khan's teams suppressed most hostile fire. Lee recognized a no-win situation and began formulating a plan. He leaned close to Bosco and Breezy. "You two flank 'em uphill to the left. The Paki and I will keep 'em busy."

The two friends looked at one another, tapped right fists together, and began to move out. Lee grabbed Breezy. "They might be flanking us—be alert."

Breezy nodded, then was gone.

Lee grabbed his notebook from a vest pocket, scribbled a message, and used duct tape to secure it to a rock. He told his new partner, "Shoot!"

As the Pakistani soldier began firing semi-auto, Lee raised up and heaved the rock at Khan. One of his men saw the message inbound and rose to catch it. He drew immediate fire, taking bullet fragments off a boulder, but hauled in the missive. Khan read the printed note:

TWO FLANKING LEFT. SEND FLANKERS RIGHT.
Khan called out. "Message received!"

Glancing over his right shoulder, Lee saw two or more of Khan's team disappear around some boulders.

———

Bosco and Breezy had their moves down. They covered one another, keeping eyes and guns swiveling through 190 degrees as they advanced uphill. They heard the RPD and some AKs firing from the crest of the hummock and swung farther to their left in order to approach from behind. Reaching the decision point, they paused long enough to coordinate their move onto the skyline.

An armed man appeared twelve meters in front of Breezy. The former paratrooper raised his AK from low ready, got a quick sight picture, and pressed the trigger. Four rounds struck the gunman, who collapsed with his mouth agape. It happened before Bosco could react.

Both men realized what had happened. They had experienced what professionals call a meeting engagement: when two maneuver elements collide unexpectedly. The Americans were flanking the al Qaeda flankers.

Seconds later two more figures emerged from the boulders uphill. One saw what he saw, spun on a heel, and fled. The other opened fire from waist level, hip shooting on full auto. His burst went low and left. Breezy's and Bosco's sighted rounds left red gouts on his torso. He was a big man, probably 250 pounds, and somehow stayed on his feet. Breezy was aiming a head shot when the terrorist dropped to his knees and pitched forward, downhill.

Breezy called "Cover!" and dropped to kneeling. As he executed a tactical reload, Bosco replied, "Covering." After Breezy stashed his partly used mag he nodded to his partner. Bosco said, "Set."

Breezy knew the drill: he shouted, "Go!"

They continued uphill, pushing hard because they had been spotted.

Topping the crest, the SSI men saw the geometry of the ambush. The machine gun was sited improperly, perpendicular to the trail rather than at the head, where the gunner could have fired down the enemy's route of advance. One or two riflemen were positioned over there, engaged in occasional fusillades with Lee. Farther "upstream" were at least three more shooters trying to keep Khan's men pinned down.

"Look!" Bosco pointed out the survivor of the recent shootout, sprinting for the safety of the RPD nest. Both Americans began shooting at the running man at least fifty meters away. Bosco was first on the trigger, firing while standing. Breezy plopped into a hasty sitting position. Their bullets impacted ahead and behind the fleeting bandit. Breezy realized he was pumped; he forced himself to breathe deeply and concentrate. At a quartering aspect, he put his front sight one width ahead of the target and pressed the trigger straight back.

The man seemed to stumble, regain his balance, and continue ahead. Then he slowed. Bosco's next round knocked him down.

Now aware of its peril, the MG crew swung toward the uphill threat. Before the belt-fed weapon could open up, more firing erupted behind the RPD. The loader was badly hit, rolling on the rocky ground. Then the gunner was cut down by 7.62 rounds from two of Khan's team. The Americans recognized Blake O'Neil and a Paki, who waved from about 120 meters. They advanced cautiously on the gun crew, rifles pointed at the two "items" while covering forty meters of open ground.

Bosco began searching the enemy bodies for information. Finding only al Qaeda propaganda, he handed the papers to the Pakistani NCO.

O'Neil kicked one of the prostrate gunmen in the ribs. The man groaned loudly and O'Neil shouted, "We got a live one here." Then he bound the man's hands. Khan sprinted to the scene and pulled back the gunman's robe and vest. "Femur, through and through. He can talk." Khan motioned for the Paki medic, who went to work.

Breezy toed one of the corpses with his boot. "Man, they shoulda had us."

Bosco held out his hands; the left was steady but the right had a tremor. "Bad setup, dude. I wonder why they put the belt-fed uphill. They coulda hosed the length of our column from the head of the trail."

"Come on down!" Lee shouted from the trail, eager to regroup his small force. He could not assume that all the opposition had been killed or repulsed. The SSI men picked up the enemy weapons and alternately stepped and slid down the hummock.

Lee did a quick head count. One mule handler was dead and one was missing. Norton, the radioman, was seriously hurt and the radio was destroyed. "Our spare radio was on the second mule, and he's long gone."

Khan produced a hand-held radio. "Major Lee, not to worry. This is a short-range set but I can pass a message to the district commander. He can notify Quetta for us. It may take some time, however."

Dr. Chaudhry pulled a blanket over the dead Paki soldier. "What about our casualties?"

Lee exhaled audibly. "We can't bury the KIA in this soil, Doctor. Maybe our remaining mule can pack him and Norton off this mountain tomorrow. That leaves one handler missing as well."

Lee looked around again. Finally he asked, "Where's Padgett-Smith?"

BALUCHISTAN PROVINCE

Carolyn Padgett-Smith looked around. She felt a shiver between her shoulder blades. She was alone.

Not just alone, but stranded in remote, hostile territory: a European woman without communications or food, who spoke no local dialect. She spent fifteen fervent seconds berating herself. *You stupid, stupid twit. You clot! You vain, unthinking female! Chasing after a mule—as if you could ever catch one. And if you did: then what? You can only hang on to the brute's lead rope.*

CPS looked back in the direction she had come. Or thought she had come. With her focus on the scampering pack animal bearing her supplies, she now realized that she had paid little attention to the terrain. *You didn't even make note of trees or boulders. Twit.* Looking at the sky, she realized that daylight was an expendable asset: she could use it to search for Lee and company, or she could climb to a protected position before darkness descended. She decided to seek high ground and find shelter from the wind.

· Padgett-Smith recalled Breezy's comments: *Fire three shots one minute apart. Sit tight and we'll find you.* She wondered if she should try the signal, but thought better of it. By the time anyone could reach her area, night would have descended, and she knew something of the risk in stumbling around a combat zone in the dark.

While scaling a rocky slope she took stock of her assets: a coat and gloves and the Klimov that Frank Leopole had insisted she take. *Thank you, Frank. You were right, you sweet man.*

Once settled beneath a protected outcropping, Padgett-Smith tried to get comfortable. She knew it was an impossible task but she wanted to sleep sitting up, if she could sleep at all. In the tight quarters she checked her AKS to ensure it was loaded and set it aside. Then she drew her Browning, chambered a round, and applied the safety. It was going to be a long, lonely night.

BALUCHISTAN PROVINCE

After securing the area, Lee deployed lookouts on each side of the ravine. He was discussing where to proceed when Khan ambled into the group, limping slightly. Most of the talk was about Padgett-Smith. "I saw her about forty meters northeast of me," Khan related. "I was going after her when my foot slipped into a crack in the shale. My ankle won't support my full weight for a while."

"What was she doing?"

"I do not know. I just looked up and saw her out there . . ."

"She was chasing the damn mule," Hendricks exclaimed. "It must've broken loose from its handler when the shooting started. I guess she was worried about her microscopes and stuff."

Lee focused on the former policeman. "If you saw that . . ."

"Well, sir, I was kinda busy. You know, shooting and reloading and shooting." Hendricks kept a level tone in his voice. "I saw Major Khan headed that way and figured he'd catch her. I didn't know he twisted his ankle."

Lee checked his watch. "That was barely thirty minutes ago. She can't be very far away."

O'Neil interjected. "Well, we can't go stumbling around in the dark, calling her name. The gooners would find her . . . or us."

Lee rubbed his bearded chin. "Concur. She's a smart lady. She'll fort up somewhere and stay put. We'll go find her come sunup." He looked around. "Meanwhile, let's leg it out of here while we still have some light. We'll find another spot for a night defensive position. Cold camp: no fires, no lights, and damn little talking."

BALUCHISTAN PROVINCE

Kassim sized up the mule handler as a man who would respond to reason.

"Son of a whore! You take the Americans' money and lead them to us!" The Syrian made a show of drawing his knife. Eight inches of honed, rusty steel glinted before the captive's eyes.

The Pakistani noncom watched the blade waving before him. He almost admired the way the steel weaved and danced. He found himself speaking freely, completely, and honestly. The interrogation lasted less than ten minutes before the man's knowledge was drained.

Ali, who had remained concealed during the process, consulted with Kassim after the prisoner was led away to an uncertain fate. "What do you think?"

"I believe that he held nothing back." Kassim gave his wolfish grin. "Bare steel and loud voices frequently produce results."

"Well?"

"The team is composed of a Pakistani major, a doctor, medic, and two other animal handlers. There are six Americans and the English woman. That vermin"—Kassim nodded toward the departing noncom—"says the mules carried very little medical supplies. Mostly camping equipment, food, water, and some fodder."

Ali shifted his weight and folded his arms—a sign of agitation. "Kassim, what is their purpose?" His voice was flat, urgent.

"Presumably they were providing medical assistance to the poor in this area. The bought dog believes they had another purpose related to the woman but he says he was not informed of the details. I tend to believe him."

"Surely he must have overheard something more."

Kassim leaned slightly forward for emphasis. "Brother, I have much experience in such things. I tell you, he held nothing back."

Ali accepted his colleague's professional judgment. He began thinking ahead. "You say we lost six men?"

"Seven, counting Loal. He will live but he is useless for now."

"You realize that we must press them tomorrow. As hard and as fast as possible. They can be flown out almost any time."

Kassim spread his hands. "More men are on the way here. They should arrive before morning, but as I have said: concentrating against the Americans leaves us weak elsewhere."

Ali nodded his understanding. "Yes, I know. But this is the decisive point at this moment." He jabbed a bony finger earthward. "If we kill more Americans tomorrow, they will almost certainly leave. It will give us more time to send the next couriers to their destiny."

The Syrian veteran bobbed his head in assent. "I hear, brother, and I obey." He turned to go.

"Kassim!"

"Yes?"

"I want the woman. Alive if possible, but dead if you must."

"As you wish, Doctor."

SSI OFFICES

The Pandora Project had turned to hash.

Derringer read Mohammed's email, then read it again out loud. "Lee's SSI-Pak search team ambushed late yesterday border area near Chaman. One Pak KIA, one MIA, and Norton WIA serious. Padgett-Smith missing. Lee searching this AM and will advise ASAP. Interrogation of one POW indicates probable aQ connection. Helo extraction likely today depending on CPS results. Suggest withholding notification of NOK until later. Omar."

Derringer shoved back from his console and stood up. Then he realized that he had no idea where he was likely to go. He sat down again, staring at the screen. He wondered if he should call Phillip Catterly to announce Padgett-Smith's disappearance, then thought better of it. If she were not found today, there would be ample time to pass the word to her colleague in Maryland and her next of kin in Britain.

BALUCHISTAN PROVINCE

Dr. Carolyn Padgett-Smith awoke with a start. She did not know what had stirred her, but the knowledge came edging up with the gray dawn. *I did sleep after all.*

It had been a hard night, literally and figuratively. Though the rocky depression was mostly out of the wind, there was no way to get comfortable in her stony sanctuary. She scooted her bottom across the hard, flat surface and heard a faint ripping sound. She knew immediately that her favorite Gore-Tex parka had torn again but she barely gave a thought to the 180 Pounds she had invested in it. Her hideout was full of snags, and another ripstop hole could hardly matter.

The crest was growing more discernable in the faint light, but most of the hill remained hidden in shadow. With her knees drawn up, she realized that her pistol had fallen between her feet. She retrieved it and laid it beside her. In a little while the hillside below would become visible and she could deploy the Klimov.

Water. She realized that she was thirsty but she also wanted to rinse the night taste from her mouth. Having no canteen, she put the thought out of mind. As per her training and inclination, she reviewed yesterday's events, cataloging her list of errors. *I was such a twit. I wanted to keep up with the young men so I put most of my kit on the mule. Damn it! I know better than that! In terrain like this you always, always keep water and some rations on you. Imbicile. Idiot. Twit.*

She began wondering what she would say to Lee and the others— assuming they found her. *No, stop it, Carolyn! Figure what you will say when they find you.*

Breezy. His short description of the gunshot signal forced its way to the front of her consciousness. She had not thought of it since beginning her climb last evening. She risked a glance around the corner of her hideout, trying to see into the narrow path below. It was still dark. She decided that when she could see the trail she would fire the shots, evenly spaced. Undoubtedly the SSI team would be looking for her by then.

Undoubtedly.

BALUCHISTAN PROVINCE

Kassim was taking no chances. False foot or not, he led the impromptu band of fighters toward the scene of the previous evening's firefight. He had neither requested permission from Ali nor informed him. Sometimes a leader had to lead from the front.

The point man came across the spot where the infidels had been ambushed. He knelt down, as it was now light enough to read the evidence. Spent brass littered the ground, with occasional hoofprints where laden mules had left their mark. The soil was too hard in most places for mere humans to make an imprint.

The infidels had left the holy warriors' bodies in a row. At least there was no desecration, and someone—probably a Pakistani—had covered them with blankets and a tarp. The scout pulled back one corner to study the lifeless faces of his fellow *mujahadin*. He recognized only two. Mohammed and Weanus had fought at his side a time or two. The others were newer recruits. One appeared to be about fifteen. Now, all were honored in Paradise.

Kassim followed the point man by less than five minutes. When he appeared, they briefly consulted on the best course to follow. The scout, a twenty-six-year-old laborer named Dualeh, noted where two mules had run off, frightened by the sudden gunfire. The third emerged from the hard ground onto a softer path, obviously walking rather than running. A few bootprints indicated that the animal had been under human control.

"This way," Dualeh said.

The twelve men began following the trail northeasterly, keeping intervals with flankers on each side, according to Kassim's orders.

A single gunshot split the crisp morning air.

The hunters stopped in place, then spread half and half to each side of the trail, rifles pointed uphill. They were somewhat slow, but Kassim was pleased with their response. A little training could go a long way.

Another shot. Kassim thought that it was a pistol. Somewhere behind them.

About one minute passed. A third shot, then nothing.

Kassim turned to Dualeh. "That is no coincidence. It must be some kind of signal." Without waiting, the Syrian jogged to the rear of the column, his awkward gait evident but of little hindrance. He shouted, *"Aana!"* Come! The others turned to follow their leader, now up front again.

———

Half a kilometer northeast, Steve Lee and Rustam Khan heard a faint sound. Abruptly they stopped and listened. Bosco and Breezy were close behind. Bosco asked, "What's up, dude?"

Breezy raised a hand for silence. He heard the next pop and checked his watch.

Sixty-one seconds later another shot cracked out, ringing off a canyon wall. Breezy paced the distance to Lee. "Sir, that's gotta be her. Remember? I told her to cap off three rounds a minute apart."

Lee regarded Mr. Brezyinski with newfound respect. *Maybe he's not such a juvenile delinquent after all.* "All right, you convinced me. We'll hustle off that way with six of us. The rest will stay here with the mule and the casualties."

Breezy asked, "Should we shoot three in reply?" As soon as he spoke, he realized the answer.

"Negative, Brezyinski. There could be hostiles out there. No point in telling them where we are. Besides, she'll repeat the signal in ten mikes, right?"

"Uh, yessir."

Lee turned briefly to face his team. "Combat check, gentlemen. Round chambered, safety on, drop your rucks. We may have to move fast."

Lee, Khan, Breezy, Bosco, Hendricks, and O'Neil set a quick pace with the rising sun at their backs.

———

Padgett-Smith waited nine minutes, then hefted the pistol again. She was disappointed in hearing no response but realized that her friends might not be within earshot yet.

Once again she ran the math. With ten rounds remaining she could fire the three-shot signal for thirty more minutes with one round left. *Save the last one for yourself*, she gloomed. Then she looked down at the shorty AK, mindful that it held thirty more rounds. At that moment, how any female could object to firearms was far, far beyond her.

She held her watch close, waited the final minute, and raised the Browning once more.

———

Another shot echoed off the rocks. Dualeh walked forward while Kassim raised a hand, signaling a stop. Again his men deployed to either side of the road, forming a rude skirmish line. Kassim thought to look at his wristwatch. He seldom gave much thought to time—it was either a precious gift or a useful commodity, depending upon circumstances. He had experienced events in which men literally lived a lifetime in a few ticks of the clock—and the celestial sweep hand came to an abrupt stop.

He had also witnessed strong men praying aloud to their deity for time to end.

However, there were occasions when one badly wanted chronological precision. Coordinating troop movements or noting the routine of guard changes could be most useful. In this instance, he thought he discerned a pattern. He stood to one side of the path, watching his Russian timepiece. The second shot came approximately sixty seconds after the first.

The third was exactly on schedule.

Dualeh was facing southwesterly, his educated ears sensing the compass arc of the gunshots. He raised his AK's muzzle and said, "This way, brother." Then he was jogging down the trail.

Kassim whistled to his men. He would lead them in a fast walk for the next several minutes, then stop to listen again.

———

Lee raised a hand. He sensed his five men kneeling in a semicircle behind him, weapons pointed outward. "You heard that?" he asked.

"Yes," Khan replied. Both men checked their watches. "She is punctual, this lady." He smiled beneath his well trimmed mustache. "Like clockwork."

Lee grunted in appreciation of the humor. It was not what he expected of most Pakistani officers, who in his experience tended toward the studious. The team continued walking, gaining more ground before the next two shots.

At the third round, Lee stopped again and raised his pocket binoculars. He knew he was still too far to see the doctor but he wanted a better idea of the terrain. More to himself than to Khan he said, "She'll probably be in the high ground where she can see us coming."

"Or them," Khan added.

With a start, Lee realized that CPS would have a hard time distinguishing friendlies from hostiles. Both sides dressed much alike and bore the same weapons. Without explaining, he broke into a trot, leaving the others to catch up.

———

Padgett-Smith capped her twelfth round thirty-eight minutes after the first. The sun was well up, but she had seen no indication of any people on the trail some 220 meters downslope. She holstered the Browning with its one remaining cartridge and picked up the AKS. She wondered how much of her precious ammunition she should continue expending with no result.

———

At the fourth set of shots, Kassim's searchers had closed the distance toward the English woman's rocky tor. His focus had increasingly been drawn to the most prominent overhang on the south side of the ravine. He turned to one of his men. "Koali, you speak English." It was a statement but was meant as a question.

Achmed Koali, an erstwhile engineering student, stepped forward. "Yes, brother."

"When they fire again, I will reply with three fast shots. You be prepared to call out."

"What shall I say?"

Kassim's face reddened in the slanting light. "Young fool! Just call to them. Ask where they are. Ask if they need assistance. Anything!"

Koali absorbed the mild rebuke with a nod and downcast eyes.

There they were!

Padgett-Smith caught the movement along the trail. Shadows appeared before the shapes of the men, their drab clothing blending with the surroundings. "Thank you, God!" she exclaimed aloud. She pointed the AK upward and fired three rounds spaced a few seconds apart.

Kassim stopped and turned his face upward to his left front. He could not see anyone but there was no doubt. The mysterious person or persons had to be somewhere near the military crest of the hill. He elevated his AKM and fired an identical response: three spaced rounds. Then he gestured to Koali.

The youngster raised a hand to his mouth. "Hello! Where are you?"

Padgett-Smith's pulse spiked. She raised herself from the cramped position and waved both arms over her head. "Up here! Up here!"

From barely a klick away, the Americans heard three shots followed by three more. Steve Lee turned to Rustam Khan. "Oh, shit." Both men took off at a dead run. The others pounded along behind them.

"Let them come to us," Kassim said.

He deployed his men in a skirmish line, prepared to meet the strangers with numbers and firepower in his favor. Once the shooter or shooters emerged into the open he would have a much better idea of what he faced. Meanwhile, his men would have the advantage of cover. One or two of the fighters—new to the trade—showed an edgy mixture of eagerness and tension. They knew what had happened the previous evening and Kassim resolved to keep an eye on them.

One figure emerged from the outcrop near the crest. With irritating slowness it made its way downward in a cautious, tentative descent that piqued the Syrian. He realized that if this person belonged to the Americans—which seemed nearly certain—the others would be looking for him. They undoubtedly would have heard the gunshots and were likely to appear from any quarter. Kassim made an adjustment to his perimeter, turning his flankers to face outward.

Padgett-Smith reached a short stretch of almost level ground. She stopped a moment to get her bearings, as the easier way down took her angling away from the men below. She looked at them while inhaling, allowing her heart to settle down.

Something was odd.

The numbers were about right, but she could not identify anyone. From 180 meters faces were indistinguishable, but after weeks with SSI she knew the men's stance; their tactical moves. She tried to pick out Steve Lee or Breezy Brezyinski. She could not.

There were no mules.

Chasing a runaway mule had got her stranded all night, but surely at least one of the animals would have been caught by now. Wouldn't it want to rejoin its friends or masters?

She felt a coldness descending upon the original flush of hope.

Cupping both hands to her mouth, she carefully called out. "Who . . . are . . . you?" The words rebounded off the rock wall.

Kassim turned to Koali. "What did he say?"

The youngster shook his head. "I cannot tell."

"Well, reply to him. Tell him to come down."

Koali turned and shouted back. "Come to us. Quickly!"

Padgett-Smith heard the man's tone better than his words. She looked to both sides, hoping for more familiar figures that did not appear. At least the people below spoke English. She proceeded slowly down the slope, keeping her Klimov slung around her neck; she would stay outside of easy shooting distance until she knew more about the armed men below.

Kassim was not pleased; the process was taking too long. He glanced at his men and noted more signs of nervousness. New recruits that they were, the youngest *mujahadin* realized their exposed position along the trail.

Kassim gestured to Koali. "Take one man and go meet this infidel. Tell him you are looking for some missing Americans."

The former engineering student called to a partner and took a quick pace uphill. He stopped occasionally to wave in friendly fashion to the stranger, calling generic greetings.

Padgett-Smith allowed the two men to get within eighty meters—she thought it one hundred. *That's close enough.* She stopped beside a four-foot boulder that afforded good cover. "Who are you?" she shouted again.

Koali heard the words more clearly this time. It was odd: the voice was almost feminine. He raised his hands to his mouth. "Pakistani Army. Searching for the Americans."

———

CPS was taken aback. The response made sense—surely Lee or Khan would have called for help. But the apparent rescuers were dressed like tribesmen. Why no uniforms? And they mostly carried Kalashnikovs instead of the Heckler-Kochs she had seen with Paki troops.

She backpedaled uphill, working behind the boulder while unslinging her rifle and extending the folding stock. "One of you. Come closer!"

Koali spoke to his friend, who dropped into a shallow defile. Keeping his own weapon pointed low, the erstwhile engineer walked within fifty meters of the stranger.

"That's far enough!" she shouted. Now he was certain. *She.*

The young Pakistani thought fast. "Please come. It is dangerous here."

"Who . . . are . . . you . . . looking . . . for?"

"Americans. Missing from last night."

"Who . . . are . . . their . . . leaders?"

Koali heard the question plainly. He shook his head, playing for time. "I do not understand."

She knew this game could last indefinitely. If they were hostile, it would give the others time to get behind her. She called, "Drop your weapon and come closer."

Koali looked back toward Kassim, who stood with obviously

growing impatience. The young man laid down his AK and walked forward.

At thirty meters he could see her face. Quite an attractive face.

"Stop there," she said.

He raised his hands. "Lady, please come. No time."

"If you're from the army, why don't you wear uniforms?"

Koali was quick on his feet. "We are special unit. No uniforms."

That seemed barely plausible. But if the searchers were looking for SSI people, some names would be known. "Who leads the Americans?"

"I do not know. My leader knows."

"Then who is the Pakistani officer with them?"

Koali shook his head. "I do not know. But please. Come." He gestured in a friendly manner.

Keep him talking. "Then go to your leader. Come back with the name of the American or Pakistani officer."

With little option, Koali bowed politely, turned and walked downhill, retrieving his AK-47 along the way. His partner remained in place.

"What is happening?" Kassim asked.

"She wants to know the name of . . ."

"*She?*"

"Yes, yes. A woman."

"English?" Kassim demanded.

Koali thought for a moment. "Probably."

Kassim looked uphill nearly 150 meters where the lone figure stood behind the rock. "Allah be praised. The doctor will have his wish."

"She does not believe we are with the army. She wants me to tell the name of the infidel leaders we seek."

The Syrian paid tacit tribute to the British woman's caution. This was no trusting female to be cajoled or bullied. "Return to her. Say that headquarters knows the names but our radio is in a truck nearby. Say that al Qaeda fighters are in the area. We will escort her to safety or we must leave."

As Koali turned to go, he heard Kassim giving orders to three men. "Keep low but work uphill behind that boulder. The doctor wants her alive."

Come on, come on, you twit. Padgett-Smith mentally urged the young Pakistani to walk faster. She realized the incongruity: the longer she stalled the men below, the more time for Lee and Khan to find her. But the tension grated on her.

At length the Pakistani was back in talking distance, carrying his AK muzzle low. "Lady, my leader he does not have names. We can call on radio in truck." He gestured vaguely to the east. "We call when you come down."

A thought pushed its way to the front of her mind. "Who is *your* leader?"

The sharp, unexpected question caught Koali off guard. "What?"

"I said . . . who is your leader?"

Koali was nonplussed. He decided to take the path of least resistance. "He is Kassim."

"What rank?"

"Rank?"

"Yes, rank, you clot! Sergeant, lieutenant? What rank in the army?"

"Oh, he is . . . captain."

"Captain Kassim."

"Yes, yes. Please, lady. Come."

Not bloody likely. Padgett-Smith flicked her safety to semi-auto. "Thank you for your offer. I believe I will stay here."

Koali had enough of the foreign woman's damnable games. He took two steps closer. "You come! You must come! Danger here!"

She kept her voice clear and firm. "No. I will stay."

The gunman felt his hackles rising. "Woman! Enough! You must come!" He started uphill.

Padgett-Smith raised the Klimov's muzzle and placed the front sight on the man's chest. "Go away."

Koali had been shot at but never threatened by a female, armed or otherwise. His eyes went saucer-wide as the 5.45mm bore seemed to expand to 12-gauge diameter. Reflexively, he raised his own AK.

His guardian, still crouched in the depression fifty meters downslope, saw the apparently deadly pantomime. He responded as a fighting comrade would.

The first 7.62 round snapped past Padgett-Smith's head, eight inches left. Frightened and angry, her own reflexes kicked in. She pressed her trigger twice.

———

Lee's team heard the first three shots. After that, the hillside a few hundred meters ahead of them erupted with gunfire.

The SSI men deployed into a skirmish line and advanced as fast as the contradictory concerns of urgency and prudence dictated.

———

For the first time, Carolyn Padgett-Smith had made a life or death decision on behalf of herself. She briefly registered the fact that she felt coolly detached after shooting the young man with whom she had conversed. Then she was concerned with his partner, firing at her position from fifty meters downslope. The incoming fire from the group on the trail did not immediately bother her; it was rapid and ill directed.

Kassim hobbled on his prosthesis, trying to control his men's fire. The distance was greater than normal and about thirty degrees uphill. He hoped that at least it would pin the she-devil to her boulder, allowing his flankers to gain position. He sent two more men wide to the right. He knew that the two teams might shoot one another, but it was worthwhile if it delivered the female scientist to Dr. Ali.

Though relatively safe from frontal fire, CPS realized that she was vulnerable on both sides. *If I go back uphill, they can shoot at me in the open. But if I stay here they'll surround me.* She leaned out the left side of the rock and fired two rounds at the nearest gunman. Then, keeping the rock between herself and the shooters, she scampered uphill toward the next defensible position.

Dodging left and right, hearing rounds cracking past her and ricocheting off rocks, Padgett-Smith flopped into a depression sixty meters above her previous site. She tried to control her breathing, knowing she was doing a poor job. Fear aggravated the physical effort of running uphill, spoiling her concentration. She knew that the ammunition remaining in her rifle was as important as the blood in her veins: the curved magazine was growing lighter as she fired cautionary shots at vague figures even as her lungs experienced oxygen debt. She breathed in mouths full of mountain air, willing her heart to settle down.

A round snap-cracked from the right front, farther downslope. She looked over the top of her berm, trying to spot the shooter. He was well hidden. Her focus swung back to her previous boulder, where she thought that the English speaker's partner might appear. So far he remained out of sight.

I'm so . . . winded. But can't stay here. Must reach my night position. Last stand there. With an athlete's ego, she willed herself onto her feet and moved again.

————

Kassim was almost livid. The men he had sent uphill to flank the English woman were acting like females themselves. Whenever she fired at them, the fighters went to earth. The uphill chase was taking far too long. He had to move two men to his rear to watch for the Americans who must have heard the shooting by now.

————

Padgett-Smith reached her goal with seventeen rounds to spare. Sliding beneath the rocky outcropping, she almost felt at home. Though she had never heard the term, she had chosen the military crest of the hill—the last defensible position before the physical peak. The overhang that had helped keep the wind away meant that the pursuers could not shoot at her from behind. They would have to approach from the front or sides, where she had a decent view from sixty to ninety meters.

Kassim's two flanking teams converged on the outcrop from left and right. They had no way of coordinating their movements but realized that while one group fired at the woman's position, the other could advance.

It worked—up to a point. The teenager rushing forward from her left was as healthy as he was young, and he dashed straight uphill toward a protected position.

Padgett-Smith swung on him, got three seconds' tracking time, and pressed the trigger. The boy took an A-zone hit below the notch of the sternum and went down hard, his spine broken. For an instant

he raised his head and the enemies locked eyes. From thirty-five meters the British doctor saw the Pakistani youngster mouthing unheard
words. Then he went limp.

The boy's death affected Kassim's flankers in different ways. Of
the four remaining, three were enraged and one grief stricken. The
trio kept firing at the infidel's position but she had proven herself:
they had to respect the threat. The fourth sobbed aloud, repeatedly
calling his brother's name.

By alternating rushes, the three effective fighters tried to gain a
favorable angle on the flanks. Each time one of them appeared, the
English woman fired single shots, halting the advance or forcing a
move to cover.

During a lull, CPS withdrew the rifle's magazine. She saw three
rounds, with one in the chamber.

Plus the salvation round in the pistol. Then she had a dreadful
thought: *What if it's a dud?*

No time to speculate. The *mujahadin* were moving again. She focused on her front sight as Tony had drummed into her so long, long
ago at Credenhill. She decided to ignore the bullet impacts on the
surrounding rocks. Two men were rushing her at once. She put her
sight on the nearest one and fired twice. He ducked or dropped; she
couldn't tell. She swung on the other. He was so close. She fired once,
twice, and felt the bolt lock back.

Carolyn Padgett-Smith dropped the AKS and grabbed her
Browning, knowing what she needed to do.

What if it's a dud?

A sonic wave swept uphill from the trail: a surging, roiling volume of
gunfire.

Lee's team arrived within range of the al Qaeda men with mixed
assets: good position, almost equal numbers, plenty of ammo, and
short of breath.

Kassim's rear guard had seen them coming, fired several hasty
shots, and dashed back to the trail. The Syrian was turning his remaining force to confront the newcomers when aimed 7.62 fire began re-
ducing his numbers. Two men dropped almost immediately. Another

scrambled down the trail; had there been time Kassim would have shot him in the back.

With a hostile force of unknown size behind him, Kassim recognized a no-win setup. He organized a fighting withdrawal, leap-frogging his remaining men into the rocks and boulders on the near side of the trail with a steep dropoff. He cast a longing glance uphill where the English woman had held out so long. *May Satan take her.* His men up there would have to fend for themselves. Then he was gone.

———

Bosco and Breezy had plopped into hasty prone positions as soon as they had targets. Like everyone else, they were out of breath but at sixty to eighty meters, they made good use of the steady position. It was over in seconds. Hendricks, the least fit of the military athletes, felt jilted: trailing by forty meters, he never got a shot.

Khan took Blake, pursuing the *mujahadin* to the rim of the trail. Once the fighters were over the lip, they could slide and roll downhill for a few hundred meters. There was no point pursuing.

Lee had his binoculars out, scanning the uphill slope. "I don't see any . . . wait!" He pointed to a prominent boulder about eighty meters away. "Looks like a body there. You, you, you—check it out. Search to the top if you have to."

Bosco, Breezy, and O'Neil eagerly complied. They began the climb, calling for Carolyn Padgett-Smith.

———

Bosco was back twenty minutes later, carrying an AKS. He handed it to Lee. "Sir, this was in the den near the crest. Lots of brass and two *muj.* One dead, one crippled. Breezy's working on him. No sign of her."

Sick at heart, Lee accepted the Klimov, noting that the magazine was empty. *She didn't want to carry a reload.* He nodded glumly, then turned to Khan. "Major, I suggest that we search the reverse slope. She might have gone downhill from the top."

Khan tweaked his mustache. "Of course, we should look. But we may still be outnumbered, and our force is divided. I suggest that we send a runner to bring the others here in case the terrorists regroup. The med-evac helicopter should have picked up our casualties by now."

Lee considered his colleague's argument and decided it made sense. "Very well. Can you contact Quetta and request one or both of our Hips?"

"Surely, Major. It shall be done."

Lee sat on a flat boulder and gathered his thoughts. He was still fighting the queasiness in his gut—the gnawing thought that he may have lost Dr. Carolyn Padgett-Smith. *Damn freaking stupid thing to do—bring a civilian female out here. What in hell was Frank thinking?* He caught himself. *Hell, what was I thinking?*

He pulled his canteen and took a long gulp of water. Whatever happened, he was going to taste something stronger back at base.

BALUCHISTAN PROVINCE

Three SSI operators spent nearly an hour combing the crest of the hill, easing their way down the far slope. They called frequently for Padgett-Smith, but got no response.

By the time Terry Keegan arrived in Helo One, the searchers were looking on the reverse slope. In order to coordinate the rescue effort, he landed briefly on the crest and the crew chief handed out two radios with frequencies compatible with the Hip's gear. Then Keegan pulled pitch, lifted off, and pedal-turned down the face of the slope.

Lee, belatedly arriving at the crest, keyed his mike. "One, this is Lee. Copy?"

"Copy, Major."

"Say status Helo Two. Over."

Keegan's voice crackled in the handset. "En route in three-zero . . . make that two-zero mikes. Hydraulic problem. Over."

"Ah, roger that. Status of our casualties?"

"Dustoff was inbound when we took off, sir. Over."

Lee double-clicked to end the discussion. He turned to Khan. "The med-evac flight was about to land when Keegan left Quetta. Hip Two should be here in twenty minutes or so."

———

Keegan slowed to forty knots and surveyed the terrain before him. He assumed that Dr. Padgett-Smith would take the easiest route downhill—assuming she went that way—and planned his search pattern accordingly. His Pakistani copilot used a colored pen to trace the Hip's flight path, avoiding duplicate effort when Marsh arrived.

Ten minutes later the noncommissioned crew chief pointed to the right and called over the intercom. "Sir, what is that?"

Keegan turned to the heading and saw what he saw. Closing to one hundred meters, he gave a huge grin behind his lip mike. "Lee, this is Hip One. Over."

"Ah, copy."

"Call in your dudes, Major. I'm returning with Charlie Poppa Sierra."

———

Padgett-Smith got out of the helo and walked briskly to the edge of the crest. She pulled her Browning, pointed it downhill, and pressed the trigger. The Hi-Power recoiled and the slide locked back. She holstered the empty pistol and looked at Steve Lee. There were tears on her dirty cheeks and a grim smile on her lips. "I just had to know . . ."

Lee wrapped his arms around her and felt her start to tremble. "I know, Carolyn. I know."

He hadn't a clue.

SSI OFFICES

Sandy Carmichael read the email first. She emitted an Alabama shriek and dashed out of her office, bound for the board room.

"They found her! Padgett-Smith is alive!"

Derringer, Wolf, and some others turned in their padded chairs. Carmichael logged the different responses. Smiling broadly, the admiral pounded his right fist into his left palm. Joe Wolf crossed himself and briefly bowed his head. Everyone else hollered and congratulated one another.

Derringer broke in: "Sandy, what happened?"

"Well, sir, there's an email from Frank. He'll send an after-action report but here's the short version. After the ambush last night, Dr. Smith found some high ground and stayed put. At dawn she started firing a prearranged signal. But the al Qaeda gang got to her first. Evidently there was quite a firefight. She held them off for quite a while and even killed a couple."

"You go, girl!"

Carmichael turned to see Sallie Ann at the door. She had heard the excitement.

Derringer and Wolf exchanged knowing male glances. Nobody needed to state the obvious: two women affiliated with SSI now had shot for blood. The admiral made a mental note to caution his colleagues against making too much of that fact. Male *or* female.

"Anyway," Carmichael continued, "she was out of ammo so she ran down the far slope of the mountain. That was when Steve Lee's team arrived. They chased off the terrorists, and Terry Keegan lifted them back to base."

Wolf spoke for many in the room. "I don't care if I have to buy a ticket to London. I want to meet that lady."

The sentiment was widely shared as the meeting disintegrated into animated conversation. Derringer decided to let it go for a while. Leaning back, both hands beneath his chin, he mused about the situation. *Was it a good idea to take a woman into the field? Was it worth the risk? What if we'd lost her?*

At length, he decided not to second-guess his field commander from the comfort of the nation's capital. *That's how we screwed up Vietnam.* But he was grateful that he could now pass good news to Phil Catterly, to say nothing of Charles Padgett-Smith.

As he watched his effusive staffers, Michael Derringer defaulted to his commanding officer programming. Yes, there was reason for gratitude, but not for celebration. In a way, the operation was similar to so many Vietnam episodes: a mission with a specific purpose had turned into an SAR exercise. The search-and-rescue phase was successful but the enemy was still out there—still undetected. He had been engaged and defeated tactically, but the strategic objective remained unmet.

We'll have to try again.

BALUCHISTAN PROVINCE

Ali was happy to see Kassim.

And angry.

"I told you not to go," the doctor intoned. "You defied me."

Kassim was prepared. "In fact, Doctor, you prohibited me from the first operation, not the second."

Ali grunted, acknowledging the truth of the matter but mentally sneering at the lawyerly evasion. "You were devilishly lucky to escape, Kassim. I have told you that I cannot spare you. I do not expect it to happen again."

The veteran fighter accepted the mild rebuke with a slightly bowed head. Two seconds later he locked eyes. "We were within meters of her, Doctor! Meters!"

"The men we lost would have been worthwhile had they seized her, but they did not. What do you make of that?"

"It was not a lack of courage or desire, Doctor. The woman chose her position well. We would have needed twice as many men at the crest to kill or capture her."

That was not quite true. Kassim knew that if he had been at the peak, he might have directed a successful enfilade. Given the strength of her position, it would have been difficult to capture her, but at least she would have been dead.

The Syrian was not given to self-pity for the foot he left in Afghanistan. But once in awhile he had reason to rue its loss.

Kassim decided to change the subject. "Doctor, what should we do now?"

Ali sat back and sipped his tea. "I have been thinking of your friend—Sial? It is time for me to meet him and his son and nephew."

"I shall arrange it."

Ali called after his colleague. "Kassim! It must be done quickly. We may havè little time, and I must arrange for travel plans and documents."

Kassim knew from experience that the doctor seldom allowed himself to be overtaken by events. Most likely the passports were already forged, only awaiting the couriers' photographs and signatures. As for airlines, Ali frequently made contingency reservations just to keep options open. It was a simple matter to cancel or provide alternative passengers as a continuing check on security measures.

Few opportunities were ever lost, if one knew how to exploit them.

QUETTA

Leopole knocked on the door at the Serena Hotel, a four-star establishment in the cantonment area. Briefly he wondered at Omar's largesse in lodging CPS in such luxurious digs, but the onetime marine could not begrudge the Briton a couple of nights to recover. There was certainly no lack of dining options: a Chinese restaurant, barbeque, and coffee shop.

Proper ladies did not dine alone, so tonight Leopole had the duty.

The door opened and CPS smiled broadly. "Frank. Please come in."

He returned the grin. "Wow. If I may say so, Doctor, you slick up really nice."

She stepped back and let him in. "Well, thank you, Colonel. Of course, a black dress does contrast with baggy trousers and a vest."

Leopole fingered his blue blazer. "I only brought this because I thought I might have to meet with some defense ministry people." He laughed. "I can't remember the last time I wore a tie. Must've been a wedding or a funeral."

Padgett-Smith pondered the American's appearance. His beard was gone but the mustache remained, and his haircut, while not high and tight, screamed "military." She had learned that some men appeared uniformed regardless of what they wore. Like Tony.

Tony. What a story I shall have for him!

"Carolyn, I'd like to talk to you just a bit before we go down to dinner."

She sat on the sofa. "Surely." She knew what was coming.

He sat opposite her, across the glass table, and leaned forward, hands clasped on his knees. "I don't want to discuss company business in the restaurant, so it's best done here." He cleared his throat. She thought: *He's nervous.*

"Carolyn, do you really want to stay with us?"

She blinked. "You mean, complete my assignment?"

"Yes."

"Well . . . of course I do! Why wouldn't I?"

Leopole spread his hands—a helpless male gesture. "After what you've been through, and no end in sight, I just wondered if you'd like to be released from your contract."

"No, of course not." She recalled the conversation that had gotten her what she wanted—at rock bottom, a chance to be shot at. "Frank, what I said before was based on a lack of activity. As I see it, we're closer now than ever."

He nodded decisively. One time. "Okay, you've got it. I'll inform HQ."

"Thank you. Now, may I ask you something?"

He shrugged. "Shoot."

"Frank, I deeply appreciate all this." She waved a hand at the well-appointed room. "It's marvelous to have a real bath and tuck up in a big, soft bed. But I was reluctant to accept Omar's offer because . . ."

"Because none of the operators got a couple of days here."

She nodded. "And I'm sensitive as a woman receiving preferential treatment."

"Okay, I can understand that. So why'd you accept?"

The corners of her mouth turned up, and he admired Dr. Padgett-Smith's dimples. "Because I'm a woman who accepts preferential treatment now and then."

"Carolyn, if I read you correctly, you're worried that you might lose some of your trust and good will with my door-kickers."

"Exactly. I mean, I made such a good start, and then . . . well, I made such a shambles of things out there. We didn't come close to completing the mission." She bit her lip. "Because of me."

Leopole leaned back against the cushion. He almost called her "honey." Instead, he intoned, "Carolyn, let me tell you something. The mission went away the minute we were ambushed. It was a risky operation from the start: we knew that. Hell, I think *you* knew that."

She swallowed hard, assembling her thoughts. "Yes, I thought so, too. And I should have done. But I learned the difference between intellectual knowledge of what's possible, and the visceral knowledge that comes . . ." She inhaled.

He knew.

She swallowed again. Outwardly she was composed, those violet eyes steady and focused. But no words came.

Okay, I'll finish it for you, babe. "That comes with combat."

She looked down, nodding slowly. "Yes."

He risked a touch on her arm. "Carolyn, everybody feels that way. Everybody. Well, just about. I've known a couple of guys who really were fearless. But they were abnormal. Down deep, they didn't care if they lived or died." He squeezed her forearm. "You feel like you do because you have so much to live for."

She looked up. "Thank you, Frank. I tried talking to Steve and Omar but . . . it was hard, you know?"

"Well, sometimes it takes awhile to get it out. My god, Carolyn. Some people never get it out. They spend the rest of their lives second-guessing themselves or indulging in survivor's guilt. So don't you ever feel you've got to be strong all the time. Believe me, even Marines cry once in awhile."

"You know, I'm trying to decide how to explain all this to Charles. We talked for ninety minutes last night but I told him hardly anything about what really happened." She paused, then continued. "I wonder if I have it in me to go out again. But I don't want to let you down."

"Carolyn, whatever you decide, it'll be fine." On a hunch, he took a different tack. "There's something else. I mean, if you're worried about the guys and what they think. Consider the men you're working with. Most of them are professionals—full-time warriors. They have what I call the red meat attitude. Believe me—and don't take this wrong—but the fact that you notched three or four terrorists impresses the hell out of those boys." He decided not to relate what he'd overheard. *Hey, dude! Doc Smith's a killer babe!*

Padgett-Smith smiled inwardly. Odd, the terminology these friendly, violent men employed. Notched. Greased. Capped. Wasted. Hardly ever "killed."

She patted his hand. "Thank you. Again. I'll get my purse."

BALUCHISTAN PROVINCE

Kassim made the introductions.

The father was graying in a dignified way that impressed Ali, and they established an early rapport. It did not take the scientist long to push the boundaries of courtesy and address the reason for the meeting.

"Sir, I wish to thank you for your support of the *jihad*. Kassim has spoken your praises in such a way that surely you will be blessed."

Razak Sial nodded gravely. "Thank you, Doctor. Your own dedication to God's work and to the less fortunate has earned you a throne in Paradise."

Ali sensed something—what? Too early to tell; he bided his time.

"Before I speak with these young men, I would know more of them. Please tell me of their education and their devotion to The Word."

Sial tasted the doctor's tea again, then set down the cup. "My wife was a good woman who died too young. But she left me with four children of my own and her nephew. It was necessary for me to leave my family for a time and make a living as best I could . . . on the other side of the border."

"Yes, Kassim spoke of your service."

"When I returned from fighting the infidels, I was able to pay most of my debts and even to expand my herd. But, alas, honored doctor, the cost of raising a large family is always high." The farmer allowed the sentiment to dangle in midair.

Ali shot a glance at Kassim, occupied with the boys outside. *Does he know? Does he even suspect that this excuse for a man accepted money to fight God's enemies?* Ali suspected not, but the point would require clarification.

Sial continued. "Even though I was often absent, I saw to the boys' religious education, as their mother and aunt desired. These two are the most devout of my sons, and they wish to serve in the holy war, if only my family can work without them." Ali's pulse spiked briefly. His reservoir of goodwill was rapidly draining. *So! The old goat will sacrifice two of his kids for the benefit of the herd—and himself.*

"And what would you require to complete the boys' transition to sacrificial warriors?"

Razak Sial spread his calloused hands in a move so fluid and emotive that it seemed rehearsed. "Doctor, I would not deem it worthy of myself to name a cost. Surely the value of two young lives is measured in more than rupees."

You shrewd bastard. Place the burden on me. Ali thought for a moment, then said, "For the worth of two fine young men, whose service will be brief, I suggest the working wages of five years each—a value of ten years labor."

In the rude hut overlooking the valley, thus were two souls purchased. They were delivered in the living bodies of Hazrat Sial and Miam Ahmed.

PART

III

BALUCHISTAN PROVINCE

Ali was pleased with his purchase.

The older boy, Sial's son Hazrat, was the more devout. Obviously he had given some thought to what was expected of him. "Doctor, The Word prohibits us from suicide, does it not?"

The veterinarian was well versed on the subject. "Truly. *Surah An-Nisaa, Aayah* 29 says, 'And do not kill yourselves. Surely, Allah is Most Merciful to you.' Furthermore, a noted scholar said that one who intentionally kills himself will suffer the Fire of Hell. However, most of our warriors are already fatally stricken. They will die regardless of what happens, which is why I have selected them."

"But, Doctor . . ."

"But you are different, my brothers. You have chosen to die while you still may live." He smiled benevolently. "Yours is the shortest and truest path to Heaven."

Sial mused upon that information and seemed satisfied. "Have others done so?"

Without mentioning the American, Ali cited an example of those who chose self-destruction. "Only one other, and he came to us from a foreign land."

The twenty-year-old farmer had a good mind for such an apparently simple boy. "But he—and we ourselves—have chosen our end. Therefore, how do we attain Heaven?"

The veterinarian was well versed on that point. "There is scholastic evidence that one who sacrifices himself in a *jihad* may be accepted into Paradise. The choice was Brother Ibrahim's, for example. Because he chose to die in our cause, I believe it is nothing against the rest of us."

Ahmed, reticent by nature, ventured a question. "Doctor, can you tell me—tell us—how our sacrifice will serve the holy war?"

Ali almost smiled. A naïve question from a naïve young man. "We are blessed to participate in the origins of this *jihad*. None but God knows where it may lead, but we may feel kinship with those who brought The Faith to the doorstep of the Crusaders and abided in Spain for eight hundred years. May our efforts lead to success so that eight centuries from now, the true faith will have spread over the earth."

Enough philosophizing for now, he told himself. *Let us address the main points.* "You know what is required of you?" He looked both young men full in the face.

Ahmed nodded solemnly. Sial almost smiled.

"There must be no doubt. Say it!"

"To sacrifice ourselves in the *jihad*, and with our deaths inflict a greater loss upon the enemies of The Faith."

Very good, young man! Ali was so impressed that he neglected to pursue the question with the younger man. He took each by the right hand in turn, welcoming them to the holy war. "My brothers, permit me to explain how you will ascend to Paradise."

BALUCHISTAN PROVINCE

"That's gotta be the place." Foyte glassed the farm from a safe distance, noting the layout of the house, sheds, and pens. "Goats and some other animals. The VW bus also fits the description." He passed the Zeiss to Lee, who adjusted the focus.

"No visible security, Gunny. You'd think they would have a sentry. At least a rover."

Foyte completed his range card and closed the olive drab notebook. "I don't think many places around here have generators, but that one does. You can hear it running. We'll talk to Major Khan and see what he says, but I think this is our target."

Both men bellied down the shallow hummock and jogged the quarter mile back to the dirt road.

Foyte and Lee returned to the staging area and convened a meeting with the rest of the brain trust. Leopole conducted the session but deferred to Foyte, who explained the layout based on his sketch and laser distances.

Leopole turned to Khan. "Major, what's your assessment? Is this likely Sharif's place, and if not, will we alert him if we break in there?"

"It is unusual for a small farm to have a generator, and the vehicle looks promising. Therefore, I believe it is his current location," Khan said in his precise English. "But we should not act hastily. There is a way to confirm if he is there."

"Yes?"

Khan tugged at his uniform shirt. "I will change into my peasant garb. I can stop there and ask for 'Doctor Ali' on behalf of 'my' animals. Even if he is not there, the other people may have information." He shrugged. "It should do no harm and may save us time and effort."

Leopole looked toward Foyte and Lee, who both nodded.

"Major, I like it."

Khan stood up. "I should return in less than sixty minutes."

———

Lee poked his head in the rude doorway. "Khan is back."

The SSI leaders crowded around the Pakistani as he stepped inside the building that served as temporary headquarters. He nodded decisively. "He has been there most of the day. He was called away shortly before I arrived but he is expected this evening."

Mohammed interjected. "How will we know if he's back? We cannot risk going before he returns."

Khan took a swig of bottled water and replaced the cap. "He is driving his van with the refrigerator unit. He keeps veterinary medicine in it, so we will wait for him to complete his rounds."

Leopole inhaled, held his breath, then exhaled. "That's it, then. We go tonight. Briefing in three-zero mikes."

At that, Leopole motioned to Lee. They walked several paces, then stopped. "Steve, who's your rear entry team?"

"Ashcroft, Green, Henderson, Jacobs, Olsen, and Pace."

Leopole thought for a moment. "Okay. Ashcroft and Green are top shooters, though I think Green's slightly nuts." He shrugged. "But that's okay with me if it's okay with you. Henderson and Jacobs are solid; Olsen and Pace seem pretty laid back." He looked his old comrade in the eye. "We just don't need any hotdogging on this job. There's too much at stake."

"Yes, sir, I know. And so do they."

––––––––

The briefing began before sundown. Thirty operators crowded the building where Leopole had set up an easel with a blackboard. He preferred a modern whiteboard that accepted different colors, but that might draw attention. Besides, he could still erase the briefing points and wash the board clean of any residual markings.

"People, this is why we came. This is what our friends died for." He took time to scan the room, taking in each man's face, reading the owner's demeanor. Most were impassive; two or three already had their game faces on. "One thing this is *not* is payback. We need the doctor alive and talking, and it may not be possible to pick him out of a crowd. So it's Roy Rogers time. If you have time, use a Taser. If not, shoot to disable if possible."

It was obvious that nobody liked the ROE, but most understood the need.

"For this mission to work, we need to surprise those people." He paused, then added, "No, that's not quite right. We need to *astonish* them. Here's how we'll do it: White Team is the entry team with Red on security. The Whites in the entry team will wear bio suits. You may not need 'em, but we just don't know what's in there."

Leopole turned to the blackboard. "Here's the setup. A small house with a couple of outbuildings and some stock pens. There are goats and sheep, and probably some dogs. Expect them to cause a ruckus. If we can get close enough without them smelling us, we'll use suppressed weapons to take them down. Otherwise, the security element will neutralize them as quickly as possible."

"We'll take a quick look at the situation before we deploy, but right now we don't expect many bad guys. Sharif doesn't seem to have much of an escort, apparently to avoid drawing attention to himself. You have his description. I wish we had a current photo but the sketch is close. He's tall, thin, late forties, reportedly with a full beard. Just remember that info may not be current. Things could have changed since Johnson saw him."

Leopole drew the perimeter he wanted. "Red, you'll deploy in a 360 around the farm, about hundred meters out. Even with part of White, that means a lot of open space between each man. But our bird may fly the coop, and if he gets out, we need to shortstop him ASAP."

Foyte raised a hand. "Colonel, I was discussing the arrangement with Major Lee. We risk friendly-fire casualties with the full-circle perimeter."

"I know, Gunny. But it's unavoidable. Besides, that's why you get the big bucks." Leopole waited for the perfunctory laughter to abate, then added, "If you have to shoot into the compound, try to hold low. That's the best we can do."

He turned back to the board. "Okay, whatever happens inside, we want to get out as quickly as possible. We'll take any prisoners by air to avoid interception in case they have backup in place. When I give the word, our primary bird will land here in the open just south of the house." He drew an X on the board and circled it. "It'll fly to a spot I've arranged with General Hardesty before returning to base. That way, any unfriendlies at Quetta won't see anything except night helo ops."

Breezy whispered to Bosco, who nudged him hard. The minor feud prompted Leopole to interject. "Something we need to hear, gentlemen?"

Breezy looked at the floor. "Ah, nosir."

Bosco shot his partner a frosty glance. He chose not to respond to

Breezy's observation that people accidentally fell out of helicopters all the time.

"Okay, one other thing," Leopole added. "If there's any reason to believe the house is a hot zone, we'll get the entry team out as soon as possible. At that point Dr. Padgett-Smith will look at the evidence and make a determination. We have some biosafe boxes to transport any cultures or other lab items. In the unlikely event there's more than we can handle, we'll notify the Pakistani Army, which will take over."

Padgett-Smith rose to speak for the first time. "Colonel Leopole, we may need decontamination measures."

"Yes, ma'am. The helos will bring in the equipment, including chlorine and portable pumps. We'll bag all suits and clothes and triple wrap them in the bags you brought, Doctor." She nodded and sat down.

Leopole erased the blackboard and dusted his hands of chalk. "Any more questions?"

There were none, as he expected. "Right. We have this one shot, gentlemen. Let's make it work."

BALUCHISTAN PROVINCE

"Maqsad and Badlah are ready, Doctor."

Ali looked up from the wood table. He was triple-checking the boys' travel documents when Kassim interrupted. Glancing at his watch, the veterinarian reflected that, as usual, his colleague was punctual. The timetable for transit to the departure point had been computed with forty minutes to spare.

The doctor tapped one of the passports upon the table. "Truly, I hope that they are ready, Kassim. This is the most complex plan yet. It requires some people we do not know to fill their part of the bargain in three other countries." He leaned toward his friend. "What do you think?"

The veteran shrugged. "The boys are as prepared as time has allowed. As for the others, I believe they will serve us through faith or money."

Ali nodded slowly, visualizing the young warriors abroad in a foreign, hostile land. "Yes, I would prefer another month of English language and instruction on travel and security procedures. I believe that Badlah will be satisfactory. Maqsad will rely heavily upon him."

Both men had taken to calling the recruits by their *noms de guerre*. It made for better security among the other cell members, let alone any strangers who may pass within earshot.

Kassim asked, "When do you expect them to start showing signs of the virus?"

"Based on the usual dormant period, no more than one week. However, Badlah's poor health may cause him to break out sooner than that. I would prefer it otherwise, as Maqsad will not function as well without his adopted brother to rely upon."

"It would be preferable to send them to different destinations, but I understand the need to keep them together."

"There are several things I would do differently, Kassim. But time is short. The Crusaders are certainly still hunting us. We would know if they had left Quetta. This may be our last opportunity to dispatch biological warriors against the Zionists, so we must do what we can while we can."

Kassim shifted his weight onto his good leg. "You believe they will find us?"

"Almost certainly. I am mildly surprised that we have not been betrayed from within." Ali raised a cautionary hand. "I mean no disrespect to any of your men, but it has always been a risk."

"Yes, I know."

Ali stood up. "We should send our couriers on their way with their message. When do you expect to return?"

Kassim had the schedule well in mind. "Probably no later than one in the morning. My contacts in Islamabad will inform me when both fighters have boarded their airplane. With two changes of vehicles and drivers, it should be nearly impossible for anyone to track the boys."

"Good. Then we only need wait two days before they board their plane."

"Yes, Doctor."

"Then let us send them on their way to Paradise."

BALUCHISTAN PROVINCE

Leopole checked his watch: 2317 on a night with a quarter moon. He keyed his mike. "Comm check. Three minutes."

"Red. Check."

"White. Check"

"Perimeter. Check."

With everyone in place, Leopole scanned the target area again. The landscape and buildings glowed crisply green in his night-vision scope. The Litton showed nothing moving except a couple of goats in a nearby pen. Then a movement caught his attention. A dog uncurled itself from a hay bale it had been using as a bed. It rose, lifted a leg . . . and stopped. Leopole froze. He realized that the wind had shifted; he felt it on the back of his neck.

The dog—a mutt of indeterminate origin—raised its snout and sensed the wind. Leopole made a quick decision. He called White Team's snipers. "White Scope, take the dog."

"Roger that." Furr's voice was subdued, controlled. Six seconds later Leopole saw the animal drop. The effect of the 190-grain flat-tail bullet was dramatic, as if a switch had been thrown. There was almost no sound as the eight-inch AWC can on the end of the barrel absorbed the violently expanding gases of the .308 round. One hundred thirty meters out, prone behind the Robar SR-90, Robbie Furr ran the bolt and recovered from recoil, his crosshairs on the dog's inert form. His spotter, Rick Barrkman, called the shot. "Shoulder, a little high."

Leopole resumed his observation, listening as much as looking. As his illuminated watch flicked over to 2320 he made the call. "Red and White. Go!"

White Team deployed quickly, ghosting along the ground, moving smoothly toward the front door. Red went to the rear. Leopole was mentally congratulating his operators on their efficiency when lights snapped on in the house. A window opened facing Leopole's overlook. He saw a man silhouetted there.

Gunfire erupted from the front and side of the house. Muzzle flashes competed with blue tracers slashing the darkness.

Things quickly turned to hash.

———

"Crusaders!"

The sentry would never have a chance to tell, but he had dozed off. However, when White Team's lead pair stepped through the rough gate in the rail fence, the motion detector betrayed them. Its audible warble awakened the al Qaeda guard from his light slumber, and he shouted the alarm.

Ali had been asleep in the back room. Almost simultaneous with the front warning, the rear approach's laser beam was broken as an American passed through it. Realizing that the house would be breached in at least two places, Ali rolled off his cot, grabbed his ancient .455 Webley, and dashed to the refrigerator. He took two syringes off the shelf, placing one in each vest pocket.

Silently, Ali gave thanks for the simple anti-intruder devices that Americans sold for less than twenty dollars.

Then he grabbed his cell phone and punched in the two-digit number for Kassim. Marvelous bit of technology—one had to hand it to the Americans. Speed dialing definitely had its advantages. For no particular reason, with gunfire all around him, rounds incoming and outgoing, Ali recalled a philosophical argument he once had with a fundamentalist imam. The holy man eschewed modern inventions, deeming them unworthy of The Prophet's followers.

But the Muslim priest had never needed reinforcements against hostile ghosts that could see in the dark.

―――――――

"Don't stop in the kill zone! Don't stop!" At the head of White Team, Breezy threw an M8 smoke grenade, knowing it would provide two minutes of screening from enemy view. The inevitable confusion had set in, however. Some men advanced without urging while others waited the order to keep moving. Breezy clapped one operator on the back of the helmet—he couldn't tell who it was in the dark—as the man was vulnerable in the open, even while prone. Breezy aimed short, crisp bursts at window height, moving his muzzle horizontally in an effort to suppress the fire from the house. He had no idea how he avoided being hit during the dash to the building.

Five meters out he dropped on his side and rolled against the exterior wall, right of the door. He dropped his near-empty magazine, tugged another from his vest, and fumbled the exchange. Finally he forced himself to look at the MP's mag well and completed the reload. A few feet away somebody was blasting with an AK. The muzzle flash was impressive, the high, sharp bark of the 7.62 rounds pained the ears.

Breezy decided against a three-foot shootout with the AK gunner. Instead, he lifted a cylindrical flash-bang from his harness, pulled the pin and let the spoon go. He counted one-potato, two-potato and made a sidearm toss on the third potato.

The stun grenade cooked inside for 1.5 seconds, then erupted like a miniature volcano. The flash—one million candela mixed with 175 decibels of sonic violence—blinded and stunned anyone within five feet.

The grenade burst with a concussive effect magnified by the building's walls. Gunfire from the front room immediately slackened. By then Delmore was beside Breezy. He shouted, "Cover!" Breezy hefted his MP, aimed at the window, and responded, "Covering!" Seconds later

Delmore slapped the charging handle with a palm-downward motion, chambering the first round off the fresh mag. "Ready!"

Sporadic gunfire resumed from inside the house. Several rounds punched through the wooden wall above their heads. More rounds splintered the boards on either side—additional suppressive fire from Leopole's perimeter team.

Breezy made the call. "Control, this is White. We're goin' in!"

Seconds dribbled past. Then Leopole's raspy voice was on the air. "Roger that. We're lifting our fires. Wait my word, over."

Breezy knew that the perimeter shooters would raise their aim points to reduce chances of friendly fire casualties. Then Leopole was back in his ears. "Red Team, ready, ready, ready. Go!"

———————

At the rear, Red Team met less resistance. Only two of Ali's men were stationed there, hosing long, optimistic bursts at the shadowy figures in the barnyard. Jeff Malten noticed that they were disciplined, however, alternating their shooting so that only one had to reload at a time. *They've done this before.*

Malten tossed a smoke grenade and prepared to lead his team to the rear door. He stood up to go, looked back—and saw Olsen take a hit and go down. Malten was momentarily stunned. *My god, where'd that come from?* Then he saw muzzle flashes from the small barn fifty meters to his left.

Pace low-crawled to Olsen and checked him. A .303 round had struck the ballistic chest plate near the bottom. Three inches lower and it would have hit flesh. Olsen was breathing hard, bruised but otherwise unhurt.

Malten made a snap decision. He motioned part of his team to deal with the unexpected threat from the barn. He watched as Ashcroft, Green, and Jacobs threw more smoke grenades and scrambled wide to the left. Henderson and Pace swapped gunfire with the shooters in the barn while Malten turned his attention back to the rear of the house.

The occupants of the barn expected a flanking movement and deployed to meet it. They nearly hit Jacobs but he had been a track man in school and sprinted across the open space left by the smoke.

When the three reached the rear of the barn, they quickly scouted the layout: there was no rear access. Ashcroft reloaded his G3 rifle and prepared to assault around the corner when Green grabbed him. "Never fight anybody when you can execute 'em."

"What?"

Green held up an M34 grenade, light green with a yellow band. He had been hoarding two of them since leaving Arlington. "Cover me."

With his friends watching left and right, Green dashed ten strides along the wooden wall and threw the white phosphorous grenade inside. Rather than dash back, he withdrew several steps, holding his rifle at shoulder height. Seconds later a garish white flash erupted inside, setting a smoky blaze that burned at five thousand degrees Fahrenheit. It spewed particles on the walls and roof, and in barely a minute half of the barn's dried wood was burning.

Green heard Ashcroft's HK around the corner. Three, four, five rounds. Jacobs swung that way to lend a hand, but it was unnecessary. Ashcroft held up his left hand, two fingers extended. "They ran out on this side. One of 'em was on fire."

Jacobs asked, "Where'd they go?"

Ashcroft pointed in reply. Twenty to thirty meters away lay two bodies, one smoldering.

Green reappeared, hefting his second grenade. "Damn!" Jacobs exclaimed. "I gotta get me some of them."

———

Between the barn and the house, Malten threw his last smoke, waited for the cloud to expand, and watched the suppressing fire drive the shooters from the windows. Then he led his half team to the rear of the house. Henderson placed a breaching charge on the door, twisted the dial for a quick fuse, and turned away. The small charge exploded with a loud, hollow noise, and the door swung on its hinges.

Pace tossed a flash-bang. So did Henderson. Malten was instantly inside, the others two steps behind. One of the shooters lay on the floor, rolling in pain from the horrific noise of the stun grenades. Malten kicked the man's AK away and watched the entrance to the next room. Henderson dragged the casualty outside where Pace secured him by the simple expedient of sitting on him.

The second shooter was deafened by the grenades, but retained most of his vision. Kneeling behind the doorsill, he extended his AK sideways and triggered a long, unaimed burst that went high and wide. Malten raised his fourteen-inch Benelli and fired two slugs from fifteen feet. The first one-and-a-quarter-ounce projectile splintered the doorsill, sending wood pieces into the shooter's face. Reflexively, he turned to avoid the shotgun blast, exposing his torso in the process.

The second slug took him in the notch of the sternum. He went down hard. Malten covered him, reckoned he was dead, and by feel thumbed another slug into the five-round tube.

"Clear!"

Two more of the rear entry team joined Malten while the rest guarded the rear approaches.

At that point they heard gunfire from the front of the house.

————

After White Team's flash-bangs detonated, Breezy and Delmore led their sections through the door. Breezy went left, Delmore went right. Two al Qaeda men rolled in agony on the floor, deaf and blinded by the stun grenades. The rear man in each section immediately secured them.

Three other Muslims chose to fight.

One popped up behind a wicker chair fifteen feet from the door. Breezy's front sight settled on the man's torso and the operator pressed the trigger. Six rounds impacted the target. *Got 'im!*

The AK shooter slid down the back of the chair; Breezy's muzzle followed him, as per doctrine.

Across the room, another jihadist was already shooting. His suppressed Uzi clattered a long burst at Delmore. Two 9mm rounds clipped the big man, but were stopped by his Kevlar vest. He returned fire, advancing in a combat crouch: two bursts. One to the chest, one to the head. The target collapsed and sprawled in a spreading pool of blood.

"Clear!"

"Clear!"

The entry team followed its well-rehearsed minuet, two pair

"running the walls" while the third duo secured the first room. Breezy and his partner held the survivors at gunpoint, ensuring that the men on the floor made no furtive movements.

With weapons raised, the operators spread out, searching behind furniture and opening doors.

A thin, bearded man emerged from the middle room. He raised a revolver toward Breezy, who saw him one second too late. Breezy's adrenaline spiked as he realized he could not beat the drop. He did the only thing he could: he fell to the floor and rolled for cover.

Bosco saw the threat at the same time, but distance lent options. He shouted *"Wodariga!"* as he raised his MP-5.

The target ignored the stop command.

Bosco got a flash sight picture and held the trigger down. It was a quick and dirty burst, and he knew that it went high. But two rounds connected as the man was turning to the greater menace. Gouts of blood erupted from the Pakistani's left arm and shoulder and he stumbled backwards, losing his balance and falling on his back. The Webley clattered to the floorboards.

"Clear!"

"Holy shit!" It was Breezy's tail man, checking the first shooter near the door. "Six torso hits and this dude is still breathing."

"Cuff him!" Breezy was on his knees, fighting his way back to standing. He did not realize it yet, but he had not breathed in fifteen seconds. He forced himself to inhale, bringing fresh oxygen to his bloodstream.

More "clear" calls came from the back of the building. The second team emerged, slung weapons, and began cuffing the prisoners.

Breezy bent over the bearded man with the shoulder wounds. Looking at Bosco, the ex-paratrooper murmured, "Thanks, man."

The victim lay on his back and raised a bloody hand. "Friend," he rasped. "I am a friend."

Breezy was taken aback. He did not expect anyone to speak fluent English. Then he recovered. "Yeah, everybody's my friend when they been shot." Breezy whipped out a tie wrap from his belt.

The man raised himself on an elbow. "Dr. Padgett-Smith. I must talk to her."

Sharif saw that the English woman's name registered with the

American. *Keep the initiative.* "Please! I know about the Marburg virus!"

Breezy stood up, still holding the tie wrap. Obviously the man at his feet had valuable information. The operator spoke into his headset. "Frank! We got a virus connection here. Send in Doc Smith!"

————

Fifty meters outside the house, Leopole turned to CPS. "Doctor, you're wanted inside. Evidently there's some information about the virus."

As the immunologist trotted toward the building, Leopole alerted the entry team. "CPS is inbound. Copy?"

"Copy that," Breezy replied.

Moments later Carolyn Padgett-Smith stepped inside. She made her way around the corpses and the bound prisoners being searched. Breezy motioned to her. "Over here, Doc. This guy knows you!"

"What?"

Sharif looked up at the figure approaching him. Despite the full biohazard suit, he saw that the features were feminine.

He held his left shoulder with his right hand, propping himself on his left elbow. Apparently he was in pain. She knelt beside him.

The veterinarian inhaled deeply, savoring the moment. He lowered his voice, knowing she would have to come closer. "Dr. Padgett-Smith?"

She was on both knees, leaning toward him. He saw the large, violet eyes that had caught his attention on the website. *I have her!*

"Yes. I am Carolyn Padgett-Smith. Who are you, and how do you know about the Marburg?"

The wounded man gave her a crooked smile. She wondered why he looked at her that way. She began to turn toward Breezy, standing behind her.

"My name is Saeed Sharif. But I am known to you as Dr. Ali."

Before she could react, the man raised himself more, reached behind him with his right arm, and brought it forward.

Carolyn Padgett-Smith felt a sudden, sharp pain below her left hip. Startled and confused, she looked down. She saw a 3cc syringe protruding from her suit and realized what had happened. Then she looked closer. It was a large-gauge needle and the plunger was three quarters of the way down.

Without thinking, she drew the Hi-Power from its holster and pushed the muzzle beneath the man's right eye. She pulled the trigger three times, then dropped the pistol.

She looked up at Brezyinski, who was astounded at the previous few seconds. His MP-5 was still at low ready. Her voice was a whisper. "My god, he just killed me."

Carefully, Padgett-Smith withdrew the syringe from her hip. The resistance told her what she already knew: her muscle had absorbed the contents, creating suction that resisted withdrawal.

CPS called over her shoulder. "Jeffrey! With me!"

Holding the syringe level with her left hand, she levered herself off the floor with her right and slowly walked to the rear of the house. Malten followed, uncertain what the doctor wanted him to do.

"Close the door," she said. As he did so, she laid the syringe on a wood table. Then she said, "Help me off with this."

Malten set down his weapon and stepped to her. He noticed that her hands trembled as she rotated the bubble helmet. He said, "I'll get it, ma'am." He wanted to call her Carolyn but thought better of it.

With the helmet off, she pulled the tape from her left wrist and Malten removed the right. She pulled off the outer gloves, then turned around. He tugged the orange suit off her shoulders and freed her arms. "All the way down," she said.

Malten undid the tape around the ankles and pulled off the lower half of the suit. Down to her scrubs, she quarter-turned again and untied the pants, pushing them to her knees. With her left side to him, she covered herself with her right hand and pulled up the scrub top with her left. "What's it look like?"

Jeffrey Malten realized that CPS had probably chosen him because he was a medic, but he still had to force himself to concentrate. He knelt down, looking at the reddening skin where the needle had penetrated, three inches below the hip bone. "It's intramuscular, Doctor. I don't think it got a vein."

She rubbed the spot; it still stung. "Small blessing," she said. "If only I . . . I hadn't . . ." Her voice cracked and she stifled a sob.

Feeling vastly helpless, Jeffrey Malten reached down and pulled up her scrub pants. He tied the strings for her and stood up. Her arms went around his neck and the tears came. That was bad enough. Then she began crying openly, without any effort to hold back.

The former SEAL hugged her close, feeling the hot tears run down her cheeks.

Leopole made the call to Black Team. "We have positive items for pickup. Start your approach now."

In the lead Mi-17, Terry Keegan descended toward the designated LZ, marked by yellow smoke. He told Eddie Marsh to remain in the holding pattern: no sense risking both birds on the ground at once. There was little wind so he set the Hip down with the nose pointed north, port-side door facing the house about seventy meters away. With his Pakistani copilot staying on the controls, Keegan unstrapped in anticipation of a quick briefing.

Leopole scrambled aboard and picked up a headset behind the cockpit. He gave Keegan a thumbs-up. "We have three items and one priority passenger."

Keegan's eyes widened in the red light. "We got the doctor?"

"Well, yes and no. Let's go discreet."

Leopole pulled off his headset and exited the helo. Keegan double-checked with the warrant in the left seat, then joined the ops officer thirty yards from the Hip.

"What gives, Frank?"

Leopole leaned close. "We got Ali alright, but he's dead. He stuck Padgett-Smith with a needle and she thinks it's Marburg. She's pretty shook."

"Holy shit! How'd that happen?"

"I'll tell you when we RTB. Main thing is, Terry, we have three prisoners and I'm sending Carolyn back with you. There's nothing we can do for her because of the incubation period. But I want to get her out of here ASAP in case she shows symptoms sooner than expected. She said she wants to talk to a colleague in London as soon as possible—apparently a homeopathic researcher. In any case, we need to get her to London immediately."

Keegan nodded. "Concur. I'll make arrangements as soon as we offload at base."

Breezy and three other operators emerged from the house, herding the captives. The men were bound and blindfolded, directed to the Hip and helped aboard. Two were wounded, requiring extra assistance. Finally Jeff Malten appeared with Padgett-Smith grasping one of his arms.

Feeling like an intruder, Leopole caught her attention. "Doctor, we're going to get you to London just as soon as we can. But we need to know if you found any biohazard in there."

She took a moment to focus on the American. In the Hip's strobing light her face alternately flashed red and dark, red and dark. Leopole felt as if her eyes were sunk in deep sockets like trapped animals regarding a dangerous world from their dens. "I found two syringes, including the one that . . ." Her voice trailed off. She cleared her throat and added, "Both are in the transport box with Omar."

Leopole patted her arm. "Okay, thanks . . . Carolyn."

She walked past Leopole and boarded the helo. Keegan noticed that Malten had to fasten her seat belt for her.

As the twin Klimov turboshafts spooled up and the Hip got light on its wheels, Omar Mohammed sprinted to the LZ. He lurched to a halt and waved animatedly. "I wanted to say good-bye to her."

Leopole regarded his Muslim colleague. "You can say good-bye back at base."

Mohammed looked at the receding Hip. "Perhaps." He turned to Leopole. "I wonder if I will ever see her again."

SSI OFFICES

Michael Derringer took the call from Quetta. His first comment was a heartfelt "Oh, my god." For three minutes he jotted notes as Leopole explained the situation. Then he signed off.

Ten minutes later Derringer convened a meeting in the boardroom.

"Okay, here's the hot wash from Frank. We'll have details later." He inhaled, cleared his throat, and began. "Our team was spotted closing in on the house. The Marburg cell was better organized and equipped than we anticipated, and maybe that's my fault. We should have treated them with more caution.

"Anyway, there was a brief firefight before our guys kicked in the doors. Four al Qaeda operatives were killed; three captured. No serious casualties on our side. Somehow—it's still uncertain—Ali or Sharif was able to hide a syringe. Maybe because he was seriously wounded.

He convinced our people that he was friendly and asked for Carolyn by name. When she arrived, he jabbed her with a needle."

"Oh, no." Sandy Carmichael's voice was hushed, fervent.

"Unfortunately, Carolyn reacted in self-defense and shot him dead. At that moment he posed no further threat, and we should have been able to interrogate him. As it was, I don't suppose we can blame her very much. She believes she's likely to die, and she knows what that means."

Joe Wolf leaned forward. "Mike, do we know what's actually in the needle?"

"Not yet, but it stands to reason. Carolyn is analyzing the contents while waiting for a ride home." Derringer folded his hands on the tabletop. "I'll tell Phil Catterly and I suppose he should call Charles Padgett-Smith."

Sandy asked, "How soon can she get to England?"

"Oh, Frank's arranging that. Probably the quickest way is commercial air. She seems to have an attachment to Jeff Malten and he'll travel with her. I told Frank to make it first class."

Wolf returned to business. "Okay, but what do we know about the bio threat? Is it over or not?"

Derringer consulted his notes. "Omar conducted a field interrogation on each of Ali's men. None of them admitted knowing about the lab or the virus carriers. They may be telling the truth. One of them indicated that Ali's deputy is still at large, and the Pakis are following that angle."

"That's not much to go on, Mike."

"Yeah, I know, Joe. But it's what we have for the moment. Frank said that his Pakistani liaison officer will take up where Omar left off. Ah, I suggested that no SSI personnel be present, if you know what I mean."

QUETTA AIRBASE

Major Rustam Khan gestured to Leopole and Mohammed. The three ducked into an unoccupied office in the hangar and Khan closed the door.

"There are two others."

"Two what?" Leopole shook his head, perplexed.

"Oh, no . . ." Omar Mohammed considered the options and defaulted to the worst.

"Yes, I fear so," Khan said. "Our, ah, interrogation of the prisoners confirmed it. Two young men left Sharif yesterday or the day before." He shrugged. "The information is somewhat contradictory . . ." Mohammed could well imagine the reason for the informants' lack of unanimity, given the likely methods of interrogation.

Leopole's frustration was audible as he blew the air from his lungs. He sagged against a desk. "Just when I was starting to think we'd wrap things up and head home." He looked at the Pakistani. "What do we know about these two?"

Khan unbuttoned his chest pocket and produced a paper. Leopole noticed that the meticulous officer rebuttoned the flap. "We have names, or partial names, but they are likely false. Remember that for months we only knew Sharif as Ali. Descriptions are similar enough to be accurate but they are also generic. Mid to late twenties, slight build, one short beard and one longer. 'Regular features,' whatever that may be."

Mohammed's mind was racing, trying to play catch-up. "Very well, Major. We have two suspects, presumably infected with the virus. They have one or two days' lead on us. Perhaps both reports are correct: Sharif may have dispatched them on consecutive days to different destinations."

Leopole was upright again. "Did the prisoners see them together or separately?"

"I shall have to consult the transcript. But I thought that you should know this much immediately."

Leopole looked at Mohammed. "Omar, we won't get to bed anytime soon. Major Khan and I'll get on the horn to Buster Hardesty while . . ."

The Ph.D. was on his way out the door, checking his watch. "I'll call headquarters. The admiral should be in the office about now."

ARLINGTON, VIRGINIA

Dr. Phillip Catterly arose early. He had not slept much after receiving the call from Derringer. Finally he threw off the covers, eased himself out of bed, and slid into his slippers. It would be dawn in barely an hour, and he wanted to reach Charles Padgett-Smith before Britons left for work.

Catterly descended the stairs to his office and closed the door. He took his time dialing the international number, and fidgeted while the phone rang. *Buzz-buzz. Buzz-buzz.* He fingered his pajama top. *Why'n hell do they put collars on PJs?*

At length a British voice answered. "Hallo?"

Catterly inhaled, then exhaled. "Charles? Hello! This is Phillip Catterly."

"Who?"

"Dr. Catterly in Virginia. I'm a colleague of . . ."

Recognition dawned. "Oh yes! Phillip. Carolyn has mentioned you. Terribly sorry—I'm not at my best before breakfast." While Catterly formed the words in his mind, he could almost sense Charles Padgett-Smith putting two and two together. "Phillip, Carolyn is not here. But I expect you know that." The voice remained level, controlled. But there was an urgency. "Is there . . ."

"She's coming home, Charles. I want to give you the flight information."

"Oh. Awfully good of you. I have pen and paper."

The American carefully enunciated the flight number and arrival time. Padgett-Smith repeated it and began to ring off.

"Charles, there's something else. Ah, something you need to know."

"Yes?"

Catterly inhaled again. Then he began to speak.

HEATHROW AIRPORT

Carolyn Padgett-Smith had barely hugged her husband before she made a phone call to a homeopathic researcher. Meanwhile, Malten offered to collect the luggage. Charles waited until his wife was on the phone, then caught the American. "Mr. Malten, please . . ."

"Mr. Malten's my father, sir. Call me Jeff."

An appreciative nod. "Done. If you call me Charles. I'm not been knighted, you know."

Malten unzipped a smile. "Sure thing."

Padgett-Smith's face turned immediately sober. "How is she? I mean, emotionally."

"She didn't talk much during the flight." The commando shrugged. "She took a couple pills and slept most of the time."

"But you must have some idea . . ."

Malten's gaze went to the polished floor. He was seeing events days and weeks old, things that Charles Padgett-Smith would never glimpse. "Well, your wife is one hell of a lady. She's humped a ruck with us when it was uphill in both directions. She shot it out with bad guys in the mountains and she helped find the specimen that put us on the terrorists' trail. She never complained, got along with a bunch of male chauvinists, and far as I know, she did everything asked of her. But after the needle, she sort of collapsed." Malten paused, frowning in concentration. Then he said, "No, that's not right. More like de-flated. The spirit just went out of her. She's got to be worried sick but she won't say so. At least, not to me."

The financier touched the operator's arm. "Thank you, Jeff. It's about what I expected."

Malten was anxious to be away from the awkward situation. He remembered a good excuse. "I'll check on the luggage, then I'll get something to eat."

"But surely they fed you on the airplane?"

"Well, yeah. I mean, they served dinner but I couldn't eat very much."

"Why not?"

"Well, she held my right hand most of the flight."

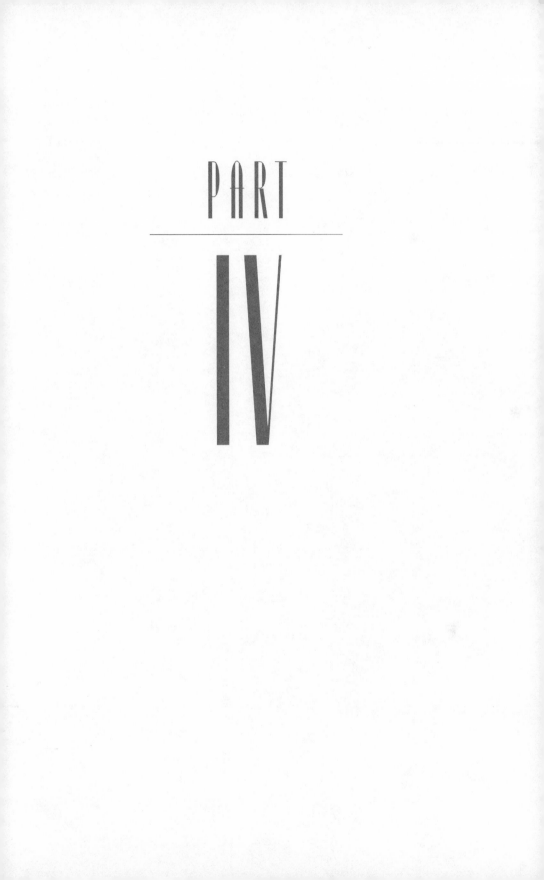

PART

IV

32

SSI's braintrust was summoned to an emergency meeting less than an hour before closing. When Joe Wolf shut the door on the secure room, Derringer got straight to the point.

"Nobody in this room is going home this evening. We have to find two more human bombs."

Sandy Carmichael was the first to react. "You mean, our team didn't get all the Marburg plotters after all?"

Derringer raised his hands, palms up. "Oh, we think we got all the big fish, or at least we know who they are. It's the last two little fish. Evidently Frank's guys missed them by a few hours."

Wolf did not bother to sit down. "I've already talked to the applicable agencies." He ticked them off with his fingertips: "DHS, FBI, NIS, HHS, DoT and FAA, a lot of the the federal alphabet. Evidently some word leaked out of Pakistan because Defense and Health and

Human Services already had an idea that something was headed our way. Now it's a matter of coordinating all the players."

Derringer shook his head. "Never happen, Joe. Not on so short a notice."

Wolf slid into a chair. "Yeah, I know, Mike. I know." He rubbed his graying temples.

Carmichael was mentally cataloging the growing list of tasks before her, including a call to a neighbor to check on the girls. "Admiral, just what do we know right now? And what do we have to assume?"

"Good questions, Sandy." Derringer raised himself from his seat and paced to the whiteboard beside the conference table. He flipped back a cloth covering his briefing points and went down the list. "Frank and Omar are convinced that their Pakistani liaison officer and General Hardesty are being forthright. Once the field interrogations revealed that two infected men had left the farm we raided, our embassy was immediately notified. The Pakistanis 'interviewed' the prisoners at Quetta and found similar enough stories to believe them. Hardesty has confirmed the basics: two men in their twenties, one who may have a fatal disease. We do not know their names but according to the interrogators, they're known as Maqsad and Badlah. I'm told those are Urdu words for 'purpose' and 'revenge.' "

Sandy looked at her boss. "That's it?"

"Pretty much. As you asked, the rest we have to assume." He tapped the whiteboard again. "We assume they're Pakistanis, but we don't know if they're traveling on Pakistani passports. That seems unlikely, considering they must know we'd be suspicious. We assume they have something between hours and days before they develop full-blown Marburg. We must assume they're headed here, but it could be any place from Philadelphia to LA. It's unlikely they're traveling together."

Wolf sat up straight. "Mike, what are the chances of getting Islamabad to cancel all flights out of the country? Maybe just for a couple of days. They could say, truthfully, that there's concern of communicable diseases."

"Hardesty and the embassy people are supposed to be working that angle. Same with bus and rail, but I doubt anything will come of it. The kamikazes have a head start, and they may be driving to another country before flying here. The best we can hope for is that all ports of entry will screen all Muslim males under thirty or so."

"Damn!" Wolf's mild expletive was uncharacteristic. "The minute INS or anybody else tries to do that, the civil libertarians will shut down the whole scheme with a discrimination suit. All it takes is one huggy-feely judge."

Derringer smiled for the first time—a small, ephemeral smile, but a smile nonetheless. "That's right, Joe. No profiling allowed—no doubt about it. But I, ah, wouldn't be surprised if the government has written appeals ready to file within minutes. Depending on specifics, all that's required is the necessary signatures."

"Whose signatures?" Carmichael asked.

"Well, I wouldn't be surprised if it was one of my college friends."

"You mean Secretary Burridge?"

Derringer leaned forward, hands on the table. "It's already gone from President Quincannon to Justice *and* Homeland Security."

Wolf's grin was in fact wolfish. "The ACLU will go spastic."

"I suspect you are correct. But even if the appeals are denied, at least there'll be time to look for the suiciders while the lawyers haggle it out."

As usual, Carmichael was thinking ahead of the game. "Admiral, if the government is dealing with all this, what's our role?"

Derringer sat down again, drumming his long fingers on the tabletop. *Paradiddle paradiddle, tap-tap-tap.* "Basically, we're backup. Remember how we got into this job in the first place? Plausible deniability! No U.S. military personnel were involved in hunting down the Marburg cell in a foreign country. Same thing applies right here. In case there are legal or operational problems, our people can step in and do what needs doing. The feds are welcome to the credit, if in fact there's any credit to be taken. So far everybody in the executive and judicial branches would be happy as hell if there's nothing to report, and therefore nothing to deny."

Carmichael was scribbling notes to herself. "Admiral, with our primary teams in Pakistan and secondary crews in Iraq and Afghanistan and Central America, we're going to be hard pressed to field many more operatives."

Wolf interjected. "Sandy's right. We can't get Frank's people back here in less than two days, and this is likely to be over by then."

Derringer made a point of loosening his Annapolis tie. "Actually, Omar is coming back tonight—he'll be badly jetlagged by the time he hits Dulles tomorrow, but he can be the most use, especially with his language skills. As for the rest of us, well, it's like I said. Nobody's going home this evening."

———

During a coffee break Sandy Carmichael and Sallie Kline got together for a bit of female bonding. Sallie confided, "You know, I don't tell many people, but some of the Patriot Act makes me nervous."

"What parts?"

"Basically, the whole attitude that American citizens are just as suspect as foreigners from hostile nations."

"Yeah, I know," Sandy replied. "I've had this discussion with David. He agrees with you, and he's active duty. But what's the alternative?"

"How about common sense? I mean, grandmothers taken aside for searches! My best friend had her wedding gown spread out on a table in Phoenix. I've even seen mothers with babies made to unload their bags with diapers and things. That's done because the government's terrified of being accused of profiling." She shook her head. "Damn it, Sandy, the threat is Muslim males—not people like you and me."

"Girlfriend, I spent over twenty years in the army. Don't hold your breath waiting for common sense."

Sallie Ann's empathic powers tickled her emotional sensors. *David Main: Sandy hasn't mentioned him lately.* She sipped her coffee and modulated her voice into a casual tone. "Speaking of Colonel Main, have you seen him since . . . ?"

"Since the attack? Just once, and a couple of phone calls."

After an awkward silence, Sallie risked another question. "How's he doing? I mean, he seems like a really nice man, but he must have some issues, coming that close to being killed."

Sandy bit her lip and lowered her gaze. When she raised her eyes again, they were misting over. "He's a wonderful man, Sallie. My god, he loves me enough to risk his life for me. But he also loves his wife." She shook her head. "Nothing's simple, is it?"

"Sandy, I think that love is simple. It's the purest thing there is. But romance can be a real bitch."

SSI OFFICES

Wolf convened the meeting. "Okay, people. What do we know? I mean, what do we *really* know?"

Omar Mohammed gulped more coffee to stay awake. He looked almost as bad as he felt—he had never been able to sleep on airplanes. "Here's my interrogation notes from the Pakistanis. Major Khan was present and he thinks the information is accurate."

Wolf spread his hands. "Go ahead, Omar."

"Two young men, about twenty. There's complete agreement on that. They seem to be related, but just how is uncertain. Brothers, cousins, whatever. One apparently speaks some English, but we don't know about the other.

"Names?"

"They received code names, apparently from Sharif before he was killed." Wolf made a mental note. *Omar's really tired. Of course Sharif gave them names* before *he was killed!* "The Urdu words are *maqsad,* or *purpose,* and *badlah,* which is *revenge.* Obviously, that indicates a depth of commitment consistent with suicide bombers. As before, the real trouble is lack of evidence. If they're carrying the virus—and we must assume they are—it's undetectable. They will probably have minimal luggage." He looked around the room. "They won't plan on living very long."

The former FBI man absorbed that information. "Okay. What else?"

Mohammed plopped his notepad on the polished tabletop. "That's it. At least for now."

Carmichael emitted a low, pensive whistle. Wolf bit his lip, staring at an ornamental ashtray that would never be used. Finally he said, "Is there any chance this could be disinformation? We need to consider all the angles."

"I don't think so, Joe. As I said, Khan was present, and I learned I can trust him. After all, his family has suffered from terrorists.

There's also the political aspect. Whatever many Pakistanis think of us, the government does *not* want to have some of its citizens spreading deadly diseases in the U.S." Mohammed knew that the reasons were tacitly obvious, mainly spelled with dollar signs.

Mohammed rubbed his eyes, then added, "There's one other thing. Pakistani security forces brought in another suspect shortly before I left. Khan felt he's potentially a good source, but evidently he's a hard case. It may take some time to break him down."

"My god, Omar. We don't even know how much time we have! They need to lean on this guy, now!"

"Well, the embassy is aware of him. Or at least General Hardesty is, which amounts to the same thing. I believe he's monitoring things as closely as he dares."

Carmichael cleared her throat, casting sideways glances at both men. She knew the implications: the interrogation methods were unlikely to withstand congressional scrutiny, so Hardesty would keep his distance. "Ah, gentlemen . . ."

Wolf nodded. "Yes, Sandy."

"Couldn't some of our people . . . you know . . . provide technical assistance?" She etched quote marks in the air around "technical."

"I suppose so . . ."

Mohammed interjected. "You're suggesting drugs, Sandy?"

"Sure. It's the quickest way, isn't it?"

Mohammed replied, "Sodium pentothal has been erratic. The evidence I've seen indicates that stronger means are needed. Maybe psychoactives or hallucinogens."

Wolf looked back to Mohammed. "Do you know who the prisoner is?"

"No. Only that he's a foreigner. Khan said they caught him by accident, a little after our raid on Sharif 's hideout."

"Well, as you all know, it is not SSI policy to use or advocate illegal methods, even overseas. But right now we're looking at a hell of a big job. Either we get a break or we try to coordinate with several agencies in identifying and tracking every young Muslim male who enters this country for the next month or so."

Sandy said, "That's the admiral's call, isn't it?"

"Yes, it is. I'll give him the info as soon as he returns from meeting with Burridge."

FORT MARCY PARK

The government limousine turned off the road between Chain Bridge and Langley, entering the park within two minutes of the appointed time. Michael Derringer exited his Jaguar and walked the short distance to the Cadillac.

Homeland Security Secretary Burridge opened the rear door. "Hi, Mike."

The former classmates shook hands, then Derringer asked, "Inside or out?"

Burridge extended his basketball player's legs and eased himself from the seat. "It's good to get out of the office. Let's take a walk."

After pacing through the blowing leaves, the friends stood at the perimeter, watching the Potomac flowing 275 feet below them. Derringer, who usually read history when he had time to himself, recalled that New York and Pennsylvania artillerymen had enjoyed the same view from 1862 onward.

Burridge got to the point. "Mike, I understand your concern over security. But we do have secure comm at DHS, you know."

"You still log most calls, though, don't you?"

"Well, yeah. Most of them. Why?"

Derringer turned ninety degrees to face his friend. "Bruce, what I have to say is not anything that you want known on the Hill—by your friends *or* enemies."

The DHS czar nodded solemnly. "Okay. Fire away."

Derringer inhaled, then expelled his breath. "The Pakistanis have a valuable asset. They nabbed him a couple of nights ago, and there's every reason to believe he knows about the last Marburg kamikazes. Or, at least what we think is the last. The doctor who injected the volunteers is dead."

"Yeah, I got that word. But what about this other asset?"

"He's a Syrian called Kassim. That may or may not be his real name, but he's been positively ID'd as one of Sharif's men. Apparently he lost a foot fighting the Russians in Afghanistan, and he's been in more or less continuous combat since then. Our contact says that a couple of the interrogators openly admire the guy."

"What's he know about the volunteers?"

"It looks as if he escorted them to their point of departure from the border. Evidently he was returning to Sharif when he ran into a Paki patrol. There was a brief shootout and he was captured." Derringer did not bother mentioning that the veteran fighter had killed one Pakistani and wounded another.

"So we missed the two guys by just . . ."

"Probably a few hours."

"Then," Burridge concluded, "this Syrian knows what they look like and probably knows their names."

"That's right. Although they could travel on forged papers."

"And Hardesty at the embassy knows all this?"

"Check."

"So, what do you need from me, Mike?"

Derringer glanced around to ensure no one overheard. "The Syrian hasn't said much yet—and believe me, that means he's hardcore."

Burridge began to understand. He did not ask for details about third-world interrogation techniques but he knew the figures: three to five percent of al Qaeda prisoners would die rather than reveal information they held dear. "You're asking me to make a back-channel request via our embassy to use—ahem—extraordinary measures to interrogate a third-party national deemed a major security risk."

"You got it, shipmate."

Burridge turned back toward the river. He had seldom been to the park, and only knew of its recent history. *I wonder where they found Vince Foster's body*, he mused. He recalled the news report: the Park Service spokesman had actually declared, "It's a suicide because we say it's a suicide."

"The locals aren't going to use extraordinary means unless we request it?"

"That's the word from our Pakistani liaison and General Hardesty. As I said, some of the interrogators admire the Syrian."

DHS nodded slowly, staring at the Potomac. "Well, it's my potato and I can't toss it up the line. The president needs to maintain deniability."

Derringer nudged his friend with an elbow. "Hey, that's why we get the big bucks."

Burridge did not smile. "Alright. I'll pass the word immediately." He looked closely at Derringer. "What do you think they'll do?"

"My guess is drugs. Something a lot better than pentothal."

The secretary turned to walk back to his limo. "You know, Mike, if this works out and we grab the couriers, probably nobody will ever know. On the other hand, if we don't get them in time, and a lot of people die, the public will demand to know why we didn't do more. But if . . ."

"If they die on us and word leaks about the interrogation, we're the bastards who torture prisoners in other countries."

Burridge stopped a few paces from his vehicle. "Hell of a business we're in, shipmate." He shook hands again. "I'll call our people right away. What's the time difference?"

Derringer thought. "Oh, nine, ten hours. Plays hell with coordination, doesn't it?"

"Until we ID those two guys, I don't think that time is going to matter very damn much."

LONDON

Dr. Carolyn Padgett-Smith opened her violet eyes. She had trouble focusing and did not recognize anything, but her nose told her more than her vision. The antiseptic aromas spoke clearly to her: *Hospital.* Judging by the near absence of sound, she thought she was in a private room, perhaps in a private clinic.

Padgett-Smith felt the clammy texture of her skin and cataloged the other symptoms: a rash, temperature, nausea and vomiting, plus the onset of diarrhea.

Early stage two. I have the virus.

Without dissecting that knowledge, she placed her emotions in a separate mental file for the moment. A glance at the wall revealed no windows. That was useful intelligence. It led to another conclusion. If she had contracted Marburg, which seemed almost certain, then she was in no ordinary facility. *They moved me to an isolation ward. They must have done. But . . . when?*

What day is it?

What's the last thing I remember?

Charles. Where is Charles?

Something turned over behind her navel: a liquid urgency. *Oh, god, no.* She reached her left hand from beneath the covers and grasped the call button clipped to her pillow. She pressed the button once, twice. It was surprisingly difficult to do. *How can I be so weak?*

In less than one minute a nursing sister arrived. She wore a disposable outer garment and a mask with gloves. Her clothing did nothing to inspire confidence in the patient, but CPS was grateful for the attention. "I need the WC, now!"

The nurse—a short, confident angel named Sister Beatrice— flipped back the covers and, with deceptive strength, pulled Dr. Padgett-Smith to her feet. Supported by the good sister, CPS managed the seven steps to the water closet and slid onto the toilet.

When finished, Padgett-Smith examined her gown. Like all hospital attire, it was calculated entirely for function. It was tied only at the neck and mid back, with elbow-length arms. While steadying herself at the basin, the immunologist allowed herself to dwell upon small things. *Will I ever wear a bra and panties again? Right now I should be glad for hiking shorts and boots.*

Tucked up in bed again, she accepted some water and ordered her thoughts.

"Sister, how long have I been here? What do you know about my husband?"

Beatrice patted the doctor's arm. Despite the latex between them, the human gesture was reassuring. "You've been here two days, my dear. You collapsed at home and your husband brought you here directly. He only left a few hours ago."

"Oh, yes . . ." Some of the last forty-eight hours fell into place. There had been a row about staying at home. Charles had insisted that Carolyn enter a special care facility but she resisted, noting that no symptoms had yet emerged and the test results were pending. She felt the onset of potentially massive guilt. Charles was exposed to her nearly every hour of the day: he was at risk, but she had been so self-absorbed that she only wanted to remain in familiar surroundings. *I was such a twit—I felt that if I were at home then I must be healthy. I knew better. Truly I did.*

Charles, I'm so sorry.

"When can I see him?"

"I don't know, love. But the charge nurse will ring him to let him know that you're awake. After that, it's up to the doctor."

CPS rubbed her forehead, as if forcing memories to the front. "I can't remember very much before . . . what? Day before yesterday?" She turned her focused stare back to Sister Beatrice. "I must have slept most of the time."

"You were sedated for several hours. You had a bad dream or two, apparently."

Padgett-Smith shook off the grim memories, knowing they would return. For the present, she had more urgent concerns. She asked, "Did we hear from Dr. Keene?"

The sister checked the chart. "I don't see that name here. Is he a consultant?"

"She's a leading researcher in homeopathic medicine. Margaret prepared some *Crotalus horridus* for me, but I only took a couple of doses before . . . coming here."

"What is *crotalus* . . . horribilus?"

"*Horridus.* Rattlesnake venom."

33

SSI OFFICES

"Admiral, Secretary Burridge on line two."

"Thank you, Peggy."

Derringer punched the button and picked up the receiver. "Go Navy."

"Beat Army," the familiar voice crackled back. "Ready to copy?"

"Affirm. Uh, are we going discreet?"

"No need, Mike. I'm giving you a one-time pad—a password that'll get you into one of our secure email sites. Each following message will contain the next password in case there's updates. It's open ended so you can check it as often as you like."

Derringer tapped with his pencil. "Ready."

"Okay. Our class year minus the hull number of your first ship, plus my varsity number, divided by *nul*."

Michael Derringer chuckled aloud at the ingenious device. His first ship, USS *Lindsay* (DLG-48), and Burridge's jersey cancelled one another; *nul* was German for zero. Anyone eavesdropping on the semi-secure line would spend at least several minutes chasing the information, by which time it would be useless.

Derringer rang off and swiveled to his computer screen. In two minutes he was looking at the secure email with distilled information from the interrogation recently concluded eight thousand miles away. Apparently the Syrian knew relatively little, but at least the hunters now could look for two names: Miam Ahmed and Hazrat Sial. Unfortunately, there was not enough difference in their descriptions to be useful. Both were young and slightly built, Ahmed somewhat taller and Sial with a beard. The latter distinction undoubtedly would have changed by now.

For a moment Derringer pondered how to use the information. Certainly Immigration and Transportation Security would be informed, but the hard-won intel probably was outdated. It was unlikely that either Marburg courier was traveling under his own identity.

Derringer reached for his console and buzzed Wolf's office. "Joe, we have some names. That's the good news."

The former FBI man knew the drill. "Okay, I'll bite. What's the bad news?"

"We don't know if those names are on their passports—if they have passports. But at least we can coordinate with INS and TSA and the rest of the alphabet. What do you suggest beyond that?"

"Well, nobody has enough agents to tail every young Muslim who enters this country, even with the artificial delays being imposed. Best we can hope for is enough of a pool from several agencies and plainclothes officers from PDs in the major metro areas."

Derringer thought for a moment. "That's a hell of a lot of people to keep a secret very long."

"You got that right, Boss."

"I'm headed for the cafeteria. Let's huddle there."

Joe Wolf was fifteen pounds overweight and could hardly care less. "Like I always said: you're a great American."

ISLAMABAD

Buster Hardesty did not have time for the full report; that could follow. But Rustam Khan's highlights received priority attention.

The Pakistani officer's usual aplomb had worn thin in two days. Hardesty had never seen Khan with a pocket unbuttoned; now the major was almost disheveled. Not that it mattered. They found a secluded corner in a government building and got to work.

"General, we have a breakthrough. Kassim has slept very little since he was captured, and not at all in the past thirty hours. Sleep deprivation combined with the chemical agents produced this." He handed over a notepad with Khan's impeccable English script.

Hardesty scanned the lines, then glanced up. "Who are these?"

"The intermediate handlers. They delivered the infected men to the final escorts: the ones who put our suspects on their airplane."

Hardesty blew an audible breath. "Good work, Rustam. Excellent. But it's going to take awhile to follow . . ."

"Already done, sir."

"What?"

"It's in the rest of my notes, General. The pieces fell into place. One of the final handlers escaped but we caught the other. He was offered two choices: he could disappear or he could become wealthy." Khan gave an ironic shrug. "Fortunately, he is motivated by personal gain rather than philosophy. The temptation of easy riches."

"But, when did all this happen? We planned on coordinating with . . ."

"I must apologize for that, sir. But we had an unexpected opportunity and we took it. In the circumstance, I did not think it wise to follow protocol. There was not time."

Hardesty risked a familiar tap on his colleague's shoulder. "Well, you did exactly the right thing, Rustam. Thank you. On behalf of everyone in my country, thank you."

Khan sagged into his chair, visibly exhausted. "Remember, sir: my countrymen also suffer from terrorists." He did not need to mention the loss his family also had sustained. "But we cannot rest yet. Look at the travel itinerary."

Hardesty read to the bottom of the page. What he saw created a chilling sensation that prickled between his shoulder blades and widened his eyes. He looked at Khan. "Oh my god."

Rustam Khan nodded slowly. "Yes, it is worse than we thought."

Hardesty read the summary again. "From Islamabad to Morocco to . . . Brazil?"

"That is how it looks, sir."

Hardesty's response was instant comprehension linked to surging distress. He met Khan's obsidian eyes. "Oh, no . . ."

SSI OFFICES

"Here's the latest intel," Derringer began. "Two young Muslim males matching the descriptions we got from Khan were on an Air France flight day before yesterday. They left Rabat, Morocco, for Santos Dumont Airport in Rio de Janiero."

Wolf asked, "Names, photos?"

"Our INS and DoT contacts are working on that, and will share any intel. However, it's a cinch that by the time our suspects get to this country they'll have new identities.

"So, we can make some assumptions, or at least educated guesses. Once they're on this side of the pond they'll avoid regular transport. They'll likely use a chartered plane to fly into Mexico, where they'll meet their local guides—*coyotes* who know the smuggling business inside out."

Wolf emitted a low whistle. "Gotta hand it to 'em: it's a beauty of a plan. In one jump they circumvent our entire airport security apparatus. All the agents and undercover people we alerted and put in place are useless. They'll be focused on every young Muslim arriving by air, and it won't matter. Meanwhile, our suspects will cross somewhere between San Diego and Brownsville. What's that? Eighteen hundred miles?"

Derringer nodded. "Just about. But you know, they could just as easily enter by sea, on the Pacific coast or in the Gulf."

Sandy interjected. "Just a minute, sir. Couldn't they also fly in? Or take a boat to Florida or somewhere else? After all, they have at least a few days before—"

Derringer shook his head. "I don't think so, Sandy. Under other conditions you'd be right to consider that, but time is crucial. Far as we know, this is the last chance to get infected couriers into the country. I think they'd take the most direct route possible. Besides, SSI can't do much about port security or airline passengers—unless we're put on somebody's tail so the feds can maintain their anti-profiling charade."

"So where does that leave us, sir?"

"It leaves us somewhere in the Sonoran Desert. We know for certain that al Qaeda has sent recon parties through various border areas. Hell, it's entirely possible that they've already infiltrated terror cells that way. In any case, I think that Sharif or somebody in his organization would have contacts with experienced smugglers: professionals who will work for anybody if the price is right."

Wolf said, "Mike, if I may play devil's advocate: what's the proof? As you said, if this was Sharif's last chance. But we need to be right the first time, too."

"Fair enough." Derringer stood up and walked to the front of the room. He selected one of several pull-down maps and revealed the western hemisphere. Tapping South America he said, "The geography. If our two guys flew from Morocco to Brazil, and it's almost certain that they did, ask yourself why."

"Well, sure," Wolf exclaimed. "The geometry of the situation points to the border. But there could be factors involved that we have no way of knowing."

"Concur. But we have to start somewhere, and I think we can make some basic assumptions." Derringer raised a hand and began ticking off points on his fingertips. "One: they're on a schedule, and probably a pretty tight one. After all, some of their previous Marburg couriers fell sick or died en route. Two: we know about this entire scheme because the first case literally spilled his guts at Heathrow. So they want to avoid control points. Three: the current suiciders are both young, probably inexperienced travelers. It's not even certain that both speak English, and I doubt like hell that they speak Spanish. That means they'll need help. Four: all the foregoing indicate a likely covert border crossing."

Derringer touched his thumb. "Five: they want to optimize their chances by placing both Marburg bombers in a major population center. To me, that means two likely targets: San Diego and Phoenix, maybe LA."

Sandy Carmichael tapped her pencil against her chin. "Sir, I agree. But do we try to operate in both areas? We're spread awfully thin . . ."

"I agree, Sandy. I'd feel better if we could pull Julio's team out of Guatemala, especially since he has most of our Spanish speakers. But there's no time to redeploy. So, lacking other information, how would you proceed, Joe?"

Wolf raised his hands, palms up. "Ya got me, Boss."

Derringer scanned the room, visually polling the other staffers. Receiving no additional input, he raised the hemisphere map and pulled the one showing the western United States.

"Very well. Here's our new theater of operations. It's nearly two thousand miles across an east-west front. It's the most porous border in the industrialized world. Thousands of illegals cross it every day, and not all of them are looking for work. Some of them want to destroy this country.

"So . . . we need maximum coordination, especially with intel. Frankly, that's what worries me the most. Oh, we'll get the info, all right, but maybe not in time to use it. There's just too many irons in the fire: too many agencies that should be sharing information but don't or won't. The new intelligence hierarchy may be a good idea, but it needs time to mature . . ."

"Time we don't have." Carmichael completed Derringer's thought.

"Correct. Therefore, we need to rely on our own resources as well as whatever the agencies send us." Derringer looked at Wolf. "Joe, maybe we need to call in O'Connor. What do you think?"

"Well, he's certainly well placed. But Mike, you know that . . ."

"Yeah. I know." There were ironic grins and a few chuckles around the table. Ryan O'Connor had entered the State Department in the Carter administration and fervently clung to that naïve worldview, despite decades of evidence to the contrary. But he was SSI's point of contact at State, and that situation would not change.

Derringer sought the silver lining in the diplomatic cloud. "One thing about this case: it's largely apolitical. No human rights abuses or questionable governments to muddy the waters." He nodded at

Wolf. "Okay, give him a call. But only tell him as little as necessary. What we want from him is back-channel contact with the Mexican government, especially their transportation and public health people. Emphasize the medical aspects, and get gruesome if you have to."

Wolf scribbled himself a note, smiling all the while.

Sandy Carmichael raised her pencil. "Sir, speaking of the medical aspects, who do we have for bioterror advice now that Padgett-Smith's sidelined?"

"Gosh, that's a good question, Sandy." Derringer had not thought about the stricken immunologist lately. "I don't have anybody in mind except Phil Catterly. He's professionally qualified, but he's no field operative. However, since he's already read in on the Marburg threat, I'd say he's our man. I'll phone him today."

Wolf looked up from his notepad. "That still leaves us to find enough operators." He turned to Omar Mohammed, who had sat quietly through the meeting thus far. It was obvious that he was still tired.

Taking the cue, Mohammed sat upright. "Frank and Steve's teams are inbound. We got them out of Pakistan as fast as possible, but they're going to be tired and jetlagged. Most of the shooters are looking forward to some down time; they figure they've accomplished their mission."

Derringer asked, "Any Spanish speakers among them?"

"I don't know." He shook his head. "I should know, but I don't. I'm sorry, Admiral. I'll have to check the computer files."

"Well, we can't assemble another team and bring it up to speed in less than a week. Looks as if we're forced to recycle the Pakistan crew."

Wolf leaned forward. "Uh, technically, none of them are required to conduct more work. Their contracts were written for the overseas job, though I can check with Corin for specifics. But I'm sure I'm right." He spread his hands. "We might not have enough guys to field a useful team."

Derringer finally sat down. He wanted to rub his temples but he suppressed the urge. Image counted for a lot at such times. Instead, he cleared his throat. "All right, looks as if I'll be working the phones tonight." He punched his right fist into his left palm. "Damn! I wish we had in-flight communication with our bird. I floated a SatCom proposal to the board last year but they thought it was a nice-to-have rather than necessary. Now we'll have to spring this news on the boys when they land."

Sandy Carmichael ignored what could not be helped and focused on upcoming contingencies. She flipped through her briefing book but did not find what she sought. "Sir, what can our people expect in Mexico? I don't see that data here."

"There wasn't time to include that in the packet but the research department has some basics." He nodded to Sharon Carper, who knew her way around the internet as few people did.

"I focused on likely Muslim contacts in the country, but there's not much evidence," she began. "Mexico has a very small Muslim population—probably under two thousand or so. Apparently most are converts to the Muribatun movement."

"Anything else?" Carmichael asked.

"Well, there are relatively few embassies in Mexico, and the only Islamic country there is Malaysia."

Wolf felt the information was of marginal utility. "It doesn't take many operatives to handle two people. Hell, they don't even have to be Muslim. In fact, I'd bet the contacts are local smugglers."

Carper added, "It'd make sense for them to proceed via Mexico City. It's the third largest metro area in the world: eighteen to twenty million. They could hole up there for quite a while without being noticed."

"Yes, they could," Carmichael responded. "But they'll want to get to the border as soon as possible."

Joe Wolf was tired and irritable, yet he wanted to get to work. "Well, that's right. After all, the clock's running." He stood up.

Derringer rapped his pen on the table. "Meeting adjourned. Until after dinner."

CHIAPAS, MEXICO

It had been a long, tiring trip. Neither young man was accustomed to air travel—let alone from Pakistan to Morocco to Brazil and Ecuador.

Dealing with strangers who could only converse in the infidel language was a constant strain, but at least the current handlers were members of The Faith; new friends who managed some Arabic in addition to English.

The elder host called himself Aamir: a handsome trader in his thirties. He did not explain his connection to Doctor Ali's organization, nor did Sial or Ahmed inquire. He did, however, express concern for Ahmed's health. It was apparent that the youngster had not endured the charter flight very well from Quito to Chiapas. The dawn landing at an outlying dirt field had been exciting enough—the pilot nearly clipped the treetops before flaring and dropping the twin-engine turboprop onto the packed earth—but now the couriers were within range of their target. Officially, they ceased to exist in Quito, where their forged passports ended the paper trail.

Now the travelers had only a vague idea of their location: somewhere in southeastern Mexico, with the Pacific to the south and Guatemala to the east.

Aamir showed the travelers to their room in his house. They took in the whitewashed walls, rugs on the floor, and two inviting beds. "It is still twenty-five hundred kilometers to the border," their host explained. "You will rest here tomorrow and fly by private plane to Sonora the next day. I shall explain the procedures after prayers and dinner."

DULLES AIRPORT

"Hey, lookit. There's the admiral."

Breezy's observation turned heads in the leased hangar. Hidden from outside view, the operators were beginning to unload critical gear from the 727 when Derringer stepped into the access door with Omar Mohammed. Some of the door kickers had never met the firm's founder and CEO, who warmly greeted Terry Keegan. Then Derringer motioned for the men to gather around him.

Frank Leopole stepped inside the circle and approached his employer. "You didn't need to pay us a visit, sir. We know how busy you are, but the guys sure appreciate it."

"Thank you, Frank. But I'm not here just to say welcome home." He turned his head, searching the recesses of the building. "I don't see any Charter people. Are we alone?"

"Ah, yessir." Leopole knew the admiral's intent. SSI shared the hangar with Charter International Airways; otherwise the rent would be prohibitive. The firm's initials were a perennial cause of mirth.

"Good. What I have to say is close hold."

Steve Lee turned to his team. "Hey! Listen up!" A tentative silence fell upon the operators. A few looked around, and Lee read the signs. *Thirty-six left; about twenty-eight returning healthy.*

Derringer began. "Guys, welcome back. It's really good to see you again. I wish I could treat all of you to an extended vacation, especially after you did such a fine job. But the fact is: Pandora is not over."

The operators exchanged querulous glances. Some expressed concern; a few betrayed dismay.

"This is close hold," Derringer continued. "Even though you broke up the Marburg cell, the doctor sent two more suiciders our way. They left just hours before you took down the farmhouse."

Leopole waved down the rising voices. Derringer gestured to Mohammed. It was a calculated move: the training officer had bonded with the shooters over the previous weeks. Many of the men felt closer to the naturalized Iranian than to the retired admiral who wrote the checks.

Mohammed stepped two paces forward. "Gentlemen, we're asking you to go one more round. The intelligence is firm: our two suspects did get away and flew to South America. We are convinced that they will enter this country via Mexico."

Gunny Foyte grasped the implications; frequently he could read between Frank Leopole's lines. "But our Latin American team is committed, isn't it?"

"Yes, it is. We have discussed pulling Julio's people back but even if we did, they would need days to reposition, get briefed, and learn the bio gear." He motioned around the hangar. "Whereas each of you . . ."

"Already knows about Marburg."

"Quite correct, Gunny." Mohammed rarely used the familiar title, but this time he wanted to make a point: unit cohesion. "You . . . we . . . have worked together and we know each other's moves, as you say. That is why SSI is asking you to extend your contract for as much as two more weeks."

Bosco raised a hand. "Excuse me, sir. I mean, does the same scale apply over here?"

Omar Mohammed was fluent in colloquial American. He smiled to himself: *Gotcha*. He looked to Derringer.

"Yes, Mr. Boscombe. Everyone who re-ups will work for the same bonus: foreign pay, combat pay, and the bonus for exceptional hazards. Full insurance coverage continues. That's definite."

Leopole and Mohammed exchanged knowing glances. They knew that Mike Derringer would wrest the extra funds from the board of directors if he had to mortgage the Arlington building to do it. However, both felt it far more likely that the United States Government had already committed to the extra funds.

Foyte looked at Leopole and winked.

Bosco glanced at Breezy and grinned hugely. Both imagined themselves on a clothing-optional beach carpeted with Victoria's Secret and *SI* models.

Jeffrey Malten thought of a comfortable house with one woman: The Woman. Whomever and wherever she was. He said, "When do we need to decide, sir?"

Derringer was ready for that. "Before you leave this hangar, son. We need a team in Arizona tomorrow."

Derringer turned his attention to Terry Keegan again. "I understand you've flown about fourteen hours in less than two days. How are you guys holding up?"

"We're okay, Admiral. Legally there's no problem because we're under Part 91 regs. As long as we're corporate rather than commercial we can pretty much set our own hours."

"Would it help to hire another crew just as backup?"

"Well, that could be a problem on short notice. Not many corporate guys are current on the Jurassic Jet these days. Maybe I can find some freighter dogs, though."

"Okay. Tell them we'll pay top hourly rate and buy their return fare."

As Derringer walked away to consult with Leopole, Keegan turned to his copilot. "You know, Eddie, in all my time in the Navy, nobody ever asked if I felt okay to fly. I was expected to down myself, but nobody ever asked."

Marsh grinned. "Nice to know somebody cares, ain't it?"

COCHISE COUNTY, ARIZONA

Agent Runnells needed a pit stop.

Based on fourteen years of Border Patrol experience, Robert Runnells knew that around 0100 hours, he would have to stop somewhere to relieve the pressure in his bladder. His wife and doctor both told him that he drank too much coffee—the nightly caffeine intake did more harm than good. Privately he was grateful for his swing shift assignment: he had worked graveyard before and that was a non-starter.

"Ah, Katie, pull over, will you?"

Agent Branch knew the drill by now. In the two weeks she had been partnered with the veteran, she had developed a grudging admiration for his professionalism, if not for his un-PC attitudes. She considered it a definite sign of progress when Bob Runnells had suggested that they alternate driving the Dodge SUV.

Branch slowed and turned off the packed-dirt road. In deference to her training officer's thin veneer of modesty, she turned off the lights but left the engine running. Runnells opened the right-hand door and exited, walking twelve paces rearward.

Katie Branch rolled down her window and looked at the sky. One nice thing about USBP work: it allowed an agent to enjoy an uncluttered view of God's handiwork. She smiled to herself. Burly, curmudgeonly Bob Runnells believed in a supreme being but fortunately he kept the evangelical rhetoric to a minimum.

Agent Branch did not share his confidence in a higher power. Between them, the Baptist and the agnostic had worked out a tenuous truce. Tonight the stars were clear as diamonds on black velvet, twinkling at Kathryn Branch across thousands of light years.

Sometimes there really did seem to be a Plan.

———————

Sixty meters south of the parked SUV, three men watched with rapt attention. Their night vision equipment—Gen III—was adequate for their purpose. Fourth-generation NVGs afforded more clarity and detail, but the price also soared commensurately. Tracking *La Migra* was a professional necessity, but smuggling was a business and, like any firm, the one run by Pablo Ramirez tried to keep the overhead to a minimum.

Lying atop a hummock, Ramirez scanned the area to either side of the white and green Dakota. After a few moments his partner whispered, *Quantos?*

Ramirez held up two fingers. *Dos.*

By tacit consent, they edged downward, reaching the bottom of the rise. Ramirez had seen one man relieving himself while the other remained in the vehicle. The leader signaled to his team: *We wait.* It should not be long.

Getting across the border had been relatively easy. A few minutes' work with pliers and wire had removed a section of cyclone fence nearly one meter wide. Previously prepared for that purpose, it had been replaced upon crossing to the American side. The egress route half a kilometer away was similarly ready. Even in daylight, one had to look closely to pick out the clipped segment.

Ramirez settled down to wait. At twenty-nine he was a fifteen-year veteran of his trade; in that time he had learned the ultimate value of patience. It was his major advantage over the *Norteamericanos.* For all their wealth and vehicles and helicopters and surveillance gear, they lacked his sense of time, the most valuable commodity on earth. It was an asset to be accumulated, saved, and expended when profitable.

Of course, it also helped to buy information now and then.

Ramirez gave a tight-lipped grin in the shadow of the hummock. The *Yanquis'* new intelligence structure, intended to produce greater efficiency, had yielded new vistas. Ramirez had predicted that with greater information sharing among federal and state agencies, more windows would open on the American government's operations. Ramirez's uncle, who taught the boy his trade, had always been an advocate of informed planning. Were he still living, *Tio* Guillermo would be astonished at the extent and the means of acquiring intelligence about one's enemies.

That was, after all, how Ramirez knew that this stretch of border would be lightly patrolled tonight. Two groups of emigrants led by expendable *coyotes* ensured that most of the *Yanquis'* attention was focused on areas well east. It was just another part of the overhead.

Bob Runnells finished "wringing out the sock" and walked back to the SUV. He opened the door, illuminating the dome light, and Katie Branch could not resist a jibe. "Feeling better, sir? A couple pounds lighter?"

The senior agent summoned up a loud, clear belch. "Why, yes. Thank you for asking. And how's your itty-bitty bladder?"

She responded with a dramatically sour expression. "Men!"

"We're disgusting, ain't we?"

"All I can say, sir, is that you're lucky there's no third sex. Sir."

While Runnells pondered the biological and physiological possibilities, Branch turned off the engine and slid out of her seat. "I feel like having a snack. What do you think? Sir?"

Runnells checked his watch. "Well, it's a little early for dinner, but I don't see any harm. Whatcha got tonight?"

"Honestly, Bob, I don't want to play Trade the Lunchbox again.

I brought what I like, and since I'm a vegetarian, you wouldn't want any of my food anyway."

Female and *vegetarian. What'n hell's the BP comin' to?* "Well, I don't know about that. Didn't you bring some dessert? I have some of Betty's oatmeal raisin cookies."

"No dessert for me, sir. I'm dieting. Gonna make a personal best in the physical fitness test next month." She produced a bag of what Runnells was pleased to describe as trail mix and unscrewed a bottle of green tea. By mutual consent they walked aft and turned the rear door into a tailgate party.

Runnells secretly admired Katie Branch's athleticism. At twenty-five she was slim and fit, a far better physical specimen than he had ever been. The downside was, the girl couldn't shoot to save her life—so to speak. She carried the standard-issue Beretta 96 because she had to, and twice had been sent to remedial marksmanship training. Runnells, a lifelong hunter, had shot on the USBP pistol team. More than once he had told the trainee, "I spent a lot of time and effort learning to shoot so I wouldn't have to run."

Katie Branch could not envision herself shooting anybody: probably not even to save her own life. She had joined the Border Patrol for a variety of reasons, chiefly to bring some informed sympathy to the undocumented workers who were the agency's reason for existence, and to enjoy the outdoor work environment.

Pablo Ramirez heard the Dodge's engine shut down. The silence was entirely unwelcome.

He bellied up the hummock again and turned on the Litton NVG. Both agents were standing at the rear of the vehicle, apparently eating. Occasionally he could hear their voices. One was higher pitched than the other—a woman?

Ramirez checked the illuminated dial of his watch. He could wait a few minutes longer but if the unexpected SUV did not move on, his schedule would be jeopardized. The station wagon that would transport the two Muslims to wherever they were headed lay nearly two kilometers northwest. Ramirez knew that the driver would not overstay his appointed time, and that meant loss of the delivery fee: half the potential revenue.

The two human forms glowed greenly in Ramirez's scope. They were damnably unconcerned with the passage of time—the value of which increased with each passing minute. *Bastards. They should be reported for slacking off.*

That would be something: a Mexican criminal reporting two American agents for idling away the night, impeding the righteous progress of the smuggling trade.

Ramirez waited another minute, then returned to the base of the hummock. "Listen," he whispered. "We cannot wait any longer. We will take a detour to the west about a hundred meters and pass behind the vehicle. Everyone crosses the road at the same time—understand?" He drew silent nods from his two immediate accomplices. They had worked with him for periods varying between months and years. All understood the rationale: by crossing together, total exposure time was reduced to the minimum. And though crossing in front of the SUV would largely block the Americans' view of the road ahead, the seven men in Ramirez's party would leave a noticeable cluster of footprints. Crossing behind the vehicle eliminated that danger.

Ramirez dispatched Jorge to bring up the two "packages" with their escort. In minutes the group was ready to move, swinging south-westerly, keeping to the defiles and occasional hummocks.

———————

"I'll take a little walk before we go," Branch declared.

"You too?" Runnells could not resist a jibe. "I thought you gal athletes never had to go potty. Muscle control or something."

"Where'd you hear that? Sir."

"Uh, must've been locker room talk in grade school."

Branch stuffed the remains of her dinner into the Ziploc bag and secured it in the truck. Then she walked into the darkness behind the SUV.

Thirty meters out, she glimpsed—something. A shadow, a movement ghosting through the periphery of her vision. She froze in place. Her instinct was to call out: issue the usual challenge. *Alto!* But she could not be sure what it was—perhaps a coyote or javalina.

She pulled the Maglite from her duty belt and shone the tight, powerful beam ahead of her. Two men were caught in the white band, twenty meters away. One stopped briefly; the other sprinted out of view.

It did not register in Kathryn Branch's mind that both were armed.

She found her voice. *"Alto! Migra!"*

The second man reacted in a most peculiar fashion. Instead of fleeing or raising his hands, he dropped to the ground, facing Agent Branch. She noticed something long and black in his hands, and her brain finally defaulted to the recognition mode. *Rifle!*

She realized her mortal peril. With her right hand holding the light, she could not draw her Beretta. She switched the light to her support hand, fumbled for the pistol and managed to draw the weapon from the thumb-break holster.

It did not occur to her to move.

Two loud reports shattered the desert air.

The first round went wide to the left, its aim spoiled by the bright light. The next, more carefully directed, struck Branch in the solar plexus. She seldom wore her ballistic vest, but it would have done no good against a rifle. The 7.62 round from a stolen Mexican Army G3 did what it was meant to do. It delivered 2,300 foot-pounds to her 125-pound body.

Because Branch was shot through and through, she did not absorb the full energy of the projectile. But the massive disparity was enough to drop her instantly. She lay on her left side, stunned and gasping for air. As she exsanguinated into the dirt, crumpled beneath a mesquite tree, she barely registered that she was dying.

———

When Bob Runnells heard the shots, he dropped his sandwich and called "Katie!" He found himself eight strides toward her direction when he realized that he should call for help. His Beretta had assumed its familiar position in his dominant hand; left wrapped around the right with the muzzle low. He paused momentarily, fighting a two-front war between Duty and Honor, and opted for Honor. He turned forty degrees left, running bent over, hoping to flank the shooter.

He badly wanted his Remington 870 with six Hornady 12-gauge rounds, but field agents were prohibited personal weapons.

Kneeling behind a depression, Runnells pulled his light and laid it alongside his pistol's frame. His thumb rested on the button, ready to illuminate any threat. He was conscious of his breath as he sucked in desert air, his eyes swerving left and right, near to far as much as possible in the dark.

He left cover again, searching the night for some sign of his partner. Something moved ahead of him; he stopped, knelt, and waited. He heard Spanish. *"Quien es?"*

Runnells resisted the urge to shoot the Mexican. Bracing his light against the pistol, he thumbed down the switch.

Eighteen paces ahead of him were two men, one with a G3. Years of training kicked in. Framing his black sights in the white light, Runnells shouted, *"Alto!"* as he stroked the trigger once, twice, thrice.

Struck by two .40-caliber rounds, the man dropped his rifle and swerved away, out of view.

Another alien appeared, then a third. Two were armed and both opened fire: one with a G3, the other with a Ruger pistol. The three combatants exchanged gunfire within shouting distance. It lasted less than five seconds.

Runnells' vest stopped two 9mm rounds, but the 7.62s bored through him and knocked him on his back. Then he was aware of someone standing over him, and the eruption of an impossibly bright light in his face that ended all cognition.

Pablo Ramirez cursed long, silently and fervently. A firefight with the Border Patrol was the last thing he wanted on Planet Earth. The only positive aspect was the conclusion. Two dead *Yanquis* versus two of his men wounded; one seriously.

Ramirez forced himself to focus. He sprinted to the Dodge and noted the doors shut, the radio apparently unused. He dashed back to his men, finding one receiving rudimentary first aid. "Jorge, take Casique home. The rest, come with me. Now!"

Supported by his friend, Casique Estrella looked at the first dead

American. He realized the body was female. He muttered, "I never killed a woman before."

Jorge de la Cruz pulled his partner's arm around his neck. "Amigo, I never saw a cow in a bull ring, either."

Ramirez turned to gather up his group and counted heads. He heard soft moaning. *"Donde es..."*

Joaquin pointed toward a prostrate form. One of the couriers was bent over the other, wailing an incomprehensible dirge that penetrated the night air.

SSI OFFICES

SSI had an early morning call from Burridge's deputy.

"Derringer here."

John Demeter's voice still carried the flatland tones of Nebraska though he had not lived there in nearly thirty years. "Admiral, the secretary is attending a meeting at State but he left standing orders to notify you immediately of any change."

"Yes, John. Go ahead."

"There was shooting on the Arizona border last night. Two agents were killed and apparently at least one of the perpetrators was hit. No body but quite a blood trail."

"Yes?"

"Well, it was a small group—the field supervisor puts it at six or seven. There were two larger groups farther east, and they may have been decoys. Anyway, the killers left a fair amount of material behind. Probably a lot of confusion with the shooting in the dark. Anyway, one of the items was a prayer book."

Derringer felt himself growing testy. *Cut to the chase!* "So?"

"Oh. Well, apparently it's a Muslim prayer book. Not Arabic, either."

"Pakistani?"

"We've not had it fully analyzed, but I'm told it could be Urdu."

"Where'd this happen?"

"Between Bisbee and Nogales."

"GPS coordinates?"

"Ah, we don't have that yet: just the preliminary report. But I checked the map, and it's roughly 110 west by 31.5 north."

Derringer recorded the lat-long, then asked, "What time?"

"Apparently about 1:00 A.M. local. Call it . . . five-six hours ago."

Damn it to hell! Derringer made a conscious effort to ease his grip on the phone. "John, that means they've got a big jump on us. My crew landed at Tucson last night, expecting to operate across the border. I'll get right on to them and deploy to Phoenix, unless you think we should continue as planned."

"Well, Admiral, I've consulted with our operations office and they say this could be an elaborate ruse. But if so, it's very well planned. There's blood on the prayer book. We recommend that you keep a small team to watch Tucson and send the rest to Phoenix. You have the contact info there?"

"Affirm. It's in the contingency plans."

"Very well, sir. I'll have the secretary call you ASAP."

"Right." Derringer punched the button, ending the call and buzzed his secretary. "Peggy, have everybody meet me in the conference room immediately. Things have turned to hash again."

LONDON

"Mr. Padgett-Smith? I am Dr. Singh. We spoke on the phone."

"Ah, yes. Thank you for your call, doctor."

The Indian physician spoke excellent English with precise diction. But he did not want to leave anything uncertain. He extended an arm down the hallway. "We can speak more comfortably in my office."

Charles Padgett-Smith had not made a small fortune by missing the nuances. "What is it, Doctor?"

Singh glanced around, unwilling to speak in public. He cradled his clipboard in both hands and regarded the Englishman. "Sir, your wife's condition is quite grave. It worsened overnight."

The financier swallowed. Hard. Finally he found the words. "Is she going to . . . die?"

Singh had years of experience with such things. It did not matter. Without intending to, he looked at the floor.

SSI OFFICES

When Derringer entered the conference room Sandy Carmichael got up and poured another cup of coffee. Derringer noted that her hair could use some attention, and there were unaccustomed wrinkles in her blouse. Joe Wolf, who typically ran toward disheveled, was rubbing his temples again—another sign of fatigue. Most of the other staffers also showed signs of working late-late. Or, more accurately, early-early.

"Ladies and gentlemen," Derringer interjected, "let me say something." He paused, waiting for the staff's full attention. "Most of you look like hell."

His quip had the desired effect. The laughter was neither forced nor polite. "Just remember, regardless of how you feel, think about our operators. They had one night back in this country before taking off for Arizona. Along the way they've had to junk their plan for cross-border ops and now work out a discreet surveillance routine in one of the world's busiest airports." He spread his hands. "Basically, they left on a camping trip and now they're attending a convention. I checked with Phil Catterly, who's still with them, by the way. He estimates most of our people have forty-eight to sixty hours of useful work in them. After that, they're going to start crashing."

Carmichael absorbed that information, then asked, "Given the limited time we have to work with, what're our priorities?"

"Sandy, you said it. We have to think fast and work fast. We're going to improvise like hell today."

Derringer explained the overnight developments and waved down the comments from astonished staffers. "I've called Frank and Terry in Tucson and told them to leave some guys there to cover the airport in shifts. But I think that Phoenix is the target because it's a much larger facility. If the Marburg gets a grip there, the effects could be devastating. Closing down one of the six biggest airports in the country is just a start."

The phone, fax, and email traffic was relentless. Joe Wolf tried to make sense of it and declared it an impossible task. "It's what I was afraid of," he said. "Information overload. We just don't have time to sort it all out." He held up a sheaf of emails and notes from phone conversations. "After this is all over, people will look at the record and think, 'My god, they were dumb. It was right there!' "

Derringer conceded the point, then conned the SSI vessel back on course. "Joe, we can't worry about that now. Let's stay focused on our operating area." He used PowerPoint to produce a map of Phoenix. "This is the fifth largest metro area in the country. There's always public events; just look at this weekend's schedule." He ticked off several items from a website. "The Diamondbacks are in San Diego, but ASU hosts Oregon State. There's also a trade show at the civic center and a big gun show at the fairgrounds."

"Any of those events draws thousands of people," Carmichael said.

"That's right. But look at it from the suiciders' perspective. Sure, there's thousands of people at those events. But they're mostly local. Anybody infected here mostly stays here. At the airport you get it both ways: people coming and going. Somebody exposed to Marburg here can be in LA or Boston or London in a matter of hours. And there's no need for the suspects to go through security. Just wander around, spreading the virus by contact with doors, lavatories, escalators. You name it."

Mohammed nodded in agreement. "We can't cover many places so we concentrate our people at Sky Harbor?"

"That's right, Omar. All our eggs go in the airport basket."

TUCSON, ARIZONA

Hazrat Sial, aka Baldah, felt more comfortable than any time since the night on the border. Poor Mian; he died in pain in a strange place, without a known grave. But Sial took comfort from Imam Taamir, a Los Angeles congregational leader who was obviously capable yet personable, as far as his position allowed. He was not given to small talk, and spent much of the trip in silence beside the holy warrior while one of two aides drove the Mercedes.

At length the cleric said, "I marvel at Dr. Sharif's vision, my friend. To think that he conceived this plan before he even met you."

"Is it true that he is dead?"

"Martyred. He is martyred."

"As is my brother, Mian."

"Truly. They are both with God."

Sial sat quietly for a moment, sensing the first stage symptoms: fever, chills, and a pulsing headache, all as the doctor had foretold. Then he found the words he sought. "I can feel the disease growing inside me. Shall I really be with Allah, wise one?"

Taamir knew enough of the plan to take precautions. He did not touch the courier, though if the cleric absorbed some of the virus, that was God's will; part of the *jihad*. He nodded—sagely, he hoped—and replied, "It is so. He who spends himself in a righteous cause earns entry to Paradise."

For all his devotion and study, Hazrat Sial was still a twenty-year-old farmer's son from the hills of Baluchistan. "I . . . I confess. I am afraid."

Taamir turned to survey the biowarrior. "That is understandable, my brother. You are bound on a journey which few have the courage to undertake. For that, you deserve all praise."

"I expected to die with Mian. We were to have one another's comfort. Now . . ."

The imam was quick to respond. The boy needed handling. "Now you are receiving the comfort of God himself. Take that, accept it. Believe it!"

The young Pakistani made no reply. He merely turned his head, watching the desert landscape cruise past at a hundred kilometers per hour.

"Remember another thing," Taamir added. "You shall not be truly alone." He gestured to the front seat where an aide rode in silence. "Mohammed will stand vigil over you. As I explained, he will not be able to provide direct assistance, but he will observe your actions and the response of the infidels. He can deceive them, delay their efforts perhaps. And report the fulfillment of your work."

The passenger looked over his shoulder at Sial. The man's name was not Mohammed, but that was of small concern. As the imam had directed, the aide would maintain his distance from the courier, but remain in sight to lend encouragement should the jihadist waver.

At least it sounded convincing at the time.

SSI OFFICES

Derringer walked into the conference room. "Carolyn Padgett-Smith is critical. She's not expected to live."

"Oh, no . . ." Sandy Carmichael's voice was hushed.

Omar Mohammed's reply was muted. He had not believed she would live this long.

"I just heard from her husband," Derringer continued. "He said she's rallied a little after last night when a naturopath visited her. She seems to think it'll help but Charles . . . well, he doesn't."

Sandy shook her head. "Why would that veterinarian want to kill her? Was he just spiteful? I mean, it was over!"

Mohammed found his voice. "We shall never know, Sandy. But I can speculate. Sharif spent many of his formative years in England. He lost his way from the righteous path, and he may have blamed British women in part. After all, he committed the sin of fornication, and there is evidence that he developed the Marburg virus as a means of proving his conversion."

"By becoming a holy warrior."

Mohammed nodded. "Exactly."

PHOENIX, ARIZONA

Leopole and Catterly convened the briefing in their suite at the Skyview Inn on Van Buren Street near the airport. The room was crowded as twenty-two operators arrayed themselves on sofas, chairs, and the carpeted floor. The door kickers were augmented by Terry Keegan and Eddie Marsh, who had to fly the 727, plus Wolf's investigators, Sherree Kim and Jim Mannock.

Leopole made the introductions. "Sherree and Jim know the basics of the case and interviewed the original Marburg volunteer's parents. They flew out here commercial to join us." He allowed a slight grin. "Beyond that fact, I wanted them here just because they don't look like any of you guys."

When the chuckles died down, Leopole turned to business. "Guys, I'll say it loud and clear: this entire operation is about deniability, as much as in Pakistan. We've been contracted because the government is not permitted to target ethnic groups or individuals, even if the rest of the world knows who poses the threat. Yes, it's stupid and it's counter-productive. But that's the way it is.

"Officially, we're just passing through the airport, and if we happen to see something suspicious, we notify the security people or we take direct action: our call. As soon as you have a suspect in hand, turn him over to the authorities—and vanish. If there's any reporting at all, the media will be told that security forces made the arrest or that private citizens noticed suspicious activity, depending on the immediate situation. In any case, nobody is to connect SSI with this operation.

"Schedules: we're going to spend rotating shifts in each terminal or riding the shuttles: eight hours on, six off, until further notice. If nothing turns up in a couple of days, we'll probably go home.

"Now, we have liaison officers who officially don't know what we're doing but who can run interference. Check your notes: you have Mr. Timmons and Mr. Meagher from TSA plus Mr. Shub and Ms. Calthrop from DHS. If you have any problems—any at all—call or page them and they'll clear the red tape for you. At least one of them will be available round the clock. The ID you've been given should get you through any security gate in the airport, but only show the badge if you're questioned."

Bosco fingered his badge in the laminated plastic holder with the metal clip. As instructed, he would keep it hidden unless needed.

"As far as the gatekeepers are concerned, you're all members of the airport security detail. But our bigger concern is keeping you from being noticed by our suspects. That's why I asked most of you to wear travel attire and to carry a valise or suitcase. You have ticket envelopes for the appropriate airlines in your terminal, and at this rate, we can keep teams in each terminal for the next twenty hours or so."

"Comm. You have hand-held radios in your bags. We'd like something less conspicuous but that's what we've got so that's what we'll use. Pay attention to the public address system. If you hear a call for me or Dr. Catterly, that probably means somebody's spotted a suspect. If your radio's down, tap in the access code on a white courtesy phone or dial the 800 number at a pay phone. At that point, we'll establish a rotating surveillance of the guy so he doesn't spot one operator in particular. If he does something overt, use your judgment. That could mean anything from tackling him to shooting him. If it develops into a chase or there's multiple suspects, use your respirator, goggles, and gloves. By then we won't be playing like tourists anymore."

Leopole gestured to Catterly, who rose to speak. "I can't add much to what I said before, but I'll review the basics for the new members. As a frame of reference, Marburg has a similarity to streptococcus. 'Step B' kills healthy tissue by breaking down the body's protein matrix. The infected area creates a growing number of dead cells, which gives the bacteria more room to grow, creating a vicious cycle. The more they grow, the more toxins are produced and the more cells are affected. It's a lot like gangrene: the dying tissue has to be amputated before the infection proves fatal."

"So how's that different from Marburg?"

Catterly shook his head. "In that respect, it's not. Strep B is most common in babies and pregnant women, but across the board the main difference is the degree of virulence. You don't get twenty-five percent mortality from strep. You do with Marburg. You could say that it's Strep B on steroids: more aggressive and it works faster." He made a face. "I don't even want to think about Ebola right now."

Sherree Kim raised a hand. "Doctor, what are we looking for? I mean, what kind of action could be called overt?"

"Just keep this in mind: the virus is best spread by direct contact with body fluids of the carrier. So anybody who spits on door handles, railings, or phones is a suspect. If he licks his hands and rubs them on a surface, that's a red flag, too. If he pours something or drops a liquid, notice where. HazMat teams are standing by. They can handle just about anything from a bite to decontaminating a bus." He paused for emphasis, then added, "I just pray they don't have to decontaminate an airport."

Mannock spoke for the first time. "When do we start?"

Leopole checked his watch. "First shift hits the airport in twenty mikes."

MARICOPA COUNTY

"Stop at once!" Hazrat Sial shouted to the driver.

The limousine urgently braked to a stop along I-17, and Imam Taamir guessed the reason. He was quickly proven right. Sial had barely opened the rear door before voiding his stomach onto the ground. He dry heaved several times, emitting gagging and retching sounds that caused the cleric to turn his head.

When the Pakistani recovered his composure, he sat upright again. "Water," he croaked. "Mohammed" passed a bottle to the jihadist, who rinsed his mouth and spat out the remnants of his previous meal. From ingrained habit, the youngster replaced the cap and offered the plastic container back to his accomplice. The man in the front seat waved a hand. "You may keep it."

Sial grasped the meaning. The response had far less to do with manners than with the donor's welfare.

The biowarrior shut the heavy door and laid his head back on the upholstered seat.

Taamir nodded to the driver and the Mercedes pulled away.

PHOENIX, ARIZONA

Terminal One at Sky Harbor Airport was typically bustling. Departing passengers unloaded on the north side while most arrivals awaited transportation on the south. Among the former were three SSI operators: Breezy, Bosco, and Delmore. Each went to his assigned sector, knowing that the other on-duty teams were deploying in the other terminals.

Breezy took in the semi-modern ambience: Southwestern murals, bright lights, and industrial grade carpeting. The irony struck him: presumably the terrorist plan was designed to avoid heightened airport security but now the confrontation—if it came—would occur in an airport. He walked to a remote area and opened his innocuous-appearing suitcase. At the appointed time he made the comm check with his handset and received "up" responses from his partners and Leopole. He sat down, produced last year's *Sports Illustrated* swimsuit issue, and began his surveillance. The gorgeous mannequins' forms had long since been etched in his memory.

Across the concourse, Bosco established his own routine. He took care to place his ticket folder in his front pocket, ensuring that his airline matched the appropriate gate. Two lines of travelers were queuing up at the security gate, indulging in the routine of removing shoes, emptying pockets, and placing their possessions in gray plastic trays for examination by TSA screeners. No Middle Eastern passengers were visible yet.

Bosco gave Delmore a subtle nod, releasing the body builder to patronize one of the fast food emporiums.

It looked like a long night.

———

"There, to the right."

Jim Mannock nudged Sherree Kim, who looked out the window of the shuttle bus. She saw two targets among the throng of travelers entering Terminal Three: apparently Muslim males, one young and one mid to late thirties.

After five hours on their shift, the investigators faced a quick decision: should they make the call and continue riding the bus? Send one inside, retaining the other as the rover? Or should both disembark and tail the two suspects?

Mannock glanced around. No likely Muslims rode the interterminal shuttle. As the senior partner it was his call. "I'll bail out, Sherree. Call Team Three and tell them what you saw. But watch for other suspects, too." With that he unlimbered his six-one frame and stepped off the bus moments before it resumed its route.

Sial and Mohammed walked into the building from the north side and skirted the baggage claim area. With his long legs, Mannock had little trouble catching up. He noted that the two were together but trying to appear apart. The taller, older man stayed eight to ten steps behind the other. The youngster was focused on getting through the building; he exhibited no tradecraft. Mannock assessed the other as an escort: not terribly well trained, but possessing rudimentary skills. The man avoided obvious turning of his head, likely using his peripheral vision, and occasionally stopping to tie a shoe or check his ticket to look around him.

Mannock stepped to a phone bank and pulled out his radio. "Frank, this is Jim."

"Copy, Jim." Leopole's voice snapped back from his command post in Terminal One.

"I'm in Three, looking at two suspects. Sherree is talking to Team Three from the bus. Our items of interest headed straight through, north to south. Looks like they're trying to shake any tail."

"Stand by, One." Mannock suspected that Leopole was contacting Team Three in case Kim was unable to reach them. The gangly ex-cop scanned the area, looking for Ashcroft or Green, but did not see them.

Moments later Leopole was back on the air. "Jim, Frank."

"Jim here. Go."

"Three is on 'em, Jim. They split up. Green's tailing the older guy and Ashcroft is waiting to see what the other one does."

"Where are they?"

"Stand by. We'll go common in ten seconds."

Mannock switched to the common frequency that placed Leopole, himself, and Team Three on the same channel.

"Green's up."

"Ashcroft here."

"Mannock here."

"Frank's up. Bob, where's your target?"

Ashcroft's drawl came across the circuit. "He left the restroom, then went to baggage claim. He's got a valise in one hand and a handkerchief in the other. Looks like he's wiped it on some doors. Right now he's on the shuttle island."

"Roger that. Mark the spots for HazMat. Break-break. Phil, what about your guy?"

"He's just walking around," Green replied. "Looks like no threat."

"All right. Stay on him. Jim, tail the primary and let me know where he goes."

Mannock acknowledged, stowed his radio, and walked to the back of the line at the shuttle stop. From twenty feet away, he assessed the young foreigner. The skin had taken on a pallorous sheen, as if the man was perspiring from a temperature. Occasionally the target raised his handkerchief to his mouth, either to wet it or to keep down something that wanted to rise above the tongue.

While boarding, Mannock went to the rear of the bus and took an aisle seat. Discreetly, he tugged on a pair of latex gloves and watched his mark, seated three rows forward. The young Muslim kept his hankie in hand but did not seem to wipe it on the seats or rails. *Too many people nearby*, Mannock thought. *We'll see what he does at the next stop.* The jihadist did nothing for the next twenty minutes. He rode the shuttle, clutching his handkerchief in his right hand with his valise in his lap. Once he stood up as if to leave, but merely changed seats. Mannock stayed put, unwilling to commit to a move until certain of his mark's intention.

Hazrat Sial turned in his seat and looked at James Mannock. *Busted*, the copper thought. *It was bound to happen.*

At the next stop the Pakistani exited the bus. Mannock resisted the impulse to chase his prey, instead calling Leopole with an update. "Frank, Jim. He's just gone into Terminal One."

With little else to do, Terry Keegan and Eddie Marsh arrived early to relieve Team One and received a radio briefing from Leopole. Then they made visual contact with Bosco and Breezy, who had just seen a young Muslim enter near the ticket counter. Marsh asked, "Is that the guy? By the Great Southwestern sign?"

"Yeah," Bosco replied. "He's wearing what Jim Mannock described."

Keegan did not want to take chances. "Have you seen any other Muslim-looking guys?"

"There was a mama with some young 'uns," Breezy said. "They wore white turbans but I'm not sure if they were Muslims or Sikhs or something."

Keegan's blue eyes parsed the lobby, searching for other suspects. "Well, I don't see anybody else right now. You guys go get some rest. Eddie and I will take it from here."

The new team dispersed to begin surveillance, watching Target Alpha while remaining open to others. Minutes later Leopole was back on the air. "Be advised, there are multiple items in Two but they're currently no threat. A mixed pair in Four, apparently leaving. However, a single is exiting the bus at One, north side."

"I'm there," Marsh replied. In a few moments he was back: "Got him. Mid thirties, heavyset, no beard, tan jacket and dark pants."

Leopole checked his notes. "Ah, roger, Ed. That's Target Bravo. He was tagged as escort for the primary before the shift change."

Mohammed was back.

———

In Terminal One's security office, Leopole summarized the situation for his TSA liaison. "We have two targets, both in the main lobby, ground floor. The younger one is the likely threat; the other seems to make eye contact with him about every thirty to forty minutes, wherever they are. Obviously they're on some sort of rotation. They've met in two terminals now."

Dennis Meagher watched the TV monitor, picking out the two Muslims amid the crowd. "Have they done anything unusual?"

"Target Alpha has rubbed his handkerchief on some railings and doors, but that's it so far." The SSI operative shrugged. "Of course, that's all it might take to spread the virus."

"You know I can't initiate action against someone without probable cause."

"Well, that's why we're here, Mr. Meagher." Leopole smiled. "Deniability."

"What do you propose, Colonel?"

"I'd like to press Alpha a bit. Let him see one of our guys obviously tailing him and watch what he does."

Conscientious professional that he was, Supervisor Meagher declined comment.

Mission-oriented operator that he was, Frank Leopole accepted silence as consent.

"Comm check," Leopole called.

Keegan, Marsh, Mannock, and Kim all checked in.

"Okay, here we go," Leopole began. "Alpha's already tagged Jim, so we'll use him to goad the target. Terry and Eddie maintain a roving perimeter around him. Sherree, watch Target Bravo. We will not act until he breaks off again. Acknowledge."

"Keegan, roger."
"Marsh, roger that."
"Mannock, right."
"Kim, okie-dokie."

When Mohammed left the terminal, he failed to notice the young Oriental woman tracking him.

However, Hazrat Sial immediately became aware of the towering presence of James Mannock, six meters behind him. After three abrupt direction changes, the Pakistani realized he could not lose the big infidel who had ridden the bus with him. Sial returned to the men's room and entered a stall.

He was perspiring more freely now, and the obvious surveillance heightened the churning in his stomach. The headache was persistent, and growing worse. He felt himself failing physically; his heart beat faster to maintain blood pressure. He could walk normally, but he realized that he no longer possessed the strength to run very far.

In the rare moments when his body had permitted him some equanimity, Sial absorbed the enormous contradiction called America. The infidels' technical marvels were plain to see: huge airplanes that spanned continents and oceans; bright, gleaming buildings of steel and glass; a communications system previously undreamt of. Yet the place was built upon determined decadence and studied stupidity. Every magazine rack paraded beautiful young women who exposed themselves to the world through a camera lens. It seemed that one-sixth of the young men slouched through life, so addled that they were incapable of wearing a cap properly.

Yet for all its varied faults and contradictions, the land that spawned the twenty-first-century Crusaders had somehow overwhelmed the world. Its mongrelized, hedonistic culture had become the global standard. How did that happen? Violent, unclean motion pictures and unhealthy fast food emporiums cropped up around the planet, including places such as Baluchistan. It was appalling. And for that transgression, America would suffer long after Hazrat Sial's pain had ended.

His time had come.

Sial unzipped his valise and withdrew a spray bottle. He pressed the plunger twice, directing the contents onto the toilet's handle and the lock on the door. From his pocket he drew a three-inch switchblade. Once his actions drew attention, he could fend off the Zionist lackeys long enough to spread more of his lethal essence onto doors, railings, and people.

The martyred doctor had explained that the virus did not live long outside the body, so the contaminated places had to be refreshed. Sial had widely deposited his saliva in two terminals but he remembered the big American who had so obviously dogged his trail. Had the balding giant noted the spots and cleaned them up? If so, at least he could not neutralize what was about to happen.

Sial opened the door to the stall and glanced around. Three infidels were cleansing themselves, paying him no attention. He went to the next stall, sprayed the door and the toilet, then went to the next. He was repeating the process when he heard a voice.

"Hey, man, what're you doing?"

A Hispanic gentleman approached Sial; one of the oppressed victims of the Jewish power structure. Well, there was nothing else to be done. The living martyr raised his bottle and sprayed the pitiful wretch in the face.

Hazrat Sial dashed for the exit, determined to empty his weapon onto as many westerners as possible. There! The big, ugly American blocked his path; latex covering his hands and a respirator with goggles on his face. The hands came toward the Pakistani with surprising speed. Instinctively, Sial sprayed his enemy but the mist only struck clothing. A hand closed on his right forearm, controlling the bottle. Sial reacted instinctively, bringing his left hand up and forward. The serrated blade sliced into James Mannock's ribs, causing the American to release his grip. Sial spun away, half turning to the right where he saw an opening near the food court.

Mannock registered a deluge of emotions: pain, anger, and fear. He felt warm blood running down his side but that did not bother him immediately. *What'd the bastard put on his blade?* Momentarily taken aback, he could only call, "Stop that guy!"

Sial sprayed and slashed his way into the crowd. Men shouted;

women screamed; children wailed. The closest people tried to flee, colliding with others. The result was a milling, noisy pandemonium.

———————

Keegan and Marsh had staked out the restroom. Whichever way Target Alpha turned, one of the SSI men would be on him. But in the noise and confusion, neither kept sight of him. They knew that Leopole would have a god's-eye view from the security office, but tracking the target's movements on remote cameras and relaying the information via hand-held radios in a panicky crowd was a major challenge.

Terry Keegan motioned with his left hand, directing Eddie Marsh to loop wide to that side of the aisle. Then the senior pilot sprinted toward the center of the churning crowd.

A middle-aged woman blocked his path, sagging to her knees and holding her abdomen. Keegan veered around her, knocked over a shrieking child, and swept his eyes methodically left to right.

Opposite the men's room entrance, Keegan noticed something odd: women fleeing the ladies' room. He spun on his heel, shoved a rabbi out of the way, and reflexively uttered, "Excuse me, Father."

The women's facility was empty. Mirrors shone; tile gleamed; blood drops tracked the floor. Keegan looked behind him—*Always check your six in a combat zone*—but he seemed alone. He eased against the wall, protecting his back while willing his breath to abate. He used the opportunity to pull on his respirator, then lowered his valise to the floor.

Deep breathing; almost sobbing. Far end of the room.

Keegan backtracked to the entrance and took a quick look. He saw neither Marsh nor Mannock, and no cops or security people. The crowd was still writhing inward upon itself. Keegan took off his shoes and padded to the last stall. The door was closed but no one seemed inside. The strained breathing told him that Alpha was there, probably perched on the commode, catching his breath.

Two college-age women came in, chattering animatedly about the mysterious confusion. They saw the gloved and goggled male and stopped in their tracks. Keegan's first instinct was to raise a finger to his face, signaling silence, but he had a better idea. He crooked a finger at them in a come-hither gesture. They screamed and ran for the exit.

Keegan backed into a stall, left the door mostly closed but still ajar, and waited.

Hazrat Sial appeared from Keegan's right. Drawn by the prospect of more infidels, he broke cover and stalked carefully down the line, proceeding past Keegan.

Shoes on the floor. Men's shoes. In the women's room.

Sial pivoted on one foot, raising the spray bottle as Keegan tackled him. They went down hard, rolling once. Keegan felt a stabbing pain as the back of his head impacted the tiled floor. *Damn! Hurts! Gotta keep in the fight.* He shook off the blow, increased the pressure of his grip on Alpha, and began leveraging an advantage. Though younger, the terrorist was smaller and weaker than the American. But Sial possessed an inherent advantage: he fought to die while his opponent wanted to live. Keegan got hold of the Pakistani's wrists and rolled him onto his back. Now on top, the aviator had neutralized the fight. It occurred to him that he was like the proverbial Great Dane that chases sports cars—what to do when you catch one?

Keegan could not release either hand without giving Sial a no-miss shot with the bottle or the knife. His mind racing, the erstwhile sub hunter decided to accept the lesser hit in order to prevent the greater damage. He shifted his right hand to his opponent's left, and began a heartfelt effort with both hands to snap the younger man's wrist. The spray bottle was constantly in motion. Keegan felt the mist against his exposed skin, behind the respirator and below the goggles. At some point in the fear and rage and violence, he realized that the bottle was empty.

Gotcha, ya little bastard.

Without intellectualizing it, Keegan employed an engineering concept: opposite torsion. He twisted in different directions with each hand, finally forcing the knife from Sial's grasp. The terrorist now was spitting into his assailant's masked and goggled face, and when the knife hit the floor, Keegan used his right fist to smash the man's nose. Momentarily stunned, Hazrat Sial did not see the infidel scoop up the knife. The living martyr only glimpsed its arcing descent an instant before its point entered his trachea.

Hazrat Sial, age twenty, transitioned to full-fledged martyrdom on the floor of a women's restroom far from Baluchistan.

WASHINGTON, D.C.

Cabinet members seldom bother reading press releases, but Secretary Bruce Burridge wanted to screen this one. He adjusted his reading glasses and read the draft press release. It was the product of two deputy undersecretaries in his outer office.

> The Department of Homeland Security has completed its investigation of the alleged terrorist incident at Phoenix International Airport two weeks ago. After consulting with other federal, state, and local agencies, DHS has concluded that original reports about terrorist activities were issued before a thorough evaluation was concluded.
>
> Following dozens of interviews with airport officials, security officers, and air travelers, DHS determined what actually occurred during a brief but confusing disturbance at Sky Harbor Airport on the nineteenth. The incident was limited to one

terminal, and passengers on other airlines were not subjected to unusual delays.

The only fatality was a foreign national who apparently was carrying forged documents. His identity has not been positively established, though competent observers testified that he exhibited signs of mental instability. Federal investigators concluded that the man, reportedly in his twenties, was not an airline passenger and never breached the security gates for any of the airlines in that terminal.

The only confirmed injuries were inflicted on six people who sustained knife wounds. Most were treated and released from area hospitals that evening, though one woman was being held following surgery. All are expected to recover.

Homeland Security Secretary Bruce Burridge praised alert travelers and the quick response of security personnel in limiting the potentially deadly effects of the apparently deranged man's attack.

Media reports about chemical or toxic sprays wielded by the assailant are not sustained by available evidence, Burridge added.

Burridge grasped his trademark green pen and made a notation. "OK for release. BB." He dropped the sheet in his out basket.

The secretary plopped his spectacles onto the desk and leaned back in his overstuffed chair. According to the medicos, the Marburg incubation period had passed, and then some. Fortunately, none of the exposed individuals had come down with the disease, largely because nothing was found on the assailant's knife blade. The spray with diluted blood was ineffective, but penetrating wounds could have carried the filovirus deep into living tissue. Like that gallant British lady—something Smith.

Burridge briefly mused about the late Hazrat Sial. That name would never be made public, nor would the body ever be claimed. It could not be—the infected corpse had been incinerated within hours and the ashes given a proper burial.

The U.S. Government occasionally had need of patriotic Muslim clerics.

SSI OFFICES

"That's quite a list," Wolf muttered.

"It keeps growing," Derringer replied. "I guess it always will."

"Well, at least we don't have to use anonymous stars like the memorial at Langley."

Derringer nodded, making no comment. Both men had conducted professional dealings with the CIA. The gray stars precisely carved into the marble wall bore silent tribute to the casualties the agency sustained in the shadow world of the Cold War.

The two friends looked again at SSI's honor roll, newly updated in the briefing room: seventeen men and two women killed in the company's employ. Five had died in accidents—three in an Iraqi helicopter crash—proving that combat often involved the lesser risk.

In Honored Memory

John F. Robison	Croatia, 1994
George H. Doherty	Guatemala, 1998
Fred M. Herrig	Iraq, 2003
Allyn L. Capron	Iraq, 2003
Tilden W. Dawson	Iraq, 2003
Marcus D. Russell	Iraq, 2003
William T. Erwin	Iraq, 2004
Harriet A. Billingsley	USA, 2006
Thomas H. Grant, Jr.	USA, 2006
Aaron L. Marks	USA, 2006
Rebeccah Nielsen	USA, 2006
Raymond H. Treater	USA, 2006
Charles K. Werblin	USA, 2006
James S. Boyle, Jr.	Pakistan, 2006
Emiliano Cashius	Pakistan, 2006
Joel R. Hall	Pakistan, 2006
Harold H. Haywood	Pakistan, 2006
Darryl Logue	Pakistan, 2006
Jacob W. Swetman	Pakistan, 2006

Wolf knew that one name was missing. He looked at his friend and boss. "Emily's family still won't let her name go up?"

Derringer shrugged. "I guess not. Her brother said they'd let us know if her mother changed her mind."

"I thought they'd be glad that somebody wants to remember her."

"Yeah, you'd think so, Joe. I mean, she was doing a really fine job in Mexico, beyond the translator work. But . . ."

"I know. We have to honor the family's preferences." Wolf caught the scowl on Derringer's face, knew what was behind it, and risked a question. "Mike, I never knew. Did the police ever catch the guys who took her?"

Derringer shot a sideways glance. "No." After a pause he added, "Not the federales, that is."

Wolf was satisfied with the partial answer. He had heard reports, and he could read between the lines of expense vouchers. There were thinly disguised entries from Mexico and Guatemala for three months after Emily Castillo-Beltran had disappeared on assignment. Michael Derringer had a long memory—and SSI had a long reach.

Derringer stepped back a few feet and regarded the plaque, arms folded. "You know, some board members didn't want us to put this up. They said it could be a security risk but I don't buy that. I think they just didn't want it known that we lose people."

"Well, it's no secret that PMCs take casualties. But I don't think the public has any idea how many have been killed in Iraq alone. Must be hundreds by now."

Derringer turned toward his colleague. "I'll tell you something, Joe. I damn well *want* people to know our losses. Everyone who walks into this building needs to look at that list and consider what it means—what's behind it." He stopped for a few seconds, focusing his thoughts. "I don't know about you, but I think it's part of our responsibility to the people we hire."

The retired admiral turned on a heel and marched away, his purposeful steps echoing off the polished tile.

LONDON

"She certainly looks better," Charles Padgett-Smith said.

Margaret Keene, Doctor of Naturopathic Medicine, almost smiled. Carolyn's husband was a dear man, but still steeped in the stiff-upper-lip tradition. *Or maybe he's afraid of being let down after weathering such a terrible siege. We almost lost her.* "Yes, she's much improved." She gestured toward the cafeteria, just down the hallway. With a sideways glance, Keene assessed the man's mental state. In that regard he was more at risk than Carolyn.

"Charles, it's a complex situation, as you know. But I'll try to summarize. Generally, Marburg is twenty-five percent fatal. As filoviruses go, that is not bad odds. But Carolyn's case was compounded by the means of exposure. The deep injection of a particularly strong strain ensured rapid dispersal throughout her body. She really was quite foolish to remain at home those extra two days." Dr. Keene's expressive eyebrows furrowed in a mild rebuke toward an indulgent husband.

He inhaled, exhaled, and nodded. "Yes, I know that now. She seemed to prefer dying at home rather than entering hospital, even if it meant risking exposure throughout the house. If she hadn't called you when she landed . . ."

Keene permitted herself a rare pat on the man's arm. "When she got off the aeroplane, she was still thinking clearly. But when the virus went active, she lost some of her reasoning ability. I can't blame her entirely. We have both seen people die of hemorrhagic fever. It's terrible—just terrible."

"Well, your snake blend must have done the trick."

Keene shook her head slightly. "I like to think so, but as I say, this was a complex case. Carolyn may have survived without the *Crotalus*, but she also might have suffered more debilitating effects—possibly permanent. In any case, I suspect she's going to be a case study for quite some time."

Charles realized that he knew little about Keene's medicine. "Doctor, just what is this *Crotalus?* I mean, other than it's derived from venom."

"*Crotalus horridus* is a homeopathic remedy for disorganization of the blood. That includes hemorrhages plus tropical and semi-tropical diseases such as jaundice, yellow fever, plague, and cholera."

"My lord, does it cure the common cold, too?" He grinned. "How does it work?"

"Well, many of those symptoms are similar to rattlesnake or viper bites, so some of my colleagues and I realized that *Crotalus* might help fight Ebola. Logic said that if it could work against Ebola, Marburg must be worth a try. So we proceeded accordingly."

"Thank God that you did." He shrugged. "Honestly, I never gave much thought to naturopathy. I was only vaguely aware of it, though Carolyn used to mention it."

"Well, the medical establishment is slow to accept new thinking. Doctors are trained in the allopathic way, and frequently they treat symptoms rather than causes. My friends and I believe there's room for both methods." She paused, ordering her thoughts, then looked at her friend's husband. "Charles, let me ask you a question. Once she's recovered her health, how are you going to deal with Carolyn's emotional trauma?"

"I've wondered about that. She's a strong woman but she's been through so much—a war zone, really. Professional soldiers aren't immune, you know: post-traumatic stress and all that." He raised his hands. "If we need professional counseling, we'll get it. Meanwhile, I think it best for me just to be available. I'll listen as long as she wants to talk. If she doesn't want to talk, I'll encourage her to do so."

"Good. That's what she needs. It also might be helpful for her to see some of the people she worked with over there. I know that travel is inconvenient, but when she's ready, you might suggest a week or two in America. She really is quite fond of some of those chaps."

"I've had calls once and twice a week from Dr. Catterly in Virginia. Carolyn respects him, and that chap Omar Mohammed, too. But there seems a real affection for some of the others, though they're just names to me. Blokes like Frank and J. J. and Jeffrey." He grinned despite himself. "Then there's a rare pair called Bosco and Breezy."

Dr. Margaret Keene arched her eyebrows. "Americans!"

SSI OFFICES

Derringer plopped the morning paper onto Joe Wolf's desk. "Read all about it! Not only were we not involved, it wasn't even a terrorist act." The admiral's gray eyes held a trace of a gleam.

Wolf barely registered the page-two story below the fold. "Hell, Mike, your pal Burridge wouldn't want to draw undue attention, would he?"

"I suppose not. But he might wait til later. You know—budget hearings and jockeying for position in the counterterror hierarchy. Bruce is a good guy, but that doesn't mean he can't play the game."

Wolf was philosophical. "Well, he does have Homeland Security to look out for. Besides, at St. Mary's I learned from Sister Agatha that there is no limit to the good we can do if we don't care who gets the credit."

Derringer, an occasional Lutheran, grinned despite himself. "Sister

Agatha? Seems that every other nun I ever heard of was Sister Mary Margaret."

"Oh, we had a couple of those. MM1 was deadly accurate with an eraser, clear to the back of the room, and MM2 was hellacious with a ruler. Sometimes we used to debate if it was a sin to duck a nun's punch." He gave a thin, tight-lipped smile at the recollection. "But you know—I got a hell of a good education."

A knock on the open door interrupted the discussion. Derringer and Wolf turned to see Terry Keegan's crew-cut head. "Uh, sorry if I interrupted something. I just wanted to let you know the Jurassic Jet is up and running again. We're caught up with the deferred maintenance."

Derringer motioned the aviator in. "No, you didn't interrupt much. Joe was just explaining the benefits of parochial schools."

"Hoo-boy. I still have scars on my knuckles. Sister Teresa caught me reading unauthorized material in class."

Wolf swiveled in his chair. "Let me guess: *Catcher in the Rye*."

Keegan chuckled at the thought. "*God Is My Co-Pilot*. I figured it was okay because General Scott was, you know, religious."

"The good sister did not share your ecclesiastical assessment?"

"Not only no but hell no."

Derringer decided to leave his colleagues to their Catholic esoterica. "Well, excuse me, gentlemen. I'm going to take my paper and read between the lines about the bioterror threat." He paced to the door, then stopped and turned. "You know, without getting denominational about it, we have a lot to be grateful for. I don't want to minimize the losses we sustained, but things could have been awfully damn worse."

Wolf nodded solemnly, staring at the carpeted floor. "I think I'll go to midnight mass and light some candles."

Terrence John Keegan, who decades ago had shunned the Church of Rome, thought of the deliverance he had sustained on the restroom floor. He heard himself say, "I'll go with you."

Michael Derringer and Joseph Wolf traded glances, knowing the full meaning of those four simple words. *Forgive me, Father. It has been twenty-six years since my last confession.* The retired admiral walked out of the room, a buoyancy in his step that matched the gratitude he felt about one man's return to the fold, and one woman's return from the edge of the grave.

On the way to his office, Derringer passed Sallie Ann Kline. "Hi Mike!" she exclaimed. "Hey, Frank's already putting together another contingency team for the next contract. He says that J. J. Johnson should be back in a couple weeks." She regarded her uncle and mentor. "What are you going to do now that the excitement is over for a while?"

The less-than-retired admiral patted his niece's elbow. "Honey, I'm going to call Cap'n Bob. I have some unfinished business with a blue marlin."

AUTHORS' NOTE

Most of the locales and conditions described in this novel are accurate. The major exception is Terminal One at Phoenix International Airport, as Sky Harbor only has Terminals Two, Three, and Four.

The situation along the Arizona-Mexico border is much as depicted. Illegal aliens, smugglers, and terrorists are able to enter the United States almost at will, owing to a continuing lack of national resolve to address the problem. The fact that no overt act of terrorism has occurred since 9-11 must be attributed at least in part to a great deal of good luck.

Of course, that situation could change tomorrow morning.

And some morning, it will.